SIXTH PRECINCT

In New York's Greenwich Village, the downtown neighborhood where crime is rare—but brutal.

SIXTH PRECINCT

The new headquarters of Detective Joe Dante, the hip, smart hero of MIDTOWN SOUTH.

SIXTH PRECINCT

The sensational new novel of crime and cops by a hot new author,

CHRISTOPHER NEWMAN

Fawcett Gold Medal Books
by Christopher Newman:

MIDTOWN SOUTH

SIXTH PRECINCT

SIXTH PRECINCT

Christopher Newman

FAWCETT GOLD MEDAL • NEW YORK

For Roger and Alyce Rose,
with love and thanks

I would like to express additional appreciation for
their help and patience to my wife, Susan, Lieutenant
Bill Caunitz NYPD (Ret.), Knox Burger, and Kitty
Sprague.

". . . but screw your courage to the sticking-place and we'll not fail."

—Lady Macbeth
Macbeth, Act I, Scene VII

ONE

Joe Dante wasn't sure exactly what caused the little tingling in his gut. He didn't know the metaphysical implications. But after learning the hard way that there was
trouble afoot when it went off, he listened. It was going
off now. A tall, stringy black kid lounged against the
fender of a Grand Prix as Dante approached the deli. There
was something in the way the kid was trying to look
nonchalant and disconnected. Trying too hard maybe. It
contradicted his body attitude and the way his eyes darted
furtively. They weren't seeing passersby but seemed to be
searching instead. Undersized red felt bowler, cocked toward one ear and pushed forward on a close-cropped head.
Nike high-top basketball shoes gleaming white in the light
of the storefront. Matching flower-print jams hanging loose
on his bony frame with the collar button done, even in the
dog day heat. The tingling worked like a stretching finger
to probe Dante's adrenal cortex, kicking his respiration
into overdrive. He took a couple of regulating breaths,
stretching the constricted muscles of his abdomen.

As he approached, Dante locked peripherally on the kid

while his gaze swept the scene. A Korean with an intelligent face and athletic build stood under the deli awning astride an open array of fruit and cut flowers. He was watching the shifty black kid like a hawk. Joe angled toward the door, moving past the vigilant Korean and trying to make eye contact.

"Everything okay?" he asked out of the side of his mouth.

The Korean took Joe in with a brief flicker of recognition before refocusing on the object of his concern. There was no way he might have guessed that the tall, sandy-haired regular was an off-duty detective. Since his undercover narcotics days, Dante had purposely maintained a low profile. On the street, he believed it gave him an edge. The Korean simply shrugged, indicating that he believed the situation was under control.

Joe pushed through the door to the interior of the store. Since the surly Cypriot who once owned the place lost his lease, a thorough face-lift and a refreshing change of attitude made the extra dime the Koreans charged over supermarket prices a little easier to take. They sold convenience with a smile instead of a snarl. The six-pack of beer he was after was in a cold case to the rear.

The store was a deep, narrow affair with fruit, vegetables, and dry goods along the left wall as you went back. In addition to beer and soda in the rear, there was a dairy case up the right wall toward the front counter. A salad bar ran up the middle under a plexiglass canopy. A second Korean, tougher-looking and older than the guy outside, was working the register. He had his eye on something around to the right toward the dairy case as Dante entered and walked past with a nod of his head. They knew each other by sight but no more. This new breed of shopkeeper was not unfriendly but tight-lipped and insular. Astonishingly industrious. Fastidiously neat.

2

Joe worked his way past a nurse from St. Vincent's scooping salad greens into a plastic container before he spotted the object of the counterman's attention. A second black kid, this one shorter and built like a baby bull with peach fuzz, loitering next to the dairy case and looking shifty as hell.

An innocuous soft-rock rhythm filtered from an inexpensive stereo rig above the counterman's head. Beneath it, the muscular Korean was moving away from the register to stare at the shifty kid like a mongoose sizing up a cobra. The young woman at the salad bar snapped the lid closed on her plastic case and carried it toward the register. The move forced the proprietor to drop his guard a moment and take her money.

The vibes coming off the loitering kid were electric. As the muscles in his own gut struggled to tighten against a controlled breathing pattern, Dante could see tension run through the kid's muscles like a plucked cello string. His fingers flexed as he darted furtive glances back and forth. His eyes fell briefly on Dante. The woman at the counter, having paid, was moving off.

Dante turned to face the glass door of the ice box, the reflection of the entire premises now visible to him. He could see the burly black kid in his knit shirt, slacks, and ball cap, watching as the nurse pushed open the front door to exit. Joe knew what brand of beer he wanted, but right now, taking a cold six-pack home was the farthest thing from his mind. If he lingered here long enough, pretending to be unable to make up his mind, the kid would sooner or later show his hand. He was primed and pumped. There was only so long he could keep it bottled up.

It didn't take long.

"What you starin' at, motherfucker?"

Dante watched the reversed reflection as the kid rounded the end of the deli counter. The Korean held his position, occupying the high ground and staring wordlessly.

"I asked you who the *fuck* you think you starin' at, you yellow-ass chink!"

The second Korean at the front door eased it open, moving inside slowly in a flanking maneuver. The kid reached inside his shirt—fast—and pulled out a nickel-plated .32 snub-nose revolver. He swung it rapidly back and forth between the two Orientals.

"Back off, you motherfuckin' gook!" he snarled. The muzzle of the gun zeroed in momentarily on the man flanking him. The younger Korean froze.

Dante was removing a six-pack of Dos Equis from the refrigerator as the taller, skinny kid in the red hat hurried in from the street. With the beer cradled in his left arm at belt level, he used the salad island to shield his movement. He worked the little Walther P-5 from his waistband and hid it behind his purchase.

"You!" the skinny kid yelled. He had a gun as well and was waving it toward the rear of the store where Dante stood. "Get the fuck out here where I can see your stinkin' white ass! Now!"

Dante started forward. The burly black kid had the younger Korean by the upper arm, the barrel of his pistol at his temple. He turned to the guy at the register.

"Empty it, motherfucker. Fast. Give me any shit and I blow this gook's ugly face off."

The tough-looking proprietor stared at the nervous gun-man impassively, eyes moving to the gun, then back into the wide, darting eyes. With painful slowness, he pushed the drawer release.

Dante saw it coming. The two blacks didn't. He admired the Koreans for their guts, but the move was crazy. The drawer release was a prearranged signal between the two. With it, they launched simultaneously, the man behind the counter coming over it as the younger guy stomped hard on his captor's instep and shot a fierce elbow into his ribs.

At that moment, another nurse from the adjacent hospital was pushing through the front door, oblivious to what was going down inside. The burly kid's gun went off. The counterman, in mid-hurdle, suddenly lurched in the air. The woman screamed.

For Dante, time stood still in bunches. He was moving forward quickly, searching for a line of fire that wouldn't endanger the three innocent parties. As played before him, the action broke down into flashes of perception, each flash producing a comprehension of events. In this flash, the nurse cowered next to the counter, wedging herself against the bakery-goods shelf. The wounded Korean fell over the front lip of the counter, his momentum taking him toward the floor.

The heavyset black spun, looking for a target. He brought the shiny pistol around, his finger already exerting pressure on the trigger. He seemed to pick up Dante and his six-pack out of the corner of his eye before moving on to focus on the now hysterical nurse. The customer with the beer and the screaming nurse seemed to cancel each other out. More immediately, the younger Korean was whipping a foot into his skinny partner's solar plexus. The little red bowler hat was jerked loose and flopped to the floor.

Dante went into a low crouch, the Dos Equis thrown aside and shattering on the floor. With the nurse now safely below his line of fire, he brought the automatic up. The impact of his 9mm slug at that range lifted the stocky kid off his feet, slamming him backwards into the deli case. The younger Korean, unscathed, stood over the skinny black, lining up to kick the hatless head through the goalposts of sweet eternity.

"No!" Dante shouted, coming up out of his crouch. The downed man was on his knees, incapacitated in gurgling gasps for air that wouldn't come. The Korean froze in mid-kick, his foot poised in the air. His head turned, and he saw the tall, athletic customer now gripping an automatic trained in his general direction. It took him a confused moment before he realized that it was this man who had shot the other assailant. Slowly, with the adrenaline surge easing up, he lowered his foot.

"It's over," Dante soothed, moving forward.

The downed counterman was trying to move, groaning in a pool of his own blood. Blood was everywhere; spattered across the counter, the deli case, the floor, the front door. The nurse, a redhead who couldn't have been more than twenty and was now white with shock, started shakily to her feet. Bright blotches of crimson stained her starched smock.

"You okay, miss?" Joe asked. He stood over the man he'd shot, staring down into unseeing eyes. There was no question of his being dead. With no margin available to try to wound him, the detective had been forced to put two shots in the middle of his chest. Unlike the wounded Korean, the muscular black kid hadn't bled much.

The nurse began to sob, taking quick, jerky little gulps of air. Bright white fluorescence intensified the scene of carnage. Joe grabbed the gagging skinny kid on the floor and hoisted him by his shirt to slam him face-first across the counter. There was no fight left in him. He stayed where he was as Dante lifted the receiver on the wall phone and dialed 911. After reporting the incident, he motioned to the nurse.

"This man might appreciate it if you'd run over to Emergency and see if you can scare up some help for him."

It was an hour before Dante was able to leave the crime scene and another hour before the duty captain at the Sixth Precinct was finished with his questions. While he was there, they received word that the wounded Korean was

6

going to make it. The bullet had missed any vital organs and he'd been stabilized. Both the nurse and the younger Korean had given statements and been gone for twenty minutes before the detective was given the green light. When a cop kills a member of a racial minority, the circumstances are carefully scrutinized in detail.

Captain O'Mallory knew Dante from a stint he'd done more than six years ago as a squad detective here at the Sixth. That made it a little easier. Joe gave O'Mallory the facts, and the captain recorded them.

"Okay, Dante," O'Mallory grunted. He pushed back from his desk and stifled a yawn. It was almost two A.M. and both men were bushed. "Why don't you get the hell out of here so we can both go home and get some sleep? Next time, see if you can't wait another fifteen minutes and let Martinez catch it. I had one foot out the door, and I don't think the lieutenant has had the pleasure of recording one of your glorious exploits for posterity."

Dante stood and reached to pick up his gun from the patrol force commander's desk. An automatic was a non-regulation NYPD firearm, and was considered less reliable than a revolver. He'd been cleared to carry it during his Narcotics days, and had since grown too accustomed to the lightweight, flat profile to give it up. As long as his ten-card authorized its possession, he cleaned it religiously and was willing to stake his life on the reliability of its tight German engineering. Now he stuffed it back into his waistband at the small of his back.

"What did your jokers do with my beer, Cap?"

"Check in back. I think it's in the fridge."

As a detective, Joe Dante often found himself having trouble with the big white lines painted around the field of play. If he was running hard in a direction and the play ended out of bounds, well, it was a thing that happened. It was also a thing that made the guys with scrambled eggs

7

on their caps irritable. They had an occasionally outraged citizenry to contend with. The way they saw it, the cop on the street was supposed to be bending over backward to make their lives easy. They'd put in the time and put up with the shit. They'd earned it. They also tended to come down pretty hard on the people who didn't see it precisely this way.

Nine months ago, Dante had drawn a six-month suspension for some rule-bending in a particularly hairy homicide case. The suspension itself, even though it involved having to sit on his hands without pay, went smoothly enough. Joe spent a lot of time with his sculptor buddy Brian Brennan, working up a sweat in Brian's big funky loft, getting his hands dirty. It was only the actual return to the job that had been difficult. Fed up with a set of rules that had him out trying to nail killers with his hands tied behind his back, Dante had put in for a teaching assignment at the academy. It was something he hoped he might enjoy. The hours were regular. The phone never rang, dragging him out of bed in the middle of the night. After a couple weeks of it, he thought he might go out of his mind with boredom.

He was in no particular hurry to get home. He hadn't been *before* the bloodbath, and he still wasn't at two in the morning. With a new six-pack of Dos Equis tucked up under one arm, he wandered back up Tenth Street from the station house, jogged left on Bleecker to Bank, and then back to the scene of the shooting on Greenwich. The sidewalk was cordoned off with yellow crime-scene tape, and a blue-and-white was still parked out front. True to its reputation as the city that never sleeps, this stretch of New York sidewalk was almost as crowded with pedestrian traffic now as it was at midday. He eased slowly past, letting the series of events come in rushes to his mind's eyes: the slumping counterman, the gun coming around, the finger on the trigger. He'd had no choice, but then again, he could choose not to carry the fucking badge at all. The world would keep spinning. People would continue to kill each other. His girlfriend, Rosa, would probably have moved out that afternoon regardless.

Dante shrugged the weight of the six-pack to his other arm and decided to head home to survey the damage.

Rosa Losada was as stubborn in her single-mindedness and intense in her focus as Joe was. She'd proven that she was a cop's cop on the street. Now she was intent on getting as far up the job's brass ladder as a bright, beautiful, college-educated woman could. Beneath his clean-cut Manhattanized exterior, Joe Dante was still the kid from Canarsie. As long and hard as he may have chipped at them, a number of the rough edges remained. Ingrained were a traditional northern Italian Catholic upbringing, a strong work ethic, and a third-generation American's civic pride and sense of accomplishment. The cop son of a cop father, Dante just didn't see the job the way Rosa did. He was unable to comprehend her brand of ambition. He wanted her to marry him, quit the rat race, settle down, and have kids. She wanted to become the first woman chief of detectives. Their experiment in cohabitation had been a disaster. Her argument for leaving was not that she no longer loved him; she simply needed her ''space.'' Joe was having trouble determining just what it all meant.

Across town, at University Hospital, Benjamin Crowley was wheeled into the recovery room under heavy sedation. His suboccipital craniotomy had taken a grueling fourteen hours to complete: an auditory tumor, and very tricky business. Neurologist George Scully and ear, nose, and throat specialist Phil Neisbaum were both dead on their feet.

''I wouldn't exactly call it a piece of cake,'' Neisbaum grunted, surveying the patient's chart.

Scully peered over the ENT man's shoulder. The neurological assessment sheet appeared as near normal as could be expected at this juncture. The next several hours would tell the real story. Blood pressure was slightly elevated, but that could be any number of things. He patted Neisbaum on the shoulder.

"Why don't you head on home, buddy. No sense in both of us hanging around."

"BP is one-sixty over ninety. That's borderline."

Scully rolled his eyes. "I'll *watch* it," he insisted. "That smart-ass new wonder-boy resident . . . what's-his-name?"

"Gelasco."

"Yeah. He's due on any minute now. I'll take it from here. Hang around maybe an hour until this old buzzard stabilizes and then catch a few hours shut-eye at the office. Not much sense in driving back to Connecticut tonight."

"Thanks." Neisbaum nodded gratefully. "I've got a tonsillectomy at the crack of dawn." He stifled a yawn. "Nice work in there, pal. Too bad you can't play golf like that."

With Neisbaum gone, Scully drifted into the surgeons' lounge for a quick cup of coffee. While there, he called his service for messages. There were two from his receptionist—one telling him that a wad of monthly bill payment checks were on his desk awaiting his signature and another saying his wife, Joan, had called. There was a message from Joan directly—something about someone from the country club with recurrent dizziness. Jesus, she'd known he was going to be in OR all day. Couldn't this wait? A final message was from Fiona, simply asking that he call. He punched her number.

"Hiya," he rumbled in response to the nurse's sleepy hello.

"George!" There was the sharp edge of irritation there. "I left a message three hours ago."

"Long day," he replied. "Had the old fart under the knife until an hour ago. He's going to be fine, but I'm not so sure I am."

Fiona Hassey's tone changed quickly. "Rub your feet?"

"The old man's pressure is elevated a little. I'm here for another hour."

"I'm not sure if I can wait that long," she teased. "Why don't you run over here, we can take the edge off, and then I can rub your feet when you come back later."

In addition to the practice he maintained in a ground-floor office of a building directly across First Avenue from the hospital, he also owned two cooperative units upstairs. Recovery room nurse Fiona Hassey was conveniently installed in one of them, a mistress possessing one of the singularly spectacular physiques on the planet, a healthy sexual appetite, and an unflagging devotion to the man who paid the rent. His imagination drifted to her there, eagerly awaiting him. What the hell? He could tear off a quick piece and probably be back before he was missed. If they wanted him, he could get back across the avenue almost as quickly as he could catch an elevator up from the cafeteria.

"I can't hang around," he said tentatively.

"C'mon, George. It's a hundred and twenty yards to pay dirt, and I'm sitting here without a thing on."

Fiona Hassey cradled the receiver and rolled onto one elbow. On the nightstand lay a pocket mirror and the last scattered traces of the half gram she'd dumped on it after work. She picked up the single edged blade lying alongside and scooped the cocaine into a little pile. The clock radio told her she had five minutes, tops. When Scully had a head of steam up, two elevators and First Avenue rarely slowed him very much. She snorted the last of what lay on the mirror before picking it up and slipping it into the drawer below. Scully knew about the nose candy but didn't approve. Not that she much cared. Half a gram of the stuff over an evening was still working on her cortex, and this last little dusting only served to boost its cumulative effect. When George came storming over like a goat in rut, she liked to have a headful to jack up her own intensity. Going full bore from a standstill always seemed easier for men. Then again, George was promising to divorce his wife, and George would be her ticket out. She was going to keep him convinced that Robert fucking Redford couldn't look any more appealing if it were *him* coming through that door.

There was a little Chardonnay still in the bottom of a glass on the coffee table in the front room. She drained it and stood, catching herself in the large wall mirror. George didn't need the silk peignoir. He'd be ready. She slipped the straps off her shoulders and let the filmy thing fall. It slid over her nipples and down across her hips to the floor. No fuss, no muss. Her doctor wasn't much of a romantic when he had all night; with only fifteen minutes, he'd hump her like a stud horse and be fully dressed before he caught his breath. Long or short haul, she made him pay by the mile. Aurora, Lutèce, and the Four Seasons at least twice a week. And spending money. You didn't run an eight-ball-a-week coke habit on a nurse's salary. The man's poor wife. Hell, she probably even loved him.

Scully stepped out of the lounge and back into the recovery room. The very competent and able Nancy Rankin was the head nurse on the unit. He approached her, wondering if the resident had checked in yet.

"He called from the cafeteria. Should be up in ten or fifteen minutes. You want him paged?"

"Don't bother. I'm thinking about getting a bite to eat myself. The consult can wait until I get back." He nodded toward Crowley. "How's my patient."

"Holding steady. We did another BP and it's still a little elevated."

Scully reached to his belt to make sure his beeper was switched on. He stepped to Crowley's side and did a quick check of his pupils. Suboccipital was rough on a patient because it required operating in the sitting position. On the other hand, it beat hell out of translabyrinthine for results. Less chance of total hearing loss on the affected side. This guy was going to be fine. George never doubted for a minute that he was good. So good that he surprised even himself sometimes.

George contemplated the image of Fiona sitting in anticipation of his arrival as he hurried from the hospital and across the all-but-abandoned avenue. Conjuring Fiona's amazing body helped prime the pump; not that it really needed all that much. Fiona's body was the stuff dreams and expensive divorces were made of. Just the thought of a roll with her, even after fourteen hours of exhausting cranial surgery, sent the blood coursing.

A contemplative Joe Dante watched a cloudburst sweep across the patio as he sat propped in bed. Naked, he had a bottle of beer clutched in one hand as he scratched his cat, Copter, behind the ears with the other. The little guy was all freaked out, what with things being moved all around and Rosa gone. Some animal sense told him she wasn't coming back, even though she worked many a late tour in the past, arriving home at all hours. Tonight it was different, a sadness heavy in the air.

Joe didn't even think about trying to get some sleep. Until he met Rosa Losada, relationships were for other, steadier psychologies than his own. This thing was something he had initially resisted. Then it happened in a rush. He was already stripping line off the reel before he knew he was hooked. Maybe that was the problem. They'd moved too quickly. Gotten too intense too fast. It wasn't until they both started talking about what they wanted, individually, out of life, that the wheels started to wobble. Dante had lived as a bachelor in Manhattan for almost seventeen years now. He no longer talked and swaggered like a kid from "da neighborhood," but he was still the boy from Brooklyn, deep in his sentimental self. Rosa, also from a close-knit Catholic family, should have fit into his dream. *Should have*, if only a pack of animals hadn't raped her mother in front of her father and then brutally murdered them both when she was nineteen. It was an act that would change how she perceived the world forever. How she perceived the idea of family. Of intimacy with people you love. She could no longer bring herself to trust those feelings. Closeness was a transient thing. Her inability to see herself as Joe Dante's wife and the mother of his kids clashed directly with his inability to see their relationship moving in any *other* direction.

Joe was angry now. Alone with his anger and an incredible emptiness, he set the equally empty beer bottle on the nightstand. With the cat curled up next to him, he switched off the lamp and rolled over to try for the oblivion of sleep. As he closed his eyes, the unseeing eyes of the man he'd killed stared back at him.

Your life's so fucked up because of the fucking job, he told himself. You're a cop.

Two

All hell broke loose for Nancy Rankin no more than three minutes after Dr. Scully checked in on his patient and left the unit. The machine monitoring Benjamin Crowley's vital signs suddenly triggered an alarm indicating a sharp rise in blood pressure. The arterial line now gave a readout of 180 over 100. Pulse was down to 60 and respiration was slightly irregular. The head nurse quickly checked Crowley's pupils, finding one markedly larger than the other.

"Get hold of X-ray," she ordered the closest staff nurse. "Tell them we're bringing him in for a C-T scan. Stat. Then call the OR and have them stand by. Page Dr. Scully and the resident."

Even as she calmly gave her directions, the patient's BP rose to 200 over 110. There was little doubt in her mind that the man was suffering increased intracranial bleeding. It was all a question of how quickly they could move now.

"Twelve milligrams of Decadron," she directed another of her staff. They had to deal immediately with brain swelling. "And hang a Ni-Pride infusion. Stand by."

"They've located Dr. Gelasco," the staff nurse informed her. She was cradling the receiver between cheek and shoulder, her hand cupped over the mouthpiece. "Dr. Scully hasn't answered his page."

Nancy Rankin watched the blood pressure go to 240 over 120 and made a decision. "Infuse him with the nitroprusside," she ordered. "A ten-minute time-out." She glanced at her watch. "X-ray ready?"

The nurse on the phone nodded.

The head nurse nodded to the now hyper-alert staff. "Let's get him rolling. Stat!"

George Scully had wasted no time getting down to business in Fiona Hassey's arms. His pants lay thrown haphazardly over a living room chair, his beeper hanging from his belt. Now, heaving like some great, frenzied piston, he rammed home and came in a surge of spasmodic relief. Fiona writhed and cried out beneath him. For a moment, he feared he'd hurt her with his intensity. Upon his arrival, she'd been sitting there spread-legged on the sofa, for crissakes. Moments later, when she went down on him, he was so primed that he nearly came in her mouth. That was a Fiona Hassey no-no.

"God*damn*!" she exclaimed as he collapsed. "I thought you said you were beat."

Breathing hard and sweating profusely, he rolled off her and sat up to swing his legs over the side of the bed.

"You okay?" he asked, panting. "I didn't hurt you, did I?"

"I'll live," she replied. She reached to the nightstand for a cigarette. George was already on his feet and moving toward the shower. "There's a message on the machine from Joan."

Scully's private line in the office downstairs had an extension and answering machine in Fiona's second bedroom. The neurosurgeon turned at the bathroom door. "Something about dizzy spells? One of those tennis-playing barracuda at the club?"

Fiona nodded.

"I got it."

"Speaking of Joanie," Fiona started in.

"Not tonight," Scully dodged. "Dinner tomorrow, huh?"

"Why not tonight?"

With his arm outstretched, Scully pointed at his watch. "I slipped out for fifteen minutes exactly fifteen minutes ago. I'm running late as it is."

Fiona shrugged. "All right. But come prepared to talk about *us* tomorrow night."

"I will," he promised. "It's going to be soon, baby. You've got to be patient on this a little while longer and trust me on it."

Five minutes later, while pulling on his pants, Scully's beeper fell to the floor. In retrieving it, he noticed that the switch was in the off position and thumbed it back on. A loud, insistent pulsing filled the room. He stared at it in surprise, his brow furrowed. Worry began to rain on his parade.

"Oh shit," he grunted, reaching to grab the phone.

Neurosurgery resident Nick Gelasco rushed into the X-ray unit. Recovery's head nurse, Nancy Rankin, and two of her staff stood by as a late-middle-aged male was wheeled away from the just completed C-T scan en route to OR.

"Whose patient is he?" Gelasco demanded. There was as much worry as irritation in his voice. He hadn't been briefed on this guy, which could only mean that he was the craniotomy just out of the OR when the previous resident, Larry Pentell, went off duty.

"Dr. Scully," the head nurse informed him. "He was supposed to be on call in the cafeteria." As she spoke,

Nancy Rankin handed Gelasco Benjamin Crowley's chart. "He can't be located and apparently isn't answering his beeper."

"Great," the resident grunted. He scanned the post-op assessment sheet and subsequent notes, moving toward the attending radiologist. Together they ran over the results of the C-T scan.

"Definite posterior fossa bleeding," Gelasco mumbled. Pressure buildup from bleeding in the brain had to be relieved in a matter of minutes in order to prevent serious neurological damage. Every second counted. With the attending physician out of the picture, it was up to him. "Let's get him prepped, people," he ordered calmly. Inside, his stomach was doing back flips.

George Scully had learned by phone that Benjamin Crowley was going sour on him. Almost thirty minutes had elapsed between the time he'd left the recovery room and the moment the downstairs elevator doors finally opened to whisk him up to the sixth floor. By the time Scully could reach the OR, scrub, and burst in upon the scene, forty-two minutes had ticked off the clock since Crowley's crisis began.

Nick Gelasco had the patient up in the sitting position, under anesthesia, and was just starting to crack him when a flustered Dr. Scully arrived.

"Why the fuck wasn't I called immediately?" he demanded, anger flashing in his eyes.

"Where the hell were you?" Gelasco retorted, not allowing the exchange to interrupt his precise movements with the knife. "Your post-op blows a gasket and you don't answer your page for twenty minutes. This son of a bitch is dying here, *Doctor*."

Scully's anger turned to confusion tinged with fear as he pictured the position of his beeper when he picked his pants up off the chair. The implications began to sink in.

18

* * *

Forty-three minutes. It wasn't a lot of time in the cosmic scheme of things, but in neurological terms it could be as good as an eternity. A human brain, suffering stem pressure from excessive bleeding, can go from perfectly healthy to dead in that amount of time—or go to any number of places in between. Patients have been known to fully recover from massive brain trauma with few or no visible aftereffects. More often, the lingering effect of paralysis, speech impediment, memory impairment, or a host of other complications result. Benjamin Crowley, male, age sixty-three, as the result of postoperative complications bled into the head for close to an hour before pressure was finally relieved. His life was saved due largely to Nick Gelasco's decision to go in when he did. In such cases, it would be impossible to determine what effect an earlier assessment may have accomplished in terms of limiting damage. As it was, the attending physician proved to be unavailable during this most critical time period. Benjamin Crowley, as the direct result of extensive postoperative trauma, emerged from this second, emergency surgery paraparetic. He was able to feel but unable to control the motor functions of his limbs and torso, a condition that would leave him confined to a wheelchair for the rest of his life.

The first Thursday evening after the Korean deli shooting Dante was just winding up his weekly lecture on surveillance technique. Most of the attendees, selected by their squad commanders, were there in order to collect overtime. The class required the academy theater because of its size.

As Joe packed slide carousels into carrying cases, the cavernous room filled with murmured conversation and the echo of shuffling feet. He didn't notice as Manhattan

South Detective Commander Gus Lieberman lumbered up to the apron of the stage. Inspector Lieberman was a big, overweight bear of a man. An ex-Fordham Rams linebacker from the glory years, he'd gone to seed behind a gray metal desk. In his day, he'd been as tough a street cop as they came. Tough and smart enough to avoid the promotional pitfalls of petty jealousies, arrogance, backstabbing and other assorted enemy-making in the upper echelons of the job. His current command was considered the direct stepping stone to chief of detectives, and that made him, in terms of power within the job, something akin to the Angel Gabriel in the Judeo-Christian hierarchy. When Gus Lieberman set out to cut a swath, people got the hell out of his way.

"Nice little talk," the inspector commented. "I managed to catch most of it."

Dante glanced up, startled by the familiar baritone.

"Gus! What the hell are *you* doing here?"

"Just dropped in to see if I could buy you a beer."

The two friends sat at the bar in one of those sidewalk fern and mahogany places on Second Avenue. There was a heat wave outside that hadn't broken in over a week. The choice had been to opt for an air-conditioned, albeit smoke- and perfume-laden, atmosphere or walk another block in the August soup. Dante was drinking a beer while Lieberman sipped a double Dewar's on ice. The dinner crowd behind them was noisy enough to make them feel comfortable conversing in normal tones. Down at one end of the bar, a couple of off-duty guys from the Thirteenth were putting the make on a blonde and a redhead. The two women weren't looking like they minded the attention too much. There were a lot of empty stools between, and the bartender was mostly busy making drinks for tables.

"How long we known each other now, Joey? Eleven, maybe twelve years?" Lieberman asked.

"Something like that," Dante replied.

"For the first time since I've known you, I saw you looking like a fish outta water up there tonight. Good talk. All the facts, and real good attention to the details, but no heart in it."

"You expected *heart* in it?"

Lieberman ignored him. "I read O'Mallory's report on the deli shooting."

"I knew it had to be something like this. What *now*?"

The inspector smiled. "You're getting a little edgy in your old age, my friend. This ain't the naughty detective's rabbi come down to play the heavy for his friends in the big building. What I'm sayin' is that I read the report and it looks to me like you may have saved a couple of lives."

"I killed a man."

"Justifiably."

"Who are you now, God?"

A look of irritation crossed Lieberman's face. "We took you down off your cross quite a while back, you long-suffering little prick. You broke the rules, Joey. You got your hand slapped. End of story. Time to move on. You don't like the assignment at the academy? Well, if I recall correctly, you asked for that, too."

Dante shook his head. "Sorry. I guess I'm a little keyed up."

"You *guess*? Okay. What I'm here to ask is whether you intend to spend the next fifteen years teaching shitheads how to wipe fanny."

"Thirteen years, three months, eight days," Dante countered. This time, at least it was said with a grin. Then he shrugged. "Beats me, Gus. Right now, I don't have anything better to do."

Lieberman took a long pull on his drink and eased a cigarette out of the pack of Carltons on the bar. Stuffing it between his teeth, he lit it and inhaled, disgust crossing his face. Lieberman hated smoking Carltons, but it was a concession he'd made to his wife when giving the butts up altogether made him too ornery to live with.

"You're a street cop, Joey," he said flatly, smoke escaping with the utterance. "You'll always be a street cop. You're maybe the best this city has to offer at the moment."

Dante smiled ruefully. "I'm not sure everybody'd agree with that assessment."

Lieberman snorted. "Fuck 'everybody.' Since when do you live your life based on what other people think of you?"

Now Dante's smile cracked the touch of sadness that lay around its edges. "Sorry, Gus. I don't need to be dumping on you. I guess I've been a little out of sorts the past couple days. Rosa moved out."

Lieberman stubbed his cigarette after only a couple of puffs and exhaled. "Sorry to hear that. Where to?"

"An apartment on St. Mark's Place."

"Rough one. I don't think it changes the underlying reality, though. In my own experience, a man is happiest doing what he does best. You? Well you sure don't belong teaching night school. Where you belong is back in my command. On the street."

Dante was genuinely surprised. "You're shitting me. Where?"

"Anywhere you want to be. I need you. I ain't gonna argue over the fine points."

Dante got a sly look in his eye. "I've had this fantasy about being able to walk to work again."

Lieberman smiled. "Vic Manley just took over as whip of the Sixth a month ago. You and him always got along, didn't you?"

"We were practically in love."

"I'll see what I can shuffle around. Seems like some-

22

body's getting ready to retire outta there. McNulty." He sipped his drink, lifting one of the fingers wrapped around it to point. "You're goddamn lucky you're as good as you are, pal. Not many guys in this lousy job got big-shot pull coming round and begging them to get their fingers out of their ass and make themselves useful."

Dante stared at the near-empty bottle in front of him, a crooked grin on his face. "You know? By the time I hang it up, I don't think there'll be anyone who's had a stranger tour on the job. What the hell's wrong with me, Gus? What makes it so hard all the time?"

"You always cared too much, Joey. Beneath that shell of resentment, I think you still do."

"Think maybe I could stop?" Dante asked, grin widening. "Get into something like real estate?"

"Who you think you're fucking kidding?"

"What about the classes I'm teaching?"

Lieberman snorted. "There are guys who could teach that shit lobotomized. I suspect some of them are."

"I guess this is the point where I get on my knees and thank you for this wonderful opportunity to volunteer for the chance to get my head blown off."

The inspector chuckled. "You just keep on volunteering and I'll make chief of detectives yet."

Ten minutes later, Gus Lieberman slid off his stool and headed for the door. Dante remained behind with a fresh beer on the bar. The prospect of being back on the street was something he wanted to sit and savor a moment. It was giving him a much-needed lift. He'd heard that Vic Manley had made lieutenant, but he didn't know he was the new whip at the Sixth. A big, heavy-framed black man with street savvy, good investigative instincts, and an easygoing manner, Manley was stand-up in Dante's book, and Dante's book read like the phone listings in Antarctica.

"Hi."

It was melodious, definitely female, and it came from his left. He turned to survey the face behind the voice, confronting the friendly-looking redhead who'd been playing cat and mouse with the two off-duty cops at the end of the bar.

"Anyone sitting here?"

He shrugged. "It's yours, free and clear." She was short and pixieish, maybe five two and around hundred pounds. Not his type at all but with a nice smile and a compact, well-shaped little body.

"Thanks," she said, climbing aboard. "You're the most interesting-looking guy in the place, and I just love interesting-looking guys."

He regarded her with amusement. "What are you drinking . . . ?"

"Patsy. G. and T."

Dante waved to the barkeep and ordered a gin and tonic for the lady.

"What happened to your friends?" he asked.

She grinned and waved them off. "Those guys? Did you *look* at them? They're *old*." She said it like even Dante might be teetering on the brink at thirty-nine. "*And* fat. I'm not into fat. It really grosses me out."

"You're into interesting," he said matter-of-factly.

She nodded. "Right. You got it. But not interesting and fat."

"Interesting and *slim*."

"Yeah." Her eyes were twinkling with soul-felt communication as the bartender set her drink on the bar before her. She lifted the glass to him. "We understand each other. I really love that. What's your name?"

"Joe. What do you do, Patsy?"

"I'm a receptionist at a brokerage house. Downtown. But I'm really an actress."

It had been four days since Dante last talked to Rosa. His idea. He wanted it this way, at least at first. He did *not* want to have dinner with her in the new apartment. He didn't want to sleep with her there. She'd invited him to do both those things, contending that the new distance might help them sort out their real feelings. Hell, he knew what his feelings were. He was pissed off.

Right now, fueled by his resentment toward Rosa, this little redhead who wasn't his type looked good enough to eat. He needed to blow off a little steam. She wanted interesting? With minimal effort, he could do interesting as well as the next guy.

"Listen," he said to the bright-eyed little "actress." "I'm getting a little tired of this place and I've got a cat at home who's getting mighty hungry. Feel like taking a ride?"

She looked a little surprised. "I hardly know you," she said quickly.

"Didn't stop you from climbing up on that stool," he said. "Besides, I'm Mr. Interesting. Remember?"

"I said you *looked* interesting."

"So how're you ever gonna find out?"

She frowned a moment. "Where do you live?" she asked at length.

"Perry Street in the Village."

She brightened a little. "That's a nice neighborhood."

"It's a *great* neighborhood. I'm a great guy."

Three

It wasn't as though George Scully hadn't known it was coming. On the other hand, unlike a speeding car or an inside fastball, it was not the sort of thing he could dodge away from. Benjamin Crowley's attorney filed a malpractice suit shortly after the hospital's Morbidity and Mortality Conference announced their findings. The case had been slated on the conference's agenda for two weeks after the claimant's catastrophic incident. After a review of surgical records and interviews with OR personnel, the anesthesiologist, and the surgical team, they agreed that the surgical procedure had been pro forma. The workups and tests had been properly administered. The surgical strategy was deemed appropriate under the circumstances. Crowley's post-op complications were not in themselves extraordinary. What they *did* find inexcusable was that the attending physician was not available when the crisis arose. The malpractice action named Scully, Phil Neisbaum, and the hospital as co-defendants, asking one million dollars in lost earnings and an additional one and a half million for pain and suffering. Crowley was a very successful investment portfolio manager, and such a claim was not unrealistic under the circumstances. Above all else, by leaving the immediate area without briefing the neurosurgical resident for consultation and then not responding to the recovery staff's attempts to reach him, Dr. Scully had failed in his responsibility to his patient. Because Crowley was initially Dr. Neisbaum's patient, and the hospital carried both men as affiliates, both the ENT man and the institution were named as co-defendants.

The summer sun broke through the clouds, dazzling George Scully and Phil Neisbaum as they strolled down the eighth fairway of Scully's Pound Ridge Country Club. Eight weeks had passed since Benjamin Crowley went sour in post-op. Eight difficult weeks for both men. The inquiries, depositions, and constant legal consultations. Now, for the moment anyway, most of it lay behind them. It might be as much as two years before the case actually got to court.

This was their usual Monday afternoon game; they alternated visits to each other's club. It had rained for about twenty minutes just moments earlier, with attendant thunder that sent them scurrying for the cover of the clubhouse. Now, as the sun was refracted in the billions of water droplets clinging to blades of grass, they pushed on to where they'd marked their balls.

"That drink wasn't such a bad idea," Scully commented. He moved along easily, taking deep breaths of the country air. "I've been tight as hell lately."

Neisbaum nodded. "Can't say as I blame you. It hasn't been easy."

Scully, farthest from the pin, addressed his ball and sliced a seven iron well to the right of the green and into a deep bunker. Neisbaum fared quite a lot better, his eight iron lofting him into a sweet little hollow on the apron of the green about fifteen feet from the cup. Phil was the better golfer as a rule, but today they were playing half a dozen strokes farther apart than usual.

"It's unbelievable," Scully complained as they strolled together toward the green. "Fucking insurance companies won't underwrite any more than a million in coverage, and these bastards sue for two and a half. With the climate in the courts, my carrier is going to offer settlement, and it's bound to be in the ball park."

Neisbaum pulled up short. "Not without your approval, they can't."

"Want to bet? Things've been a little tight lately. I changed my coverage from occurrence to claims-made last year."

"You did *what*?"

"It saved me almost twenty grand. I didn't think I could come up with it at the time."

A snort escaped Neisbaum's lips. "Give me a break, buddy. I know some guys who can cry poor, but you aren't among them. What were you, out of your mind? Afraid you might have had to drive last year's model for another six months or something?"

Scully shook his head. "You don't know the half of it." he pointed. "See that ball over there?"

Neisbaum squinted. "Nope. Afraid I can't."

"You'd call that a shitty lie then, correct?"

"*Real* shitty, if you have any hope of getting down in two."

"Well, the shit I'm in right now is three times as deep as that sand trap."

Phil chuckled. "C'mon. The house alone's gotta be worth close to a million. It's all but paid for, right? And how many apartments do you have in the city now? Six? And paper in the market?"

"Paper is about it," Scully said dully.

"What?"

"Paper. I took out a second on the house and the co-ops. They all belong to the bank."

Neisbaum's mouth dropped open. "What are you, crazy?"

The ENT man's ball could be seen resting on the apron of the green, just three or four yards from the flag. He let it be for the moment and followed Scully to the lip of the trap as the neurosurgeon climbed down into it. The front edge of the trap fell off from the rough just below the green about as steeply as the Jersey Palisades meet the Hudson. George was tucked right up against the base, presented with a near vertical trajectory of escape.

"It didn't seem crazy at the time," Scully contended. He bit his lip, wiggling his sand wedge and trying to fathom how the hell he was going to hit the damn ball. "Milt had that offshore fund recommendation. I went in pretty heavily, and then along came Biotechnics. I was already leveraged to the tits. The only equity I had was in the real estate. Took a fucking second note on the house. *Forged* Joanie's signature on the papers."

With this pronouncement, he chopped down hard, sending sand in all directions and blasting his ball directly into the face of that mini-Palisade. The ball careened wildly off an overhanging clump of turf and skittered back across the trap to the hollow of a Scully footprint.

"Fuck me!" George groaned.

Neisbaum had barely noticed the errant shot. He stared at his friend of fifteen years. "Biotechnics?" he heard himself ask.

"The herpes vaccine," Scully replied hollowly.

"Holy Christ."

"You got it, friend. The FDA flushed the whole project down the shitter. Milt wanted me to get out a month earlier. The fucker'd quadrupled and was going through the ceiling. I wouldn't let him cash me in." He paused to address the ball in its new location, slashed at it, and managed to push it up onto the verge, about forty feet from the pin.

"I mean, Jesus, Phil. The sons of bitches *had* to know about those side effects. They *had* to."

Neisbaum was silent as he moved slowly toward his own ball. He studied the green from down on his haunches as Scully stepped up to remove the flag.

"Your shot," Phil said.

"Fuck it," Scully waved him off. "Go ahead. The way I'm playing, I'm going to six-putt the fucking green anyway."

"How much did you lose?" Phil asked.

George shook his head. "My initial two had turned into eight three. Now the shit isn't worth the paper it's printed on."

"Two *million* dollars?" Neisbaum asked, incredulous. "Who do you think you are? T. *fucking* Boone Pickens?"

"You kidding?" Scully snorted. "I was riding the crest of over four hundred percent profit. Up to the point when it went down in flames, it was looking like a great bet. Hell, even after being left out to dry for a million and a half in liability, I was *rich*."

Neisbaum abandoned any attempt at the cup for the moment. He leaned on his putter and shook his head. Facing him, Scully held up two fingers, their tips just a quarter inch apart.

"I was this close to being able to tell Joanie's dad to kiss my ass. I was going to give that self-righteous prick his med school money and his down payment back with interest. Tell him to go fuck himself. Now if he finds out about the forged mortgage papers, he'll want her to have me arrested."

Phil turned away, shaking his head, and addressed his ball with an attempt at concentration. When the club head met it at the end of a short, fluid stroke, it ran true to within a foot of the cup and then broke left to miss the rim by a mere half inch. After stepping up to tap it in he turned to eye his old friend. "You were with Fiona, weren't you?"

Scully, on the way across the green to his own ball, stopped in his tracks.

Neisbaum pressed him. "The night you were supposed to be attending. You were across the street, right?"

"What the fuck's that got to do with it?"

"The same thing as trying to get rich quick like you've got a wild hair growing up your ass. Fiona Hassey. She's got you thinking with your schlong."

"Leave her out of this, Phil," Scully retorted hotly.

"Why? It's like leaving the chocolate out of hot cocoa. You're liable for a million five in a malpractice suit, Georgie. You just got done describing to me how thoroughly your ass is hanging in the breeze. Haven't you stopped to try and figure out why? Jesus, man. You've all but committed professional suicide for a piece of ass from *Akron*!"

For a moment, Neisbaum thought Scully might swing at him. There was real fire in his eyes. Then, as quickly as it had flared, it was gone.

"You've got it a lot easier than you know, friend," Scully said quietly. "You took the rough road up. Got used to the bumps and scrapes along the way. Me? I was a lazy fuck. Got myself a debutante with perky tits and a tight ass and said to myself that life is a series of compromises. She was crazy about me, probably because her daddy wasn't. You married a woman because you thought you were in love with her, Phil. I didn't. That was just the first of many mistakes."

Neisbaum eyed him. "You make this up recently because you're feeling sorry for yourself? Or do you really believe it?"

Scully shook his head. "If you think I'm going to follow it up with a declaration of passionate love for a certain nurse, you can stop cringing. That's not it. Fiona's an escape. She's hot. When I'm with her, I don't spend a lot of time worrying whether or not I can get my dick hard. It's always hard when I'm around her. The grass is always greener."

"She thinks you're gonna divorce Joan."

Scully glanced at him sharply. "She *told* you that?"

"She didn't have to. She's acting like she owns you. She goes out of her way to kiss my ass every chance she gets because I'm your buddy and the only real competition for your attention once you ditch Joan and the kids."

"I *am* going to divorce Joan," Scully insisted quietly. "Or at least I *was*, until this load of shit hit the fan."

"To marry Fiona?"

Scully shrugged. "How the hell do I know? I was going to play it by ear. String her along a little. Hell, she's already got free rent and a paid-for nose habit. And that's another problem. I can't see myself tying the knot with a fucking dope fiend."

George continued toward his ball, dispensed with studying the green, and took a sloppy shot in the general direction of the hole. The results were to be expected. He ended up about six feet wide, with a steep downhill lie. Behind them, in mid-fairway, the trailing foursome was close on their heels. Scully stooped to mark his ball and waved them to play through. Both men wandered off to the side of the fairway and climbed up to sit in their cart.

"You're sure they'll want to settle?" Phil asked, changing the subject.

"The insurance company? They haven't said, but you figure it. What's their percentage in fighting a thing like this? One of their insurees inexplicably fucks the big, fluffy dog. They know that if they go to court, the plaintiff's attorney wheels this sorry vegetable up to the jury box and asks the nice people to take a good look at what happens when some asshole doctor steps outside for a little "fresh air." They look at me, dressed nice and able to walk anywhere I want to catch all the cool breeze I can get my lungs on. Hell, they'll want to drive that wheelchair up my ass. They'll settle all right."

The foursome played through, and with the green once again vacant, they approached to see how many more strokes it might take George to drop his ball. The rain clouds were now moving well out toward Long Island Sound. Sunshine poured down across the Westchester landscape. All along the fairway rough, the club groundskeepers had planted a riot of late-blooming color. To look at the setting, it would be easy to believe that anyone with a free afternoon to enjoy it couldn't possibly have a care in the world. George replaced the little plastic marker with his Top-Flite and then hunched over it, his putter gripped in well-tanned and meticulously manicured surgeon's hands. With brow furrowed in fierce concentration, he poked at the ball with a stroke that sent it scurrying directly into the cup.

Detective Joe Dante had been at the Sixth Precinct for almost two months now. His boss, Lieutenant Vic Manley, was grateful to Gus Lieberman for pulling the strings necessary to land him there. Manley knew Dante from almost eight years back, when the two of them had worked this very same squad together. He'd followed Joe's subsequent moves through the job grapevine. A lot of what he heard was not terribly positive. The picture painted in certain quarters was of a cowboy cop with a hard-on for authority. Manley knew better. He'd been on the street with him. His hunches were often uncanny, and he worked leads with the tenacity of a pit bull. Partners who had toured with him would go through the gates of hell with Joe Dante as backup.

With the retirement of long-timer Petey McNulty some five weeks back, Dante had been teamed with McNulty's two partners. After a couple of weeks the old hands had gotten used to the new guy, and things were settled into a smooth-running routine. Art Campo was an old-fashioned northern Italian like Dante who *hadn't* left the old neighborhood. Beasley "Jumbo" Richardson was an easygoing black man from East New York. The chemistry among the three seemed good from the start.

It was a Thursday night in late October. Dante's team was preparing to swing out for seventy-two hours after finishing a tour on the four-to-midnight. All three men had just finished the laborious job of whittling down the mountains of paperwork on their desks and were trying to stretch the kinks out of desk-bound muscles when the whip poked his head out of his office and gestured them inside.

"The commissioner and C of D have gone into their juggling act," Manley announced. "Artie, baby, guess what?"

"No," Campo groaned. "Not again."

"You guessed it. This time it's the exciting long-term parking lot at JFK."

Once upon a time, Art Campo had had some luck stumbling into a ring of high-end car thieves who procured for shipment to the South American market. Ever since, whenever there was a rash of luxury car thefts in a concentrated area, the so-cursed Artie would be flown off to join a special task force aimed at cracking the case. With each success, the label "expert" became more firmly attached.

"Starting when?" Campo moaned.

"Starting Friday morning. You report to a Captain McNeal at Queens Borough Command."

"Numb-nuts," Campo grunted. "They could steal a Rolls-Royce stretch limo with him asleep on the back seat and he'd be halfway to Buenos Aires before he realized it wasn't all a bad dream."

Manley ignored him, turning to the other two. "That'll leave you guys a little short, so they're flying in some guy to be assigned temporarily. Don't have a name yet and probably won't until he shows up on our doorstep Monday."

Out on the street, Campo hurried off around the corner of Bleecker while Dante and Richardson ambled along at a slower pace.

"Got time to let me buy you a beer?" Joe asked.

Richardson shrugged a pair of massive shoulders and grinned.

"Why not? I go home, I gotta face a mother-in-law who quotes from *Watchtower*."

Richardson was a big-boned black man of forty-five who, at just under six feet, was carrying in excess of two hundred eighty pounds. His size and easygoing manner had earned him the nickname "Jumbo," and almost everyone in the squad preferred it to Beasley. Unlike most other detectives on the job, who either lived in suburbs outside the city or in the nicer neighborhoods, Jumbo chose to remain in the East New York section of Brooklyn where he grew up. Dante liked working with him. He was street smart, easygoing but no pushover, and a lot quicker on his feet than he looked.

Even at midnight, the tables on the sidewalk outside the White Horse Tavern on Hudson Street were crowded. Dante and Jumbo pushed inside, grabbed stools at the short end of the bar, and ordered a couple of drafts.

"How do you afford to live in this neighborhood?" Jumbo asked. They'd just taken that first satisfying sip after clicking glasses. "I got trouble payin' the rent in the ghetto."

Dante smiled a sneaky little smile. "I'm one of those assholes you hear about who has a rent-controlled apartment. One that would otherwise be going for eighteen hundred a month. It was quite a bit less than a hundred when I moved in seventeen years ago."

Jumbo whistled and shook his head. "The more power to you, partner. You ain't got no kids, right?"

"No kids, no wife. I *do* have a cat."

The big man sighed. "That must be nice."

"At least the cat doesn't have a mother-in-law who reads *Watchtower*."

"That's what I mean."

"How long's she here for?"

"Just another couple days, and then *my* mother comes and that ain't a whole lot better."

"Why East New York?" Dante asked. "What have you got in now? Twenty-five? You're making better bread than that."

Jumbo sipped his beer.

"I don't know how it was where you grew up, but that place was a shithole then and it's *still* a shithole. When I got to thinkin' about finally makin' my move out, I started looking around me and wonderin' how much further it's gonna slide if all the kids got for role models is crack dealers, pimps, and whores. I dunno. I never talked about it or made a conscious stand. I just stayed."

Dante shook his head. "I don't know whether you need a shrink or a cardiologist. It sounds a little like softening of either the brain or the heart."

"Maybe a little of both."

"Did I hear you telling Campo about a Pop Warner team?"

Richardson nodded. "My oldest boy plays linebacker, and I'm the head coach. We got us a kick-ass bunch of little hooligans that ain't lost a game yet this year. Got a string-bean kid playing quarterback who could end up bein' great. You find the time, you oughta come check it out. Great fun and pretty good franks.''

Dante left Jumbo and started for home about twenty minutes later. He had known he liked the big guy, but this was the first time they'd had a chance to drink a beer together and shoot the breeze. It was like that most of the time when you were the new guy on the squad. The thaw took time. Richardson was black and he was white. That took time too. They were different people with different lifestyles, but there'd been a growing mutual respect for the important things. Coolheadedness on the street. A certain natural sync that either came or it didn't. They seemed to have it, and that felt pretty good. In fact, Dante couldn't remember the last time he'd felt this good about the job.

The village blocks between the White Horse and Dante's building were teeming with foot traffic, even at that hour. He didn't really mind the crush of humanity at all hours. He was sort of a student of people, peering into their faces as they passed, knowing better than most the human potential for good and evil.

It was just before he reached the low wrought-iron stoop gate that he realized he was out of milk and cat food. After a pause to mentally inventory the contents of his refrigerator, he continued on to cut over to West 11th on around the corner to the deli. The humidity was so oppressive the air seemed as though it couldn't hold even another molecule of moisture without the heavens opening in a torrential downpour. Even at his slow, easy gait, the effort was producing sweat. His shirt clung to him across the shoulders, and a rivulet of sweat tickled his spine as it crept toward the small of his back. Real strange weather for so late in the year.

On the corner of West 11th and Seventh Avenue South,

the nighttime circus was swinging in all three rings. Across the way, two ambulances and a squad car from the Tenth were pulled up to the emergency entrance of St. Vincent's Hospital. A filthy, bearded drifter asked Dante for a dollar, and a fresh-faced blonde with hope and idealism sparkling in her eyes asked him if he was a registered Democrat in Manhattan. A couple of loud gays in tight, shiny clothes and coiffed hair passed arm in arm, hands in each other's back pockets. Greenwich Village: cultural carnival. For Dante, as a young kid from Canarsie, it had taken some getting used to. Now he would never think of going back. Guys from the old neighborhood who visited his Perry Street pad seemed as though they'd crossed over from a foreign country. This was life with the intensity knob cranked all the way up, and Dante loved it.

The shooting victim of August's robbery attempt was back working behind the counter of the deli; he was pale, weak-looking, and hollow-eyed. It was the first time Dante had seen him since the one visit he'd paid at the hospital after his surgery. The guy brightened a bit at the sight of the detective, telling him that he was feeling fine now while pumping his hand. Joe bought his quart of milk and cans of cat food and got out of there. As the Korean feebly shook his hand, he couldn't get out of his mind the image of those hard, rippling arm muscles coming over the counter. On the way out of the store, groceries in hand, he felt a lot less high on life than he had going in.

George Scully didn't go directly home from the country club. That hot little number in the cocktail lounge had been leaving just as he was pulling out of the lot. Gretchen. Tall, tanned, and auburn-haired. Her TR-4 was refusing to start when Scully eased by to offer her a lift. One thing led to another. George found himself atop an Indian-bedspread-draped waterbed in a caretaker's cottage in Lewisboro.

Gretchen was one of those eager young nonverbal things who thought a neurosurgeon or some other fat cat might want to marry her just because she spread her legs and gave enthusiastic head. George left her fairly late in the evening with the obligatory promise to call and get together again soon. He guided his Porsche 928 off Route 35 and into Ramapo Road in Ridgefield about twenty minutes later.

Surrounded by stately oaks and one-point-three acres of manicured lawn, flower beds and ornamental shrubs, the Scully house rambled for two hundred feet along a slight incline above the road. All three stories of it. White clapboard and fieldstone. Giant verandas to the south and north. It was Joanie's pride and joy, that place. A portrait of Wasp gentility. It was also little more than a paper kingdom, prevented from blowing away by two signatures— one authentic and one forged.

"George?"

It was Joan, from in front of the television in her favorite little den. Scully stopped in passing and looked in on his wife. Medium height, perky and athletic, the former Joanie Cox was the essence of country Connecticut from her bobbed brown hair and unadorned, fresh-scrubbed face to her pleated linen jumper and understated handmade flats. She played a lot of tennis and did the Jane Fonda workout religiously in the privacy of their master suite. At forty-two, her body was tanned and tightly muscled. But then, as far as George was concerned, everything about Joanie was tight. Too tight. Like a clock wound too many turns of the key. Instead of moving from place to place, she seemed to dart.

"What's that?" Scully asked vaguely. He'd had a couple of Scotches at the lounge and another few with Gretchen. It wasn't easy to focus.

"Where have you been? It's after one o'clock."

"Something came up. I had to run back into the city after my game."

"You couldn't have called?"

George shrugged and rubbed his eyes. "I thought I asked Amy at the office, but it may have slipped my mind. I think I'm fighting off a bug or something. Tired all the time."

Joan was concerned. "George, you've been acting awfully strange lately. I think we have to talk."

Scully felt a sudden impulse to blurt out the truth—that the house wasn't theirs and the investment properties weren't theirs and all his investments had gone down the crapper. He was screwing a gorgeous blond bombshell who snorted cocaine and was just now returning from a rendezvous with a cocktail waitress who'd helped him prove yet again that social station and self-respect had very little to do with each other.

Christ! Joan was going in and out of focus in front of him. He was dizzy and felt like he might pass out. In another second, his stomach did a quick little flip-flop and he was running hard for the powder room down the hall before he puked on the wool pile. Joanie was behind him in the hall, looking on in concern as he dry-wretched into the bowl. In time, he backed away and stood on wobbly knees. His face was ashen.

Joan shook her head. "I keep trying to shake the idea that there's something terribly wrong. Come on, George, if there is, I'm your wife."

Scully regarded her through watering eyes. "There's really nothing wrong," he insisted. "Lot of pressure lately. Got some money in something that's a little shaky at the moment. It'll all work out."

"Shaky?" she asked, interest piqued. "I just talked to Dad this morning. He says you ought to be getting rich off those tips he gave you last fall."

The mere mention of Pete Cox made Scully's blood boil. He was always trying to butt in, never letting them forget how much he'd done for "you kids" over the years. Rarely a month went by when the old man didn't find occasion to make reference to the support he'd given George's medical education. That, and the grubstake here in Ridgefield. To make matters worse, Joanie worshiped the ground the arrogant ass walked on. Instead of being critical of him, George went out of his way to bite his tongue. With the way his private affairs were moving, it seemed important to keep Joanie mollified.

"This was just a little something of my own," he said amiably.

Joan sniffed. "Something Milt Carpfinger gave you?"

George closed his eyes, pressing his thumb and index finger to them. "I'm really beat, baby. The man *is* our financial planner. He's given us good advice."

"Dad insists he doesn't know his ass from his elbow."

"Milt and I have kept you and the kids in shoe leather," Scully reminded her, forcing a wan smile. "I've got to hit the hay, honey. The schedule of emergency occurences lately is about to murder me."

George had swigged a good mouthful of the waitress's Listermint and popped a Certs before pushing through the front door. Between them and the incident in the bathroom, he felt it was safe enough to hold his breath and peck her quickly on the cheek.

"G'night, huh?" he mumbled and moved off for the stairs.

Four

Joe Dante got a jolt when he returned to the squad Monday morning. The temporary replacement for Art Campo was a former narcotics detective named Vinnie Arata. While Dante was assigned to the Manhattan South Narcotics Division, Arata was working Manhattan North. They'd crossed paths occasionally but never actually collaborated on anything. Later, when shifted back to regular precinct duty, Arata was one of nearly a dozen detectives rotated out of the Tenth in a corruption shake-up that occurred only months before Dante worked his own short stint there. As Dante entered the squad, he became the focus of Arata's jovial attentions.

"Joey Dante. Paisan. How you been, guy? Long time no see."

Dante nodded. "Hiya, Vinnie. I heard you decided to crawl back out of the sewer a couple years back. Join the rest of humanity. Kinda lost track after that."

A dramatic shrug propped up both sides of Vinnie's shit-eating grin. "Only so long you can take it, right? Hey, I

42

was sorry to hear about the six the brass made you pull on the outside. Fucked-up bunch of politicians.''

Dante winked. "Still got my tin."

Lieutenant Vic Manley stepped out of his office and strode across the squad room. "You can enjoy old-home week later, gents. Let's take a ride."

Jumbo Richardson hopped down from his perch atop a desk; no mean feat. "What's up, Vic?"

"Uniformed patrol just called in a corpse on West Eleventh between Fifth and Sixth. Some old dude hacked to death in his bed. Guy on the scene says it's grisly as hell."

The lieutenant and his team were hustling downstairs when he glanced back over his shoulder at Arata. "Sorry about the welcome, Detective. You met Beasley Richardson?"

"No sweat, Vic," Vinnie answered amiably. "We both got in a little early and had a quick java together."

They gained the ground level and hurried out back toward the tight little parking area.

Manley approached the front passenger door and tossed the ignition key to Jumbo. "Unfortunately, we gotta save all the lie swapping for later. Damn inconsiderate of whoever this asshole with the pigsticker is."

"Something we'll have to remember when we finally get him in the elevator," Jumbo said.

The block of West 11th Street between Fifth and Sixth avenues in Greenwich Village is partially lined with Federal townhouses constructed of brownstone or red brick. On the north side of the street, toward Sixth Avenue, the New School for Social Research intrudes on the period architecture for a couple of hundred feet. On either end of the block there are a couple of restaurants. For the most part, though, the street is commerce-free, tree-lined, and quiet, and the townhouses are individual residences. One, with a modern front built at a slight angle to the sidewalk, marks the scene of a Weatherman bomb factory, the original facade erased in a basement explosion in 1970.

"Check it out," Jumbo grunted. He seemed to be in slightly ill humor this morning. An obvious case of in-law overstimulation. "The vultures have descended."

In addition to the two squad cars from the Sixth, an ME's sedan, an ambulance, and a forensics van already on the scene, there were a pair of camera crews from local news teams. Within minutes there would be more. Like vultures, some were slower than others to locate carrion and swoop.

On the sidewalk in front of the place, two uniforms were stringing the characteristic yellow tape along a low wrought-iron fence, marking the perimeter of the crime scene. Another man guarded the top of the wide stoop, barring access. Jumbo eased the unmarked sedan in behind a squad car, and the four detectives climbed out to approach the gate. Manley led the way, nodding to the uniforms and wading through reporters, grumbling "No comment." He beckoned to the man at the top of the steps, encircling his shoulders with one meaty paw and putting their heads together. He asked for a status report.

"No one's been in or out but our people and the maid, Vic. The ME's in there with the stiff. I've never seen anything like this."

Manley nodded and told the patrolman to keep the jackals at bay. "I don't want them getting anything unless I give it to them," he said, glancing around at his three-man team for emphasis.

Inside a pair of ornate and beautifully preserved antique oak doors was a foyer, its marble floor done in big white squares with smaller green squares at each point where four corners met. Dante noticed that the green marble was slightly veined and resembled both the color and texture of money. The ceiling was vaulted to what must have been fifteen feet, making the room seem narrower than it really was. At the far end, a polished mahogany staircase returned back on itself as it swept grandly to the second level of the house. From the sound of things, all the real excitement was up on that floor. On the other hand, there was plenty for an imaginative detective to sink his teeth into right where they stood.

It had to be blood, even though it was now dried to a dull brown, almost the consistency of watercolor. A message was scrawled in it, in letters nearly a foot high: "DEATH TO THE ART IMPERIALISTS"—whatever *that* meant. There were six framed paintings in the foyer. Dante didn't know much about specific painters or periods, but one of his famous hunches told him that these were almost certainly masterpieces of one sort or another. They were lavishly framed and individually lit. Each had been slashed once diagonally and splashed with blood.

"Jesus motherfucking Christ!" Arata stared wide-eyed at the scene. "Somebody's gone off his nut."

"The man is obviously a detective," Dante cracked. "Stick around, Vincent. You're gonna fit right in."

Arata jerked halfway around to scowl, betraying his good-natured facade for the first time. Manley absorbed this and waved them ahead.

"C'mon, you Sherlocks. The *real* action seems to be upstairs."

As they ascended, strobe flashes lit the walls of the stairwell. The victim, one Oscar Wembley, age seventy-nine, had gotten it in the master suite, hacked to death in his bed. The corpse was still in position, though hardly recognizable as anything more than so much dead meat. There was blood on every surface of the room; the walls had been heavily spattered in the frenzied attack, the floor was awash in it. Five more paintings in the room were

45

slashed diagonally and smeared with yet more blood. There were more crazed messages.

LIBERATE ART–EXTERMINATE CULTURE VULTURES!!
ART IS LOVE–KILL HOARDING PIGS! GENTRICIDE!!

As the lieutenant checked with the head of the forensics team and the medical examiner's man, Dante moved slowly around the room with the lumbering Jumbo at his side. Right then, neither of them was ready for a closer look at the body. You just never got used to a sight like that. The color was drained from their faces. A nasty knot in Joe's gut threatened back flips. The nauseating odor of death filled his nostrils: the primary stages of decay.

Together, the partners tried to focus on the messages and the ruined paintings. If Dante was right, each of them had to be worth up into the hundreds of thousands of dollars. Perhaps more.

"The new guy is right," Jumbo mumbled. He was sweating, the perspiration forming droplets on his brow that he mopped with a handkerchief. It was air-conditioned in there. Cool as a tomb. "Somebody *did* go off his nut."

Dante nodded, turning from the walls. He was ready now to force himself to examine the corpse. He knew he had to get the grisly reality fixed in his mind's eye. On a slab at the morgue, the insanity of the act would be lost. The intensity of it. He had to capture that now, lock in on it, in order to know in his gut what they were up against.

From across the room, Vic Manley watched Dante step to the bed and stare down at the mutilation there. Seconds later, Jumbo joined him. Together, they simply contemplated in silence. Behind the two, Vinnie Arata stood regarding his new teammates. From the way his shoulders were set, Manley guessed that the new man was willing his partners to show some sign of weakness here—an indication of being unable to handle it. That was the sort of cop Gus Lieberman had described this guy to be. Arrogant and marginally disruptive. Not a team player. *Not* what Manley or any other commander needed. He had to smile to himself now. Dante and Jumbo were both smart, tough cookies. If Vinnie thought he might see some weakness, he would be disappointed. These guys may have been an unlikely pairing upon surface inspection, but they both had all the tools it took to be good detectives, and they respected the hell out of each other.

With his jaw set, Dante watched calmly as the ME men lifted the butchered corpse and slid it into a plastic body bag.

"What do you think?" he asked Jumbo. "See anything I didn't?"

"You don't do that just to off a dude," the fat man replied. He wiped his brow again with his handkerchief. "The cat was crazy mad."

Dante turned to spot Arata standing idly by. "What do you get from the lab boys?" he asked. There was the hint of challenge in his voice.

Arata shrugged. "The ground ain't trembled. No signed confessions wadded up in the wastebasket."

From across the room, a familiar voice hailed Dante. "Joey! You catch this mess?"

Dante turned to spy Rocky Conklin advancing on him. Rocky was a forensic pathologist who did most of his work in the basement of the morgue.

"Hey, Rock, welcome to the bright light of day."

Conklin, a grisled, stocky character with gray hair and a ghoulish grin, paused to spit the bitten tip of a new cigar into a Kleenex before lighting it. "Boys called me over special," he said. "Craziness, huh? One of the worst I've ever seen."

Dante regarded him pensively. "So? Anything you can

tell us? Have the walls whispered anything we might want to know?''

Conklin shook his head. "Not even a good stock tip.'' He stopped to wave another guy over with his cigar. "Hey, Bernie. C'mere. You know Bernie Horvath, Joey?''

Dante nodded. "We've been down the garden path a few times. Howzit, Bernie? Nice to see a lab *pro* at a scene for a change.''

He turned, introducing Jumbo to the ME and the forensics man while he was at it. "Rock says the guy didn't leave much.''

"Left the murder weapon,'' Horvath said. "Right here on the floor. Not much good. He stole it from the kitchen along with a pair of rubber dish gloves from under the sink.''

"Mind if we pay you a visit at the lab a little later?'' Dante asked. "You know, look over your shoulder while you tear your hair out in frustration.''

Bernie patted his bald head. "Did that yesterday,'' he grunted good-naturedly. "Sure. Why not? I'll probably be knee deep in this shit all afternoon and most of tomorrow.''

Distractedly, Dante scanned the walls. "What do you make of all this? Ever seen anything like it?''

"Not me,'' Bernie replied, shaking his head. "Real Charlie Manson stuff. Fucker went haywire.''

Dante sighed. "Maybe that computer of yours will give us something. I hope so. I hate to think of somebody doing this sort of thing again before we can get to him.''

Jumbo pointed to a little gizmo attached to the pane of glass in an adjacent window. "You checked out the alarm system? One of them jobs where all the stations broadcast to a central unit. You gotta figure if the perp forced entry, the thing would'a been tripped.''

"Not necessarily,'' Bernie said. "We haven't found any evidence of forced entry yet, but the maid tells us the old guy sometimes forgot to activate it. The thing wasn't on when she showed up for work this morning."

Dante cocked his head. "Then there's a chance our man knew the victim."

Horvath nodded. "There is that chance, sure."

Vic Manley, overhearing the conversation, now stepped over to join their brainstorming. "The central unit is directly linked to the alarm company. Uniformed patrol called the number on the sticker. When the thing goes off, they're supposed to send a car around, pronto. They confirmed that the old man was a little absentminded. A couple of times a month he'd forget to turn the fucker on."

Jumbo considered this information. "That'd be some nice coincidence, yeah? A couple days outta thirty and our friend picks one of the lucky few."

"Unless it was an inside job," Vinnie interjected from a few feet away. "Someone who worked for the alarm company would sure as hell know what the old fart had stashed here. Whadya figure all this shit's worth? More than a couple million is my bet."

"Easily," Bernie Horvath confirmed. "But I've been through the place pretty thoroughly, and I'd say the motive wasn't theft. There's nothing significant missing, as far as the maid could tell us."

Arata shook his head. "Maybe it was somethin' else then. The old bastard forgot his Christmas tip or somethin'. A nut don't have to do somethin' that makes sense, somethin' you just figure out. And lookit this shit on the walls. Loony-tunes, babe."

Dante was still trying to follow his new teammate's logic when a commotion on the landing outside interrupted them. A woman was wailing hysterically.

"What's going on?" Manley barked.

The cop at the door gestured helplessly. "Next of kin,

Vic. The victim's niece. Showed up for her weekly visit or something.''

"She can't come in here," Manley said firmly. "Dante. Take her down to the kitchen and see what she can give you." He glanced over at Horvath. "You boys finished down there?" When the lab man nodded, Manley waved Dante on. "Other family and all that shit. You know." He then turned his attention to the room at large. "All right, I'm puttin' a lid on this thing. Them vultures outside the front door don't get shit, got it? They've seen the body bag. Let them draw their own conclusions. They probably already got a name. Fine. I don't want them selling their yellow fucking rags with our madman's MO."

Dante stepped out onto the landing to find a sobbing middle-aged woman in a chair. She was elegantly dressed and coiffed, a blonde with aristocratic features and a good body. Joe guessed that she'd had her face done at least once, judging from the smoothness of her skin compared to the backs of her hands.

"Ma'am?" he said, approaching. "I'm Detective Dante from the Sixth Precinct. If you don't mind, I'd like to talk with you downstairs."

The woman looked up, eyes vacant. Even in her makeup-smeared distress, Joe could see that she'd been a stone-cold knockout in her prime. She was still very pretty.

"Please," he prodded. "Maybe we can get you a cup of coffee or something. Believe me, you don't want to go in there."

The woman rose without a word and allowed herself to be led to the floor below. A slight, wounded utterance escaped her lips as she momentarily focused on the message scrawled across the foyer wall. Joe steered her quickly away and through an unscathed dining room to the kitchen. The lab boys had made quite a mess of it, with print powder dusted over every surface in sight. Beyond the

50

kitchen was a tiny maid's room, and Dante opted for its less disturbed interior. With the door propped open, he set a kettle to boil as the woman sat heavily on a shabby little daybed.

"Call me Joe," Dante suggested. He moved to sit opposite on a straight-back chair.

The woman dried her eyes with a monogrammed hanky. "You must forgive me," she sighed, sniffling. "I guess I'm not being very strong."

"You've just had a terrible shock. It's understandable."

The woman tried to smile. "I'm Jane Goodell. Oscar's niece. He was the only family I had left."

"We're going to catch the animal who did this"—Dante spotted the simple wedding band—"Mrs. Goodell. There may be a way you could help. How close were you to your uncle?"

Jane Goodell appeared to consider the question as though for the first time. Dante knew she was asking herself all the questions a person in her situation invariably asks. Questions involving a lot of senseless self-recrimination.

"I would visit him at least twice a week," she replied. "To make sure the little things got done. Uncle Oscar was frightfully forgetful. He wouldn't pay bills or perhaps forget to sign a check before he sent it off. That sort of thing."

"Did he have any enemies you know of?" Joe asked. "Maybe a disgruntled employee or a business associate?"

His subject managed a wan smile. "My uncle has been retired from business for many years. Before that, he wasn't very good at it and only dabbled. They were less than fruitful enterprises. His employees loved him. Ask Marta, the maid."

For some reason, it surprised Dante that a man of Oscar Wembley's obvious wealth hadn't been involved in earning it. He wasn't sure why it should. New York was full of people who lived on inheritances.

"The perpetrator seems to have focused much of his wrath on your uncle's art collection. Do you have any idea what that might be about?"

She shrugged expressively. "It's absolute madness. Oscar Wembley's collection of Impressionist paintings is one of the finest private holdings in the country. He was considered an authority on the period. Quite respected. Any number of buyers would come to him first before purchasing a work at auction."

Dante nodded, absorbing this information. "Would you have access to his financial records? With the full knowledge and cooperation of his accountant, of course. We will need records of disbursements made to tradesmen and anybody else who might have had access to the house during the past year or so. If you intercede as the sole heir, we could avoid the usual subpoena procedure and save valuable time."

Jane Goodell straightened, trying to hold her head high.

"Of course. That would make sense, officer. A bookkeeper by the name of Stewart comes from the accountant once a month to do the ledgers. I believe they're kept here. On the premises."

Five

At three-fifteen on the afternoon following Oscar Wembley's murder, George Scully was catching up on his professional reading and going over notes on an upcoming procedure when his receptionist entered to hand him his personal mail. Prominent among this batch of letters was correspondence from his malpractice insurance carrier. They were putting him on notice that they had reviewed his case in the greatest detail and saw no avenue of approach other than to offer settlement. In order to avoid the increased costs of executing further depositions and continuing preparation toward litigation, they were prepared to offer one million to the victim. In any subsequent negotiations, Scully would be on the look for the rest.

Wonderful. After slamming his fist into his blotter in disgust, Scully buzzed his receptionist and told her to get his own attorney, Weeb Caruthers, on the phone. As he waited for the call to be put through, he tapped a pencil on the edge of his coffee cup impatiently, stopped, gripped it between thumb and forefinger, and snapped it in half.

"Dr. Scully," the lawyer rumbled in his mellifluous baritone. "What can I do for you?"

Without much preamble, Scully read Caruthers the insurance carrier's letter.

"I've looked over your policy, George," the attorney replied in a more informal tone. "They can do it. This is claims-made you're carrying now. Not the old occurrence."

"It's two goddamn years before the thing would ever come to trial," Scully complained. "I don't get it. Why now?"

"Court costs. Overhead. You dangle a number at them now because the other team knows that a significant amount of any court award is eaten up by the clock. This way, you save both them and yourself the time and expense."

"You're telling me that there's nothing I can do about it? That sixty days from now, I'm possibly out a million bucks?"

"That's what I'm saying. You can fight them yourself, of course. As your attorney, I can notify them that they would be making settlement over your strongest objections. Lot of good it'll do us. They're ready to hang your fat out to fry, my boy—and believe me, no insurance company is willing to give away a million bucks unless they're convinced it's a *very* lost cause."

Scully thanked Caruthers, hung up, and stared blankly at the letter in front of him. Thanks for nothing.

Fifteen minutes later, the neurosurgeon still couldn't get his mind back on the procedure he was scheduled to perform the next day. Another human life hung in the balance, all nicely detailed in the notes jotted in the file, and he'd gone completely blank on the facts of the case.

They were willing to offer their full exposure! It actually said that right in the letter. It boggled Scully to even attempt imagining where he was going to come up with his end to it. Hell, it might as well be a *hundred* million for all the hope he had of raising it.

In fury, George swept his desk clean with his forearm, scattering paperwork across the carpet.

At the end of the shift, Dante offered to buy the whip and the rest of the team a beer. When Vinnie Arata begged off, asking for a rain check, Joe, Jumbo, and Manley headed for the Corner Bistro at West 4th and Jane. All three were drained by the day's events, but none of them, for various reasons, was eager to hurry home. Vic Manley was recently divorced and faced the prospect of returning to a half-furnished apartment on 102nd Street. Jumbo had mother-in-law to the eyeballs. Dante had a couple of hours to kill before his buddy, Brian Brennan, showed up to watch the Monday-night game between the Jets and the Patriots.

Manley had a copy of the *Daily News* spread on the bar in front of him, open to the stats page of the Sports section. Dante was trying to peer past his forearm to the results of Sunday's second game of the World Series between the Mets and Red Sox. The hometown squad was down two zip after a fabulous season and a hair-raising playoff with Houston. nobody was hitting, and Doctor K looked shaky in the opener.

"How'd your team do on Saturday?" Dante was elbowing Jumbo.

The big guy, contemplating one of the Bistro's famous bacon cheesburgers, suddenly lit up. "We whipped ass," he said enthusiastically. "My boy Arthur had six solos, and this troublemaker kid I been workin' with ran for a hundred and sixteen yards." He paused to signal the bartender and *did* order the Bistroburger, rare. "We're playin' some pantywaist team of rich kids from Forest Hills this week. You oughta come. They got a couple ringers and are undefeated, but I snuck over and caught them two weeks ago. We'll make dog food outta them."

The fat man's enthusiasm was contagious. Before he knew what he was doing, Dante found himself saying he thought he just might swing by and check it out.

The barman ambled over and set a large order of fries in front of the lieutenant. Without a word, Dante slopped a little ketchup along one side of the plate and dipped one as Manley pried himself away from the sports to glare at him. Dante smiled and had another.

"Have all you want," the whip grumbled.

"No thanks. Don't want to ruin my dinner."

"You're a real fuckin' piece of work."

Dante shrugged, caught the bartender's eye, and circled his finger over their glasses for another round.

"I can't figure why an eighty-year-old man would let someone into his house at two in the morning," Jumbo mused. He picked up his beer and downed what was left in the glass.

"Maybe he didn't," Dante countered. "It could have been someone he spent the evening with."

Manley joined in, shaking his head. "The maid said he ate alone and she left unusually late. Nine fifteen."

"And he generally turned in when?" Dante challenged. "Late, right? He was supposed to be some sort of art historian—and not much of a sleeper. The Goodell woman gave us that much. She said he would sit up reading into the wee hours. Look at the room. There were half a dozen books on the nightstand and a yellow legal pad with a lot of notes jotted on it." Joe took a swig of his own beer and fingered another fry. Just then, an attractive blonde entered with a fairly run-of-the-mill guy. Joe tried for eye contact and got nothing but cool indifference. You couldn't win them all. "I wouldn't discount the idea that he knew the guy."

"Resentment toward him, you think?" Jumbo asked.

"Or art collectors in general," Dante replied. "Either way, I like the idea that the perp knew him."

Manley mulled the idea over. "Your buddy Arata is all hot and bothered over the alarm company angle."

Dante rolled his eyes. "*My* buddy?"

" 'Hey, paisan!' " Manley mimicked Vinnie. " 'It was like old-fucking-home week.' "

"Just between you, me, and this french fry," Dante said, snagging another one, "that guy's an asshole. His badge may say detective on it, but he couldn't find his dick behind his own fly."

Dante's indictment of Arata surprised both of the black cops. On the job, racial subgroups tended to gravitate together, a phenomenon reinforced by various heritage organizations, the most famous of which is probably the Irish Emerald Society. The Italian Confederation was also one of the job's strongest.

"He's not looking at this thing logically," Dante insisted. "Think of all the contacts the old guy must have had in the art world. Museums, dealers, individual collectors like himself. Shit, the ledgers the niece turned over list some pretty heavy acquisitions over just this past year. He has long-term loans with at least a dozen institutions. That would put him in touch with lots of the same types of people. Any one of them could have gone over the edge."

Manley nodded. "I kind of like it. Seems like as good a place as any to start. Where's this dude's money from, did the niece say?"

"His father invented some sort of hydraulic valve or something. I guess almost everything that flies has got to have it. The dough is still rolling in."

The whip picked up his beer and drained it; he refolded his *News* and tucked it under his arm. "I'm gonna fly. I'll see you two in the A.M., huh?"

"What about your fries?" Dante asked.

"You seem to be doing a pretty good job on them."

Dante grinned, picked up another, and shamelessly slipped it into his mouth. Manley, meanwhile, paused about halfway off his stool, frowning over something.

"Am I hearing you say that there might be a little personality conflict between you and the new man?" he asked.

Dante shook his head. "I'm not saying that, Vic. You're asking me whether I'll work with him? Hey, I've rocked enough boats on my own account. I just wouldn't ever ask him to feed my cat."

How long could he maintain his sanity? George Scully was asking himself as he left his office at six and started upstairs to Fiona's apartment. Joanie'd had little choice but to accept his "staff meeting" and "early surgery" excuses for staying in town. Now, in the elevator, Scully struggled to get a grip. It was a situation that had already gotten out of control *before* the insurance company's letter that afternoon. It was simply the nudge that threatened to push him over the brink. The malpractice suit had been a reality for the better part of two months. In there somewhere, Biotechnics went belly-up. At the same time, Fiona started really putting the screws to him; shit or get off the pot. Christ, he'd brought it on himself by moaning something about being in love with her while in the throes of passion. Fiona, confident in the knowledge that he wasn't happy with his home life and that she was pushing all the right buttons, pushed the wrong one in demanding a more definitive declaration of intent. Scully remembered making just such a promise that same night. He would ask Joan for a divorce. But how could he? There was the matter of a forged mortgage note and the heavily leveraged community property. Meanwhile, things had gone from bad to worse. Paying off the note on the house and suffering scrutiny of his other dealings was out of the question. If Joan didn't have him thrown in jail outright, she'd leave him a pauper, indentured to her for the rest of his life. Somehow, Scully sensed that Fiona wouldn't be quite as interested in life with a pauper. Already, she was quick to voice displeasure and was more openly demanding. Two weeks ago, in a fit of jealous anger, she'd almost answered the guest-room extension phone Scully maintained in her apartment. He'd managed to calm her down, but it'd cost him dinner at Aurora and the cash to fly her to Nassau with friends for a long weekend. The sex was still good. Great, in fact. But there was something creeping in around the edges of their "arrangement." A hostility. Fiona wanted to marry a secure professional. Someone who could show-case her good looks and provide a niche in the world where she felt she belonged. Scully had always accepted this. A woman like Fiona was a commodity to be purchased. His was the rare, exclusive currency: standing, security, tanned and athletic good looks. It had been like an electric current arcing between them that first time in the packed hospital elevator. She hadn't been coy about it either. And let's face it, dalliances with cocktail waitresses aside, George Scully was as addicted to her as she was to cocaine. Now he didn't know what the hell to do.

Fiona had a shift running to eight and wouldn't be home for another forty-five minutes. George let himself into the apartment, checked for messages with his service, and made himself a double Scotch and soda. An hour later, he was sprawled on the sofa, barely comprehending the news in an alcohol haze when his statuesque mistress walked in. A bottle of Dewar's sat on the coffee table at his elbow, a couple of inches down from where he'd found it earlier.

Fiona took in the scene as she tossed her handbag onto the entry table and stood with her hands on her hips.

"Trouble in paradise?" she asked, eyebrows arched.

George focused on her. White uniform dress, stockings, and shoes. He'd never seen anyone fill out clothes like she did.

"Something like that. Joanie really started getting on my nerves last night. This afternoon, the insurance carrier sent a letter advising me they plan to offer settlement."

"What time's your morning call?"

"Six thirty."

"You look like you'll be in fine shape for it."

He nodded, grinning, and held out a hand. It wobbled uncertainly in the air. "Steady as a rock. Check it out."

Fiona rolled her eyes and crossed to the bedroom door. With a shoulder against the jamb, she braced herself on one foot and removed a shoe. Alternating, she finished the job.

"How long are you going to let this eat at you before you do something about it? I thought you were a tough guy, George. Mr. Success. Mr. Ambition. Right now, you look like Mr. Pathetic."

Scully craned his neck to contemplate her, anger in his eyes. "You never used to talk to me like that."

"You always had control, George. Telling me how you were going to make your own decision without the help of your meddling father-in-law. Is that what you're doing? You look drunk to me."

She reached to unzip the dress, peeling it back from her shoulders and pushing it down over her hips. She wore a garter belt and stockings instead of pantyhose. Her brassiere was a lacy little half-cup number, just enough to give her minimal support. Even wasted, Scully felt a stirring in his pants. Not that it would do him much good. When she was in this sort of mood, Fiona could be cold as ice, and George, no matter how much he wanted it, had one hell of a time pulling the trigger when he got this drunk. She was teasing him, popping the clasp on the bra now and shrugging out of it. God almighty!

"You're lucky, you know that?" He was speaking slowly, working to forge his thoughts into words. "You've got no idea what this is like. One day everything is fine and you're sitting on top of the world. The next day, not one or two things but *everything* falls on your head."

In the middle of this little speech, Fiona disappeared into the bedroom, only to return seconds later and sit across from him in one of the two armchairs. On the glass-topped table she placed a small, folded paper packet. Next to it she set a shortened soda straw and a razor blade.

"You're a drunken mess and I want to get laid tonight," she said matter-of-factly. "I don't want to listen to you whine and feel sorry for yourself, George." With the paper packet now open on the table, she lifted cocaine out of it with the corner of the razor blade and dumped it on the glass. Slowly, she started crushing it with the sharp edge of the blade. George watched, fascinated. Fiona knew he disapproved and until now had kept her little vice ostensibly under wraps. Now, all but naked, those magnificent tits staring across at eye level, her perfume wafting to him and the whole package making him crazy, she was flaunting it. She was also quite expert at what she was doing, lining the powder up into little piles.

"Here," she said, handing him the straw.

"What?"

"Do some, for Christ's sake. Courage in powder form, George. You need it."

Scully stared at her and then at the cocaine on the table. He'd always been anti-drug. Pot, coke, pills, whatever. Other doctors he knew smoked a little, a couple did coke, and more than he wanted to admit hit the bennies and tranquilizers. But him? He was a social drinker, who prided himself on his propriety.

"I don't think so," he said, shaking his head slowly.

Fiona smiled for the first time since she'd walked in the door. "You know what your problem is, George. You're chickenshit. You're a wimp." She eased back in the chair and unclipped the garters and wriggled out of her panties. After slipping them over a slender ankle, she wadded them into a ball and tossed them in his face. "But you see," she continued, "I've already got too much invested in you to sit here and watch you self-destruct."

Scully could smell the warmth emanating from the lingerie now sitting on his chest.

"I don't want to self-destruct," he assured her. "Do you think I chose all this shit?"

"Take a snort, George. It'll give you a whole different perspective. Scotch is a down. This will help you focus on something I want to talk to you about."

"What's that?"

"Saving your ass, George. Saving *us*." Standing, she held out the straw to him.

Scully stared at her towering over him. Even through the Scotch haze, he'd begun to ache for her, his ardor throbbing in his pants. He took the straw.

"How the fuck am I supposed to do this?" he asked.

"Sniff like you're doing nasal spray, and for god's sake don't exhale."

He rolled off the sofa and onto his knees. Hunched over the table, he eyed the little piles of powder. What the Christ did he think he was doing? With the straw lined up, he snorted quickly, eyes squeezed shut. The stuff burned a prickly sort of burn, surprising him. He reared back, eyes coming open wide and watering. Fiona was grinning at him.

"Do one more up the other nostril," she instructed.

Already the burning in his nose was gone, replaced by a pleasant, tingling numbness. He did another line.

"Now sit back and relax," she ordered. Rounding the table, she eased back next to him on the sofa and reached to run her hand across the erection in his pants, fingers squeezing it gently. Scully moaned with pleasure. She worked to unzip him before slipping to her knees and doing two lines with practiced swiftness.

This was her meal ticket. She'd spent the better part of a year cultivating it. Unlike a lot of other fat cats she'd run across at the hospital and around town, Scully was at least not repulsive to contemplate naked. He had a nice body, as a matter of fact, something she considered now as he lay back with his eyes closed, her fingers caressing him. On a lot of levels, he was just as much of an object as she was. When she looked at him, she saw more than a physique. She saw the life of ease this particular physique could afford her. Now all he needed was his confidence back, and in a couple of months he could put his problems behind him. Fiona didn't want to lose this shot at the brass ring. Not without a fight.

George Scully was confused at first. The drug was nothing like he'd anticipated. Within minutes, his alcohol haze had vaporized and he was sitting up above himself. A feeling of elation lifted him. His stomach fluttered, while below it, a heated desire was being stoked by the firm fingers of his mistress. The delicious weight of free-hanging breasts brushed his thighs as he was suddenly engulfed by the hot wetness of her mouth. The shock of contact was heightened by a crystal clarity inside his skull. He didn't think he'd ever felt so ready, so primed. Her mouth seemed to sense this as she began to work him feverishly, slipping a hand into the act as well.

She'd said she wanted to get laid. The thought flitted through George's consciousness as he lay there, unable to stop the flow of events. His back arched as he came in great shuddering spasms. Fiona stayed with him all the way, never breaking her rhythm, doing something that was repulsive to her.

"God*damn*!" she gasped, suddenly throwing back her head and gulping air. "I thought you were going to drown me."

Scully was breathing hard, leaning forward to clamp that blond head in his hands, smothering it with kisses. "What can I do for you?" he whispered.

"I want you in me, George. I want you to feel your own power. It excites me, George. I can't believe you'd let a man in a wheelchair take it all away." She climbed into his lap and straddled him, grasping what remained of his enthusiasm and mounting it. With the mention of Benjamin Crowley, their eyes had locked.

Scully panted, trying to keep up with her. "What am I supposed to do? Have him killed?" The drug and the way she was moving against him, trying to extend the pleasure of the act, made his perception fuzzy.

"What would you be killing? You've already risked your fortune and your reputation trying to save his life. *You* didn't cause him to hemorrhage. Why should you have to pay? Just because some shyster lawyer can pin phonied-up blame on you?" She stopped moving and settled to stare deep into his eyes. "Ask yourself why *we* should have to pay for this, George. The man needs to have an accident."

What she'd said took a while to sink into Scully's consciousness. The drug was taking a nasty turn on him, the bottom of his euphoria suddenly falling out.

"Do you think I could have just a little more of that?" he asked, pointing at the table.

She smiled and lifted off of him to retrieve a little pile of the powder, scooping it with the help of the blade into one of her fingernails.

"Exhale and hold your breath," she instructed. She

brought the drug up under one of his nostrils. "Now sniff."

George didn't feel the burning so much this time as he watched Fiona refill the nail, take a quick one of her own, and then carry more to his other nostril. He snorted again and sat thinking.

"Not an accident," he said at length, shaking his head. He was staring at his hands. They were hands which would work early the next morning to preserve another life. "In order to get the malpractice dogs off my back, it would have to look like he was murdered." He paused. "Jesus Christ. What am I saying?" In some removed space he was wondering if it was really him thinking the thoughts that now ran through his head. The same George Scully who paid lip service to the Hippocratic Oath. Father of two young sons. Then again, what alternatives did he have? Ruin? The reality, as cold and harsh as it was, acknowledged the desperation of his situation. If Benjamin Crowley lived to be rolled into a courtroom, he and the insurance company would quite certainly lose any decision. In settling, they were doing the same thing as asking Scully to stick a loaded gun in his mouth. With Crowley dead, there was half a chance that he might recover his position in the market; at least enough to pay the note on the house and get *that* monkey off his back. It wouldn't really matter if Joanie discovered they were broke once he'd filed for separation. She would get the house and not much else. He still had a four-hundred-thousand-dollar offshore fund investment that she couldn't touch. It wasn't enough to cover his malpractice exposure, but it could prove a nice little nest egg if he were free and clear of it. Hell, if Crowley were dead, he'd have a fighting chance.

Fiona stood and stretched languorously above him. God-damn, there were times when she could make him do almost anything.

"I'm taking a bath," she announced. "You look like you ought to think about getting some sleep."

"How?" Scully asked, for the moment ignoring her advice. "*I* can't kill him."

"I have a friend who's told me that if I ever needed anyone's legs broken, I should just let him know," she said matter-of-factly. "I think he knows some pretty heavy people."

Scully considered this, sitting on impulses of jealousy and curiosity. "My name never comes up," he said. "Not to anybody."

Six

Dante's sculptor buddy, Brian Brennan, represented a sort of window into a completely other reality. They did a fair amount of off-hour hanging out together, Dante glad to get away from the immense private fraternity of the job and Brennan enjoying the gritty grounding that Dante's daily experience could afford. Tonight they occupied Dante's living room, eating pizza and getting set to take in the Monday-night game between the Jets and the New England Patriots.

Brian emerged from Joe's kitchen with another pair of cold beers. He was a robust Irishman who ran religiously and looked real good for his early forties. A fair amount of fame and good fortune hadn't done much to affect the gregarious side of his otherwise intense demeanor. He grinned now as half the cheese from Dante's slice drooped into his lap as he reached for the offered beer. On the screen of the cop's 27-inch Sony set, Frank Gifford was busy singing the praises of Jet quarterback Kenny O'Brien. Brennan grunted at the mess in Dante's lap and took his own seat next to him. Before the sculptor left for the kitchen, they'd been arguing about Joe's foundered relationship with Rosa Losada.

"Maybe I'm wrong," Brennan suggested. "She just might want a guy who's house-broken."

Dante scowled at him. Around the room, two months after her departure, there were still bare spaces where Rosa's things had been removed and nothing had been shifted to replace them. If asked, Joe would claim the holes didn't bother him. Brian knew better.

"I still don't get it—why she thinks it's me who's copping the attitude." He twisted the cap off the bottle and tossed it onto the coffee table next to his sneaker-clad feet. "I mean, I was the one who bent his ass over backwards to make her feel like this was her home too. Shit, I washed my share of dishes and took out the garbage, and *she* left."

Brennan grinned, shaking his head. As much as they'd talked about it, he was forever amazed at how basically unconscious his friend could be in approaching this thing.

"I've said it before and I'll say it again. You've never really listened to her side of it," he countered. "She never argued that you didn't do all those things. If you opened your mind and faced the music, you'd know that isn't it at all. You're too smart to sit on that line of shit forever. Her leaving put a giant goddamn dent in your ego, and now you're telling yourself what your wounded ego wants to hear. Get *past* it!"

"What?" Dante returned hotly. "Get past what? That the woman I gave my heart and life to doesn't want to marry me? Doesn't want to have my kids? Doesn't even want to *live* with me?"

Brennan grinned. "Your infinitesimally tiny Italian brain insists on equating that with her not being in love with you. *I'm* the one who had dinner with the woman last night, and last week and the week before that. I'm also your fucking friend. Diana and I have heard both sides of the story, and I wouldn't even be wasting my breath if we didn't think that there's some monumental mis-communication here.''

Dante shook his head. ''I don't think so. I've heard all the bullshit—how she's afraid that if she trusts a commitment, the cosmos will snatch it away again. But you see, I was *there*. I *felt* her feeling it. Trusting it.''

At an inch under six feet and a little more heavyset than Dante, Brennan somehow appeared to be roughly the same size as his taller friend. They both occupied space with the same sort of authority.

Brennan raised a hand. ''But you *won't* allow that maybe you couldn't see her fighting all that shit from her past at the same time. Something else could have been at play while you were seeing what *you* did. For a smart guy, you can be amazingly dumb sometimes. Look at this mess.'' He swung his arm around the room in demonstration, his blue eyes flashing in challenge. ''It's like nobody has lived here for the past two months. I *know* how you feel about her. You can't hide it. What you refuse to do is accept that there might be another way of seeing your involvement with her. You're willing to make both of you miserable because what you *could* have doesn't conform to some outdated romantic ideal.''

''Are you going to shut up and watch the fucking game?'' Dante asked. A frown of irritation knit his brow.

Brennan turned to glance at the screen. A good-looking blonde was stroking a handsome, heavy-jawed guy's face, affection triggered by the slick shave he'd just gotten from something disposable or out of a can.

''They haven't even kicked off yet.''

''They're gonna any second.''

''I'm finished with what I had to say. Everybody's different, Joe. Look at us; like night and day. My thing with Diana is different than you and Rosa. I'm neat, she's a slob. I'm an introvert, she's an extrovert. The problem with you and Rosa is that you're both so much the same. Pigheaded. Assertive.''

''I thought you said you were finished,'' Dante growled, eyes still fixed on the screen.

Brennan chuckled and finally took a seat, now also facing the tube. From Al Michaels, microphone in hand, the picture cut to twenty-two players strung out facing each other from sideline to sideline at Foxboro Stadium.

''You've got to give a lot of ground to make a thing work,'' Brian mumbled.

''I gave ground,'' Dante snorted.

Pat Leahy booted the ball into the Patriot end zone. Play started with Tony Eason beneath his center at the twenty, dropping quickly to flip a completion to Irving Fryar. Eight yards on the play.

''So tell me,'' Brennan countered. ''You refuse to return her calls. You're miserable. What do you want—Rosa on her terms, or no Rosa at all?''

Dante sighed, collapsing back into the sofa. Craig James had just been stopped for no gain, Lance Mehl and Bob Crable combining on the tackle.

''I don't know.'' He shook his head in frustration.

Copter the cat hopped up onto the coffee table, nose working the air in an attempt to locate leftover pizza. Dante reached over and pulled a little pepproni off a piece. When he tossed it, Copter pounced hungrily and wolfed it down. Dante smiled, a distant look in his eyes.

''I think you want her back,'' Brian said flatly.

Joe looked at him. He shrugged. ''I think I do too, but maybe I'm too proud. What do I do? Just pick up the phone?''

Brennan grinned. ''It'd be a start,'' he said.

* * *

The next morning when the unit came on, they had a meeting in the whip's office. Art Campo was assigned to the car theft task force out at JFK for the duration. They couldn't count on him returning soon to aid the new investigation into Oscar Wembley's murder. The other team on the same tour had its hands full in dealing with the usual autumn rash of residential burglaries. Junkies were like squirrels, stashing away sustenance before the weather got too cold to allow comfort while breaking and entering.

"Arata, I'm letting you run with the burglar alarm company angle," Manley said. "I think that if it has any validity, we'll have to discover that something overlooked was stolen. Then we can entertain the idea that somebody got overenthusiastic in trying to cover his tracks."

Dante, sitting with an ankle crossed over his knee and balancing a cup of coffee on his thigh, glanced at Jumbo and rolled his eyes. Behind Arata's back, the big man wiggled his hand up-and-down in the classic jerking-off motion.

"Check the inventory the niece is putting together," the whip continued. "Talk to the DA. They accessed a safe-deposit box that supposedly contained a list of valuables."

"What the hell are *they* gonna do?" Vinnie complained. He was twisted half around in his chair to regard his two teammates. "That's a lotta ground for one man to cover."

"You're all I can spare," Manley returned. "You guys see the papers this morning? They're building a fire under this one. Some asshole claiming to be next of kin got a look at the corpse. We've gotta move fast, and I think Joey here's come up with the best shot."

Arata flicked an irritated glance at his fellow detective, not aware of the previous night's conversation at the Bistro, nor of what this other line of inquiry might be.

"Wembley had dealings with a lot of people in the artworld. Dante thinks we might have a disgruntled peer or

71

maybe even a frustrated artist-type working for one of the galleries or museums. Jumbo, I want you to work on it with him. See if you guys can focus on that list of buys and loans the guy made in the past year.''

"Speaking of the morgue," Dante said, "have we seen a preliminary forensics work-up yet?''

Manley shook his head. "Swing by and see what's holding them up, will you? Talk to that guy Horvath.''

"You see the news last night?'' Jumbo asked.

They were rolling east on 22nd Street toward the medical examiner's office on First Avenue. Rush-hour traffic was building, heavy volume crawling out of the Midtown Tunnel. The heater in the beat-up Plymouth was stuck in the full-on position. They had the windows rolled down and were sitting in their shirtsleeves. The fat black detective was perspiring profusely, constantly wiping his brow.

"Wembley made the networks. America loves to hear about rich guys getting hacked to death in New York. Reinforces their idea that all we got is murderers and rapists runnin' wild in the streets here.''

"Any good background on the old man?'' Joe asked.

Beasley shrugged. "Usual nutshell shit. How a majority of the poor fucker's collection is on loan to half a dozen museums across the country. There's some sort of appeal from the Met for money to repair the stuff in his house. Everybody's shocked and all the other bull.''

Dante grinned. "You ever thought of writing epitaphs for a living? You're a natural.''

Richardson grunted and leaned on the horn. The snarl of traffic ignored him for the most part, and after a smart-ass in the car next to them told him it sounded like his horn worked fine, he stopped.

"The lou had me sweatin' in there for a second,'' he

said. "I was prayin' to God he wouldn't saddle me with the new guy. Somethin' about him that makes me nervous."

Dante nodded. "I guess we can both count our blessings, huh?"

"Personally," Jumbo told him, "I'm with you. I think this alarm-company angle's a dead end. I was thinkin' about maybe the delivery kids from the grocery store or maybe a plumber or somethin' until you come up with this art-nut angle." A huge bead of sweat rolled to the tip of his nose. He swiped at it irritably.

Joe shrugged. He pulled his little notebook out of his shirt pocket and flipped it open. "You may not think much of the idea after you've seen this list. There've gotta be forty people and places on it."

"Where do we start?" Beasley asked.

"At the top," Dante said. "The last contact Wembley had was with a Gloria Hoskins at Sotheby International. She came to his place Friday. I say we try her once we leave the morgue."

"If we ever *get* there," Jumbo growled. He banged the dash and the heater continued to hum. "I'm dying in here."

Assistant ME Rocky Conklin was leaning against an autopsy slab and smoking a big Casa Del Rey when Dante and Richardson pushed through the extra-wide double doors into the basement morgue.

"Look what the cat drug in," he quipped.

"Hiya, Rock. How's tricks?" Dante greeted him.

"Tricks? All these good-lookin' dead people stacked in the ice box and you think a guy like me has to pay for it?"

Dante frowned. "Guy like you? Maybe not."

Both men were at ease, Conklin with his twisted sense of humor, in his element, and Dante, an old and once frequent visitor when he was working the Lower East Side drug world.

"Don't see you for almost a year and then we cross paths twice in two days, Joey. What gives? Heard you spent a little time in the penalty box."

"That I did," Dante agreed. "Two months' medical leave with six tacked on."

Conklin shook his head. "All that after you got your fucking man. That's gratitude for you."

"Politics," Joe said. "Palace Guard didn't much dig my methodology."

The ME puffed furiously on his cigar a moment, getting a healthy glow going before setting it, with total disregard for regulation and all decency, on the edge of a human skullcap. Rocky was just that sort of guy. In his line of work, you didn't survive if you weren't a little irreverent.

"What's going on with our dead guy?" Dante asked. "The lou says he hasn't seen anything yet."

"You got to see Bernie. He's in back with his microscope. We had a couple of crack dealers whacked commando-style last night and things are sorta backed up. Got some nice tissue and hair from under the old man's nails though. Looked like he hadn't cut 'em in a month. Your lucky break."

Bernie Horvath wasn't exactly *chained* to his microscope when the two detectives entered the pathology lab. He had the *Today* show on his little Sony Watchman and was following Gene Shallit's interview of some blond bombshell more closely than anything he had under the lens. After reaching to turn the volume down, the lab man glanced up.

"Hate to interrupt you, Bernie," Jumbo said evenly, "but there's this kinda grisly murder we're trying to solve, and your friend out there in the other room says you got some tissue and hair follicles we might want to check out.''

Horvath shrugged apologetically. "Sure. Real beauties, actually. Step up and take a look."

While Jumbo bent over the scope, followed by Dante, Bernie fumbled through a little stack of slides. When they'd both had a peek, he replaced the one slide with his second suggestion and had them take a look again.

"That first you looked at was a skin sample. It's hard for a layman to glean much from it, but it tells me the melanin level is way on the low side. It ain't from the old man. I already checked. What it says is that the probable assailant is very fair-skinned. At least this part of his body hasn't been exposed to sunlight recently. No ultraviolet stimulation of the melanin pigmentation." He motioned to the slide Jumbo was currently bent over. "What you're looking at there is a hair follicle. Slightly oval. That means it's sort of wavy. Has some curl in it."

"It's red," Jumbo added.

"That too. And short. That blunt end is a scissors cut. The follicle measures just over three quarters of an inch. Even if the hair is wavy, it wouldn't appear to be so at that length."

The technician then inserted another slide, leaning over and fiddling it into sharp focus.

"This is the real find of the day. More tissue, but there's an aberration here."

It was Dante who took the first look this time, squinting to scrutinize what was on the slide.

"Blue?" he asked. "What the hell is it?"

"That's what I asked myself when I first saw it. Then it hit me, and I checked it out to make sure. Your murder victim did you a big favor with this one, gents. It was under the nails of the first three digits, left hand. Theorizing that this assailant was coming at him from the front at the time, I'd say your man has a tattoo somewhere on his right arm. There were body hair follicles mixed in with the blue tissue."

Dante stood upright and took a deep breath, nodding in appreciation of Horvath's thoroughness. "Nice work, Bernie. We've got a pale white guy with short red hair and a tattoo on his right arm. That's a hell of a start."

"In the six-foot-plus range," Horvath added. "Angle and height of the writing on the walls. Right-handed, judging from the direction of the slashes in the paintings and the thrusts into the body."

"Beautiful," Dante told him. "Mind if I use your phone?"

When George Scully awoke the morning after his introduction to cocaine, his mouth felt like the Kalahari during drought season. His jaw muscles ached from sleeping with his teeth clenched. He was due in surgery at eight fifteen. There wasn't time for sitting and dwelling on the acute misery of his condition. Three aspirin and an ocean of coffee got him out the front door and across First Avenue to the hospital. A quick cold shower, taken while still half asleep, had him looking almost human by the time he greeted the operating room staff, anesthesiologist, and surgical resident in the scrub room. No one had the temerity to mention the bags beneath his eyes. Banter went unabsorbed as he mulled over his own situation. Even after the rough night, his hands were fairly steady. The surgery was pretty routine stuff. He was clipping an aneurysm of the base of the brain in a patient stabilized from a bleed three days earlier. It took three-and-a-half hours to perform. By noon, the fifty-one-year-old interior designer from Forest Hills was on her way to a complete recovery, more or less. There would be no more of her beloved tennis. As far as the extracurricular activity she was engaged in when the incident occurred, she would have to take that up with a husband who was rumored to be distressed. She'd been seven miles from her home and in bed at noon in the Carlyle with her club pro when she collapsed with a subarachnoid hemorrhage. The whole sordid mess made page nine of the *Post*.

It was over coffee in the cafeteria that George finally found time to dwell on the events of the previous evening. He'd been drunk, sure, but he wasn't sure *that* could be blamed for his ingestion of the devil drug. Fiona was wiggling that thing of hers in his face, but she hadn't shoved the shit up his nose. And Christ, had they really talked the sheer madness of killing Ben Crowley?

"Hey, sport!"

He looked up to find Phil Neisbaum pulling out a chair and setting his coffee on the table.

"You look like you spent the night riding the roller coaster at Coney Island. What gives?"

Scully stifled a yawn. "Early surgery," he mumbled.

"So you spent the night at the 'office'?" Phil snickered. "I'm glad that it wasn't my brain you were playing with."

"What the hell's *that* supposed to mean?" Scully snapped.

"I don't know," Neisbaum replied. "After the funk I left you in the other afternoon, and now seeing you like this. . . ." He let it drift off.

"I'm a big boy, Phil. I could have done that surgery this morning with my eyes closed."

Neisbaum softened. "I'm just worried, Georgie. You haven't been yourself lately. That was the worst eighteen holes of golf you've played in fifteen years."

"Maybe you haven't gotten it yet, *pal*," Scully sneered sarcastically. "My ship is sinking. Joanie's on my case. The insurance company is planning to settle. I've got a lot on my mind."

"So you're out there burning the candle at both ends?

I'd be mending fences, buddy. Trying to stabilize the domestic situation. Joan's in a position to have your balls on a platter . . . and you're burning bridges.''

Scully pushed back his chair and stood up abruptly. "Listen, *friend*," he snarled. "We've been close for a lot of years. Don't fuck it up now by putting your nose where it doesn't belong. Sink or swim, I run my own life.'' He turned on his heel and stalked out, leaving Neisbaum to contemplate his backside and scratch his head.

Phil was worried. From the way Scully had described the situation the other afternoon, his whole life was primed to explode in his face. He chose to deal with it by running to his clutching concubine, drinking himself haggard by the look of it, and yelling at his best friend. No, he wasn't handling the pressure at all well.

Scully checked on his patient in recovery, made sure his beeper was switched on, and called the office to check his afternoon schedule. There were no appointments until three. He needed a nap in a bad way, and Fiona wasn't due in the OR until four. Leaving the hospital, he barely noticed the balmy air and bright sunshine pouring down on First Avenue. His perception seemed confined to a dark tunnel of impending catastrophe. That asshole Phil hadn't helped any with his words of friendly concern. Of course, he was full of good intention and well-meant advice, but showing concern of that sort, in his present circumstances, was like throwing a drowning man a rubber duck. The conversation of the previous night came back now to gnaw at the edges of his despair. Kill Benjamin Crowley. Was it really such a morally repugnant notion? For God's sake, the man was a vegetable. A vegetable who, by his very existence, threatened Scully's whole world. His stability. His dreams. And what dreams of any consequence could a vegetable dream? What sort of future did *he* have?

He found Fiona in her robe, stretched out on the sofa and watching *All My Children*. She hardly looked up as he entered, acting almost annoyed as he bussed her on the forehead and tried to slip a hand onto a breast. When he got no response, he frowned, feeling himself on the verge of pouting.

"I'm going to grab some Z's. I'm whipped."

Fiona nodded absently, still staring at the TV screen.

"I've been thinking about what we were talking about last night," he pressed. "About Crowley."

The beautiful nurse finally tore herself away from her show to turn a withering look on him. "Feeling a little less bold in the light of day?" she asked. "Chickening out, *Doctor*?"

The sharpness of her barbs made Scully's hackles rise. He realised then and there that he'd already made up his mind. He'd made the mental leap, and now he stood his ground.

"Why do I suspect that you'd get some perverse satisfaction if I *was*?" he asked. "Well, you're out of luck, sweet meat. I need you to talk to that friend. Soon. I need a strategy, and time is running out." he grinned a leering grin at her. "Time to grab the fucking bull by the horns."

The set of Fiona's jaw softened, and she got a little sparkle in her eyes. "I'm glad to hear you say it, George. I was starting to worry about you. What did you think of the coke?"

He waved her off. "I don't know how you do it. The immediate effect is sort of interesting, but I felt like reheated beans this morning."

She licked her lips, amused. "Last night? You've never been hotter, George. Remember?"

Dante and Richardson didn't have much luck with their list as they chased what seemed like one dead end after another for the remainder of the morning and afternoon. The Sotheby woman's visit to the Wembley home on Friday proved to have been fairly routine. Two other people on the list also confirmed that because of a severe rheumatic condition, Mr. Wembley was regularly visited by auctioneers and gallery representatives when he was unable to come in and view offerings they thought he might be interested in. He was also sought out for advice on any number of subjects from authentications to pricing. Nobody they talked to had a tall, fair-skinned redhead in their employ.

"What do you think?" Jumbo asked. He was steering the Plymouth back to the station through what was now the start of evening rush hour. The heater which had been trying to incinerate them earlier had suddenly stopped dead, a change coinciding with a sudden dip in the outside temperature. They now had the windows rolled up against a more seasonable October chill.

"I think we've still got a butt-load of names to go on that list," Dante replied.

Jumbo shrugged and gunned it to cut off a cab trying to straddle two lanes at once. "What was it the little bitch in the movie said?" he asked. "Tomorrow's another day?"

Curtis Maxwell was leaning on the handle of his mop. The CAUTION: WET FLOOR pyramids were arranged along the gleaming expanse of linoleum tile corridor. Lionel's "Say You, Say Me" filled the headphones of his Walkman. Visiting hours were over, and things had settled down for the night. Curtis preferred the swing shift to the hectic pace of days. In another fifteen minutes, with this stretch of floor dry, he'd step up onto the roof, blow a little cheeb, and maybe tighten his head with a quick one-and-one. The weed was some heavy-duty Jamaican shit—it made him melt-headed mellow. The coke would put an edge on. Oh yeah, Curtis sure liked the swing shift.

Down the hall, that truly righteous blond pussy from the OR was heading his way. Sweet God, he would surely love to tie into *that* action. Word had that Hot Tits Hassey was the property of some fat-cat surgeon named Scully. A real granite-hewn smoothie, this dude. Curtis didn't give a fuck. Woman like that shouldn't be narrow-minded. Jah surely designed such creatures to be admired and shared by all humanity. The way he saw it, he had something of an inside track. The doctor was one tight-wound machine. He didn't know how to get loose. Curtis, on the other hand, was the fun man. About a year ago, Curtis discovered that Hot Tits Hassey liked the hospital roof too.

"Got a minute?" she asked, approaching.

"Shit. You surely lookin' fine tonight," Curtis crooned. "As a matter of fact, I was just contemplatin' a little trip upstairs. It's national Be Kind to Your Nose Day."

Fiona smiled. "What are we waiting for?"

Curtis stooped, touched the floor, and rubbed thumb against forefinger. It was dry. "Nothing. Nothing at all."

It was a cool autumn evening, maybe forty-eight to fifty degrees with a light breeze coming from the west. Twelve floors above First Avenue, with the lights of the city spreading out in all directions, the roof was a little oasis atop the madness of suffering and disease beneath. On sunny days, nurses often used the roof to eat lunch and catch a few tanning rays. At night, it went unused, except by the likes of Curtis Maxwell and Fiona, huddled behind a ventilator duct, out of the breeze and out of sight of the access door some sixty feet away.

Curtis blew the Jamaican cheeb alone while Fiona fidgeted, watching him uncap the vial of cocaine and dump a little pile out onto the back of her hand. She handled it expertly, positioning it beneath her right nostril and snorting quickly.

"How's your stash?" Curtis asked.

"Getting low."

"You want, I got a line on this mighty fine Bolivian shit. What you just tasted. First-rate. Get you an eight-ball for three and half."

"I'd appreciate it," she said. "I can't get you cash until tomorrow night."

Curtis nodded. "You bring the cash and I'll have the stash. My man knows I got certain clients who are good for the bread. *Downtown* clients." he dumped another little pile of cocaine onto the blonde's outstretched hand.

Fiona snorted again and waited with her eyes closed to feel the first load kick in. It was smooth, subtle stuff. No hard edge that might indicate the cooker was cheating with chemical additives. Her front teeth started turning a little numb. A good sign. The orderly was right. This was first-rate.

Curtis watched the nurse's breasts heave beneath the tight uniform blouse as she leaned back with her eyes closed, getting off on the product. He could see her nipples getting hard and pushing against the fabric as her respiration increased. It made him crazy to watch that and not be able to touch it.

Fiona opened her eyes to find the orderly contemplating her. She smiled at him. "I need a favor, Curtis."

Maxwell swallowed hard, realizing she'd read the look in his eyes and feeling the warm prickle of blood rising to his face.

"Name it."

"It was about seven or eight months ago. We were up here and you were talking about a man you knew. You told me that if I ever needed someone . . . uh . . . hospitalized, your man could get someone to do the job. I have a friend who is in the market."

Curtis was taken aback at first. Hot Tits Hassey was a

little wild maybe, but he never suspected she might be up to playing hardball. He'd mentioned the man to impress her. Now she was actually calling him on it.

"The man ain't cheap," he said carefully. "Your friend be payin' for a clean, quiet job. The man, he pays pros. Your friend—do they want it bad enough to pay the rate?"

Fiona smiled. "I think that's safe to assume. I believe *they* are in a position where they can't afford not to."

Curtis uncapped his vial for another go-round, dumping a third little pile on the back of Fiona's hand. She horned it with little ceremony; something he had to admire in a white woman. Most of them made such a silly-ass big deal over a little whiff. This one was a cool customer. When she opened her eyes after her little communion with the buzz, she found him staring straight into them, no attempt to hide anything.

"I ever tell you what a sweet piece of ass I think you must be?" he asked her.

She met his gaze and held it, nodding. "One way or another. Sure."

Seven

When Diana Webster finally agreed that she *might* marry Brian Brennan, the rock-and-roll songbird took the first step between no and maybe by moving into his 27th Street loft. The move coincided with Rosa Losada's search for a new apartment, and they'd arranged an open-ended sublet.

When the intercom buzzer blared in the kitchen, Rosa was still applying the last of her makeup in the bathroom. She was a striking woman in her late twenties, with a muscular yet voluptuous build, fine, aristocratic bones, and flashing black eyes. If she were to be likened to any other of God's creatures, a high-strung thoroughbred horse sprang immediately to mind. With a quick final dab of light green eye shadow, she examined the end result critically in the mirror. This was crazy. She actually had butterflies in the pit of her stomach.

Joe Dante stood on the stoop outside on St. Mark's Place, wondering if he'd buzzed the right apartment. He searched his memory back to when Diana had lived there. Number six. Definitely. He was just reaching to push the button again when he heard her voice.

"Joe?"

"It's cold out here," he answered.

The door lock rattled as the mechanism released. Dante pushed his way inside and began to climb the stairs to the third floor.

Two months. It seemed like forever. There were times when he had trouble remembering what she looked like. He definitely couldn't remember what it felt like to lie next to her in bed. His mind had blotted that part out. It hurt too much to remember. All he really knew was that he missed her like crazy.

She was standing at the door, dressed in a white silk blouse and gray wool slacks, looking as nervous as he figured he must look. A flood of who she was rushed back over him. The dark, penetrating eyes and the darker hair hanging loose to her shoulders. That body that he could suddenly remember naked in a flash so hot that his skin tingled.

But now there was an awkwardness as they stood facing each other. Rosa finally indicated the hall within and stood aside, waiting for him to pass. When he did, they avoided contact. They'd agreed to meet again. Period. To see how it went.

In the subdued, tastefully furnished living room, Dante took a seat on the sofa and accepted the offer of a drink. When Rosa was finally seated opposite him, he cleared his throat. "How goes it in the big building?"

Rosa, a college grad who had more than proven herself on the street, was currently assigned as department liaison between the chief of detectives and the various media. She harbored political ambitions within the job and was already on the way up the ladder. Her post was considered something of a plum.

"Okay," she replied. "The Wembley case has kept me jumping the past thirty-six hours. I hear you caught it."

"Lucky me," he said. "Some pretty grisly shit. Not the sort of thing you ever get used to."

'Any progress?''

"For the general molification of the piranha—or job side?"

"You know me better than that," she said with a frown. "I blow smoke for a living now, remember?"

He almost smiled. "Forensics has built us a profile based on some good physical evidence. We chased our tails all day but not enough to get discouraged. Yet."

"I take it you've got a hunch."

Now Dante *did* smile. "You know me. I've always got a hunch."

"But it's not for the record."

He shook his head. "Not until it can stand on its own two feet."

Dante noticed that she was drinking something clear, with ice, in a tall glass. Gin. Rosa always drank gin when she was wound up. She said it made her a little crazy. Although she mixed it with tonic, the second *active* ingredient was nervous energy.

"I . . ."

"I . . ."

They'd both started in at once. Pulling up, they let it hang a second, mouths open. Dante waited for her to continue, and when she didn't, shaking her head, he tried again.

"I've been sort of a shit, not answering your calls."

"*Sort* of a shit?"

"A shit."

"I suppose you've been pretty angry."

He nodded. "Sure. Probably still am, a little."

"And?"

"It hasn't really made me feel much better over the long haul."

86

"Two months is a long time, Joe."

"I'm not contending it isn't," he replied. "It's how long it took."

Rosa tossed back a pretty good sized slug of her drink and set it back on the end table at her elbow. "And now you think you've worked it out?"

"No," he replied honestly. "I just thought it might be time to talk about it, before I woke up one morning regretting that I hadn't."

"I don't think it can work, Joe," she said flatly. "Not the way you want it to."

He sat a moment, searching for the words to respond. He wondered what the hell he thought he was doing here, in this room with its Rosa feel. Feminine touches. Subdued shades of ivory over walls and furniture he'd never seen or sat in before.

"I don't know how I want it to," he replied slowly. "Not anymore."

"You want a woman to be your wife. To have a home and kids with."

"Maybe. Then again, actions speak louder than words, right? And how hard have I really tried to get those things? In six months I'll be forty years old."

"My life has changed as well," she told him. "I'm involved in a whole new world now. I haven't just been sitting home, Joe. I've been going out with other men."

The green bile of envy suddenly churned in the pit of his stomach. Dante swallowed hard, jaw tightening. Two sides of him were at war with each other. The intellectual told him that he'd done exactly the same thing. The emotional asked, "How dare she?" The good old double standard. He knew he was part twentieth-century Manhattanite and part caveman.

"What are you telling me?" he asked, his voice tight in his throat. "That it's too late? That I'm wasting my time here?"

For the first time since they'd sat down, she softened a little and got a faraway, sad look in her eyes.

"No," she said, shaking her head. "A lot of what happened between us is my fault, and I accept responsibility for it. You have no idea how jealous I am of you and your old-fashioned romantic idealism. It would be so simple if I could feel the same way, wouldn't it? *I'm* the one who's carrying around the psychological baggage. *I'm* the one who has to work through whatever terrifies me about getting close. You wanted some assurance that I could, and I can't give you that."

Dante couldn't help himself. "So what about these other guys? Is any one of them better, uh, equipped to understand your, uh, *problem*?"

Rosa finally slid into an easy grin. "Trust me, Joe. None of them needs to."

"What's that supposed to mean?"

"It means that all most of them want to do is get laid. *All* of them have tailor-fit uniforms and permanently shit-smudged noses. Everybody in the big building is looking for a hook in and a leg up. A lot of them just assume that I'll be willing to spread my legs in order to get what *they* can give me. My *problem*, as you put it, hasn't come up. These assholes could care less about intimacy."

Dante's mind was jammed with questions he couldn't ask. His imagination ran the gamut. He wondered just how many times in the past year he'd asked himself, "Why this one? Why her?" The answer was sitting in the chair across from him.

They sat in silence now, drinking. Outside on the street, car tires screeched, a horn blared, and a male voice shouted at top volume in a language three or four thousand miles from English.

"Can two people as twisted up as we are take another shot?" Joe asked at length.

"Under whose ground rules?" she countered.

"Do there have to be any?"

"I don't know. It's obvious that we both still want something. On the other hand, I don't think either of us knows what it is."

Dante shrugged. "I can't see any other way to do it than to sort of feel our way as we go. Maybe it doesn't work out after all. Then again, maybe we both end up hating ourselves if we don't at least try."

Rosa sat a moment, deciding something. "Brian and Diana have invited the two of us out to the beach this weekend." She just let it hang there.

Dante shrugged. "I've got something on for Saturday morning. I could drive up after that."

George Scully hoped to Christ that Joanie wouldn't bring anything up again about his recent moods or how he'd failed to pick up the three calls she'd made to his office last night. To his great relief, it looked like she was choosing to pout instead, keeping stone-faced through the evening meal and disappearing into the bedroom shortly after the kids headed off to the public library to do their homework.

With a stiff Scotch-and-water in hand, he was just settling in to watch the third game of the Series when his study phone rang. It was eight ten, and the call was coming in on his private line—the number his service used.

"Scully," he grunted, in no mood for an emergency or any other problem.

"Weeb Caruthers," the baritone voice on the other end of the line announced. "I hope I'm not interrupting anything too important.

Scully scowled as he set his drink on the coffee table. "Just the ballgame. What's up, counselor?"

Caruthers got right to the point. "I believe I've discovered why they jumped on offering early settlement. Tell me what you know about a Roscoe Fields from Johns Hopkins."

"Ross Fields? Crackerjack neurosurgeon. Brilliant, even. Pioneered some new technique. In my game, he's as highly regarded as they come. As a matter of fact, we've been on a couple of panels together."

"How would he stand up as an expert witness?" Caruthers asked.

Scully snorted. "You kidding? The man's the best. You want me to get him? Wouldn't be a lot of trouble. I was the first guy to use his new clamping technique in suboccipital application. We did a paper together."

"Too late," the attorney said dryly. "The other team got there first."

"What?" Scully asked, pulse quickening. "Ross Fields has been engaged by a *patient* to testify against *me*?"

"I'm afraid so, Doctor. He gave a deposition last week, after his review. I don't think I have to tell you that it shifted the balance somewhat in terms of settlement."

"Son of a bitch!" Scully seethed. "That back-stabbing scum!"

"It's become a more frequent phenomenon than it once was," Caruthers told him. "I'm afraid the carrier had little choice. They are forced to shift the timetable in terms of offering settlement, Doctor. Once the damage of such depositions starts to pile up, the purpose of early settlement is subverted."

"Wonderful," Scully grunted. "Once their offer is made, how soon do we know if they bite?"

"These things can take some time. There's still a certain amount of paperwork to be executed. A month to six weeks, perhaps."

When George Scully hung up the phone, he no longer

had any interest in whether Bob Ojeda could beat the Red Sox in his former home ballpark. He switched the set off by remote and sat staring at the dead screen of the set. He drank quickly now, hoping the dulling alcohol haze would descend and cut him off from the hatred boiling inside him. His thoughts drifted to Fiona. When she'd first suggested killing Benjamin Crowley, he'd taken to the notion only in the abstract, as a sort of perverse fantasy. Even in asking her to speak with her friend, he'd known *he* had final control. It was curiosity that encouraged him to have her do it. He wanted to know if he really did have the power—and for how much money. Now he found himself in a totally new frame of mind. At this juncture, he would do anything. Sell his soul to Satan, if that's what it took. He'd been betrayed by one of his own brothers. Ross fucking Fields had testified against him. A man who *knew* the pressures of their business. The awesome risks they took. It was unforgivable that he would use his knowledge against a peer like this.

When you were down, no one was going to reach out and help you up. If there'd been any lingering doubt, Weeb Caruthers had just removed it. They'd just as soon kick you in the gut. When you were down, if you harbored any hope of getting on your feet again, you had to help yourself.

Joe Dante sat on his own living room sofa in the dark, Copter purring in his lap and a beer in his hand. It had started to rain outside, and the wind was whipping leaves from the trees in his garden. He wondered if he thought Rosa would just kiss, make up, and want to fuck his brains out. God, he knew that by the time he left, he was aching to do just that. Everything he'd forgotten about them together, the things his pain conveniently erased, flooded back the moment he saw her at that front door.

*   *   *

Jumbo Richardson looked as cheerful as Joe Dante felt. He entered the squad that Wednesday morning with a lightness in his step. Outside, the night's downpour had washed the air a crisp autumn clean. It was one of those rare sun-drenched New York days, neither stifling hot nor bitter cold. People reacted to each other differently on the street. Even the muggings and murders seemed to slack off a bit.

"You look like a guy who's just gotten rid of a mother-in-law," Dante observed dryly.

"That," Jumbo replied. "And *my* mother's postponed for another week. Jesus *does* love me."

Joe grinned. "Must be all that clean living."

Jumbo slipped out of his jacket and tossed it over the back of a chair instead of hanging it up. "You appear to be in a pretty good mood yourself."

Dante smirked. "Ain't nothing to get the spirits up like a good, grisly homicide."

Jumbo rolled his eyes, collapsed into his chair, and opened a grease-stained bag of donuts. "Jelly, jelly, jelly," he crooned, plucking an ooze-filled calorie bomb from within and eyeing it with unnatural fondness.

Dante reached over and pulled the bag his way, looking for something a little less obscene. He located a plain old-fashioned, tore it in half, and dunked an end into his coffee.

"I want to take the forensics profile back over to the crime scene and just sort of walk it around," he announced. "You know, just to get a feel now that we have a mental picture."

Beasley shrugged, a trickle of purple slime crawling perilously close to the edge of his chin. At the last possible second, he swept a finger upward, catching it and guiding it into his mouth. The man was an artist.

"Whatever you say. On, great one. *You're* the one with

the mental pictures. What'd you think of the game last night?''

"Hard to admit it, but I was sort of tied up."

Jumbo stared at him in astonishment. Joe Dante was recognized to be a near-certifiable Mets fan. "You *missed* it? You're bullshittin' me."

" 'Fraid not."

Jumbo sighed, pulling the donut bag back to his side of the desk and shaking his head. "What's the fucking world coming to when pussy proves more important to a red-blooded American male than the motherfuckin' World Series?"

Dante shook his head, grinning and nodding. "I know what you're saying, partner. In a way, I feel like I've failed the entire sex."

It felt eerie to contemplate the quiet facade of the townhouse on West 11th Street. All of the shutters and curtains were closed. The picture emanated an absence of life. Dante and Jumbo sat parked at the hydrant across the street and stared for a moment, unwilling to move.

"Looks a lot different today, don't it?" Jumbo mumbled.

"It's how our redheaded friend saw it," Dante mused, already psyching himself into the mood. "Darker and with a couple of lights on, maybe, but just another house on the block. I've been doing a lot of thinking about it. For instance, we've assumed that because the old man was sort of absentminded that he forgot to put the alarm on that night. I'm wondering if maybe he was expecting our man. If the maid didn't know anything about it, the meeting could have been something he didn't want on the record. There's a darker side to the art world. Fakes, forgeries, and all that. Something went down between these two that really set our perp off."

Jumbo nodded agreement. "Tall dude with short red

hair, pale skin, and a tattoo shows up at this old man's place sometime after nine thirty, winds up hacking him to death, even though it would appear that the victim let him in. He doesn't steal anything but destroys a couple million bucks worth of high-end art. You're try'na get inside the drama and see if you can read what went down here.''

''That's about it.''

Jumbo took a deep breath and let it out slowly. ''Then what are we waiting for, Holmes?''

''Elementary, Watson. Just trying to get a handle on the control it'll take to keep me from puking on the bedroom floor.''

The average human body contains approximately eleven pints of blood. By the time he expired, Oscar Wembley's dipstick was all but dry.

Nothing inside the townhouse had been touched. It was still the scene of a very active murder investigation. As such, the odor inside the place was horrendous—the stench of a slaughterhouse. Joe and Jumbo held handkerchiefs to their faces as they moved through the foyer and mounted the stairs. Dante remembered seeing a copy of a memo from the PC regarding a request made by the Metropolitan Museum's restoration department. They were asking to be allowed to attend to the ruined masterworks at first opportunity. He couldn't see now why the request should be denied. The idea that *anything* might be resurrected from this was in some small way heartening.

The bedroom remained exactly as it was, sans corpse. The bed sat soaked through and blackened with coagulated blood. Dante stopped after taking in the scene, unable to push the image of a bucket brimming with blood from his mind. He closed his eyes and watched a tall, gangly redhead in a crew cut move steathily across the room, the brimming bucket in his grip. He was faceless, like a Dick Tracy character whose name he couldn't dredge to mind.

"Seen enough?" Jumbo asked.

"Too much," Joe replied. "Let's get out of here."

The short stretch of 116th Street between Fifth and Lenox avenues was crawling with lowlife street-creeps and dope-hustling junkies. Every man had his attitude. Every step was a strut; every pause a pose. Hats sat at jaunty angles. Massive street radios blared rap and disco. Greenbacks were exchanged for little wrapped packets in the shadows of alleys and doorways. This was the Harlem street scene in broad daylight. It made Curtis Maxwell jumpy.

Curtis had never met the big man face to face before. He'd seen him around in that truly transcendental stretch Benz, driven by a bodyguard who used to fight heavy as Bobby "Badness" Burke. The big man had the ladies. He had the wheels. He had the protection and the goods. He was also the man who supplied Curtis's connection in midtown. This morning, the man had passed the word that he wanted an interview in person. Two o'clock, on the corner of Lenox and 116th. The man also moved quickly.

Curtis waited nervously. He preferred maintaining a low profile. He felt naked now as he loitered among the flotsam and jetsam of the trade. These were guys who'd sell their grandmas for a bag of shit. They'd shake your hand and stab you in the gut. Junkies were sharks: devour or die. Sooner or later, most of them stepped in deep shit and were left with their feet dangling from a dumpster. They called themselves players, and this was their game. In the eyes of Curtis Maxwell, it didn't look like fun. He had his pad on West 46th Street, just a couple of blocks from Times Square. He had an easy gig at the hospital, where he met numbers like Hot Tits who paid him top green for their little yuppie habits and never ripped him off. Between his paycheck and the dealing, he cleared a cool twelve hundred a week. Not bad for a kid from the South Bronx. Most of the dudes he grew up with were either dead or doing time. Not Curtis. Curtis had it dicked.

At ten after two, the big man's huge white Mercedes slid grandly around the corner off Lenox and eased to the curb. As the back window came down, Curtis moved hesitantly forward. The big man himself looked up from his deep leather seat. Reginald DuQuesnay. He nodded. "Get in, little brother. Let's you and me take a ride."

Curtis was so busy locking on the kingpin that he failed to notice Bad Bobby slip from behind the wheel. A heavy hand suddenly fell on his shoulder, making him jump about a mile, scaring the snot out of him. He spun around as Bobby's hand clamped his upper arm and his eyes bored into him.

"Easy, little brother," Reggie cooed. "Just a little formality."

Bad Bobby proceeded to give Curtis a quick once-over, patting him for heat. Convinced he was clean, he turned him loose, reaching to open the door for him. As Curtis climbed into the dark, cool interior of the car, his eyes took in the surroundings. There was a liquor bar, a little walnut-cased television, and a well-built redhead with legs a mile long in net stockings.

"Say hello to Lu-Ann," Reggie suggested as Curtis settled in. "What can I get you to drink."

Curtis fidgeted, eyes moving quickly between his host and this great-looking white girl with the cleavage and pouting lips. He shrugged. "A beer?"

Reggie nodded. "Get our friend a beer, Lu-Ann."

Curtis hadn't noticed the tiny refrigerator built in below the television. The redhead moved with dazed, liquid actions, pulling a King Cobra from the box and handing it to him. When he smiled his thanks, the look returned in his general direction was vague, bored. It changed an instant later when Reggie removed a vial from his pocket and uncapped it. Up front, Bad Bobby was getting under way, the car moving effortlessly into traffic. Meanwhile, the redhead's eyes followed every movement of the vial as Reggie dumped a little pile of powder out onto the back of his hand and extended it toward her. She leaned into the offering and horned it with eagerness. There was no boredom in those eyes now. Reggie extended the vial to Curtis, who accepted and tapped out only the tiniest hit, lest he be judged negatively by the man himself. Reggie nodded to him as he watched.

"Go ahead, my man. Treat yourself. Don't be shy. You saw how shy Lu-Ann was."

Curtis doubled the ante and snorted, returning the vial. He waited while Reggie did a quick one and returned the stash to his pocket.

"Now," Reggie said. "What's this I hear? You got a friend lookin' for a friend to do a little job."

"A client," Curtis replied, nodding. "But if that was the all of it, I wouldn't be bothering you with it. I put two and two together and come up with somethin' interesting. Just a theory."

Reggie shrugged, smiling. "I like a man who does a little thinkin' for hisself. Speak to me, little brother."

The coke was starting to bite into Curtis's nervousness now, consuming it in big chunks. He knew he was onto something the big man would want to know about. Confidence built from the pit of his stomach and surged upward as he spoke.

"There's this nurse. Dynamite-looking blonde works in the operating room of the hospital where I got this gig. She has a nice little nose habit I help her feed. It's the word out around the place that she's got a fat-cat neurosurgeon on the string. He has her set up rent-free in a lovenest right across the street. A married dude with a wife and kiddies in Connecticut. Well, last night the bitch comes to me to reorder and she mentions she's got a friend needs a little body and fender work done on an unnamed party." His mouth was going dry in a hurry. He took a big swig off the Cobra and wiped his lips. "I'd take it at face value. Everybody gots a beef against somebody. Then I'm down in the scrub room mopping up and this dude named Neisbaum is in there with this other surgeon cat. They've just finished a fourteen-hour job and they're talking about this doctor from a place called Johns Hopkins who's screwing the lid on this George Scully's coffin. Testifying against him a in a big malpractice gig."

Reggie held up his hand, stopping him. "I'm a busy man, little brother. I'm sure this history lesson's got some hidden point, but I wish you'd get to it."

Curtis shook his head insistently. He was on a roll. Tossing back another swig of his beer, he actually dared to smile at the big man.

"The point is that this George Scully is the same dude I'm talking about. The nurse's boyfriend. Couple months back he's nabbing some quick point and forgets to switch his beeper on. Patient of his blows a gasket, he bleeds inside his head and winds up paralyzed. Word is that the doc is personally on the hook for almost a million. When this nurse approaches me about getting a little specialty work done for a friend, I gotta wonder if there ain't no connection there. Fat cat like Scully's gotta be worth heavy coin."

Reggie eyed Curtis Maxwell thoughtfully as he extracted his stash from his pocket for a second go-round.

"That's some pretty fancy thinkin', Curtis. Some *nice* thinkin'. Here." Ignoring Lu-Ann's eager eyes, he handed the vial straight to his guest. He watched with amusement as Curtis, acting the gentleman, tapped a little out on his hand and extended it toward the whore. Lu-Ann took it like a hawk snatching raw meat, reappraising Curtis with a quick glance.

"You like that?" Reggie asked Curtis, jerking his head toward the woman. "She's some sweet shit, ain't she?"

Curtis was feeling good. The whore *was* some sweet shit.

"You bet," he replied.

Reggie pulled a little pad and pen from his pocket and scribbled a phone number. Tearing off the sheet, he folded it and handed it to Curtis.

"Give this to your nurse friend. Have her tell *her* friend to call that number between eight and eight fifteen tomorrow night. Have him leave a number and I'll call right back. If it turns out he wants to arrange to have me whack some paralyzed dude, I'm gonna want you to arrange for a little meeting between me and the lady. A business meeting."

Curtis nodded, shoving the slip of paper into his shirt pocket.

"And listen,' Reggie added. "I appreciate a man who recognizes a business opportunity when he sees one. Freddy tells me you been doin' some decent volume and the money's always there. I think it might be time you and me had a little talk about your future."

Eight

A gull wheeled hard on the breezes of the Sound, rolling into an inverted dive that took it into the sparkling swell just offshore. When it surfaced an instant later, a fingerling fish flashed silver in its beak. Lingering on the flat wet sand of low tide, Dante and Rosa watched from the cove behind Brian Brennan's rambling Victorian beach house. It was a bright, chilly Saturday, with winter's first breath in the autumn air.

After beginning the morning in Manhattan with a weight workout in his apartment and then a run as the sun came up, Dante had driven out to Forest Park in Queens to watch the East New York Bengals play the Forest Hills Cavaliers. It wasn't a great game by any technical standards, but there was a compelling enthusiasm apparent in everything Jumbo's pint-sized combatants undertook. The disparity in talent was near-painful to watch. Jumbo was terrific; transformed into an animated, beaming maniac as his ragtag group kicked the crap out of the their upper-middle-class opponents. As advertised, his twelve-year-old stringbean quarterback had quality tools and a cool head on his shoulders. Occasionally, his teammates would even catch one of his passes. To balance out their youthful ineptitude on offense, the Bengals played an aggressive, swarming defense. Jumbo definitely had someone to be proud of in his son Arthur. Not only did the kid like to hit, he played smart, flowing and alertly anticipating how a play would develop.

By eleven, Dante was on the road in his 1984 Corvette, crossing the Whitestone Bridge. After dodging potholes up I-95 toward New London, he arrived at Brian's by early afternoon. A cup of steaming hot coffee with Brian, Diana and Rosa, then he had led his erstwhile lover out for a walk by the rippling sea.

"You see that?" he asked. "Those little fish must be running out there."

"You're a lot happier being back on the street, aren't you?" Rosa said.

He shrugged and nodded. "Yeah, I suppose I am. It's what I seem to do best. Getting pissed off at the entire job and electing to sit out the duration in some backwater didn't do anything but make me more frustrated."

"You weren't ever serious about getting out," she said matter of-factly. "When you talked about it during the suspension, I just bit my tongue. You love it too much."

"I guess I do," he admitted.

Together, they began to walk again, tentative in attitude but huddled close against the chill.

"I saw your name on the list to take the sergeant's exam," she said. "I thought you never wanted to be a boss."

He shook his head. "I never did. Now I think that to be effective, the balance of power has to change a little."

"Did you hear I passed?" she asked.

"Through the grapevine," he replied. "Still want to be the first woman C of D?"

She was dragging one foot idly in the wet sand, leaving a trail behind. "I'm not like you. The more time I spend in the big building, the more convinced I am that off the street is where I can be most effective. I hate people with closed minds, and I intend to open a few in this department if I have to use a sledgehammer."

"Dynamic entry," Dante said, flashing a smile.

"You ought to know."

"I suppose. I've practiced at *not* being a political animal."

She nodded. "You never had to be. As hard as I might try, I can never be one of the boys. The way I see it, if I don't head for higher ground, I get buried. It's as simple as that."

"You were better than you think you were."

Rosa sighed. "That could be. But part of it has to be the way I feel about it. Like I belong. You know as well as I do that I never felt at home in a squad room. Some women like that sort of fishbowl sexual attention. I hate it. Part of what I've resented between us is how easy it all is for you."

Dante stopped and turned toward her. "You resent something you *perceive* to be true," he said emphatically. "Because it's hard for you, you want to believe it's easy for me. You read reports and press releases about the Oscar Wembley murder. I had to look at the fucking body, and it was all I could do to keep from puking my guts out." He balled his fists in frustration. "I've never argued that it isn't a man's world. I've also never stood up for what's negative about the job. You always had my support when it came to fighting those things."

A large, fragmented cloud gathered itself together to temporarily blot out the sun. What had been a brilliantly gleaming seascape only an instant before now turned dull, murky gray.

"I'm not as much concerned with what affects me

directly,'' Rosa replied calmly. She and Joe were standing face to face now, the wind blowing their hair and making their ears ache. ''You want to put bad guys behind bars, and I want to improve the way we do it. I happen to believe that there is an inherent lack of balance in any gender-exclusive society, male or female.''

''You sound like you're back at Bennington,'' he said. With it, he turned and began to walk back toward the house. Rosa fell in step beside him.

''Someone has to try,'' she countered.

''I never said you shouldn't. I only resent being treated like I'm not on your side. That I'm the enemy or something. I may not be a woman, but I'm not blind. I understand your frustration. You just have to remember that you're dealing with a lot of years of chauvinist history in this job. Change takes time.''

Fiona Hassey found herself forced to call George at home in Ridgefield on Saturday. Feigning to be from his answering service with an important emergency message, she got past the housekeeper. When Scully came on the line, she told him about the quick action resulting from her talk with her ''friend'' and that he was to call the number Curtis gave her between eight and eight fifteen that evening.

''Christ,'' George complained. ''We've got a dinner party at Joanie's parents' place. Tonight?''

''Getting cold feet?'' she asked, sharply. ''We agreed I would make this contact.''

''I'm going to do this,'' he hissed anxiously. ''It's just that . . . well, I didn't expect it to happen so fast.''

''That's the way it is, George. I think you'd better tell Joan that there's some sort of emergency the hospital is monitoring and that you could be called away at a moment's notice. I'll call you again at around five and say I'm from the hospital. She'll just have to go to the party alone.''

If Scully wanted it done, he didn't have much choice in the matter, and he'd already decided he was going through with it.

"Okay. I'll come to your place and make the call from there."

"I'll be here," she assured him.

Dante spent part of the evening after dinner with Brian in the new foundry facility he had built a hundred feet or so from the side of the house. It was a larger setup than the one the sculptor had in his big warehouse loft in New York. Fourteen months ago, the original foundry on this site had been destroyed in a propane tank explosion. In the interim, Brennan had designed a bigger wax-extraction kiln and more efficient bronze furnace. In back was a replica of the original drawing and modeling studio, now with an additional window over looking the Sound. Unlike many of his peers, Brian insisted on doing all of his own casting work instead of jobbing it out to one of the specialty houses.

Part of the initial bonding between these two friends involved the detective's fascination with the sculptor's process, which rendered bronze figures from clay originals. No amount of imagining could have prepared him for the gritty, hands-on work it entailed. Dante had thought of making art as a powder-puff occupation. Through Brian Brennan, he'd come to appreciate the absolute confidence it demanded in one's own inner vision. He'd also gained proficiency with a body grinder, welding torch, slag hammer, and any number of other tools. The mesmerizing brilliance of molten metal as it cascaded into a mold still riveted his attention the way it had on first observation. It was hot, sweaty, dirty work, and he loved every minute of it.

Rosa and Diana had a fire crackling in the big, fieldstone

hearth when the two men rejoined them just after ten o'clock. At an angle to each other and facing it, they slouched in overstuffed chairs, drinking wine and deep in conversation. Motioning them to pull up chairs, Diana reached for the bottle of Bordeaux on the sideboard behind her and asked them if they'd care for a glass. Brian begged off for the moment to hit the shower. Dante sat and accepted the drink. He liked Diana quite a bit and enjoyed spending time around her. She, in turn, liked male company and Joe in particular. Many a night when he'd been completely baffled by Rosa, Diana had served as a sounding board. She had a knack for finding common threads. Even now, as she sat there with her wildly tousled hair, bleached platinum blond and cut by an apparently blind beautician, Dante saw her as an oracle of logic and common sense.

"You two solved all the problems of the modern world?" he asked. Raising the wineglass to his nose, he swirled and sniffed before taking a sip. His hosts could well afford to have great taste in wine. Drinking something from Brennan's cellar was always a treat.

"Rosa was telling me about your case," Diana replied. "It sounds horrible."

"Pretty bad," he agreed. "This is the sort of sicko who works himself into a frenzy to get off."

"Do you think he'll do it again?"

"Nobody knows. I met a guy once from a psychiatric hospital upstate. He told me that most of the time with a killing like this, the act is the ultimate extension of a single, all-consuming hatred. The killer is fixated, and once he's done the dirty deed, all the fury dissipates. Right now, I hope to hell he's right. I never want to see another one like that."

For the first time since his joining them, he and Rosa locked eyes. They'd been partners a year ago, experiencing plenty together that would horrify others. Joe lifted his glass and winked over the rim at her.

They talked for another hour, killing off a second bottle of wine. Brian joined them after cleaning up. It was hard for Dante as the memories flooded back. The four of them had spent many an evening just like this: two couples who were comfortable with each other. Eventually, Diana stretched her lithe limbs and yawned.

"Bedtime," she announced. "I was in the studio for twenty-eight hours straight, yesterday and Thursday night. I'm afraid I still haven't caught up." In her other world, Diana was a rising star. Her band, Queen of Beasts, had a single near the top of the *Billboard* chart and was currently on the fast track, trying to pump an album out in the wake of current success.

Sleeping arrangements hadn't been discussed. In the past, both Joe and Rosa had shared the biggest guest bedroom on the ground floor. There were several more upstairs, and it was toward one of these that Dante now started to climb.

"There are clean sheets on the bed of the first room to the right," Diana told him. "I put towels in the bathroom."

The radiator in the room was hissing as he entered. After turning it off, he cracked the window a touch, preferring to sleep cool, with the Sound's salty tang on the air.

The water of the shower felt good as he stepped in to wash the grime of his evening's labor away. That afternoon, Diana had played a demo tape of one album side, and a tune was stuck in his head. He hummed it now, the water coursing over him. He felt better than he had in a long time. At least things were out in the open now. He and Rosa were talking. Neither of them had been very good at it in the past.

He was surprised to find Rosa in his bed when he returned.

"Hi, stranger. Think there's room enough for two of us in here?"

Joe felt suddenly disoriented as he stood there naked before her. It was the sort of vulnerability he wasn't sure he was willing to expose.

"Can we handle it all over again?" he asked quietly.

"I'm just asking you to try," she replied. "At least for now. I think we should just see how it goes for a while."

Letting out a deep breath, he shrugged and nodded, too played out to offer much more resistance. If the truth were known, he'd admit that he no longer had any idea of how he felt about his involvement in *any* relationship, let alone this one.

"Do me a favor," he said, pulling back the blanket and spread on his side. "The minute you think you've got us figured out, let me know. I haven't got a fucking clue."

The pay phone in the candy store on St. Nicholas Avenue in Harlem rang at eight twenty-five that evening. Bobby "Badness" Burke was standing idly by, thumbing through a copy of *Hustler* magazine. When the owner of the store started for the booth, he waved him off and picked the receiver up.

"What's your number?" he growled.

"I beg your pardon?" a nervous voice replied.

"Your number. Where you're at."

"Oh, uh . . ." and the voice read him a 212 area-code number.

"Sit tight," Badness ordered. "We be in touch."

"How long?" the voice blurted.

"You know that when the man call, now won't you, boy?" He hung up, repeating the number in his mind as he scribbled it down in his little notepad.

Outside, Reggie was waiting with the redhead, Lu-Ann, in the back seat of the Benz. Bobby slid in behind the wheel and reached around to hand his boss the information.

"Boy sounds nervous," he said.

Reggie told him to drive. Picking up the cellular phone from it's cradle, he punched in the number from the slip of paper.

"Hello?" a voice blurted eagerly.

"A warning, sir," Reggie said smoothly. "You never had this conversation or any other little talks we gonna have. Get that straight in yo head right here at the outset."

"I have at least as much to lose as you do,' the voice told him.

"Fine. Just so we're understood. You know the piers over on the West Side past Twelfth Avenue? Circle Line and that aircraft carrier shit?"

The voice answered yes.

"One of them is where they do them summer rock concerts. Nothin' happenin' there tonight 'cept for something called a floating hospital tied alongside. You meet me there at midnight. On foot. Alone. You got it?"

"On foot?" the voice asked. "It's out in the middle of nowhere."

"You can handle it, baby. Look at it this way—you *gotta* handle it if you want to see me."

Reggie hung up the phone and smiled to himself. Curtis Maxwell. He *was* going to have to talk to the little brother about his future.

George Scully parked the Porsche adjacent to the new and well-lit Javits Convention Center and got out to stand on the sidewalk for a moment. This is crazy, he thought. *What am I doing here?* At midnight, the place was deserted. Hell, the whole far West Side was deserted save for a few straggling streetwalkers and pimps. Nervously, he checked the location of the car one last time and turned to notice a night security man peering out at him through the convention center glass. Good. At least if some asshole tried to drop the hook on it or steal the radio, there would be a witness. He turned and strode west toward the Hudson.

Back in the glory days of ocean travel, before the advent of jetliners, this area was the bustling arrivals and departures terminal for the Port of New York. Even today, a few blocks up, a contemporary harkening to those days past stood to service the Caribbean cruise trade and an occasional crossing of the QE2. Down here, in the mid- and lower forties, things got less glamorous in a hurry. There was the faltering Air and Space Museum aboard the mothballed USS *Intrepid*. The Circle Line and Day Tripper sightseeing boats. And between them, on Pier 84, the temporary scaffolding and bleachers of a summer rock concert series with the Lila Wallace Floating Hospital moored alongside. At midnight, the place was desolate.

Approaching with deep trepidation, Scully tested the chain-link gate in the fence and found it locked. Confused, he scanned up and down until he noticed that the fence ended at a place where one could slip around it with minimum risk of falling into the water. This wasn't the neurosurgeon's accustomed style, but then again, neither was paying criminals to kill men in wheelchairs. He swallowed his pride and took the only way in.

Still, there was no one in sight as Scully walked cautiously toward the far end of the pier. It was deathly quiet out here, the sirens and bustle of the city a vague background din. The imposing skyline loomed behind him. Reaching the water's edge, he turned away from New Jersey and stared at the city. The view from out there was really quite remarkable. As it was, he had little time to contemplate it before a monstrous black man emerged from the shadows of a large abstract sculpture fifty feet away and started in his direction.

Scully's first impulse was to panic. Jump into the river. Run. The cool rationality that had prevailed all his life quickly kicked in and told him there'd be little sense in that. These people were businessmen. They had to hope he could afford the service they were allegedly prepared to offer. What would the percentage be in knocking him off for a couple hundred bucks and some credit cards? He struggled to regulate his breathing, realizing that his knees were quivering a bit.

"Evening," the big man said amiably. "You the party who called?"

"I am," Scully replied.

"Before you see the man, I got to pat you down for heat. Just a formality."

Scully swallowed and nodded, lifting his arms and holding them out at his sides. The big guy stepped up and ran his hands over him in perfunctory fashion.

"Okay," he said, stepping back. He reached into his jacket pocket, producing a butane lighter and flicking it once.

A second black man stepped from the shadows of the sculpture, tall, wiry in build, and arrogant in the way he sauntered. He was dressed impeccably in a white linen suit. There didn't appear to be a crease on it anywhere other than the razor-sharp one down the front of his pants. Scully wondered how one achieved such ultimate cool. He also wondered what the market value was of the gold the man wore.

"Sir," the man addressed him. "What can we do for you?"

Scully looked at the man and took a deep breath. "It's not exactly what my friend mentioned to your friend," he said quickly. "It's a little more involved than that."

"Spit it out," Reggie DuQuesnay encouraged him.

"I want to start off by saying that I don't want any

110

names involved in this. I don't want to know who you are and vice versa. I have a problem that will go away if a certain elderly gentleman in a wheelchair dies. It has to be obvious that he was murdered.''

DuQuesnay's lips pulled slowly back into a thin smile. ''Well, well. My man tells me the job is a little body and fender work. You've just told me you want your man totaled.''

Scully nodded, swallowing nervously again. ''It's important that it be impossible to implicate me. Otherwise, there's no sense in me doing this.''

Reggie chuckled. ''Impossible's a big word, my friend. What you're asking is going to cost you a whole lot of money. You see, I offer a complete, professional service. I can't hire just any leg-breaker for a job like this. I've gotta bring in a hitter. Hitters cost big bread. You prepared to have this done right?''

''How much?'' Scully asked quickly.

''Fifty,'' Reggie replied. ''Cash. Used twenties.''

''Thousand?'' Scully asked, shocked.

Reggie snorted. ''That's right, friend. For less than that, you can go find yourself a two-bit greaseball from Passaic and let him fuck it up for you. You gotta ask yourself if the bread it costs to do it right is worth it compared to the shit you're in if you don't. You ask my unsolicited advice, it sounds like maybe the shit you're in is pretty deep.''

Scully blinked. Slowly he nodded. ''All right. Fifty thousand. It's going to take me a little time to get that kind of money together in small bills.''

Reggie shrugged. ''Take a year, friend. It ain't no matter to me. On the other hand, you know what they say about striking while the iron is hot.''

''How do I reach you?'' George asked. ''Same number?''

''You *are* from the other side of the tracks,'' Reggie

snickered. "Listen. You get the bread together and have your friend talk to my friend again. Don't worry, we'll get in touch."

The hitter left his house at ten thirty Sunday morning and drove the five minutes it took to get from Sheepshead Bay to Dyker Beach. The bottom had really dropped out of a brief, balmy low-pressure system that had prevailed well into the evening before. He had the windows and moon roof of his jet-black Pontiac Trans-Am rolled up tight against the chill and the heater going. A BTO tape in the cassette player was cranked up high. He felt good. Reggie said he had a definite maybe for him. Wanted to discuss the preliminaries. The hitter was always ready to discuss preliminaries where twenty-five thousand was involved.

Slouched low and lazy in the bucket seat, he eased the black monster into the parking lot of a little clamhouse on the other side of the Belt Parkway. After lowering the volume on the stereo a little, he shut down and waited, staring contentedly out across Gravesend Bay. He was nearly twenty minutes early but didn't mind. On a Sunday morning like this, it was quiet out here. The clamhouse didn't open until early afternoon. He had the parking lot all to himself. Beyond, out on the water, ships passed in and out of the Narrows, framed in the graceful sweep of the massive bridge above. The Irish on Staten Island resented the bridge and the invasion of Italians from Brooklyn that it had brought. They referred to it as the Guinea Gangplank. Screw them. It was a free country. People ought to be able to live wherever they wanted to. Except the niggers, but then that was a given, wasn't it? Even the scumbag Irish didn't like the niggers. You had a nice neighborhood and the niggers started moving in, you better start burning them out or you might as well move yourself and count your losses.

It was fifteen minutes later that the big stretch Mercedes limo rolled into the lot and pulled up next to the parked Trans-Am. The hitter rolled the window down, flicking the butt of a Marlboro out onto the pavement. The tinted glass of the limo's back window hummed open.

"My man," Reggie greeted the hitter. "Long time. How you been keepin' yourself?"

The hitter exhaled the last of the dead butt's smoke through his nose. "I've been just fine, pal. What do you have?"

"Step in for a Sunday morning eye-opener," Reggie invited. He motioned into the darkness of the car, and a sullen black female face appeared. It was a beautiful, high-cheekboned face framed in straight, tightly pulled-back hair. "You remember Esme, don't you?"

The hitter got something close to a smirk on his face, ignoring the black man for a moment to confront the hatred in the woman's eyes. Oh yeah, he remembered Esme all right. Reggie's special stash. He reached for the release lever and opened his door.

It was warm inside DuQuesnay's custom cocoon. Esme sat across from them, alone and wearing a sheer body stocking, charms held intact with a tightly wrapped lace shawl. There was nothing subtle about what she had to offer. The hitter sat next to Reggie, directly across from her, lounging comfortably and matching cool for cool.

"So what's on your mind?" he asked.

Reggie ignored the question for the moment, placing a Bloody Mary in his hand and palming a small vial of cocaine.

"Snort?"

"Maybe a short one," the hitter agreed.

They did a little whiff and drank while Whitney Houston crooned softly on the sound system. Outside, a good-looking Chris-Craft power boat churned tenaciously through choppy seas, heading east.

113

"I got something that might interest you," Reggie said at length. "Paralyzed dude in a wheelchair. Heavyweight Fifth Avenue building in the seventies. I've had one of my people check him out. Collects art. Tight security."

For the first time since the meeting began, the hitter looked suddenly edgy. "Twenty-five thou to whack an invalid. Now I'm starting to get it. I thought it was a lot of money."

Reggie smiled easily. "My information has you close to a certain overenthusiastic snuffing down in the Village. I read the details in the paper and can't help recognizing certain obvious similarities."

"Oscar Wembley," the hitter grunted.

"Old dude," Reggie agreed, nodding. "Collects art. Doesn't get around much. Lotsa crazy shit done in blood on the walls. To copy it, the thing would have to be perfect. We both know that the cops hold back certain shit. That's why I'm offering you the twenty-five. You're the only one who *could* make it perfect."

"When?" the hitter asked.

"Soon. Customer's in a hurry. He's supposed to have his green together by Tuesday."

The hitter considered this. "With the go sign, I could do him that night—provided I get some in-depth background. You say you've got people on it?"

"It'll be together by Tuesday night. You get the first twelve and a half with the background report and the second when I read about your handiwork in the morning paper."

With a pensive look furrowing his brow, the hitter considered the logistics. "I'm gonna want to spend every minute from now till Tuesday on this without a nickel up front. You know I never go in unless I've checked it out myself." He stared openly at Esme. "How about a gesture of your good faith, friend?"

Irritation clouded Reggie's eyes for an instant before he broke into a phony grin and reached out to pat Esme on the knee.

"Go ahead, honey. Man wants to walk down memory lane." He turned to the hired killer. "Don't be all day, friend. I'm a busy man."

The hitter got an incredible rise out of doing the cocky nigger's main woman, especially knowing that he was off on the other side of the lot, drumming his fingers impatiently. It was more than a year ago, now, but she hadn't forgotten the routine. With the seat beside him shoved all the way back, she reclined and stiffly peeled the body stocking down.

He was sweating and moving hard against her when he came, his body shuddering and his fingers roughly groping the flesh of her breasts. Her eyes were shut against his maniacal leer when he pushed away and slumped back into his own seat.

"Get the fuck outta here," he panted, head thrown back. Then he closed his eyes and didn't open them until he heard the heavy *whump* of the door closing.

Nine

When Joe Dante arrived for work at eight-thirty Monday morning, he was amazed to find Vinnie Arata already there and poring over the Wembley file. He was seated at one of the desks, reports and photographs spread out before him, drinking coffee and smoking.

"Yo, paisan," Vinnie greeted cheerily. " 'Nother day, 'nother dollar, huh?"

Dante paused in mid-stride, shook his head, and then continued on. Vinnie Arata showing a little get-up-and-go was too much to take first thing in the morning. He put the bag of donuts and coffee he was carrying on a desk and pulled up a chair. "You have any luck Friday?" he asked.

Arata shook his head. "Too late. Couldn't reach nobody. Fucked the dog for half the evening and ended up doing a report I didn't finish Thursday."

When Beasley Richardson arrived, he and Dante wasted little time in hitting the bricks, heading uptown to visit a woman at Sotheby's authentication department. She turned out to be pleasant enough but not very much help. Any dealings that Oscar Wembley had recently had with the auctioneer were strictly as an expert opinion. The partners knew from ledgers obtained from the Goodell woman that most of the man's acquisitions were on the gallery level, and only one had been made at auction. It had gone straight to the Metropolitan Museum on loan and was never delivered to the West 11th Street address.

They hit the Met next, discovering that, as with Sotheby's, one or two high-level staff had made periodic visits to the man's house, but no one who fit into the frustrated-artist category; there was only one male, and he didn't have a tattoo *or* red hair. They confirmed that Wembley, getting on in years, found it increasingly difficult to get around, especially on days when his rheumatism acted up. Often, the mountain was forced to visit Mohammed. These people displayed a profound respect for the murdered man and expressed deep grief at his passing. Certainly none of them was disenchanted with the idea that he was rich. On the contrary, they appreciated the fact that he chose to focus his money and interest in their common pursuit. No one they talked to could fathom the slashing of a masterpiece.

The information being gathered seemed to point them toward the galleries.

"You seem to be in a pretty good mood today," Jumbo commented as they rolled in their unmarked Plymouth toward a gallery on Madison Avenue in the sixties. "I don't think it's because my team won. What happened? You get laid this weekend?"

Dante threw him a sidelong glance. "Something like that."

Indeed, first thing that A.M., he'd put a card with Rosa's phone number and address into the vulva file, a listing of places where off-duty cops might be found when not at home. Things between him and Rosa were a long way from being straightened out, but the weekend was a begin-

117

ning. Joe still didn't understand the ground rules and was pretty sure he didn't really care anymore.

"Give me the rundown on this place again," he said, changing the subject.

Jumbo ran his finger through his notes. "The Daniels Gallery. Contemporary American and European paintings and lithographs. He bought one painting here, for loan to the Museum of Modern Art collection. Tag on it was sixty-eight thousand. Dealt with Mrs. Daniels."

"How many more on Madison?"

"Two. Then three on 57th Street and six more in SoHo. Must be nice to be rich. He bought from all twelve in the past year to the tune of six hundred and seventy-eight thousand bucks."

"About as much as we could expect to make in twenty years on the job," Dante mused. "We're in the wrong racket."

"I'll say. Half that shit I seen at Sotheby's looked like some dude dipped his ass in paint and mooned a canvas."

"That's what I like," Dante said, grinning. "A partner with refined aesthetic sensibilities."

"The fuck you say?"

"Never mind. I say we hit the rest of these Madison Avenue galleries, break for lunch, and do the 57th Street stuff the late end of the shift. That'll leave downtown for tomorrow."

Jumbo reached for a bag of leftover donuts on the dash and nodded. "Why not? We're uptown now. You notice the Italian stallion this morning? Smart-ass acts like he don't give fuck-all 'bout any of this shit, then shows up *early* to read the whole fuckin' file. Go figure."

A hint of winter was definitely in the air as Joe Dante walked his groceries home from the D'Agostino on Bethune Street. He loved the Village this time of year. The tourist hoards of summer dwindled to a few casual shoppers strolling the sidewalks. With November just around the corner, the trees were getting a tinge of yellow in their leaves. Residents of the neighborhood seemed a little less on edge, more ready with a smile and a nod for someone they recognized as having been around for years. On Bleecker Street, across from Abingdon Square, some guy was tending tomato vines on his fire escape. Drunks snoozed on park benches, and dog walkers slid newspaper beneath squatting hind ends. There was nothing normal about any of these things, but Dante had come to see a sort of order in them.

The tour he and Jumbo made of uptown galleries that day had produced no sudden flashes of insight. Everyone mourned Oscar Wembley's passing, and no one had red hair and a tattoo. Both detectives had long since come to expect this methodical plodding as par for the course. An investigation like this took legwork—lots of it. Often, the real break came from the oddest quarter. As much as they might scoff at Vinnie Arata's burglar alarm angle, seeing it as too simplistic, they knew he was just as likely to turn something up as they were. All of them were looking under rocks.

Dante's upstairs neighbor, Rebecca, was on the front stoop, conversing with a beautiful young Oriental woman, when he eased through the low wrought-iron gate and approached along the short flagstone walk to his apartment on Perry Street. Rebecca worked in advertising as an art director, fed Copter when Dante was away, and was his oldest friend in the building. She smiled at his arrival.

"Meet a new neighbor," she said. "This is Wendy Lee. Just moved from Lotus Land. She's subletting from Carole."

Joe shifted his groceries to shake hands.

"Wendy's going to co-host a new entertainment show at five o'clock."

Dante's interest kicked up a notch. "I'm impressed," he said. "That what you did on the Coast?"

"I was anchor on the late news," she replied.

"Joe has the garden," Rebecca informed her. "When he's not home, we sneak down there and lie in the sun."

Wendy took in his casual attire, and his tall athletic build.

"What do you do, Joe?" she asked. "Wait. Don't tell me. You're a lifeguard." She grinned mischievously.

Dante smiled. "I guess I sort of am. An urban lifeguard. I'm a cop."

As Wendy's eyebrows shot up in surprise, Rebecca hastened to interject, "A *detective*."

Tall for a Chinese woman, with a body and smooth, exotic features that made her look more like a runway model than a TV host, Wendy Lee gave Dante an even friendlier smile.

"A pleasure to meet you, Joe. I feel safer here already."

Dante glanced at Rebecca and then back at the new arrival. "Listen," he said. "I don't know what you two have planned for later, but why don't you stop by for a drink after dinner?" Rosa was due to dine with him in another hour. She liked Rebecca, and Joe knew they hadn't seen much of each other since she'd moved out. It would be a nice way to make the new neighbor feel welcome. "Rosa'll be here," he told Rebecca.

Her eyes sparkled, intrigued, as the brows above them arched in question. She turned to Wendy. "I can make it. You?"

Dinner was going to be a simple fettucine carbonara and a Caesar salad. Joe had the sauce on its way and was waiting for the pasta water to boil when the phone rang. He glanced at his watch. Rosa was due by now.

"Yeah," he said into the receiver of the wall phone, which he'd quickly wedged between shoulder and ear, lifting the melted garlic bread butter from the burner before it was scorched.

"You're going to hate me," Rosa announced from the other end. "We've got a cop shot in a Bronx truck hijacking sting, and I'm stuck here till it blows over."

"Who?" Dante asked, immediately concerned.

"Brian Joley. Bronx Command Task Force. He was working undercover with Safe, Loft and Truck. It doesn't look like he's going to make it. Took one in the neck."

Dante shook his head in silent disgust. In recent years, truck hijackings, once the realm of the rackets, were being pulled more and more by a new breed of wantonly violent South Americans. The mob rarely mixed it up with the cops. Ecuadorians seemed to think that killing one was a badge of honor.

"The chief is in the middle of an impromptu press conference with the PC and the mayor. It'll be hours before I can break loose."

It was eight o'clock. Joe knew she'd be lucky to make it by midnight.

"Want to take a rain check?" he offered.

"I think I'd better." There was disappointment in her voice.

"Give me a call later and let me know if the guy pulls through."

"I will," she promised. "I'm sorry about this, Joe. I was looking forward to it."

"So was I."

George Scully was beside himself with anxiety. He'd gone to the bank early that morning, played his usual game of golf with Phil that afternoon, and then driven back to the city to hand a flashy black pimp and his thug bodyguard fifty thousand bucks on a handshake. Hell, George had never so much as given the paperboy ten dollars without getting a receipt for it. This was nuts. The goddamn insurance company was going to offer to settle any minute and he'd handed what meager assets he still had over to a man who represented the lowest form of scum in all society. He *had* to be crazy.

It was three hours since he'd done it now. He lay in that bedroom he'd come to hate, Joan slumbering easily beside him. He had a nasty feeling in the pit of his stomach. It was telling him that the flashy black man had seen him coming a mile away.

Rebecca yawned and stretched. It was almost midnight, she'd had three brandies, and she had to get up and go to work in the morning.

"Hate to spoil the party," she apologized. "But I'm whipped. Thanks for the drink, Joe. I'm going to feel like somebody kicked me in the head when I wake up."

Dante, Rebecca, and Wendy were lounging in his front room, a Pretenders tape running through the cassette deck and bottles of both brandy and port on the coffee table. The advertising woman was just reaching to gather up her handbag when the phone rang. Dante stood and crossed the room to answer it.

Rosa had just gotten home. Detective Brian Joley had died at ten twenty-eight, leaving a wife and two kids in Spring Valley. The news gave Dante the same feeling he always got when he heard the creeps had blown away another member of the job. The same little voice that guided his hunches during an investigation now whispered that it could have been him—or any of his twenty-some-odd thousand brothers.

Rebecca, realizing that it was Rosa on the other end, asked him to say hello as she kissed him on the cheek and headed for the door. When he hung up, Wendy Lee was still on the sofa, finishing her Rémy. She saw the disturbed look in his eye and quickly drained her snifter.

"Thanks for the drink. It was fun getting to know you like this. I really like your place."

Dante nodded distractedly, walking with her toward the door. He shook his head to focus as they stood there a moment in the doorway.

"Sorry. A detective was blown away up in the Bronx tonight."

She nodded, her huge brown eyes softening. "I understand. In L.A., you don't feel it so close around you. This city scares me a little. It really *is* like a concrete jungle."

"Believe it," he said quietly. "Listen, you need anything, feel free to call. We all get along pretty well here."

He held out a hand to shake hers goodnight. Instead of taking it, she leaned forward, stood on tiptoe, and kissed him full on the mouth. For a lingering moment, her tongue raked across his teeth and met his before he broke it off. Caught in surprise, Joe regarded her quizzically as she smiled boldly.

"You should feel free to call too," she said seductively. "I'm home most nights after seven. You know where I live."

Dante and Jumbo prepared to saddle up for their assault on SoHo. Nearly a week had passed since the Wembley homicide. The lieutenant was getting heat from the brass now, and he wasn't shy about letting them know about it. With a murder like this, the big building needed an occasional scrap to throw to the dogs of the Fourth Estate. Those dogs were going hungry and making one hell of a racket about it.

There were six galleries on their list with whom Wembley had had financial dealings during the past two years. His purchases ranged from minor painters on the rise to several established stars. Compounding the problem of trying to hit them all in a day was the fact that none opened before eleven o'clock. To kill time, they spent an hour going over the detailed report submitted by the medical examiner's office, learning very little new about the case. They were just getting ready to head downtown when the lieutenant stuck his head out his door.

"Richardson."

"What's up, lou?"

"Dante. You might as well be in on this too. Come on in a sec. Both of you."

The pair wandered in and sat across the desk from the whip. He looked tired, his shoulders pulled up with tension from the pressure he was under, making his suit coat look ill-tailored. There were bags under his eyes.

"We got us a problem," Manley said flatly. "The court rescheduled Jumbo's testimony on that jogger-rapist collar he and Campo made last month. Something else fell through on the calendar. You're due down there at ten tomorrow morning, Beasley."

"That leaves us short as hell," Dante remarked.

"Tell me about it," the grizzled black man sighed. "Campo's still at JFK, at least for the rest of this week. They haven't had much luck out there. Two more thefts went undetected. The whole op is headed down the shit chute, and they're scrambling to see if they can't shore it up with *more* manpower."

Dante got a bad feeling as Manley spoke.

"You can guess the rest of it, Joey. You and Arata are the only members of the team available for duty on the Wembley case. You'll be backing each other up if either of you needs a hand in your lines of investigation."

With a shrug, Dante accepted the inevitable. "That it, Vic?"

Manley nodded. "Sure wouldn't mind if you two had a bone you could throw my way. The C of D has the PC breathing down his neck."

"Nada," Dante told him, shaking his head. "I don't figure Vinnie's come up with anything?"

"You gotta be *lookin'* to find somethin'," Jumbo said under his breath. "C'mon, Dante. Let's hit it before this whole investigation turns to dog shit." He heaved himself to his feet.

"What have you got on tap?" Manley asked.

"Contemporary art appreciation, downtown style," Dante told him. "About the only thing solid we've gleaned so far is that the uptown scene looks at the downtown scene with contempt. Lack of sophistication or something. The downtowners see the uptowners as some very un-hip whores of the filthy rich. They've got a nice, healthy rivalry going."

"That's wonderful," the lieutenant drawled. "And if this wonderfully delicate balance weren't maintained, the cost of a burger and coke at Wendy's would hit the ceiling, right?"

"I seriously doubt it," Dante said.

"Then us common slobs don't give a rat's ass, do we?"

"Only when they start killing each other, lou."

Manley waved them out of his office, calling after them as they crossed the squad room, "Bring me a bone with a little meat still on it, will ya?"

They hit three galleries and struck out three times before breaking for lunch at two o'clock. Dante and Jumbo were running out of runway, and the prospect of getting tangled in the trees was discouraging. A day that had started out cool and sparkling was turning downright cold. After a couple slices of pizza and coffee, they were now walking along the west side of Greene Street between Broome and Grand.

"Nancy Epstein," Jumbo announced, pointing at yet another glass facade in a cast-iron-faced manufacturing building. All these galleries looked the same down here. According to Jumbo, they were also all crammed with the same no-talent shit. Dante wouldn't go quite that far, but he would have admitted privately that comparing some of the works represented to their price tags was a little mind-boggling.

Jumbo pulled out his notebook as they stood surveying the premises. Those big, bloodhound eyes looked less than hopeful. "What've we got here?" he asked, scanning a page. The prospect of spending the next week in court had him depressed. "Three paintings purchased, one last November and two more after the first of the year. Artist is a guy named Mennington. All three works circa 1975. Fifteen thousand bucks apiece. Acrylic on multimedia. Wood, canvas, and clay. Jesus. Who thinks up this shit?"

Dante didn't answer. He put on his best friendly policeman face and held the door for the grumpy fat man.

The layout of the place was one more variation on the SoHo gallery theme: large expanses of white Sheetrock wall, high-intensity track-lighting, oak strip flooring, support columns left rustic. At one end, along the right wall, a four-foot L-shaped wall capped with solid oak served as a partition for the attendant's counter. Behind it sat an underling, always bright, fresh-scrubbed, and attractive. From their earlier experiences in the milieu, the detectives now knew that there would be a set of offices somewhere in the back, nicely furnished with the sort of creature comforts potential customers generally enjoy: coffee urn; small refrigerator containing white wine; a cabinet full of stemware.

There would also be the obligatory potted palms and broad-leaf tropical plants.

"Can I help you?" the clear-complexioned blonde asked from behind the desk wall. She was maybe twenty-two or -three, more than likely an art history grad from Columbia or NYU, earning peanuts.

Dante approached the desk, reaching into his jacket to produce shield and ID. "Detective Dante. Sixth Precinct. Detective Richardson and I would like a word with Ms. Epstein."

At the sight of the gold detective's shield, the young woman's entire demeanor changed. She was no longer quite so confident.

"Is . . . is there something wrong?" she asked.

"Please." Dante moved to put the girl at ease. "There's no cause for alarm, miss. We're just in the course of a routine investigation and wonder if Ms. Epstein might be able to answer a few questions."

The young woman looked nervously toward a closed door in the back of a smaller room beyond. This room displayed some interesting matte black sculpture comprised of cylinders and intersecting planes. All of it looked somehow substantial, holding its own in the space.

"She's with a customer right now, I'm afraid. She hates to be disturbed."

"How long do you think she'll be?" Jumbo asked.

The woman shrugged. "Maybe fifteen, twenty minutes."

He smiled, trying hard to seem friendly. "We'll wait. If it goes much longer than that, I'm afraid we'll have to interrupt."

"I can tell her now, I suppose," she said.

"That's okay, miss. We know how nervous it makes people to hear the cops are waiting outside. We can give her a little time."

The girl smiled in great relief, obviously sweating the

prospect of arousing the boss lady's ire. "Could I get you something while you wait? I have coffee here."

Less than fifteen minutes later, Nancy Epstein's office door swung open and a young, semiattractive, obviously very well-heeled woman emerged while being gushed over by the gallery owner.

"Talk to John about it, dear. The minute I laid eyes on it, I knew it had your name on it. It's quite a splendid example of the period."

"It's too gorgeous," the client gushed back. "I'm sure he'll love it as much as I do." She got a little conspiratorial grin on her face. "He'd *better*." And then she giggled.

Nancy Epstein, in contrast to the brunette who was preparing to put her husband's balls in a vise, was a tall, lithe, well-preserved blonde. Late forties, Dante guessed. Everything about her was in the most chic and currently expensive taste. She carried herself imperiously while at the same time exuding no small amount of charisma. There was an undeniable absence of self-consciousness.

As Nancy Epstein escorted her customer to the door, she caught the look of concern on her assistant's face. With a quick sweep of the room, she spotted the two detectives, one tall and lanky in pleated slacks and a Harris tweed jacket, the other a roly-poly black man in a baggy suit with jowly face and big, watery, bloodhound eyes. Both looked out of place. As soon as she sent her gold mine trundling off up the block, she turned to see what the problem might be.

"Something wrong, Jillian?" she asked in a smooth, velvety voice, eyebrows arched in just the hint of displeasure.

"We're police officers, ma'am," Jumbo offered. He produced his shield and ID. "I'm Detective Richardson, and this is Detective Dante."

The gallery owner glanced nervously back and forth

between them before speaking. "Would you like to come back into my office, gentlemen? It's much more comfortable there."

"Whatever," Jumbo replied. He turned to Jillian and forced another smile. Dante figured he had to be running real low in that department. "Thanks for your help, miss."

When and only when Nancy Epstein had the office door safely shut behind her did she dare venture further inquiry.

"What's this about, officers?"

Jumbo nodded to Dante, ready to let him take it from there. Joe spoke to the gallery owner for the first time.

"You're no doubt aware that one of your clients was murdered, ma'am? An Oscar Wembley?"

Sudden comprehension registered in the woman's eyes.

"Yes, of course. Terrible tragedy." She was relaxing visibly with each tick of the clock now. Moving to an overstuffed armchair alongside her desk, she sank into it. "Please, have a seat. Certainly. It makes sense that you would be checking everything. I don't mind telling you that Oscar will be sorely missed by the artworld. He was one of a kind."

"I'm sure he was," Dante said, nodding curtly. He referred to his notes. "Mr. Wembley made several purchases from your firm in the past year. To be specific, three by the same artist—one last November and two in early February of this year. Can you tell us about those purchases?"

"What would you like to know? Specifically?"

"Everything. Manner of selection. Payment. Delivery. Those sorts of things."

Brow knit, Nancy Epstein considered a moment, digging back through the memory banks. "It was really quite straightforward, if I recall. Oscar didn't get out and around much, you know. Quite often, when I had something I

129

thought he might be interested in, I either had the slides of
the work sent to him or brought them myself. This time I
believe I hand-carried the slides. Menningtons always seem
to go fast, and I knew he had a special interest in the
artist.''

"Did you also deliver the paintings?" Jumbo pressed.

She shook her head. "One of the staff did that."

"Which one?"

She seemed surprised by the question. "I'm not really
sure, actually. I suppose it was probably Stuart if it was
after the first of the year.''

"What would the difference have been?" Jumbo asked.
"I mean, between February and, say, May?"

"I'm afraid we had to let Stuart go," she replied,
something close to tenseness in her voice, not from the act
but the memory.

"A problem?" Dante asked.

Nancy Epstein sighed. "Stuart Wiems was one of those
young artists who believes the world owes him a handout
until the day when he bursts full-formed onto the center
stage of the art world. He was insolent. He had a chip on
his shoulder. One nearly had to apply a crowbar to get him
to move.''

"How long did he work for you, ma'am?" Jumbo
asked, trying hard to sit on his excitement.

She thought again, finger to her cheek. "From about
this time last year until the middle of March, I guess.
Yes.''

It was Dante's turn. He shared Richardson's sudden
upswing in mood. "Would you be able to recall if this
Wiems made any other deliveries to the Wembley residence? Delivering slides or other purchases?''

Nancy Epstein shrugged. "It would be on my routing
sheets, I suppose. You see, I run my slides much like they
run the public library. Leave them off for a day or so and

then pick them up so that another client might have a look at the same work.'' She stood and moved around the desk to open a bottom file drawer, quickly fingering through manila folders until she reached one in particular. Pulling it, she returned to her seat, the file on her lap.

''Yes, here it is,'' she said, finger running down a page. ''Stuart made his first delivery to Oscar on June sixteenth of last year. Slides of some sculpture. Then again on July twenty-seventh . . . September ninth . . . skip all the way to''— she flipped a page—''the last week in November. Yes. Here it is. Specifically to deliver the Mennington. The first one. The others were part of an estate. I was engaged as broker. If I recall correctly, Oscar was feeling well enough to visit down here the previous months. Then his rheumatism started acting up again.''

''When you say Stuart Wiems had a chip on his shoulder, ma'am, would you term it anger? You know, resentment for people who *had* made it?'' Jumbo was right around the center of the target now.

Nancy Epstein's eyes widened as the implications of what they were asking finally hit home.

''I . . . I don't know what to say,'' she stammered. ''Yes, Stuart's animosity bothered me to the extent that it became very unpleasant having him around here. I suppose that's why I let him go. He was also less than courteous to Jillian. He was one of those people who seems to delight in shocking others. Jillian, I'm afraid, shocks easily.''

''Describe him to us, ma'am. Physically,'' Dante suggested.

Nancy Epstein thought a moment, distress very evident in her eyes now.

''Tall. About as tall as you are. Red hair. He had it cut in a mohawk. Very fair complexion. Oh, and he had a tattoo on his right forearm. A spider, I believe it was.''

Dante could hardly contain himself. "Do you have an address for him?" he asked.

"We must. The accountant prepared his W-2 at the beginning of the year. Just a moment. I'll get it for you."

On the street, Dante and Richardson could barely restrain themselves from embracing each other with glee.

"This is it," Jumbo said excitedly. All evidence of his earlier depression had vanished. He was walking light on his feet as he waved the three-by-five file card with Stuart Wiems's address on it. "We've found our fuckin' man!"

Dante nodded. "Maybe. Just maybe."

"What?"

"I'm *with* you friend. But I learned a long time ago not to count my chickens." He checked his watch. It was four-fifteen, and the two of them were due to go off duty in forty-five minutes. "C'mon. Let's go throw the lieutenant his bone and then I'll buy you a beer."

"Little bon voyage present?" Jumbo ribbed him. "Now that I've helped you with the rough part, you and that asshole Arata can step in and nab all the glory."

Dante rolled his eyes. "Wishful thinking, partner. With Vinnie backing me up, you'll get out of court and our man will still be on the street."

Ten

Fiona Hassey reached to cover Scully's hand with her own, reading the extreme nervousness in his voice and on his face. It was five thirty in the evening, and Fiona was due to start three days of evenings in the recovery unit at seven. They were seated across a window table from each other at a trendy little corner restaurant just blocks from the hospital on Third Avenue.

"You haven't flushed anything down the toilet, George," she insisted emphatically, attempting to allay his fears. This thing might take a couple of days. You only just gave the guy the money. Look at it this way—the insurance company isn't planning to offer settlement until next week, right? I don't think you need to start worrying quite yet."

"You think so?" Scully asked hopefully. "I can't even think straight anymore. Everything's one giant fucking headache."

"Benjamin Crowley's as good as dead, George. Start thinking about how much better everything is going to be. You'll be able to breathe again."

"It will only cure one of my problems," he said gloom-

133

ily. "There's still the Biotechnics fiasco and the notes on all the real estate."

Fiona shrugged. "What about the offshore fund? That money's still there, isn't it?"

"It isn't doing much, but sure it's there all right. That's my safety valve. My mad money."

"Listen," Fiona said. "I understand your not wanting to confront Joan with a divorce when everything's in such disarray. I'm also not asking you to."

"Oh?" he asked, surprised.

"Come on, George. I'm not *that* unreasonable. Things are going to change soon. The market's still on the upswing, and without the lawsuit threatening to clean you out, you can rebuild. How long would it take before you had the money to repay the house note? Eight months? Ten at the outside."

He shrugged. "Maybe. You'd actually wait that long?"

"I'm here now, aren't I? I want us to work, George. I'm not going to destroy all that for a few months, one way or the other."

Scully brightened noticeably. "You don't know what it means to me to hear you say that. I've felt a lot like I've been grasping at straws lately."

"You've got to give me a little more credit, George. We're in this thing together, remember? All the way to the end."

George Scully *did* remember. Rolling north in the Porsche an hour later, he couldn't think of anything else. It looked like he'd have to marry Fiona now whether he had ever seriously thought he would or not. She was playing him perfectly, and he'd gone for it. You pay your money and you take your chances, the saying went. He'd paid his money.

* * *

At two o'clock that morning, the hitter sat in his black Pontiac Trans-Am on the Central Park side of Fifth Avenue at Seventy-second Street. Kitty-corner across the avenue, opposite the Frick Collection, the target's building loomed skyward. Number 902. Fourteenth floor.

At that hour, the avenue was all but abandoned. The thermometer had dropped down into the high thirties a little after midnight and was still hovering there. All along the way, in front of each of these palaces of conspicuous comfort, uniformed doormen loitered in their overcoats beneath awnings that stretched curbward, the occasional cab stopping in front of them to disgorge passengers. Lights blazed through ornate lobbies replete with marble, polished brass, and crystal chandeliers.

What a way to live, the hitter thought. He thumbed the three typed pages of the report Reggie had delivered along with his first twelve-and-a-half thousand dollars at eight the previous evening. It was a very thorough document. For a few bucks, a brother working the service elevator had been reached for a floor plan and the details of comings and goings at the target apartment. The report detailed type of locks, service stairwell access from the lobby, the fact that there was a live-in nurse. The hitter bellyached about that one, saying he'd have to get more money for her. Reggie told him to just whack the bitch, promising him an extra two grand for the inconvenience.

He also had some notes of his own, gleaned from personal sources. After digesting Reggie's report, he read over his own information for the hundredth time, mentally quizzing himself on details he would have to replicate exactly. From the information at hand, he could see no reason why the job shouldn't be done tonight. There was supposed to be some sort of rush on it anyway. He glanced at his watch—it was 2:10 A.M. Time to kick it in gear.

* * *

When the emergency operator came on the line, the hitter cupped his hand over the receiver. He told her he was the superintendent of 902 Fifth Avenue and that his wife had gone into convulsions and was now unconscious. He wasn't sure if she was breathing or not. She was turning blue. Their apartment was in the basement. Please hurry.

Back in his car, he fired it up quickly and drove east on 70th Street to Madison and back around on 71st, searching for a parking spot. At that hour, he had little trouble, dropping it alongside the museum. Before climbing out from behind the wheel and locking up, he grabbed a corporate-looking briefcase from the seat beside him. Out on the sidewalk, he leaned against the hood and had a smoke, waiting until he heard the distant wail of an EMS ambulance siren. A passerby would have thought him a successful businessman, a little too slick perhaps in his European-cut Giorgio Armani pinstripe, but well within the range for Fifth Avenue. His wiry black hair was slicked back. He'd added horn-rims with flat glass. His South Bay fishing tan gave him the look of a high-power corporate raider who weekended a little farther east on Long Island.

As the siren wailed loud and steady now, just blocks away, he pushed off from the car and sauntered casually up the sidewalk toward the park. The lights of the ambulance cut red and white swaths in the gloom as it screeched to a halt in front of 902. He watched as two attendants hopped out, hurrying around to open the rear door and haul a rolling stretcher out. In confusion, the doorman and night porter advanced from just inside the front door, engaging the EMS people in excited conversation.

The hitter strolled casually up the sidewalk toward them, timing it so the surge of pandemonium moving to the elevators worked as distraction enough to let him slip by. Moving quickly now, he slid soundlessly across the gleaming marble to a door opposite, hoping to God that Reggie's dope was accurate, turned the knob, and pulled. Within seconds of having entered the building, he was safely inside the service and fire stairwell. He quickly opened his briefcase and donned a pair of mechanic's coveralls. With twelve flights of stairs to climb he skipped the surgical gloves and knotted nylon stocking until he got just outside the Crowley apartment service door.

One of the nice things about a high-security building like 902 Fifth was that once access was gained to the floor itself, the actual door-locks were generally a pushover. That was the case now. A dozen years ago he'd determined it wise to invest in a locksmithing course at a technical school in Brooklyn. He'd even moonlighted for a few years afterward, sharpening skills by working part-time for a locksmith in Sheepshead Bay. Knowing what sort of locks they have in a place and being called out to install and repair them gave him twice the information of a regular burglar. He knew what was inside the premises and whether or not it was worth his while. A nice way to supplement his income.

Even now, he tried to stay in practice. He had a number of locks in his basement workshop and would tinker when he had time. If you didn't keep your hand in it, picking a lock could take hours. This one, a fairly standard Weiser, took about eight minutes.

The door swung open into the gloom of a ceramic-tiled pantry area. The hitter slipped quickly inside, not knowing if anyone was close to where the light from the service area might alarm them. He closed the door behind him and sat crouched in the darkness, listening hard. Nothing. Not a peep in there. He got his bearings. Straight ahead and off to the right was the kitchen. Beyond that, the dining room in one direction and the day maid's cubicle and bath in the other. He could get from the kitchen to the rest of the house through the dining room. He needed the requisite kitchen knife and would pick that up on the way.

The tiny penlight bit into the gloom as he advanced soundlessly into the kitchen. It was a big, elaborate setup, with restaurant range, all manner of hanging pots and utensils, acres of counter space, and a prep island in the middle. There was quite an assortment of kitchen knives to choose from, all arranged, handles up, in slits down through a massive maple butcher-block. The hitter picked out the closest thing to the size and shape used on West 11th Street in the Village. Twelve-inch blade, sharp as a razor, with a substantial ebony-colored handle. He hefted it. Nice feel. Most likely expensive as hell, a sweet piece of steel like this.

There were paintings all through the dining room, with its massive mahogany table and chairs polished to a high sheen and perched on a marble floor that gleamed too. There were double doors at the other end, standing open on a sort of entry foyer that also seemed to function as a gallery. The entire area was jammed with paintings, one after the other across all four walls. Again, polished marble underfoot. There was more light here, coming from the living room ahead where the sweeping expanse of windows opened onto Central Park and the street lamps of Fifth Avenue. Hot damn, what a spread. Maybe the nicest setup the hitter had ever broken into. Everything the penlight fell on looked like it cost a fortune and change.

Still not a sound as he crept past the entrance to the living room and bore left down a long hall toward the bedrooms. There were three, along with five bathrooms in the place. Five fucking *bathrooms*. He grinned to himself. Rich people *were* fulla shit.

The live-in nurse was in the smallest of the three bedrooms, just past another room the floor plan sketch called a library. He stole up to it and stood frozen, his ear to the door. The nylon mask was making his head sweat, even though the place was temperature-controlled and cooler than a morgue. From inside, he could make out the faint, steady breathing of someone in deep sleep. He set a hand carefully on the knob and gave it a try. With a half twist, the door gave inward with an all but inaudible click.

The nurse was in this fairy-tale four poster with a canopy, sleeping naked with a sheet pulled half over her so her legs and torso were hanging out. She was big-framed and heavy-breasted, with straight blond hair and a flat, Scandinavian face. The way she slept, her neck was exposed on one side. Perfect. The hitter didn't have any time to waste wrestling with naked broads awakened while he tried to adjust his angle. He stepped up fast, dropped the big knife to intersect her carotid artery and whipped it in one clean motion, making sure to go in plenty deep. Then, as she started to thrash, he jerked the pillow out from beneath her head and shoved it down hard over her face. All things considered, especially as he had nothing to do but watch a pretty good pair of legs kicking and her hot-spot heaving around jay-ass naked in the breeze, it didn't take her too long to go.

After the nurse, the old man was a piece of cake. He was situated in the middle of this great big bedroom, looking kind of tiny and pathetic in a single, motorized hospital bed. There was a wheelchair and an oxygen rig not in use against one wall. And more paintings. Christ, these things had to be worth a load.

The old guy must have been a light sleeper, because his eyes blinked as the hitter came at him across the Persian area rug. His mouth opened, but the hitter was fast, closing the distance pronto and slapping his hand across it. There was no struggling this time. The poor old bastard was paralyzed. It made it almost too easy, slicing him into ribbons with that ultra-sharp knife. There was a lot of blood. Between him and the nurse, more than enough for what he had to do next. The hitter checked his watch. He'd been in the apartment only seven minutes and in the building just twenty, including the trip up the service stairs. With the dirty stuff out of the way, he could relax a bit, but he still had to work quickly. Hefting the dripping knife in one gloved hand, he started around the room, methodically slashing each work of art. Then he moved off to do more down the hall, in other bedrooms, the gallery, and living room. The perp in the Wembly job had skipped the dining room. Hell, he'd already wrecked ten or twenty million bucks' worth. It was time for the crazy shit with the blood.

Joe Dante was in the middle of an erotic dream involving his new upstairs neighbor when he got Vic Manley's call. The mental footage was fairly graphic, with the beautiful Chinese woman going a whole lot further than she had at his front door the previous evening. For a moment, he had trouble focusing, believing the telephone to be his alarm clock.

"Whaa . . . what's up? he mumbled into the receiver.

"It looks like our guy struck again," the whip announced. "902 Fifth Avenue. Fourteenth floor. It's a real mess. You'd better get up here."

On his way uptown, Dante had the cab driver stop at a deli on Sixth Avenue for coffee. He took it in gulps during the ride, wishing there were a way to pump it intravenously. The taste of Wendy Lee was still lingering on the palate of his imagination, but the bitter deli brew worked hard to obscure it. The cab pulled behind a medical examiner's meat wagon on the corner of 71st and Fifth. Dante paid the driver, all the while musing about erotic dreams, gift horses and Trojan horses.

* * *

The hitter was still cranked up, running on adrenaline a full two hours after the fact. Nowhere had anyone mentioned the possibility of the fucking day maid sleeping over. That wasn't in the bargain. He'd panicked, damn it. The big nigger bitch appeared out of nowhere when he accidentally knocked over a brass bucket of dried flowers in the foyer. On seeing him, his white coveralls drenched in gore, the bitch screamed. With the kitchen knife abandoned on the bedroom floor, he'd been forced to kill her with his bare hands. She went hard. After kicking her in the gut to cut off her air, he'd had to bounce her head a half dozen times off the shiny marble floor.

The building at 902 Fifth was humming with activity as Dante pushed his way through the news crews on the sidewalk. Several recognizable reporters from local stations milled about in the bright camera lights. At five thirty, day was chasing night from the eastern sky, now a faint glow on the horizon. The park across the avenue still lay in deep shadow. In addition to the Fourth Estate and the ME's wagon, there were a forensics station wagon, four patrol units from the Nineteenth, and half a dozen unmarked units. These would be primarily Borough Command Task Force detectives, called in when mayhem struck between the hours of midnight and eight A.M. A uniformed patrolman from the Nineteenth stood conversing with the doorman as Dante presented his identification just inside the lobby door.

He knew he must look like a warmed-over TV dinner. Dispensing with any notion of formality, he'd hopped into a pair of Levi's and pulled on a sweatshirt. He hadn't bothered with washing his face or combing his hair. Now he hustled over to the elevator bank and rode up to the crime scene, feeling like he'd just gone ten rounds with *Bruce* Lee instead of Wendy.

The door to the apartment stood ajar as a forensics man dusted it for latents. Dante steeled himself for what he knew came next. Directly inside, across the foyer, a dark, moody Renaissance oil was slashed from corner to corner. Beside it, in the familiar scrawl of their murdering madman, a bloody message declared: THE BLOODSUCKERS MUST DIE!

A patrolman stood outside the front door, stopping him now to examine his ID before allowing him to proceed.

"They're in the master bedroom. Myself, I ain't never seen nothin' like it."

Dante shook his head. "Afraid I have. Thanks." His stomach was knotted, the deli coffee working with his own juices to heighten his queasiness. Cold sweat dampened his forehead. He swallowed hard and stepped inside.

The first sight upon entering the apartment surprised him. A huge black woman in a simple cotton nightdress lay sprawled on the marble floor next to an overturned brass bucket. Dried flowers were scattered all around and beneath her. There was a bloody pulp where her face should have been, as though she'd been bludgeoned to death. Gray matter lay exposed from a crack in her skull. Curious, he moved forward to stare down at her. He'd prepared himself for the horrible gore of slashing death, and there was none evident here. This was an odd new twist. Hearing voices farther off in the apartment, he turned to move on.

More destroyed paintings, smears of blood on the floors, and more scrawled messages were evident as he made his way through the place to the master suite. The apartment itself was very elegantly appointed. All the doors had brightly polished brass levers instead of knobs. The wallpaper was a custom fabric, and there was extensive marble throughout. Dante found Jumbo and Vic Manley in the big bedroom at the end of the hall. They were engaged in conversation with half a dozen detectives from both the Borough Command Task Force and the Nineteenth Precinct. Rocky Conklin from the medical examiner's office had been called out of bed and looked none too happy about it. He and the area zone commander, Inspector Raul Rodriguez, stood in conversation, watching a pair of forensic pathologists at work next to a hospital bed. They screened the corpse itself from Dante's view. He spotted a wheelchair and an oxygen setup. Invalid. The room itself was a nightmare of gore and frenzied destruction—half a dozen slashed masterworks, scrawled messages, blood splashed everywhere. There was also a pool soaking a Persian area rug at the victim's bedside. In the middle of it, a heavy, long-bladed kitchen knife lay covered with blackening blood. The art and the address would definitely put the victim in the same league with Oscar Wembley, though this collection looked uniformly Old World. The sort of stuff Rembrandt and his pals did about four hundred years back. Dante stepped forward. A corpse rendered into so much flayed meat lay atop a sheet and blanket saturated in crimson.

Manley broke away from the others. He looked a lot like Dante felt, the bags under his eyes heavy and his color going a little toward gray, odd on a man who normally had a rich, walnut brown skin tone.

"What sort of wild animal has the concrete jungle spawned this time?" Dante asked hollowly.

Manley took a deep breath and let it out. "You know any of these guys?" he asked.

Joe was quickly introduced around. Inspector Rodriguez, a distinguished man of fifty with a thick mane of silver hair, perfect teeth, and a tanned, rugged face, asked him how he'd been. Once, he'd been part of the borough narcotics hierarchy while Dante was assigned to undercover.

"You want to bring him up to date?" the inspector asked a task force detective named McClellan.

The stocky redhead with a drinker's nose and florid face nodded. He motioned Dante aside. "A neighbor downstairs was awakened at approximately two forty-five by a loud crash in this apartment. Aware that the victim was confined to his bed and a wheelchair, she was getting ready to phone the doorman and ask him to make sure everything was all right when she heard a scream. A minute or two later, she heard the pantry service entrance door slam. The doorman sent the porter up with the night man. They found the service door ajar and, unable to raise anyone inside the premises, elected to enter. They found this and called us."

"Are either of them suspects?" Dante asked.

McClellan shook his head. "Negative. There was some sort of emergency call received by EMS, claiming the super's wife had suffered a stroke. Probably a diversion created by the perp. Both men were in the basement until the call to the doorman came from the neighbor. The building has a policy that personnel only enter a residence in pairs. Lot of valuable shit laying around a joint like this. If there's a complaint about sticky fingers, they want their people backed up by a witness."

Dante turned to stare around the room. The scrawling on the walls and the damage to the art seemed identical to the stuff at Wembley's place. He'd looked at those pictures in the file often enough to have most of the slogans memorized and the images burned in his mind.

Vic Manley stepped over. "They thought of us as soon as they saw this," the whip told him. "Looks like a dead ringer to me."

Joe nodded, moving away from the group to approach the corpse, staring down now at the carnage. Again, the victim had been literally hacked to death.

"There's a nurse who got it too. In the next room," Jumbo told him, moving to his side. His shirt was wrinkled and tie askew.

"How's the grand jury?" Dante asked, turning away from the grisly sight. Already, though the death was only hours old and the place was heavily air-conditioned, the close odor of primary rot was beginning to fill the room. It crawled up his nostrils.

"Same old shit," Jumbo replied. "I should be back in the squad by the end of the week."

"Not soon enough," Dante said, gesturing to the mess at hand.

They moved together from the room and wandered down the hall to the next bedroom. Instead of a hospital bed and the general air of an infirmary, this room was done more conventionally, with heavy chintz curtains, matching flowered wallpaper, and exquisite antique furniure. In the middle of it, on an ornate four-poster, a semi-nude woman lay sprawled with her throat cut. She was young, bleached-blond, and had a good body. Death apparently caused by blood loss from a severed carotid artery. Some signs of convulsion were apparent in the wild disarray of the bed-clothes and her hair, as well as in the bulging, unseeing eyes.

"God!" Dante said, losing color.

"Nasty, huh?" Jumbo said. "It's like the dude did her just so he could have the old man to himself and do his thing undisturbed."

Joe turned away and moved back into the hall. He almost ran into a sweating and agitated-looking Vinnie Arata.

"You look awful," Dante commented.

"Speak for yourself," Vinnie retorted. He pushed past a forensics man and walked quickly back up the hall to report in to the whip.

It wasn't until Dante reached the comparative calm of a vast living room that he was able to work on his breathing and get control of his churning stomach. This room, too,

145

was filled with destroyed paintings and scrawled messages. Without the immediate presence of death, they gave him a curious feeling, almost as if he were viewing perverse reruns of the Wembley thing. As he walked quietly forward, the building's air exchange system *whoosh*ed overhead. This was certainly the lap of luxury. Outside, beyond an expanse of glass stretching the entire length of the room, a woolly carpet of golden treetops spread outward toward the ornate buildings of Central Park West, now gleaming in the first long rays of morning sun.

He turned from the view, feeling a little better, and sat on a comfortable leather divan. He continued to force himself to drink in the cool, processed air in measured breaths, focusing on his center. As he did so, he stared at the wall before him, his mind clearing. Ever since he'd walked in the front door, something had been clawing at him. It was time to try and figure out what it was. Beyond the messages and the actual modus of the killer, something inexplicable was out of whack here. He tried to fathom his reaction by analyzing his response to what he was now viewing. This was often the way he managed to turn a nebulous unease into a hunch. Right now, the walls simply stared back at him.

A few minutes later, Jumbo ambled in, hands in his pockets. He paused a moment to survey the room. "Anything interesting?" he asked.

"That's just what I'm trying to figure out," Dante returned. "Something strike you as odd here?"

"Howzat?"

Dante shrugged. "I'm not quite sure. Something feels sort of . . . controlled about it. Like the guy was just going through the motions this time."

"He wasn't just going through the motions in that bedroom. Jesus Christ!"

Dante shook his head, still not able to shake the funny feeling.

"You want to elaborate?" Jumbo asked. "Maybe I'm not getting what you're saying."

Joe rubbed his face with his hands, inhaling deeply and letting the breath out. "I don't know how to put it exactly. It's just that at Wembley's place, it was like he was pouring his bottled-up rage out onto the walls. Writing whatever came to him. Look at this stuff. The words are exactly the same ones he used last time."

After Jumbo concentrated on the content of what was scrawled for the first time, he nodded. "You're right, you know?"

"Yeah, I know."

"Think it means something?"

Dante shook his head. "That's the problem. I'm not sure if it means *anything*."

"You saw the dead maid?" Richardson asked.

"Be hard not to. Practically tripped over her on the way in the front door."

"Does anything about *that* strike you as odd? He didn't kill her with a knife."

Dante looked at him thoughtfully. "He'd already left the knife behind when she surprised him," he said evenly. "The crash the neighbor heard. Then the scream."

"You ever heard of a knife man killing without a knife?" Jumbo asked. "I mean a real psycho-slasher type? And did you get a load of the size of her? Our description of Wiems makes him to be a tall drink of water. You think a scrawny fucker like that took a big woman used to manual labor out with his bare hands?"

"So he hit her over the head with something," Joe said.

Jumbo shook his head. "Your buddy Conklin says it was the floor, most likely. Beat her head in against it."

"Adrenaline does funny things," Dante mused. "If he was really jacked up and had the element of surprise . . ."

Richardson was shaking his head. "You just get done

tellin' me that you got a gut feeling about this room. Now you're tryin' to tell me a hundred and fifty pound kid took out a two hundred twenty pound woman because he was jacked up. What do you think *she* was? She screamed, didn't she?''

''Just playing devil's advocate. You're thinking what I am.''

He shrugged. ''I don't know what I think. You got a hunch about this, and the minute I walk in the front door, my instincts tell me in lookin' over the big dead woman that somethin' ain't right in *that*.''

''Copycat,'' Dante said evenly.

Jumbo shook his head. ''How could it be? Nobody knew the Wembley modus. Not in *this* detail. Just that he was hacked to death.''

Vinnie Arata had been the last of the Sixth squad's team to arrive. After a long drive across Brooklyn, he was hollow-eyed and on edge. Vic Manley saw him and asked if everything was all right.

''Yeah, lou. Don't sweat it. Ate somethin' nasty last night at this clamhouse. I been up half the night with the runs. I'm okay.''

The whip summoned them together in the front room to lay the situation out to them. Jim McClennan, his opposite at the Nineteenth, joined him.

''Looks like this one is ours,'' Manley told his team. ''Inspector Rodriguez just got off the phone with Gus Lieberman. The lou here and I concur. This and the Wembley killing are directly connected. They'll give us any support we need up here, but we've caught it.''

''Any additional manpower, lou?'' Dante asked. ''With Campo flown out and Jumbo in a legal circle-jerk, that leaves just me and Arata to work this thing.''

''I talked to the inspector about it and he's leaning on

the PC to form a task force. Meanwhile, you and Jumbo found us a suspect. We'll concentrate our primary efforts there and hope to God he's our man. Thompson and Koehl will cover some of the ground here, see what kind of tie-ins they can find between the victims. That leaves the other half of their team to catch everything else that goes down on the shift. We don't have any other choice.''

"Suspect?'' Arata asked. "I didn't hear about no suspect.''

"It was late yesterday afternoon,'' the whip told him. "Kid by the name of Stuart Wiems. We ran him last night. Two shoplifting beefs. Both dismissed. Nothing much else. We're waiting on the IRS and the bank check.''

"You're throwin' the *both* of us at some shoplifter?'' Vinnie asked.

"Until something better comes along. Right now, he seems to fit. He isn't just our best shot, he's our only shot.''

"Richardson and I were just comparing notes, lou,'' Dante said. "There are a number of things about this setup that we don't like. They're not adding right.''

Manley looked intrigued. "Such as?''

Dante went on to outline their feelings about the way the killer had gone about systematically defacing the front room. Jumbo hopped in to describe his misgivings about the way the maid was murdered, based on the theory that their perp was supposed to be a one hundred and fifty pound knife fanatic. Manley was mulling this new information over when Arata took exception to it.

"C'mon. Who can predict what a wacko'll do? He's making his break for it and the big broad shows up outta nowhere and scares the shit outta him. He reacts with what he's got. His bare hands.''

Manley was only half listening to him, staring at the walls now. When Vinnie finished, there was silence dominated by the passing of a stretcher beyond the entry arch. A gleaming plastic body bag was strapped to it. What Dante and Jumbo were saying was totally farfetched. On the other hand, he was disturbed that the idea hadn't even occurred to him.

"I'd have to argue with you there, Vincent," he said thoughtfully. He was still staring at the walls. "Sometimes, in a case like this, it's the only thing that gives you a toehold. Most of the time you *can* predict *exactly* what a psycho will do."

Vinnie Arata stood at the living room window and stared out at the park. The rest of his team had left the room. The dex he'd taken to get it going was wearing a little thin. He felt ragged as hell. He rubbed his eyes, the bile rising. He'd been born in lower-middle-class Brooklyn and lived there his whole life. No breaks; no easy leg up. Then there were the fat cat rich bastards who lived in joints like this, sitting above it all. Some poor slob in the neighborhood gets whacked and the cops just go through the motions. Maybe they get lucky. On a thing like this, half the fucking job shows up.

Eleven

George Scully looked up from the journal he was reading as his receptionist entered the office with the mail. She was also carrying a copy of a late edition of the *Post*. It ran a bright red "Extra!" streamer above the masthead.

"Have you seen this?" she asked, dropping the paper on his desk.

The headline, in huge bold type, screamed up at him: SLAUGHTER ON 5TH AVE!

He absorbed it and then looked up at her, sudden fear hitting him like a hammer blow.

"It's Benjamin Crowley," she said.

The look on the doctor's face was interpreted as confusion.

"The *victim*. One of them, anyway. They killed a nurse and a maid too. It's supposed to be connected to that murder of the old art collector down in the Village. All the same crazed stuff was inside the place."

Scully picked up the paper and forced himself to open it. The cover story was stretched across the first two pages inside the tabloid. Details were sketchy, with the police holding quite a bit back. Christ! A nurse and a maid had

151

gotten it as well. The whole story, coupled with the knowledge of his own hand in it, made him go pale. A mad jumble of questions and recriminations raced through his head.

"I guess this lets you off the hook, right, Doctor?"

He looked up, jarred by the sound of his receptionist's voice. Amy was in her mid-thirties and had been with Scully for almost ten years now. In a sense, she lived vicariously through her association with the eminent surgeon. His honors were hers as well. His distinguished patients were her patients. When Joan called and she knew he didn't want to be bothered, she ran interference. She even knew about the affair with the beautiful nurse from the hospital. Though green with envy, she covered for that too. Amy Gill, devoted handmaid. She imagined that the malpractice suit brought against her boss by Benjamin Crowley was as devastating to her as it was to the man she worshiped.

"Huh?" Scully asked, appearing dazed.

"The malpractice suit. This makes it a dead issue, right?"

"Oh," he said vaguely, closing the paper and handing it back to her. "Yes. I suppose you're right."

He'd paid for the murders of not one but three people. Could the number really make any difference now? Did it dig his personal hole in hell any deeper?

By the time Fiona called to ask him where they were meeting for their celebratory lunch, Scully was a wreck, more scattered than ever.

"I can't go out to eat right now," he said nervously. "We have to talk. I want to come over to your place."

Fiona didn't quite understand but agreed.

When Scully arrived an hour later, he was threatening to unravel at the seams.

"What in God's name is wrong *now*, George?" she demanded in exasperation. "It worked. It's taken care of."

"How can you say that?" he blurted. "Think about it. I've been completely naive. You think the cops aren't going to scrutinize the hell out of this thing? What do you think they'll find? One thing they're sure as *shit* going to find out is that Ben Crowley had a two-million-dollar malpractice suit pending against me."

"Jesus Christ, George! They can't *pin* anything on you. That's the point, isn't it?"

"Come on," he growled angrily. "I'd have to be a prime suspect, wouldn't I? And what happens whenever they catch the guy who did that first one? Then what? He denies that he had anything to do with this thing and I'll have jumped from the pan to the fire."

Fiona paced back and forth, seething with frustration.

"You deny everything. You were never there. You don't know anything about it."

"What if they dig deeper? Into my finances. If they put together the fact that I'm leveraged to the eyeballs *and* that the insurance company was planning to offer a settlement, they'll find something and make it stick. What happens if that asshole nigger gets busted selling crack to two-year-olds and decides to flip on me?"

"He doesn't know who you are, baby. You're just a guy with money in a bag."

"I'm cutting it too close," he replied hotly.

"You're fucking paranoid is what you are."

"I've got a right to be paranoid. I've been thinking about it all morning and I think I have a solution. I'll need to talk to the guy again."

"You'll need what?"

"To arrange another meeting," Scully insisted, the spark

of crazed determination in his eyes. "They've got to do it for me again."

Fiona's mouth fell open. "George, you're out of your mind."

He smiled coldly. "Am I?" he asked. "A third murder would throw a whole other set of intangibles into an investigation. I'm in this deep now, so what the fuck's the difference?"

"George . . ."

"Please," he nearly begged. "We're so close now. All I want to do is make sure."

The enthusiasm Vinnie Arata had shown Monday morning, getting into the squad early to immerse himself in the Wembley file, was markedly missing as he and Dante began searching in earnest for Stuart Wiems. Perhaps, as he had said, he had eaten something bad in a greasy spoon. That wasn't really Dante's problem. Until Gus Lieberman could fly in more warm bodies, Vic Manley only had manpower enough to put two detectives on quadruple brutal homicides, and Vinnie Arata was once again the listless boor. Dante really wondered how he'd ever made detective.

The two men were eating lunch at a Chinese place on Hudson Street, having killed the morning chasing the obvious leads, all of them dead ends. Vinnie didn't seem to have much of an appetite. He sat and picked at his food while Dante ate the lion's share.

"You really think this is our guy?" Vinnie asked.

Dante shrugged. "Considering all the other brilliant leads we've dug up, I'd say he's our best shot. We've got reports of an alienated, nasty disposition. Add to that the fact that he left his apartment on Avenue B and Third Street a week ago and seems to have disappeared."

"He's got no real record," Vinnie argued. "No psychiatric history."

"Not that we can find," Dante cautioned. "There might be something out of state—or maybe there isn't anything. It wouldn't be the first time."

They'd gotten an IRS rundown after returning to the squad prior to lunch. According to the report, Stuart Wiems failed to file the W-2 issued by Nancy Epstein. The Dollar Dry Dock account he maintained at a branch on Second Avenue near 6th Street showed a near-zero balance and hadn't seen any activity for almost a month. Another report, from the DMV, indicated that he did possess a valid New York driver's license. It was obtained a week after he started work for the gallery. That would make sense if he was required to drive a truck to make deliveries.

"Chick on the second floor of his building said the dude was heavy into the club scene," Vinnie said. "She said she used to see him around before she got a waitress job. Doesn't make the scene so much anymore. Maybe we outta check the discos."

Dante rolled his eyes. Privately, it gave him an idea. Brian's fiancée, Diana, and her band were a fixture at all the hip downtown clubs. Maybe *she* knew Wiems. He would give her a call and check it out. With a last slurp of his house special fried rice, he set his chopsticks down and glanced at his watch.

"Maybe what we oughta do is check the action over at the morgue. They should be pretty far into the autopsies by now."

The two detectives found Rocky Conklin in the big pathology theater in the basement of the medical examiner's building on First Avenue. Three different assistant MEs were working concurrently at three separate slabs. Rocky Conklin had the primary target: Benjamin Crowley, male Caucasian, six foot one inches tall, one hundred fifty-eight pounds. As Vinnie wandered listlessly around the place, looking bored, Dante forced himself to stand at Conklin's side.

"What's the scoop on this guy, Rock? I saw the wheelchair in his place and the hospital bed."

Conklin lifted the mangled head, turning it sideways to show him the scar up the back of the neck. It moved up into the hairline at the base of the skull.

"Suboccipital cranial surgery. Not too long ago, either. Scar's still a little purplish. It generally takes anywhere from six months to a year before a thing like this completely whitens. We've requested his medical records. I'd say, just off the top of my head, that he had tumor surgery. The tumor most likely caused the paralysis."

"He was paralyzed then?"

"Oh, definitely." The pathologist let the head drop and lifted an arm. "Quantifiable wasting of the musculature. No activity. With a live-in nurse and proper physical therapy, the only thing you can really hope for is a maintenance of circulation and very minimal tone."

"All because of a tumor," Dante mused, more to himself than anyone else.

Conklin nodded. "That or complications with the surgery. It amounts to the same thing."

Joe Dante hung up the pay phone next to the rest room of the Dew-Drop Inn on Greenwich Avenue at Charles Street. By the time he could muscle his way through the after-work crowd to their table, Vic Manley had a couple of Heinekens set up and was paying the waitress. Joe sat, exhausted, and lifted his beer to his lips. God, it tasted good. An afternoon in the morgue could affect a mood like nothing else. There was so much death and so little dignity. It only served to remind him of how it all eventually ended up. Worm shit.

"Brennan says Diana'll be home in about an hour," he told Manley. "I'll swing by and see what I can find out about our punk-rocking pal."

Manley nodded, distracted momentarily by a passing pair of free-riding breasts in a tight little T-shirt.

"Her mother know she goes out dressed like that?" he grunted. "Where's she think she is. Dogpatch?"

"Probably," Dante replied. "Tell me something, Vic. You were there this morning. I saw the way you were looking at those walls. How did the whole setup strike you?"

The lieutenant frowned as he turned his attention to the neck of his beer bottle. "As far as the maid goes, I'm with Richardson. Our man is a knife freak. He's seriously gettin' off on what he's doin'."

Dante had to agree. "You know, I don't think I've ever heard of a blade man who didn't carry his own personal shiv. A guy like that defines himself with his blade. It's his instant hard-on."

"And if he uses a kitchen knife to butcher someone, he's doing it because he don't want to scum up his personal pig sticker," Manley added. "If he left it on the bedroom floor and then that maid surprised him, I can't figure why he'd risk his bare hands on her. Maybe to stun her, but not to finish her off. That wouldn't be how he gets off."

"Jumbo and I came to the same conclusion," Dante told him. "That and the fact that a man of Stuart Wiems's physical description would have one hell of a time beating a two-hundred-plus pound woman's brains out without more of a struggle. You ask me, there's also something real strange about the setup in the living room."

"We checked your hunch," Manley said. "You're right. The messages are the same to the letter."

"I'd say that was almost impossible, given a man in a blood frenzy, shooting his load all over the inside of his underwear. It's too . . . *controlled*."

"What's it spell to you?" Manley asked.

"Copy cat. But—"

"But what? It's impossible? The lid was on?"

"That's right. It still *is* on."

Manley shrugged. "Never say never. Rule number one."

"Just what I'm thinking," Dante replied, nodding. "I'll be interested to see the results of the background check. Maybe we can figure out just why this Crowley might have been a target."

"At least we're thinking alike," Manley granted. "We've been looking on only one set of premises. Do they fit this? And if they don't, that doesn't necessarily mean our original theory is wrong."

Dante slumped back in his chair and scooped a fistful of pretzels from the bowl next to his drink. Damn, there were a lot of single women in this joint. It was Manley's choice. As a recent divorcee, the lieutenant liked this kind of odds.

"We need to find this bastard Wiems," he said. "We squeeze him till he pops and the whole sorry mess comes a lot clearer."

"We're turning the city upside down," Manley said. "Emergency room admissions. Credit card companies. Warrants. Hell, we even got Sanitation checking to see if he didn't scoop up after his dog."

"If he *had* a dog," Dante countered. "As far as we can get a line on him, this son of a bitch didn't have much more than the shirt on his back."

"Find him for me," Manley said flatly.

Dante parked his Corvette at the curb outside Brian

Brennan's warehouse loft building on West 27th Street and Eleventh Avenue. It was early yet, just barely seven o'clock, but already the hookers were gathering on nearby corners in anticipation of the evening's commerce. The temperature had climbed back into the mid-fifties that afternoon, and in the hour before darkness fell it was still balmy enough out to permit serious skin display if you were stoned to the wig. Almost as soon as he rolled to a halt, several girls broke away from their corner clusterings and wandered over to pitch the dude in the fancy sports car.

"Goin' out, honey?" a thin black woman asked through his open window. She was wearing little more than her underwear.

"Not tonight," he replied. He was groping around under the seat for his police business card.

"Oh c'mon, honey. You sayin' you already satisfied?"

Joe rolled his eyes. "Take off, sister, okay? I said I'm not interested."

The whore tossed her long mane of black hair back from her face, checked quickly in both directions, and then peeled the straps of the tight little singlet she wore. A pair of small, pointy-shaped breasts jutted out at the detective just inches from his face.

"You want me, baby. I *know* you do. Here, let me give you a little sample." She reached right in the window, her fingers groping at his fly.

Dante finally located the "Official Business" card, dragged it out from under the seat, and flipped it onto the dash. The hooker's face went from scorn to openmouthed apprehension. She was there with her hand on his crotch, stripped to the waist. The way her eyes and mouth worked soundlessly, trying to find words as she backed out of there, was worth the price of admission. Eventually, she got hold of the correct attitude.

"What is this?" she snarled. "You bustin' me?"

Dante smiled, shaking his head. "I told you. I'm not interested, sweetheart. Not in busting you *or* in feeling your sweet lips wrapped around my dick. Just get dressed and get lost."

Brennan was in his studio when Dante buzzed him on the intercom. He let him in, releasing the elevator with his key and sending it down to the first floor. He was the only tenant who actually lived on the premises—one of the privileges of ownership.

Dante emerged from the elevator into the huge, comfortably decorated living room of the sculptor's digs. He liked visiting here—the feeling of sheer size made it seem like he was somewhere other than Manhattan. Space is such a premium commodity in New York that this was shameless luxury. The furnishings of the room were mostly in earthtones on slate gray carpeting. It was what hung on the walls and sat around on every available surface that made the place come alive. Brennan owned an eclectic assortment of art, all of it contemporary. Much of it came from trades with his peers. Other pieces were purchases of works done by promising young talents on the way up. They added color and unusual shape to the place.

"Back here," Brian called from his studio.

Dante wandered back, spotting Brennan at one of the big worktables in the metal shop. The studio sprawled over almost three thousand square feet, divided into areas devoted to the various disciplines of a sculptor's craft. There were full wood and metal shops, both crammed with machinery and bits of work in progress. In another area, a large kiln was erected for firing wax from casting molds. Finally, there was the bright, fastidiously clean modeling and drawing studio where Brennan worked planning his projects and doing the preliminary executions in clay.

Sparks flew momentarily as Brennan, face hood down,

ground a protuberance off a blackened lump of bronze. Dante knew enough now to realize that this object clamped in the jaws of a padded vise was, beneath a charred and plaster-flecked exterior, a recently cast piece.

Brennan set the body grinder down and flipped up the face shield.

"She still hasn't shown yet. You want a drink?"

Joe shrugged, and Brian tossed the face shield onto the table before stepping to the shop refrigerator and pulling out a couple of cold beers. He popped both caps and handed one to his buddy. "C'mon in," he said, leading the way into the drawing studio. "You look a little under the weather, Joe."

"Spending an afternoon in the morgue does that to me," Dante admitted. "You hear about the triple murder on Fifth Avenue?"

"Yeah." Brian nodded. "On the news. Of course, that would be yours because you've got the Wembley killing."

"You're learning," Dante told him.

"What's this about some guy from the club scene?" Brian asked.

Joe shrugged. "Guy who worked at the Nancy Epstein gallery on Greene Street. His description fits certain physical evidence recovered at the scene of the first killing. Too early to tell about the second. He seems to have disappeared into thin air."

"You think Diana might know him?"

"I can hope, can't I?"

Brennan smiled. "Talked to Rosa since the weekend?"

"Couple times. I'm supposed to swing by later on. She's got some testimonial with the brass hats downtown."

"How's it feel so far?"

"Beats me. I'm playing it by ear now, tell you the truth."

Brennan shook his head. "I can't understand women."

161

"You seem to be doing okay at the moment."

"Pure luck, friend. I tell you the divorce came through? Nick, my attorney, called me yesterday. Lisa finally backed off the worst of her demands. I still get reamed, but I'm free."

"Great news. What's your next move?"

Brennan grinned. "Believe it or not, now that it's legal, Diana says she's in no rush. Like I said, I don't understand them."

On cue, the elevator door in the front room rolled open and the Queen of Beasts stepped out, resplendent in sweaty workout gear, hastily tied-back hair, and scuffed Reeboks.

"Joe! Hey!" she enthused. "I'd kiss you but I smell awful. Let me hop into the shower. You hear about loverboy here finally being a free man?"

"Yeah. I figured you'd have the new halter ready to slip over his head. What gives?"

"I thought I'd give him a week or two. Just a taste of the good life, you know. Then *wham*! Nuts in a sling."

"You think she's kidding?" Brennan asked.

Dante chuckled.

Fifteen minutes later, they were sitting around the living room, Diana now relaxed in a pair of shorts and a T-shirt. A former artist's model, she had the sort of body dreams are made of and a cute, friendly face. The biggest surprise to anyone who watched her perform was that a voice so big and gritty could be coming from *that* package. The second biggest surprise was how she moved in the skin-tight outfits she wore.

"So who's this guy?" she asked.

"A gallery assistant who worked for Nancy Epstein in SoHo," Joe told her. "He's supposed to be some sort of painter, and we hear that he made the club scene pretty heavily. Does a Stuart Wiems ring any bells?"

"Tall, gangly guy. Real pale, red mohawk and freckles?" she asked.

Dante nodded excitedly, leaning forward a little in his chair. "That's the guy. Exact same description Nancy Epstein gave us. And the hair we recovered from our victim's fingernails was clipped short. Maybe half an inch."

Diana nodded. "If it's the same guy, he used to be around quite a bit. Had some friends in a band called Numbnuts. Pretty terrible garage music, you know? Come to think of it, I remember him having sort of a wild red mop before the mohawk. Always wore pants with paint smeared all over them."

"Have you seen him lately?"

Diana shook her head. "I'm afraid I haven't hung out much in the past few months. I usually only go to a club when I'm playing it now."

"Do you know anybody who might have?"

"Sure. Every doorman on the circuit. They remember everyone . . . of the regulars, anyway. People who make the scene never pay the cover. That's for the tourist crowd. Wiems was definitely around enough to be a regular. Kind of obnoxious. Sneered a lot."

"Could you give me a list? Clubs and maybe the doormen's names?"

"I could do better than that. We could cruise them. They might be a lot more willing to talk if I was with you."

"You'd do that?"

She looked at him like he had a giant hole in his forehead. "Of course I'd do that. I've got this thing about people who kill other people with knives."

"Me too. Sorry, Brian. I've gotta steal your girlfriend."

Curtis Maxwell delivered Fiona's urgent communiqué to Reggie DuQuesnay via a special phone number. An hour later, instructions came back. Her friend was to enter Central Park at midnight and proceed to the Carousel. A coin phone would ring. He was to answer it.

At first, Reggie thought the man had to be crazy and was ready to dismiss immediately the idea of meeting him again. Then, the more he thought on it, the more curious he became. What could be the harm? He would have Bobby Burke with him, and this doctor chump was the king of wimps. He'd seen right through his bravado the last time they met.

Reggie sat in the Mercedes outside the park. At midnight, he dialed the Carousel pay phone on his cellular unit.

"Hello?" the fool doctor's cautious voice answered.

"Evening, friend. What can I do for you?"

"Where are you?"

"Never mind. You remember my big friend? He's watching you right this moment. Just a precaution. I want you to hang up now and walk out into the middle of the Sheep Meadow. I'll meet you there. And don't worry. You don't try any funny business and my big friend will make sure you don't get mugged by any crazy niggers." He chuckled to himself as he hung up.

"You wait here, honey. Daddy be right back."

Esme sat staring sullenly at him across the dimly lit interior of the limousine. She said nothing as he prepared to depart. Reggie grinned, dug into his pocket, and produced a vial half full of cocaine. With one hand on the door release, he tossed it to her.

"Do yourself, honey. Don't scowl so."

George Scully paced the lawn of the Sheep Meadow nervously. It was five minutes now, and the slick pimp was nowhere to be seen. Scully felt exposed out here, vulnerable. He wanted to be done and gone.

"Hello, friend," a voice greeted him from the gloom. It came from behind him, making him jump.

The gaudily dressed black man and his neatly attired gorilla emerged from shadows.

"I wonder why we're meeting again so soon," the black man said. "Something you don't like about the job?"

Scully hurried to assure him that the job was fine.

"That's not it at all," he said quickly. "It's just that I have a sort of special set of circumstances. A sort of problem I hadn't anticipated."

"What's that got to do with me?" the black man asked.

"I need it done again," George blurted.

"What?" the black man asked, a look of comical amusement twisting his face. "The dude is *dead*, friend."

"Not him," Scully said, shaking his head. "Somebody else."

"You cleaning house? Who now?"

Scully didn't know how to formulate this next part. Not exactly. "It's not a *who* like you think. Just somebody . . . like the others, that is. Art collector. Old."

The black man laughed outright. "You gotta be shittin' me, right?"

Scully stood his ground. "I assure you, I'm absolutely serious."

DuQuesnay got himself under control, looking suddenly sober. "Let me get this straight now. You want me to research this like? *Pick* some old dude at random that fits the profile and whack him, just like the others?"

Scully nodded. "That's right."

"You know what it is you're askin'? I'm supposed to pick *your* target? That's nuts."

"It's what I need to hire you to do."

The black man mused a moment, putting a business face on as though he was calculating the immensity of the undertaking in dollars and cents. Finally, he shook his head.

"I couldn't do it for a nickel under a hundred grand."

Scully was dumbfounded. "But the last was fifty. Jesus Christ! I thought *that* was high."

"You gave me a name. You gave me a place. I did a little detail work, and then . . . *bingo*. It got done sweet. There were even complications, but you don't hear me whinin' to you. Now I'm lookin' at my profit margin here. I'm a businessman. A hundred grand, friend. Same way as last time."

Scully got angry now, consumed with his own frustration.

"You saw me coming! You know you've got me over a barrel, and now you're going for the ream. It's robbery!"

With exquisite cool, Reggie shook his head. "No, chump, it's *murder*. And dig it, the troubles you got ain't my troubles, you got that? You come out here askin' me for a favor, then go gettin' indignant and accusin' me of robbin' you, you can go *fuck* yourself."

With that, he turned on his heels, collected the gorilla, and disappeared into the night.

Twelve

The doorman at the Milk Bar shrugged as he answered Dante's query. "Beats the hell out of me," he said. "They come and they go down here. Shit, this is the eighth club I've worked at in the past three years. They get hot, somebody asks me if I want to come work the door. They cool off and I get an offer from the next place down the line. Stuart? He sorta followed the same pattern. The suburban crowd is the death of these dumps. Once they get wind, the real crowd is outta here."

Dante listened with interest to this counterculture lore. In fact, though the guy failed to recognize him without his shaved head and leathers, Joe knew him from his days of working undercover narcotics. What he contended was unfortunately true—once the squares and tourists discovered the latest "in" spot, the people who made it hot would quickly abandon ship. Most of todays clubs hadn't existed a year and a half ago when Dante called it quits with the division and returned to a squad. Now, in front of these fresh, obscure clubs stood at least one heavy whose duty it was to filter the ebb and flow, leaving unworthy supplicants stranded on the sidewalks outside.

"Dude used to be a fixture around here," the guy continued. "I ain't seen him around for, oh, maybe a month. Couple of weeks, anyway. You ought to talk to the cats in Numbnuts. Stuart used to hang out with them."

Diana took over for a moment.

"You seen any of them around, Georgie?"

He thought a moment. "Not the past couple of nights. But yeah, they're in and out. Last I heard, they had a gig over in Hoboken."

The thought had occurred to Dante that Wiems might have gone out of state. It would be an easy enough thing to do in his crowd. A lot of young artists and musicians were taking advantage of the lower rents on the other side of the Hudson.

"We'll check it out," Diana told Georgie. "Thanks."

"When we gonna see Queen of Beasts in here again?" the guy asked.

Diana smiled. "We're working up some new material. We'll have the world by the throat come New Year's."

Georgie nodded. "Looking forward to it. Always."

Dante glanced at his watch as they drifted back toward his car. It was moving on toward twelve-thirty and he hadn't called Rosa yet.

"I've got to find a pay phone," he told Diana.

"Let's hang it up," she said. "That was my last good idea. Stuart Wiems has either gone totally underground or he's left town."

Dante tried to look at their exercise philosophically.

"Listen. It was a good shot. I could have wasted a lot more time if I'd done this on my own. Now I can waste it somewhere else."

*   *   *

Rosa was in a bit of a snit when Joe arrived at her place at one A.M. Her political dinner had wound up two and a half hours earlier, and she had been home waiting for him since eleven o'clock.

"One thing led to another," he confessed lamely.

Her dark eyes flashed as she stood, clenched fists on hips. "You couldn't have called?"

"I didn't figure you'd be out of your thing until at least midnight."

She shook her head, not accepting the excuse. "I have an answering machine."

Dante took a deep breath and exhaled. "Okay. I screwed up. I *apologize*. I found myself with a few hours to kill tonight, got off on a tangent, and lost track of the time. What the fuck—you've done it yourself. We're cops."

Rosa dropped her defiant pose. Turning away, she walked slowly toward the window overlooking the street and stood there with her back to him, hugging herself.

"We also can't keep using that as an excuse," she said. "Cops drink too much because they're cops. Cops screw around on their wives and husbands because they're cops. They shake down club owners, cop a free blow-job, drive shit-faced—and blame it all on the pressures of the job."

"There are assholes in every walk of life," he countered.

"But *we* start using the tin as a crutch."

Joe decided to back up and try another tack. "Maybe I never should have blamed it on being a cop," he said. "It's who *I* am. I see a helpless invalid turned into hamburger and the image sticks in my mind. I can't get rid of it. I'm obsessed with nailing the animal who did it. I think maybe I'll get lucky enough to prevent him from doing it again. When he does, and I haven't, I get upset with myself. I ask myself if maybe I haven't been pushing hard enough. In the process of pushing harder, I hurt your feelings. I'm sorry."

He shrugged in frustration, recognizing the heated edge in his voice.

"Did you have any luck?" Rosa asked quietly.

"Struck out," he mumbled.

"I heard the mayor talking to the PC about it tonight. The screws are being turned."

"Can I have a drink?" he asked.

She gestured toward the kitchen, and he moved to make himself at home. A moment later, after rattling bottles in the refrigerator, he returned with a beer.

"They can turn the screws all they want," he told her. "We've got exactly two guys chasing all the leads on this thing. I've been busting my fanny. There should be an all-out manhunt for this creep and *they* fly our manpower out to catch *car thieves*."

"After this last thing, and the pressure, they're going to form a task force," she said confidently. "It's already in the works."

Joe shrugged, suddenly realizing how tired he was as ice cold beer slid down his throat. "Tell that to Benjamin Crowley, his nurse, and his maid. I'm sure they'll find it comforting."

"You look beat," she said.

"In this case, looks don't lie."

She tapped her watch. "I'm on at nine o'clock, and tomorrow is looking like another busy day. Spend the night?"

His face was creased by a weary grin. "You realize that's about *all* I'm good for?"

The hitter tried reaching Reggie DuQuesnay at the contact number for twenty-four hours. Now, at nine thirty Thursday morning, he figured he'd had enough of being ignored. Their deal stated specifically that he never visit

Reggie's crib on Lenox Avenue. Anyone tying the two men together at that location would have too strong a link—possibly strong enough to blow a long and mutually profitable association. In parking the Trans-Am on the avenue and crossing to the lobby of DuQuesnay's building, the hitter was violating this fundamental safeguard. He was angry.

Bobby Burke's eyes opened in astonishment when he found the hitter outside the apartment door. He hadn't buzzed downstairs. He'd just appeared. When Bobby opened up, the hitter waved an impatient hand.

"Don't give me any shit, Bobby. Just get him."

"What you doin' *here*, dude?" Badness asked. "What are you, crazy?"

The man got a hard, steely look in his eyes. "I'm *here* because that motherfucker ain't answered my fucking calls!"

"You know the rules, dude. Right after some very sticky . . . uh . . . *business*, everything gotta settle out a little before—"

"Fuck you guys and settling out. I'm the son of a bitch risking the exposure here. I got a problem, I want somebody answering the phone when I call."

Badness shook his head. "Reggie's asleep right now. Late night last night, you know. As soon as he gets up, I'll have him get back to you."

The killer wasn't hearing the big man. "You fight one too many fights, Bobby? Somebody scramble your brainpan so, you know, you ain't making certain connections?" He said it quiet and silky. The next thing from his mouth was a thundering bellow. "Wake the whore-mongering cocksucker *up*!"

Bobby didn't see where it came from, but there was suddenly a .38-caliber Smith and Wesson Bodyguard

"Airweight" jammed into his midsection. The hitter's voice hissed through clenched teeth.

"I didn't come all the way up here to be turned away by the *doorman*!"

"What the fuck's goin' on here?" Reggie asked from the mouth of the hall leading back to the master suite.

Both men at the front door turned to Reggie. He stood in his bare feet, wearing only his gold chains and a pair of white satin Everlast trunks. An automatic dangled loose in his right hand. He took in the essentials of the conflict between Bobby and the irate hit man, primary among them being the pistol, and waved Burke away.

"Let him in, Bobby. Put that gun away, friend. What the fuck you doin' here anyway?"

The hitter entered the plush digs. Everything in the front room was white—leather sofas, chairs, deep-pile shag rug, walls, track lights, laquered cabinetry, and even the stereo and television set. Into it drifted Reggie in his white satin shorts, his blackness in stark contrast to everything else in his domain. Reggie still dangled the automatic at his side. Until he opened an end table drawer and placed it inside, the other man held on to his own gun. Finally, as Reggie collapsed on a sofa to lounge back and regard him lazily, he holstered the .38 inside his leather jacket.

"I been calling for twenty-four fucking hours," he snarled. "You ain't answered. *That's* what the fuck I'm doin' here."

Reggie smiled sadly, looking hurt. "But friend. Our arrangement."

The hitter glared back, furious. "The *arrangement* was for you to give me an accurate description of the situation inside the apartment. I'm supposed to go in and take care of the problem based on that. Nothing, nowhere, does it say one word about no fucking maid in the back room. I do the job, start makin' tracks, and run right the fuck into her. She's got time to scream. I gotta kill her with my bare hands, beat her to death on the floor, and get the hell out of there. You think the bulls on this case ain't gonna wonder why a knife freak kills the bitch with his hands? You got a reasonable answer they could satisfy themselves with?''

Reggie shook his head, still the essence of calm. ''The maid was unfortunate, friend. Sometimes these things happen. You took care of it.''

''I'm *exposed*,'' the hitter shot back in frustration. ''The whole fucking thing could unravel over that one *unfortunate* maid.''

''Relax, my man. Nothing's gonna unravel. You're just edgy. What do you want? A little more money? Get your dick hard with Esme? She's sleepin' in the other room. Go on, she be glad to see you.''

The hitter looked toward the hall and swallowed.

''I'll get you another five for the trouble,'' Reggie said soothingly. ''Be a day or two. After that, *you* are in the best position possible to prevent things from gettin' too far out of hand.''

The uninvited guest eyed him warily. ''Another five?''

''That's right. And all day with your favorite pussy, if that's what you want. But friend''—DuQuesnay held up a cautioning finger—''I'm very disappointed in your coming here like this. Never again.''

The hitter didn't answer. He turned to move toward the back rooms. He was keyed up as hell. Getting his nuts off might help some.

Fiona Hassey was working days in the OR that week. It was a surprise to her then to see Curtis Maxwell approaching her in the cafeteria at lunch, dressed in his streetclothes.

She never saw Curtis unless she was working the four-to-midnight, his regular shift. Now Curtis was smiling above her and asking if he might sit down.

"What's up?" she asked him, trying to seem casual. Lately, George's concern over the whole Crowley thing was really getting on her nerves. Now this, the day after Curtis's man had demanded twice as much money to work for him again.

Curtis smiled agreeably. "You like that last shit I scored you?"

Fiona's eyes lit up. "Like it? It was phenomenal."

"I got a pipeline right to *the* man now," Curtis told her. "In fact, you helped me get it."

Fiona looked confused. "How's that?"

"Your little request. I guess it all worked out. The man is very pleased. In fact, I'm prepared to return the favor."

"How's that?"

"Step aside as your middleman. Make the introduction direct. I cleared it with the man. We're talkin' highest quality for fifty-five a g-r. He'll do that for you on my say-so."

"Fifty-five dollars a gram? For what you just sold me?" she asked, almost beside herself.

"Like I said," Curtis confided. "I made out. The man made out. No reason you shouldn't ought to make out. In fact . . ." He reached into his jacket pocket, shot a quick glance to both sides, and reached under the table to press something into her hand. "A token of the man's appreciation. He'd like to meet you."

Fiona copped a look at what was in her hand under the table. It was cocaine in a plastic baggie, big chunks of sparkling flake in it. Maybe two or three grams. A freebie. Her respiration rate started climbing, cool droplets of sweat trickling down the small of her back. Fifty-five dollars a gram for shit like this?

She attempted to appear nonchalant. "When, Curtis?"

He matched her, cool for cool. "Anytime, baby. This is my night off. We could roll up there after you got off work if you wanted."

She was going to meet George at the Waldorf for drinks and then dinner at Sparks. Probably to listen to him whine all night. She could cancel; tell him something came up. Feeling lousy, anything. Right now, all she wanted to do was get that baggie into the ladies room and run a little up her nose.

"I'm off at five," she heard herself tell him. The anticipated rush was her only focus now.

"Out front? 29th Street corner?" he asked.

"Sure," she said vaguely.

After three tours on the eight-thirty-to-five, Dante swung out. He was set to start his next tour that Thursday afternoon at four o'clock. He returned home at noon after spending the night at Rosa's place and then catching a couple more hours of sleep once she left for the big building. It felt strange to wake up in that place, a sensation he figured he had better get used to. It irked him to realize what a creature of habit and inflexibility he'd become. Before forcing himself to drift back to sleep, something kept whispering that he had a perfectly good bed of his own; that he had a hungry cat who was going to be pissed off when he got home.

The weather had turned cooler and a threatening gray as he emerged onto St. Mark's Place at midday. A couple of leather-clad punks huddled on the stoop, smoking a joint. When they didn't readily part to make way, he showed them his tin and watched them scatter like leaves in a breeze.

There were several messages on his answering machine

when he got home, in addition to a furious Copter the cat. One was from his mother, one from Rebecca upstairs, inviting him to a party at her place tomorrow night, and one from Vic Manley, asking him to call the squad. He elected to avoid his mother for the moment. She'd only work the conversation around to when he was going to marry the nice lady detective. Rebecca's party sounded like another one of her spontaneous urges. They were mostly fun, and in the past, he'd even managed to drag a loose damsel off to his own place on a couple of occasions. If it was still going by the time he swung out at midnight, he supposed he might drop in.

Vic Manley sounded tired when Dante reached him.

"What's up?" Joe asked him. The lieutenant wasn't due in until his two teams came on at four.

"Nothin', really. Just got tired of staring at the walls of a half-empty apartment and figured, with this case buggin' me the way it is, I might as well come on in."

"And?" Joe asked.

"What are you doing for lunch?"

"Eating reheated Chinese food from two nights ago. Join me?"

"Maybe I will."

Twenty minutes later, the two men sat in the little alcove between the bedroom and the kitchen, nibbling at steaming heaps of house special lo mein and Szechuwan shredded beef. Stretched out on one of the two remaining chairs, Copter lounged content in the knowledge that the boss was home.

"I just finished going over Thompson and Koehl's report on Crowley," the lieutenant said. "A good job on such short notice. Financial situation, medical history, and like that. They've come up with some shit that just doesn't connect with Oscar Wembley."

"For instance?" Joe asked. He twirled a little lo mein around his chopsticks and shoved it into his mouth.

"Get this. He didn't collect hardly any of the shit hanging on his walls. Not personally. Inherited most of it from his father and grandfather. What little he bought himself was on the advice of investment people. This guy was a purely financial animal."

"He never bought from any SoHo galleries?" Dante asked.

Manley shook his head after clearing the pipes with a swig of beer. "There's nothin' to indicate the fucker even knew where SoHo *was*."

"Is there *anything* similar there?" Dante asked. "Something we haven't considered, like shared financial advice? Same broker or whatever?"

"I don't know the connection, Joey. I can't figure it. What I *do* know is that this Wiems character has got to be our guy. If we get a line on him, maybe we can ask him what the connection is."

"No if," Dante insisted, shaking his head. "I'm so close I can almost smell him now. We'll find him. What about the requests you put in for outstanding warrants—that shit?"

Manley shook his head, indicating the negative, as he chewed a mouthful of shredded beef. His eyes were watering, and sweat was beading on his upper lip.

"God*damn!*" he gasped after a swig of beer.

"You must have gotten one of the peppers," Joe sympathized.

Manley took a moment to recover, wiping his eyes with his napkin. "A big fat zip with summonses so far. Same with Con Ed, the phone company. We even got traces on calls made to his parents in Indianapolis."

"How good do you think the chances are that he's *not* the Crowley killer?" Dante asked.

"I keep tellin' myself not to think about it."

"You know it's in the back of all our minds."

Manley nodded. "Something did come up in the report. Crowley had brain surgery to remove a tumor on something called the auditory nerve. Pretty tricky, but not *too* hairy. Something popped in recovery. They couldn't find the doctor and there was some delay before he was opened back up. Poor bastard ended up paralyzed from the neck down. That was a few months ago. Crowley filed a two-million-dollar malpractice suit against his doctor."

Dante whistled, considering this new information. "Opens up a lot of new angles," he mused. "It takes years for one of these cases to work its way through the courts, right?"

"Two, sometimes three," Manley confirmed.

"Surgeon like that's gotta be insured up the wazoo. Then again, maybe there's something irregular going on with the old man's estate. He's confined to a bed. Somebody could be monkeying with his assets, see an opportunity to get rid of him. Bury something. You never know."

"Lot of new angles," Manley agreed. "What bothers me is where a second killer could get them kinda details."

Dante shrugged. "Lot of possibilities there too. Medical examiner's lab. Forensics labs over at the academy. Ambulance attendants."

"Sixteen detectives at the Sixth," Manley added.

Joe glanced sharply at him. "This is a slight change of tune. You're ready to start looking hard at a copy-cat kill?"

"You got any better theories?"

"That somebody maybe got to Wiems in the first place? That it wasn't a depraved act, but planned from the beginning to look that way? Maybe there's something in Wembley's finances or somewhere else that we've overlooked."

Now it was the whip's turn to shrug. "You said yourself

that you got a funny feeling looking at the second murder scene, Joey. That it didn't have the 'feel' of the first. What happened to the famous Dante hunch?''

''That's the problem. I've got so many, they're shorting out against each other. We need Wiems. He's the fucking key.''

Dante went on to describe his efforts of the previous evening, searching the clubs with Diana.

''Sounds like we maybe oughta tie in with the Jersey State people and see if they got anything in their recent records,'' Manley said.

''What are Thompson and Koehl doing now?'' Dante asked. ''Any chance of them digging deeper into both financial backgrounds? Maybe there's something there.''

''I'll have them start on it tonight,'' the lieutenant agreed. ''You're right. Wiems might be our ace in the hole, but he ain't the only card we got to play.''

Reggie DuQuesnay was looking forward to this. From what Curtis described, the blonde had all the requisites: greed, ambition, hunger for the product, and a build that could make a eunuch's tongue hard. He was still upset about his hitter's visit. Right now, a little sport would go a long way to ease the tension gnawing at his temples. He checked his watch. Curtis said five thirty or quarter to six, depending on traffic. It was almost five twenty now. Esme was off sulking. With practiced fingers, he spun the dial on the safe built into the pedestal of the bed, swung the door, and removed a full-ounce bag of his finest stash. He opened the bag, dipped a fingernail in, and did a quick one before wandering back into the sparkling white living room. The coffee table was a big, three-quarter-inch slab of glass perched atop four solid ivory elephants, each more than a foot high. He dumped the entire bag of Bolivian flake onto the surface, setting a single-edged razor blade and an ornate silver straw next to it. Lu-Ann entered the room, eyes widening at the sight of all that coke on the table.

"Do yourself, honey," Reggie cooed.

As she slid down to sit on the floor and worked the blade, chopping and lining up a couple of hefty ones, Reggie moved beside her and reached down to hold that mass of wild red hair out of the way while she went to work on them.

"You remember the brother we rode around in the park with last week?" Reggie asked her as her head came up, nose twitching.

She nodded. "The one with the friend who had a friend."

"That's right. He's bringin' that friend here in just a few minutes. Demonstratin' a real head for the business end of the life. I want you to show him a good time, honey. Anything he wants. Okay?"

As she smiled and nodded, he took her hand and guided it up under the white satin trunks until her fingers closed around his rising excitement. He grinned and pulled the hand gently away. His fingers stroked her cheek as she stared up at him, hope in her eyes.

"Yeah, baby. Do yourself again. Take a little of that with you for when Curtis comes."

When Bobby Burke opened the front door to admit Curtis Maxwell and Fiona Hassey to the inner sanctum, Reggie was just emerging from the back hall, a loose-fitting silk tunic over the satin shorts. He smiled a big smile of welcome, forcing himself to attend to the brother first.

"Curtis, m'man. You lookin' good. Come in, come in. You remember Bobby . . . and Lu-Ann."

The redhead was lounging on one of the sofas, looking

as interested in life as she ever could anymore. She'd done a half-dozen lines—good-sized ones. She smiled wanly as Maxwell nodded in her direction.

"This is Fiona Hassey," Curtis introduced the nurse. "Reggie DuQuesnay."

Reggie smiled a big smile and reached out to take the woman's hand in friendly welcome. He could see that she was a little nervous, eyes flicking back and forth over the room before coming to rest on his own. He just stood there radiating benevolence, giving her his full attention. The little brother was right—this *was* some righteous pussy.

"All *my* pleasure," he told her, music in his voice. "Come on into my humble place and make yourself comfortable."

Fiona was dazzled by the brilliance of the room. In the background, Marvin Gaye sang about sexual healing at volume that made the presence of melody little more than subliminal mood enhancement. The redhead on the opposite sofa was dressed in white silk pajamas, top unbuttoned to reveal some magnificent cleavage. Fiona smiled at the woman as she stepped to the offered seat. As she moved to take it, she noticed the monster pile of sparkling flake on the coffee table. More cocaine than she'd ever seen at one time before. The light of the track canister reflected off it, making her heartbeat quicken. She sat and forced herself to tear her eyes off that pile.

"Curtis," Reggie beckoned. "Why don't you have Lu-Ann take you back and show you her new tropical fish. I'd like a minute alone with Miss Hassey here.

Curtis looked at the sultry redhead, his eyes full of that beckoning cleavage. Lu-Ann gave him a hooded smile and stood slowly, reaching out a hand to take his.

Fiona watched the pair of them leave the room and turned just in time to catch Reggie nodding to the huge black man who'd answered the door. Bobby, he'd called him. Bobby turned and moved slowly from the room.

"Well," Reggie said, dropping onto the sofa at the other end from Fiona. "Curtis speaks very highly of you . . . may I call you Fiona? That's a beautiful name."

She nodded warily.

"Like to do a couple of lines?" Reggie asked. "That's what the shit's here for."

Fiona shot a look at the sparkling pile of coke.

"Don't be shy," he told her.

She tried a tentative smile, leaning forward to pick up the razor blade gingerly and cut out two tiny lines.

"Whoa," he laughed. "You worried about me running low or something? *Do* yourself, beautiful. There's plenty more where that came from."

The lines got bigger. She picked up the silver straw, and as she started to bend over the glass, a gentle hand was suddenly there to help her with her hair. She took the lines in two eager, steady runs. The drug barely even burned in her nose as she threw back her head, eyes closed, sniffing again and again to send it on its way. The black man's hand had disappeared just as subtly as it had appeared. When she opened her eyes, he was leaning back, seated at his end of the sofa, watching her.

"You like this shit?"

She grinned, relaxing, and nodded. "Love it. Is it true what Curtis said? That you'd be willing to let me in at wholesale?"

Reggie smiled easily, eyes sparkling. "If that's what you want."

Her own eyes clouded in confusion. "If that's what I *want*?"

He shrugged. "I got an open mind. That's how I came into all this." He waved a hand at the room. "I'm wonderin' what sort of an open mind you got. You want in at wholesale? I can do that for you.''

''I don't get it,'' she said after a moment.

''Do some more,'' he urged.

She did, without question this time. The hand again appeared and disappeared at precisely the correct moments.

''I'll play you straight,'' Reggie told her. She had her head back, eyes closed, and was swallowing, jaw working. When her breasts heaved up and down, he felt a stirring in the satin shorts. ''It seems that you got a friend that got put together with me, and last night I learn that this friend's problem ain't completely solved yet.''

Fiona's eyes came open, the shock of his words causing her to jerk around and regard the man with panic.

''Relax, honey. I ain't yankin' the rug on you. I just got me a thought I'd like to share. See what you think of it.''

With nonchalant ease, the man leaned forward and past her to the pile of coke, dipped in a fingernail, and pulled it to his nose, snorting deep and quick.

''You see, in talking to this man, I started to wonder to myself if his problem was ever gonna be completely solved. Some people's problems is inside their selves. Your friend is a naturally high-strung type. Once he steps off into a world he doesn't know anything about, he's lost.''

Fiona stared at him. He was talking about George. About the killing. What the hell did he want? His drugs were beautiful. He acted like a gentleman; at least as much of a gentleman as she'd expect to find in such a situation.

''I'm wondering if you recognize a profitable business opportunity when you see one?'' Reggie asked. He stopped to wave around the room again and then at the pile of cocaine. ''This is all at your disposal,'' he said flatly. ''You want it wholesale, you can have it wholesale. You want it free? You can have that, too. Me? I'm interested in an ongoing business relationship with you. The sort where both parties benefit.''

Fiona was riding a high so smooth and crystal clear that she thought she could conquer the world right then. ''And what exactly do you have in mind?'' she asked, a smile of challenge on her lips.

''Oh,'' he said, grinning. ''I'm sure you know what sort of problem Dr. George Scully's had and how he's seeking to eliminate it.''

It landed like a dead rat on the sofa between them. Fiona, angry, was just starting to open her mouth when Reggie held up a hand, smiled softly, and continued.

''Come on, Miss Hassey. It's my business to learn these things. I'd be somebody's fool if I didn't. Think about it and you'll realize that. It's also my business to profit from them. I'm offering you the choice between a life raft and a sinking ship. I seen that man. He's destroying himself. You going down with the ship? I mean, what the hell's it to you?''

Fiona was calculating quickly now. It wasn't news that Scully was showing signs of deterioration. She'd been seeing them for weeks. Steady self-destruction. Losing his grip. Then there was that big pile of cocaine.

''What *exactly* is it that you have in mind?'' she pressed.

He beamed broadly at her. ''The way I see it, you're in a perfect position to lean on the dude,'' he said simply. ''You know about what he's done but you don't know nothin' else.''

''Blackmail?'' she asked.

''In a word. You and me split. Partners. We get into him for maybe five grand a month. I throw a quarter ounce every payday to sweeten the pot.''

''Twenty-five hundred. Seven grams,'' she figured.

''That's almost thirty thousand tax-free dollars a year,''

he added. "Plus a nice steady supply of nose candy on the side."

As he spoke, Reggie slid off the sofa onto his knees and reached for the razor blade, working idly now to crunch up the better part of a gram. With a dip of his nail, he scooped a little and held it out to her. From the way her fingers were working the straw she still clutched in her hand, he could tell she was blazing.

A little too eagerly this time, she bent to his finger, bumped it, and knocked the offering all over the white shag. As she blushed, he smiled.

"What do you think it's white for, honey? No matter. Here."

He offered her more, and this time she slowed on the approach. He did her another and then one for himself before nonchalantly pushing up off the floor and onto the sofa next to her.

"Beautiful shit, huh?" he crooned, close now.

She swallowed, jaw working, smiled, and nodded. "Excellent. God, I'm high."

With casual ease, his arm drifted up behind her and his perfectly manicured fingers toyed with her hair, pulling it back from the side of her face. What a face. Great bones. Full, pouting lips. Flashing blue eyes. He slipped his other hand across his body to trace a finger lightly down her arm.

"Tell me what you think of my idea."

Eyes alive, she turned to him. "Straight split?"

"That's right. Equal partners."

Fiona's mind raced. This guy was right in his assessment of George. He *was* self-destructing. Aside from that, he was seeming more and more out of it, more *square*, with each passing day. Admittedly, she had a lot invested in him, but then again, this was looking like a much better

185

deal. In addition to the screws Reggie was going to put to him, Fiona could pressure George to let her keep the apartment and pay the maintenance. She turned to regard this muscular, gleaming-eyed stud on the sofa next to her. His growing erection was visible against the tight satin of his shorts.

"Do you want to fuck me as much as I'm dying to get laid right now?" she asked point-blank. She'd done it. She was changing horses.

There was the quickest flicker of surprise in Reggie's eyes before he could cover it. He stood slowly and took her hand to lead her from the room.

Fiona pointed to the pile of coke on the table. "Let's take some of that with us," she suggested, licking her lips.

Thirteen

Sanitation Foreman Felix Concepción sat slouched in his city-issue Chevy Chevette, observing the building at 39 Ludlow Street. For two weeks running, he had been bombarded with abuse and complaints stemming from tickets for uncontained garbage he had written on the adjacent sundries warehouse. The owner of the business swore that the garbage wasn't his; that every night when he locked up, his sidewalk was clean. Every morning when he arrived, Felix was there to issue a summons for garbage on the sidewalk in front of a commercial establishment. Under New York City law, all commercial buildings are required to engage a private carter to haul away nonresidential refuse. The owner of the sundries warehouse would point out his regulation two-yard dumpster, showing Felix how he had to keep it padlocked to prevent the "bastard heepees" in the neighborhood from filling it to capacity before he ever got any use out of the thing. That morning, they'd nearly come to blows when Felix explained that he was merely doing what the law and his job required. The warehouse owner called him a "facheest" and told him he could "chobe" his "chob" up his ass. Stinking Dominican.

Sitting there now, Felix still couldn't get over being called a facist. His *parents* were recent immigrants. He resented the abuse he took every time he gave a ticket to a Yuppie who left his dog's shit on the sidewalk instead of cleaning it up. It was the law to clean it up. It was the law not to leave garbage in front of a commercial building. There were rats and disease. Felix hated rats and disease. He hated this man who called him a facist. Tonight he would work on his own time to catch this name-caller red-handed.

When the tall, red-haired punk emerged from number 41, dragging two Hefty garbage bags behind him, Felix was almost too absorbed in his own personal vendetta to recognize the significance of what he was seeing. Looking furtively in both directions, the punk lugged the sacks to the same location in front of number 39 where Felix had encountered the previous violations and simply left them there before continuing up the street. The veins bulged in Felix Concepción's neck. This punk, this *bastard hippy* was the guilty party.

When the sanitation car screeched to a halt beside him and the enraged Puerto Rican in the green uniform leapt out of the car to all but forcibly pin him to the wall, Stuart Wiems was deep in his own thoughts. This was the only time of day he would allow himself out of the warehouse loft now. A walk to the corner deli for beers and maybe a loaf of bread and cold cuts. For better than a week now, he'd been hoping the furor over his killing that repulsive old faggot would die down. Hoping the cops would hurry up and discover what a perverted old scumbag he was and figure he'd gotten what he deserved. Five hundred dollars to touch his penis, a thousand if he let him jerk him off.

He was disgusted, but he badly needed the money. He went there thinking he'd have it done and over in a few minutes, collect his money, and get out. The old fucker led him on for much longer than that, and once he had his way, he laughed at him and refused to give him more than the first five hundred. Stuart flew into a blind rage. For that next half hour he was an insane animal, killing not only Oscar Wembley but everything his sort of bloodsucking wealth stood for. Then, just when the story started to die down in the papers and the cops were admitting they had few leads, there was this second murder up on Fifth Avenue. Stuart couldn't fathom what it meant. He knew he hadn't done it. If he'd been scared the morning after waking up with blood all over his clothes, trembling with fever, he was scared absolutely shitless now.

Which is exactly what happened when the uniformed man erupted from the car in a purple rage. Stuart defecated. He didn't even have the presence of mind to run. He just stood there, dumbfounded, submissive, while the man screamed at him about the law, germs, rats, and something about facism. He didn't even hear him when he asked him for identification.

"Huh? What?"

"ID. You don't have ID, I gotta take you to the precinct. Dumping unauthorized garbage is a misdemeanor. A *crime,* buddy."

Stuart shook his head to clear it. "Let me get this straight. You want to give me a ticket for leaving garbage on the sidewalk? That's *all*?"

His apparent lack of sensitivity toward the magnitude of the transgression launched a second tirade from Felix Concepción. When it was over, Wiems reached into his back pocket, removed his wallet, and handed the man his driver's license.

Felix scrutinized it. "You don't live here?" he asked suspiciously.

Wiems shook his head. "Third Street, like it says. I work here. I'm a painter."

Felix was about to say something about bastard hippies but managed to control himself as he wrote the punk a twenty-five-dollar summons for littering. When he was finished, he tore it out of his book with a flourish and shoved it at him.

"I got your number now, buddy. I be laying for you. Every time you leave your garbage anywhere in the whole fucking city, I'll be there."

Stuart Wiems had to return to the warehouse loft to change his pants before proceeding to the store. He was badly shaken. At the corner deli, he skipped the bread and cold cuts, buying extra beer instead. He couldn't eat after a thing like that. Back on his cot in the warehouse, he stared at his latest painting, realizing it was lousy. From under the mattress, he pulled the last of Oscar Wembley's money. He'd seen where the old man kept it when he was paid the five hundred. When he killed him, he took it all. Twenty-two hundred. Right now, he had fourteen hundred left.

A full forensics report was waiting for Dante when he reported to the squad at four o'clock. As suspected, the dissimilarities between this and the previous killing went beyond the visual. The killer had used dish gloves removed from beneath the sink in the first instance. In this case, the telltale lubricant powder of surgical gloves was found. Because Crowley was paralyzed, there were no signs of struggle resulting in tissue or hair follicle samples beneath his nails. The nurse, killed in her sleep, had produced no physical evidence either. In fact, the Wembley murderer was decidedly sloppy in his technique while this murderer was neat. A careful vacuuming of the entire premises revealed little that could be called unusual.

There were also additional bits and pieces of information to be read through: Thompson and Koehl's report on Crowley's medical history and the malpractice suit. As Dante read it, he jotted down the names of attorneys and other principals. Across the desk from him, Vinnie looked over the forensics report, once in a while comparing an eight-by-ten glossy from it to one in the Wembly file.

Dante glanced over. "Did you make a request to have Wiems's yearbook picture copied? There's no note of it in the file."

"I got it right here," Vinnie growled defensively.

"Lot of good it'll do us there. How are we supposed to find this guy? You clairvoyant?" For the past three days, Arata had been dragging tail, failing to respond to the manpower shortage for what it was and pick up some of the slack.

Vinnie got hot. "What is this? Who annointed you Pope? Quit busting my balls."

"Then *carry* your fucking end," Dante retorted. "Just in case you hadn't noticed, there's just two of us on this thing."

Manley could be heard scraping back in his chair. His head appeared from around the edge of his office doorjamb.

"What's going on out here?" he asked wearily.

Dante was already on his feet and snatching his jacket off the back of his chair.

"I'm going to Hoboken to look for a murder suspect. Someone else can babysit this jerk."

It was well past midnight before Dante returned home to the Village and parked his car in the garage. He'd just spent seven hours chasing all over the Hoboken club scene trying to locate the sum or parts of a band called Numbnuts. The process left him feeling his age, as well as empty-handed. Nobody in the entire crowd was within ten years of him in age. Nobody knew anything. Numbnuts had had a gig in a club three nights ago but was nowhere near proficient enough to find work anywhere this late in the week. With the club crowd, Thursday was the weekend already. Prime time.

As he strolled up Perry Street toward his building, a black stretch-limo eased to the curb in front. Wendy Lee emerged to cross the sidewalk and push through the front gate.

"It's nice to see someone else keeps late hours around here," he commented from behind her. She was fumbling for her door key in a big, floppy bag. At the sound of his voice, she nearly jumped out of her pumps.

"God!" she gasped, clutching a hand to her breast and trying to catch her breath. "You scared the shit out of me."

"Just a free introductory lesson to the streets of New York," he replied. "At no time can you afford to be oblivious to the immediate environment. Not until you're safely locked inside your own apartment."

"I'll remember that," she said, relaxing the frozen grip on her handbag and nodding with relief. "Do you often find yourself inclined to employ these firsthand demonstrations?"

"I don't plan them for weeks in advance, if that's what you mean. You were getting out of the stretch and I was coming up the block. The timing was there."

She looked at him, intrigued. The other night, she hadn't noticed the drawn lines in an otherwise boyish face. "You look tired."

"Whipped is more like it."

She managed to fit her key into the door cylinder and get

192

it open. As she shouldered her way in, she looked back. "Can I offer you a drink? My place is still a mess, but I think I can find the box marked booze."

"Believe it or not, I was just going to brew myself a cup of coffee," he replied.

"Coffee then," she countered. "I think I can handle that."

She wasn't kidding about her place being a mess. It was obvious that she was unpacking things as she needed them. Other stuff in the same box could wait until she found a place for it. Approximately half the boxes were open, including the one marked booze.

Wendy entered the tiny kitchen to put coffee water on. "Are you going to Rebecca's party tomorrow night?" she asked from out of view.

"I'm on until midnight," he replied. "I thought I might drop in if things are still going when I swing out. They usually are with her parties."

"Swing out. That's police talk. You guys have a whole bunch of special jargon you use, don't you?" She reappeared with a tumbler and a tray of ice.

"I guess we do. Just like broadcasters or steelworkers or any other fraternity."

"Do you like it?"

"What?"

"Being a cop. A detective."

"There are good days and bad. Today was a bad day."

Her place was bigger than his, just over twelve hundred square feet, with two bedrooms and a large bath in back. The landlord had done a typical New York paint job. She'd hung art prints on the walls to make it seem a little cheerier than it really was. Dante didn't want to know what sort of astronomical rent she was paying. With an on-camera job like she had, he figured she could probably afford it.

Wendy poured a couple of fingers of Scotch into the tumbler and put a Herbie Hancock tape on low.

"Rebecca tells me you were involved with a lady detective until recently; that it's sort of on the rocks."

Dante blinked in irritation. "Rebecca's a nice girl, but she's got a big mouth."

"So it's true."

He shrugged. "On the rocks is a little dramatic. Let's just say we're reassessing."

"I don't mean to seem like I'm prying or anything," she said hastily. "It's just that I don't know all that many people here, and I thought it might be nice if we had dinner or something, some night when you're not on until late."

It came at him like a surface-to-air missile launch out of heavy cover. It wasn't just what she said, but the look in her eye when she said it. There was absolute confidence in that look. An "Anything I want, I get" look. It set him back on his heels.

"Maybe," he said tentatively.

"I find you very attractive," she said matter-of-factly. "Would you like to spend the night here?"

Dante blinked again, but not in irritation this time. An amused smile crept across his lips.

"I'm flattered, but I think I'll take a rain check."

In the kitchen, the water began to boil. Wendy turned to get it. A moment later, he followed her over and leaned against the door. She was standing over a dripping Melitta cone, an impetuous scowl fixed on her face. If anything, it only served to make her more beautiful.

"On second thought," he said, pointing at the filling cup. "Maybe I *will* have a drink. Mind if I pour a little Scotch in there?"

* * *

Vic Manley realized that he was spending more and more of his off hours in the squad room lately. He didn't have to reach far to put his finger on why. The time he spent in his lifeless, recently renovated, and half-furnished apartment on West 102nd Street depressed the hell out of him. The old place, four blocks south on West End Avenue, was the one that held all the memories. It had been sold, with the proceeds split between him and his wife in a straight community property settlement. When he retired, she was even entitled to half his pension. She'd gone back to live with her mother in Chicago. His two grown girls were away at college. Although he kept it tight inside him, the life of a fifty-two-year-old divorced police lieutenant was proving to be dull, uninspired fare. Some nights, when he'd had too much to drink and still couldn't get to sleep, he thought he knew why so many guys in his line of work ended up eating their service revolvers.

Now at least he had something to concentrate on. He found himself actually looking forward to heading downtown to work a few hours on the grisly multiple murders that had been dropped into his lap.

On Friday morning, Manley ambled into the squad room at ten fifteen. The early shift was mostly out. There had been a rash of burglaries in one building on West 13th Street, and those who weren't chasing some detail on the Wembley and Crowley murders were busy canvassing the neighborhood. On his desk, he found copies of summons search reports from all enforcement branches of city government. Traffic, police, sanitation, health—all negative. It was a slim hope he'd held out to begin with. Locating a perp through some minor social fuck-up was always a long shot. Still, you went through the motions. Throw enough shit against the wall and sooner or later some is bound to stick.

Manley started to sift through a mountain of neglected

DD-5's and "sixty" sheets, signing them after a quick scan and tossing them into his out basket for filing. This was the thankless part of the job that every cop hated. There were mountains of paper everywhere you turned.

Two hours after he'd come in, Manley was thinking about stepping out to the deli on Hudson Street for a sandwich when Ollie Pemberton, one of the detectives on the shift, poked his head in.

"Sanit Department's chief clerk is on two for you, lou."

Manley dropped his pen a little too quickly and grabbed at the phone like a drowning man going for a life preserver. "Manley," he barked, punching the line button.

"Bob Kelley at Sanitation, Lieutenant."

"Tell me you've got something for me and make my day," Manley urged him.

"I think you'll agree that you owe me one after this, Lieutenant. It just came in on our daily update. The girl inputting it was the same one on when we ran your request yesterday. A Stuart Wiems was issued a summons for illegal dumping last night."

Manley's pulse, already racing, kicked up a notch. "Where?"

"39 Ludlow. He identified himself with a New York license issued to an address on East Third."

Manley could barely stay in his chair. His mind was stripping gears. "Listen," he told the chief clerk, "I've got to talk to your issuing officer. Pronto. You think you could get him in here ten minutes ago?"

Kelley grunted in amusement. "Can't see why not. His name is Concepción. One of the foremen. He's out in a car right now, but we'll get him on the radio."

"As soon as you can," Manley urged. "Goddamn, Chief, I can't tell you how much we needed this."

*   *   *

No sooner was his connection broken than the whip was punching in Dante's home number. He got the answering machine and was just preparing to leave a brief message and hang up when the detective came on the line.

"Sorry, Vic. I was just getting out of the shower. What gives?"

Manley related what the sanit chief had told him. "I'm getting Arata's fanny in here. I want you to go down there and check the address out. I'll see who else I can lay my hands on and send him along with you."

"Give me twenty minutes," Dante told him.

Joe entered the squad in time to catch a green uniformed sanitation foreman in Vic Manley's office, along with a guy named Pemberton from the other shift. Ollie was one of the new breed—a tall drink of water with a smart mouth, ambitions of a swift rise up the ranks, a shaggy mustache, and a soul-burst cultivated beneath a prominent lower lip. Dante knew him well enough to have filed a mental assessment. Not a bad sort but also not the guy he'd want to have backing him in a jam. His head was off somewhere in the clouds—most likely a cloud of off-duty reefer smoke. That was another problem with the new breed. They wanted to see themselves as being the same as everyone else. Same proclivities and vices. It generally took one good civilian complaint to clear up this misconception.

"What's the picture?" he asked, pulling up a chair.

"This is Felix Concepción," Manley said. "Detective Dante."

The strangers shook hands.

"He issued a summons to a Stuart Wiems last evening about seven o'clock. The description fits."

"Punk-looking kid," Concepción added helpfully. "Said he was a painter or something. He been leaving garbage in front of the building next door for a couple weeks now. I saw him come out of number 41.''

Dante glanced at Manley. The whip nodded. "As soon as Vinnie gets here. I want you two to take Pemberton with you and go check it out. This is the break we've been looking for.''

"What sort of building was it?" Dante asked the foreman.

Concepción thought a moment. "Not too big. Like all that building down there. Maybe four story. Like a warehouse, you know? But small for one.''

Vinnie Arata was none too happy about being called into the squad for overtime. He'd been awakened from a sound sleep to discover a pudgy bleached-blonde next to him in bed. The details of how she'd gotten there were a little fuzzy. He knew he'd had a lot to drink in that cop bar on Stillwell and she'd sat on the stool next to his. She was too heavy but had big, fleshy tits. Just the way he liked them. He also remembered that he'd had trouble getting hard with all the booze in him and he was sore as hell now as a result. Damn. He wondered if he'd hit the bull's-eye or strayed a little. Either way, she didn't strike him as the type who would mind.

Anyway, he had to get rid of her now. He dragged ass into the shower and turned on the cold full blast. What the hell had Manley said? He couldn't quite remember that either. In fact, he was still pretty drunk.

Four cups of coffee later, Vinnie straggled into the squad. He was bleary-eyed but sober. The whip, along with Dante and a nigger named Pemberton from the other shift were all waiting for him.

"Shake a leg," Manley snapped, anxiously checking his watch. "We've got a line on Wiems.''

"What?" Vinnie asked, head snapping around. "Where?"

"Lower East Side. Ludlow Street. Ollie is going to back you guys up."

"Let's roll," Dante told him. "You ready?"

"Meet you out in front. Got to use the head."

As Dante reached to grab a set of keys off the board, Vinnie hurried back toward the men's room.

The building at 41 Ludlow Street was pretty much as the sanitation foreman had described it. It was situated on a block of run-down tenements and warehouses in a neighborhood well out of the Manhattan mainstream. Dante suspected that a lot of the warehouses had since been converted to living space by the art community. That's what was happening to these neighborhoods, just when even the regular residents were wondering if maybe it wasn't time to get out. All part of the great downtown renaissance.

He pulled the Fury around onto Hester Street and parked just adjacent to a hardware store. From what he could see, the rear of the store would front on the gap of yards and alleys running down between the buildings on Ludlow and the ones behind them on Orchard.

"They've got to have access in through there. Which one of you two wants to watch the rear?"

Pemberton nodded. "Hang on a sec. I'll check it out." He climbed out of the car and hurried into the store, emerging a moment later with a thumbs-up. "No sweat. I can get right under the fire escape."

Dante handed a portable radio out the window. "We'll let you know as we go," he told him. "Stay awake now, huh?"

"Kiss mine, chump," Pemberton told him, hurrying back inside the store.

Dante and Arata got out of the Plymouth and proceeded on foot around the corner to number 41 Ludlow Street.

The building was a walk-up with a freight elevator in front. A narrow staircase ran up the right side from behind a metal fire door with a small pane of wired glass in it. Three of four mailboxes in the vestibule were tagged and stuffed with a recent delivery. There was a Tinker Bell Apparel Corp. on the first floor. From the look of the place, it was most likely one of the infamous Lower East Side sweatshops. Something named the Wimjay Group occupied the second floor, and Freidland Hosiery was listed as being on the third. The fourth-floor box had its labeling peeled away. Dante reached out and punched the button belonging to Tinker Bell.

"Hello?" A hollow, faraway voice crackled from the intercom box.

"Delivery. Tinker Bell Apparel," the detective announced.

The door release buzzed and they pushed in. Another door just off the foot of the stairs swung open and an owlish female face peered out at them.

"What's going on here?" the woman demanded.

Arata produced his shield, finger to his lips. "Just stay inside, please," he said quietly.

"Can you tell us anything about the occupant of the top floor, ma'am?" Dante asked.

"Some punk artist kids. Two boys and a girl, I think. They come and go."

Dante nodded. "Like the detective said, ma'am, stay inside, please. We'll let you know when it's okay to come out."

As the woman shut herself into Tinker Bell Apparel, Dante lifted the hand-held radio to his lips and called Pemberton.

"You in position?" he asked.

"Goldilocks got yellow hair?"

"Fuck you, wise-ass. Keep an eye out. We're going up."

Dante and Arata started up the long flight of stairs, guns drawn, moving quietly. The stairwell was only dimly lit and smelled strongly of mold and mildew. On the landing outside the door on the second floor, again marked Wimjay Group, they could hear the muffled ringing of telephones and a loud male voice. Further up, outside Friedland Hosiery, the steady whump and whir of machinery could be heard.

Dante, in the lead, turned to Vinnie as he pulled up about eight feet short of the fourth-floor landing. Without speaking, his eyes asked if he was set. Arata nodded. Carefully, they climbed the last dozen steps to a tight little area in front of a metal fire door. Dante stood to one side, pistol raised, as Vinnie took up position on the other.

Dante reached out and banged loudly on the panel. "Plumber!"

They strained their ears now, listening. From inside, the sound of shuffling steps could barely be made out.

"What do you want?" a voice asked.

"They got a leak downstairs on two. It's coming from up here somewhere. Gotta check the pipes."

"Nothing wrong in here," the voice answered.

"Just gotta check it out, pal. Could be somethin' in your waste stack."

A face appeared on the landing below them, staring up and taking in the two men with drawn guns on either side of the door.

"What the hell's going on up there?" the guy demanded. He was balding and pudgy in an electric blue polyester suit.

"Fuck," Vinnie muttered under his breath.

Inside, he and Dante could hear quickly receding steps.

The next sound to reach them was the scraping squeal of sash pulleys as a window was raised. A moment later, Pemberton's muffled bellow came from outside.

"Hold it! Police!"

Dante's head snapped quickly back and forth. "Shit! He'll go for the roof."

The two of them started pell-mell upstairs, leaving the astonished fat man gaping up at them from below. Roof access was through a small structure that looked like an outhouse with a steeply pitched roof. The door on it was fastened from the inside by a single, heavy-duty slide bolt. Dante reached out to slide it open, checking Arata's position over his shoulder. Gritting his teeth, he kicked hard.

Out on the expanse of black tarred roof, Stuart Wiems was nowhere to be seen. The whole view was pretty much unobstructed as Dante and Arata crept slowly into grey dull day, guns extended. Toward the front of the building, the small structure housing the elevator motor suddenly emitted a loud click and began to vibrate.

"The fucking freight elevator," Vinnie yelled.

Dante was already at the parapet wall in front, staring over it and into the street. The building next door, level with the one they were on, had a fire escape running down the facade to the street.

"You take the stairs. I'll go down this way," Dante replied.

As Arata started back toward the roof access, Joe was jumping the four-foot gap to the next roof and scrambling over the parapet onto the fire escape ladder.

It was a crisp and cool autumn morning, with a thin overcast blanketing the city. In the street below, activity was at a peak for the day, trucks loading for afternoon deliveries, men wheeling hand trucks along the sidewalks. Dante went as fast as his feet would carry him down toward this scene. The stairs inside the building next door would have to be quicker than a rusty metal fire escape with its switchbacks at every floor. Twice he banged his shins in his haste, his eyes focused on the door below instead of on what he was doing.

The door flew open while Dante was still one flight above the street. From his vantage, he watched as a gangly redhaired kid, eyes wide and limbs pumping furiously, erupted from the building and shot diagonally across Ludlow to the opposite sidewalk. Just a second or two behind him, Vinnie Arata emerged in hot pursuit.

Stuart Wiems was in a panic. In desperation, he ran between a pair of standing trucks and then moved straight up the open sidewalk. Vinnie anticipated the move almost before he made it and cut over simultaneously. He had the direct line of pursuit, only twenty or so yards back.

"Hold it right there, fuck-face! Another step and you're dead meat!"

Wiems stopped almost dead in his tracks and spun, hands outstretched in surrender. Joe Dante was stunned by Arata's reaction. The pistol in his hands jerked twice, taking the quarry square in the chest.

Dante was hanging by his hands and dropping the last seven feet to the sidewalk as Vinnie hurried to where his victim lay on the opposite side of the street, crumpled like a marionette whose strings had been cut.

"Jesus *Christ*!" Joe panted, racing forward.

Vinnie was down on one knee, bent over the fallen man. He was fumbling with something, and then Dante saw it emerge from beneath his pants cuff. While trying to shield himself from Dante's view, Vinnie had the dying kid's hand pried open. With blood dribbling from the side of his mouth, Wiems's breath was coming in short, gurgled gasps.

Ollie Pemberton came running around the corner from Hester Street as a crowd began to gather.

"Call an ambulance," Dante shouted.

Vinnie looked back over his shoulder and saw Dante staring down at him in disbelief.

Vinnie shook his head. "He turned so fast like that. I thought he was carrying. Fuck, man. I know this kind of scum. Son of a bitch has the decency to die right here, we just saved the city one fuck of a lot of money."

Joe's mouth came open and then closed again without a word, incredulity on his face.

Arata pointed at the throwaway he'd just planted in Stuart Wiems's hand. "You'll back me up on this, right?"

Fourteen

The afternoon was a blur now: Stuart Wiems rushed to the trauma unit at Bellevue Emergency where he still lingered on the edge of death. The questioning by the duty captain of the Fifth Precinct, where the shooting took place. Vinnie Arata's story. The newshounds besieging the hospital and the Sixth Precinct.

Joe Dante sat with Gus Lieberman and Vic Manley in the living room of his apartment. He had a cold beer in his hands and a churning in his guts. He'd chosen his own home because he couldn't think of another setting for something like this. Cops stood together when they made mistakes in the line of duty. They didn't rat each other out. Guys who worked in Internal Affairs were perceived as the enemy. Judases within the job. Vinnie Arata would be seen by his fellow officers as a man with fifteen years in; four of them as a volunteer working narcotics. There were commendations. Membership in the Knights of Columbus and the Sons of Italy. A guy like that fucks up accidentally, you cover for him, just like you'd expect him to do in a similar situation.

"I was still a good eight to ten feet off the ground, Gus. There's no doubt about what I saw. If that kid hadn't turned around when he did, Arata would have shot him in the back. He was gunning for him. He had the fucking throwaway in his boot."

The inspector shook his head. "Christ," he mumbled.

"He shot him in cold blood and planted the gun with me watching," Dante continued evenly. "It wasn't a mistake."

Lieberman sighed. "Nobody likes this prick, but they like what you're doing even less. You willing to go all the way with this?"

Dante nodded. "I don't suppose I'd have you guys sitting here listening to this if I wasn't."

A dreary silence descended as the three men drank their beers and stared at each other.

"I don't get it," Gus finally said. "The man's a bona fide cocksucker, but why does he risk his entire livelihood for the pleasure of triggering some poor schmuck on a sidewalk?"

"Cops back each other up on this sort of shit all the time," Manley replied. "Maybe he didn't think it was any risk at all."

Dante shook his head. "I don't get it either. Not that he'd risk his pension. It's his history. Rumor's had him maybe dirty, but there's nothing I've heard about him being trigger-happy. You *hear* that sort of thing. Nobody wants to partner with someone like that, and word gets around. Still, he carries a throwaway in his boot." He stopped and looked hard at his two superiors. "Always? Or just this once?"

"I know a leading question when I hear one," Lieberman said. "Plenty of cops carry throwaways as a matter of habit."

"So much happened so quickly," Dante sighed. "I didn't really have much chance to think about it until right now. Going over it all again. What were we doing down there? We were trying to bring in the only suspect in two separate murder cases. Only the second of the two smells bad. We can't quite put our finger on why, but we're hoping this Wiems character might help answer some of the questions, one of our theories being a possible copycat kill. Before we can put question one to him, Vinnie gets a sudden rod-on and guns him down in cold blood. He's carrying the goddamn throwaway with him.''

Manley remembered something. ''When I told him it was Wiems you were going after, he said he had to take a leak and headed back toward the can. He could have hit his locker instead.''

''What were we talking about just yesterday?'' Dante asked him. ''About a copycat. We figured that the accuracy was so uncanny that it'd have to be someone on the inside. Maybe one of the lab techs or ME guys leaking the information. Why not a cop?''

''Whoa!'' Lieberman exclaimed. ''You guys mind backtracking just a little and filling me in?''

Manley apologized and quickly brought Lieberman up to date on their progress and various theories.

''Damn! You two realize what you're dancing around?'' the inspector asked.

''If it's true, it fits,'' Dante pressed. ''Like a fucking glove. Who would be in a better position to do the job *and* make sure that we never get too close to the truth. That kid over at Bellevue ain't gonna make it. Believe me. I watched them cart him off and it'd take a miracle. Vinnie relies on the code of silence to protect him. Hell, if I hadn't been exactly where I was and seen what I saw, he would have gotten away with it.''

The three men sat staring at their hands. Copter wandered into the room and jumped up on the sofa to rub against Dante. Joe pitched him back onto the floor and stood. He headed off to the kitchen and returned with three new beers.

"What do you want to do?" Manley asked his superior.

Lieberman shook his head. "I've gotta run by the PC and the C of D with this one. They might think some sort of covert IAD investigation might be more productive than an open accusation. If Arata's mixed up in something as heavyweight as collaboration in hired hits, he might lead them to something more readily if he doesn't know he's under suspicion."

"You want to leave him in the squad?" Manley asked.

Lieberman nodded. "Maybe so. That's not my decision. Meanwhile, I want Dante here to start digging into this Crowley's situation on the QT. Look for some sort of link. Look for something we might be able to follow back in the other direction. Maybe we can make this thing boomerang on the son of a bitch."

"How am I gonna do that without Vinnie picking up on it?" Dante asked. "The man's not stupid."

Gus gave it a moment of thought.

"With Wiems in custody, we announce that both the Wembley and Crowley murder investigations are being closed. We can use that to get the media off our backs, anyway. That'll mean a lot of the pressure is off the squad at the Sixth. It would stand to reason that there would be manpower available there for other duty. I'll have you flown out for a temporary tour with the Borough Command Tasks Force. Covering for vacation time or whatever. You and Vic can stay in touch by phone."

George Scully was in the surgeons' lounge after a lengthy and exhausting craniotomy to relieve pressure on the brain of an injured construction worker. The patient was in recovery, and he was sticking around until he stabilized. He drank coffee to keep from nodding off. It wasn't all that late, but he hadn't been getting much sleep the past week. First there was the Crowley matter, and now Fiona hadn't returned his calls for two days. When he'd run across the street to see what was going on, she was nowhere to be found.

"Hey!"

He looked up to see Phil Neisbaum entering the lounge, a grin spread across his face from ear to ear.

"Hiya, Georgie. You looked whipped. I figured you'd be out celebrating for a week. Or is that *why* you look whipped?"

Scully scowled. "What the hell are you talking about?"

Phil shook his head. "You don't know, do you? You telling me you haven't seen a newspaper?"

"I've been in surgery for the past eight hours. They don't generally broadcast the news in there."

Neisbaum scanned around the lounge and then stooped to retrieve a copy of the *Post* from a trash basket. He shook it out straight and handed it to Scully, headline prominent.

"Your troubles are over, buddy. They found the fucker."

Scully stared at the big, boldface headline: SLASHER GUNNED DOWN. There was a little lead-in to the article, which was then continued on the inside page. It described how the police now felt that the Benjamin Crowley and Oscar Wembley murders had been solved. The killer was in critical condition at Bellevue and not expected to last the night.

"Amazing, isn't it?" Neisbaum enthused. "First this nut decides to carve up the albatross around your neck and then the cops save the state the cost of even prosecuting him. All nice and neat."

Scully wasn't sure that he could even speak. He felt giddy, the world a kaleidoscopic jumble of anxiety suddenly set aright. To think he was set to pay that black bastard more money to do it all again when now it wasn't necessary. It was over. Just like cutting a cancerous tumor out of an otherwise healthy organism.

"It's hard to believe," he said shakily, a smile lifting the corners of his tired mouth.

Phil clapped him on the back. "Believe it, buddy. The way I see it, we go into a guy's head with all the expertise in the world at our fingertips and the grace of God in our hearts. What happens next is fate, and when fate points thumbs-down, the legal system and the rest of the world wants *us* to fry in hell for it. Fuck 'em. Just yesterday, I read about some poor slob down in D.C. who was left hanging in the breeze for two mil on an informed consent case. Thin as hell, the argument. Patient claims she wasn't informed in enough detail about the risk she was taking in an operation that probably saved her miserable life. Whatever happened to implied risk?"

Scully weathered this outburst, hardly listening. He was free. Everything was going to get sorted out now. Joan. Fiona. The notes on the real estate.

Neisbaum glanced at his watch. "Jesus, listen to me. I was supposed to meet the old lady for dinner ten minutes ago." He threw an arm around George's shoulder and gave him a firm shake. "Be happy, buddy. When you say your bedtime prayers tonight, thank God for creating maniacs."

Reggie DuQuesnay listened to an account of the shooting on Ludlow Street on the five o'clock TV news. Bad Bobby sat with him in the big white living room. Back down the hall, the beautiful blond nurse was still sleeping off an all-night snort-a-thon. Reggie had been up for a couple of hours now and was busy easing into the day with a Schlitz Bull tall and a fat jay of high-grade Jamaican sinsemilla. They drank and passed the weed back and forth as the nice lady told them about an upcoming interview with the author of a book about good ways to entertain your kids on rainy days.

"Send your little girls to me," Reggie chuckled. "I'll entertain 'em."

Bobby pointed at the screen, suddenly sitting forward. "Look," he said excitedly.

As a reporter narrated the apprehension and subsequent shooting of Stuart Wiems, the camera zoomed in on the face of Vinnie Arata as he left the Fifth Precinct house on Elizabeth Street in Lower Manhattan. He was described as the detective forced to pull the trigger when the suspect turned a .32-caliber pistol on him. Wiems was not expected to live, as he lingered with a bullet pressing the left ventricle of his heart. Physical evidence recovered from the Wembley murder scene already tied him conclusively to that crime, and the police were calling the Crowley killings the second stop on a mad spree.

Reggie grinned at Bad Bobby through a cloud of reefer smoke.

"What can you say, m'man? That was some nice work. I see the door closing all nice and neat on this thing now. Our police friend takes care of the first loose end and now we take care of the last. It's time we begin enjoyin' the fruits of our labor. Unencumbered, so to speak."

The sleepy blond head of Fiona Hassey appeared in the hall entrance. She rubbed her eyes.

"Hey there, sunshine," Reggie greeted her gaily. "Thought you was gonna sleep the entire day away."

"What time is it?" she asked.

"Just five fifteen, gorgeous."

"God!" she exclaimed, touching her hand to her hair. "I'm due on at seven o'clock."

"Relax," Reggie cooed. "You got plenty of time. Bobby will drive you down. Why don't you hop into the shower and I'll have a little eye-opener ready for you when you get out.''

Fiona's eyes opened a lot wider just at the thought.

When Jumbo Richardson returned to the four-to-midnight after completing his brief testimony in the jogger-rapist indictment proceedings, he found the atmosphere of the squad much enlivened. After the events of that morning, the chief of detectives declared the Wembley and Crowley murder investigations officially closed. The pressure was off. The detectives of the Sixth could return to the more or less normal routine of muggings, rapes, and burglaries.

Joe Dante was slouching in a desk chair when Jumbo emerged from the lockers with a Diet Coke and dropped into the chair opposite. It was just past six, and the two of them were holding the fort. The lieutenant had suggested that Vinnie take the shift off on account of the trauma he'd suffered in being forced to shoot a man in the line of duty. Jumbo and Dante were alone, drinking sodas and eating the fat man's donuts from a paper bag.

"You talk to the lou about the copycat angle again?" Richardson asked. "I just don't get it, the way they just shut it all down once Wiems is in the bag."

"I don't much get it either," Dante told him. "Sure seems a little too cut and dried to me, but then I ain't the boss. On top of it all, they tell me I'm being flown out to cover vacations on the task force. Nothing but nights for the next month."

"What'd you do to deserve that?" Jumbo asked.

"Beats me. Luck of the draw, I guess."

At six thirty, Dante called the intensive care unit at Bellevue to inquire into the status of Stuart Wiems. A doctor informed him that Wiems had died of his wounds only fifteen minutes before.

Thoroughly depressed, Joe sat staring blankly at a cheese-cake calendar on the opposite wall. A bikini-clad woman gripped an electric drill. No one had flipped the page to November. Pushing back his chair, he drifted in to see if Manley had duplicated the Crowley file. He wanted to take the material with him when he swung out.

"By the way," he told the whip, "I just got off the phone with Bellevue ICU. Wiems died a few minutes ago."

Manley sighed and nodded. "Man did a nice thorough job, didn't he?"

Dante shrugged. "Hopefully not thorough enough. Any word from Gus?"

"Yeah. He talked to the chief and the PC. They're huddling with Internal Affairs first thing tomorrow morning. They want you at the big building at ten."

From the sound of it, Rebecca's party upstairs was in full swing by the time Dante pushed in through the front door of his place and dropped the duplicate Crowley file on the coffee table. There was loud music, the shuffling of dancing, and the hubbub of conversation seeping down through the stairwell outside and the floor above. He'd already decided not to go. He was beat and discouraged, not in the frame of mind that would make him the life of a party.

He stripped out of his jacket and kicked off his shoes before padding into the kitchen for a beer. It had been a day that seemed like it might never end. Now, after midnight, with the ache of fatigue in his joints, Dante knew that if he crawled into bed, he still wouldn't be able to sleep. It wasn't the noise coming from upstairs. Hell, there were times he was so tired he could sleep through a thermonuclear attack. Now he was just wound up tight with thoughts of hit-man cops, copycat murders, and a lot of facts floating in the soup of irrelevance. Somewhere out there, the key ingredient went begging to be added.

In his bedroom, he flipped on the lights and lowered the shades over the window and French doors. Copter was nestled comfortably between the two pillows on the bed, and the bright light disturbed him only long enough for him to bury his head deeper beneath a paw. After a long, satisfying pull on his beer, Joe set the bottle on the dresser and squirmed out of the shoulder holster harness. He hadn't exercised that day and figured that a few rudimentary calisthenics might help loosen some of the tension. After removing the rest of his clothes, he pulled on a pair of gym shorts and carried the beer back into the living room. With some old Graham Parker on the cassette machine at moderate volume, he stretched out, did fifty push-ups, a hundred sit-ups and then shadow-boxed with a pair of five-pound hand weights.

Half an hour later, he was panting heavily and dripping sweat when a knock at the door interrupted his warm-down. Upstairs, it sounded like the party was still in full swing. He eased slowly out of the plough position he was in on the floor and opened the door to find Wendy Lee on the threshold with a bottle of Cristal and a pair of fluted glasses.

Wendy looked down at the bottle in her hand. "I stole it from a sales reception at the station. Good champagne being wasted on a bunch of drunks. I also saw you on the news and guessed you were planning to skip Rebecca's party." She took in his breathless and sweat-soaked condition. "Am I interrupting something?"

Dante had to chuckle, shaking his head. "Just finishing up." He could feel her eyes moving over his torso, appraising what they saw. He was in good shape and proud of his strength. The knife scars were something else again. Some women didn't mind, and others seemed a little put off. Not that it mattered much. In his line of work, you took a few scratches. He'd survived all his, so far.

"Are you going to leave me and my bottle of champagne out here in the cold or are you going to invite us in?"

"A little late, isn't it?"

"You can sleep with *that* going on upstairs?"

He shrugged. "Good point. Some nights I'd be able to, but probably not right now." Standing aside, he invited her to enter.

Wendy set the bottle and glasses on the coffee table while Joe stooped to pick up his weights and return them to their cabinet next to the television.

"Graham Parker," Wendy commented. "Screwed around by his label. Too bad. I miss his albums. Do you always exercise at one in the morning?"

"Only when I need to unwind. Do you always visit men with champagne at this hour?"

She smiled. "Only the ones who play hard to get in the light of day."

He shrugged. "I'm involved in what you might call a complex relationship at the moment. I'm already more confused than one man ought to be."

"The other day you were reevaluating," Wendy said. "I hear she's very attractive. I *also* hear that variety is the spice of life."

"Have you always been this frank?" he asked.

"In my business, you have to be. You also have to go for what you want, because if you don't, somebody else will run right over you to get it first."

He smiled and pointed at the champagne. "I've got to hop into the shower for a minute. Why don't you see if you can get that open?"

Dante was toweling dry, after the blazing hot shower had washed a lot of his tension down the drain. The knob of the bathroom door turned, a cloud of steam escaped, and Wendy Lee was standing in the open doorway with two full glasses of sparkling wine. She smiled, her eyebrows raised as she let her eyes run up and down him. Dante dropped the towel, accepted a glass, and clicked it with hers. They both took tentative sips.

"I like your body," she said, voice low and sultry. "I knew it would be something like that. You're such a tough guy."

The hitter checked his watch as he sat in front of the Letterman show drinking V.O. It had all clicked, and there was a certain satisfaction that came when all the pieces fell into place.

As soon as he swung out, he'd driven straight to the back streets at the foot of the Brooklyn Bridge, picked up a black whore with a real set of lungs on her, and had her bring him off right there in the front seat of the Pontiac. Sore or not, it wasn't anything like it was with the fat blonde from the cop bar. Tonight, there wasn't anything that could have kept him down. Twenty minutes after he got home, Reggie called with a peace offering, telling him that he was sending Bobby by within the hour with an extra five grand for the maid trouble at Crowley's place. The hour was almost out now and the hitter with a couple of shots under his belt, was feeling decidedly mellow.

Fifteen

Every morning at around seven o'clock, Joel Taylor walked his springer spaniel Herbie in Van Cortlandt Park. Sprawling across a huge section of the northwest Bronx and located directly across upper Broadway from Joel's Riverdale apartment building, the park's sporting fields and rambling woodlands were a perfect venue for these two fast buddies and their ritualized morning romp. Neither ever knew quite what they'd find out there. In the past few years, various voodoo sects from the Caribbean, transplanted for God only knew what reason, celebrated certain rites in the park woods. Herbie might retrieve just about anything during one of his frenzied romps. Butchered chickens drained of their blood. A squirrel, rat, raccoon, or cat, similarly dealt with.

That particular morning, the day broke sparkling and a little cooler than it had been in the past week or so. Joel had slipped into a ratty old down jacket used primarily for winter chores outdoors at his weekend place in the Cats-kills. Tall and rangy, with a well-clipped beard, he cut a pretty casual figure as he led Herbie through a break in

Broadway traffic and then onto the verge of the big playing fields. He checked quickly for any uniformed city parks personnel, stooped to unsnap Herbie's leash, and let the eager little guy run wild. While the dog ran, the boss sauntered, breathing deep and enjoying the cool of the morning as he contemplated business aspects of the day ahead. Together, the pair made their way toward one of the bridle paths networking through the wooded, rolling landscape ahead. Progress was remarkably similar for the amount of energy expended, Joel's path taking him in a beeline while Herbie's was essentially a mad, moving spiral.

Joel scanned the ground for something to throw, and *bingo*. Poking just the slightest egg-white baldness above a thick tuft of grass sat a forlorn ten-inch softball. As Herbie bounded to and fro, Joel stepped into the weeds to retrieve it and then flung it far afield. Joel had a pretty decent gun on him, sending the ball about seventy yards on the fly. Herbie was after it in a frenzied scurry, all feet, madly wagging tail, and huge flopping ears. When he returned mere seconds later, the softball had been transformed into a slick, slobber-covered sphere. Par for this course. Joel merely gave it another good, gooey flip and wiped the slimed hand on his designated dog-walking pants. Idly, he ambled farther down the bridle path.

Herbie's barking did not at first occur to him as being the least out of character. The little fucker was always barking on his mad morning dashes. In a moment, his mouth would again be full of softball. The barking would then cease only long enough for him to return it for another go-around. Only this time instead of stopping it became more frenzied in pitch. Joel stopped on the path, turned, and whistled. The ball had gone into a stand of oak and sycamore.

"C'mere, Herb! C'mon, fella!"

The frenzied barking continued. Joel reversed field to approach it. Through the dense foliage, he could make out the dog scurrying back and forth, attention riveted on a certain location.

"What you got, boy?" he called, curious now himself.

The path veered off to the right, and from it Joel noticed tire tracks flattening dew-drenched weeds, leading into the stand of trees. There were more tire tracks on the path ahead. It was not unheard of for Park Service trucks to venture along the paths, but why into a dense stand of trees like this? He followed them toward where Herbie stood, frantic barking unabated. What he discovered there on the ground in front of the dog had him grabbing at his stomach and mouth simultaneously. Herbie was in a stand-off with half a dozen good-sized rats. Several were on their hind legs, teeth bared at him, while the others tore hungrily at the corpse of a thickset, stocky man with no clothes and no face. The softball was nestled almost directly where his chin should have been

Feeling ragged, red-eyed Fiona Hassey answered the incessant buzzing at her door to find a furious George Scully confronting her. It was just eight thirty, and Fiona had worked a partial double the night before, filling in for a friend from seven on and then doing her own midnight-to-eight.

"George, I'm dead. I just this minute got into bed."

"I've been trying to reach you for two days. What's going on?"

"A lot of things, George. I needed some time to myself. In case you hadn't noticed, there's been a lot going on the past couple weeks. It's got me really confused."

Scully wasn't sure he was hearing this right. *He* was the one who had paid to have a man killed. *He* was the one who'd been sitting on a volcano of anxiety. Now *she* was confused.

"What in God's name are you taking about? Have you read the papers? The cops killed the suspect in both murders without even getting to question him. They've closed the case. I'm *clear*."

Fiona sighed theatrically, hugging her arms close around herself as she paced the living room carpet in her bare feet.

"That's great, George. But it doesn't change how I've been feeling. All of this has put a heavy strain on our relationship. I've had a lot of time to think about you and Joan and a divorce. I'm not really sure it can work out between us. It's so complicated."

"What?" he asked, more amazed than angry now. "Why do you think I did all this? For myself? No, Fiona. For *us*. You and me, so we could have a life together."

She shook her head. "I'm not sure I want that. George. Not with you or anyone right now. I'm sort of reassessing everything."

"Jesus," Scully groaned. "I don't believe this. I mean, that's it? Just like that? Sorry George. It's been nice knowing you?"

"I want to stay friends, George. I just can't be your lover right now. If I've learned anything in the past couple of weeks, it's how different the two of us are."

Scully's feelings changed so quickly that he risked stripping the gears of his emotional transmission. From confusion to hurt to fury, his face turned from livid to rage-red.

"I don't suppose you've forgotten who's paying for this apartment," he seethed. "When are you planning on finding yourself another place?"

She smiled coolly now. "I don't think you understand, George. We're going to remain friends. That means you still pay my maintenance—or have you forgotten that I'm the only person in the world now who knows that you paid to have Benjamin Crowley killed?''

It took a full couple of seconds for what she said to sink in. Scully stood riveted, unable to speak or move. His hands, dangling at his sides, clenched and released furiously.

"There is also the matter of my expenses, George. It's hard to make it very far on a nurse's salary. You understand that. What do you think would be fair? I was considering something around five thousand a month."

"You dirty blackmailing bitch!" he hissed. "You planned it all along, didn't you? Where the fuck am I supposed to get that kind of money?"

"Considering the story I could tell the police, I figure you'll find a way," she said confidently.

Once Scully was gone, instead of crawling back into her bed, Fiona dug that beautiful new stash of Bolivian flake from the back of her lingerie drawer and laid out half a dozen hefty lines on her silver hand mirror. God, the stuff was wonderful. She was sure now that she'd never known what cocaine really was before she met Reggie DuQuesnay. Just as she'd never known what sex was like with an equal partner, a man whose hunger matched her own. They were a couple of wild beasts in bed together. He was uninhibited and demanding, and at the same time intent on pleasuring her beyond her furthest expectations. After one night with Reggie, she knew she could never go back to George.

Joe Dante had been up for a couple of hours and was getting ready to move on items of interest in the Crowley file when Vic Manley called at eight forty-five. Wendy Lee still slumbered fitfully in his bed. It was a Saturday, the break in her weekly programming schedule. Against a quick temperature drop outside, the radiator was on high, and it was a bit warm in the bedroom. She lay with the covers and sheet kicked off, one knee pulled up toward her chest, sleeping on her side. Dante was relieved to find that fatigue and a fair level of horniness the previous night hadn't blinded him to reality. She still looked gorgeous. Not the kind of voluptuousness Rosa possessed, but a slim, graceful elegance like the lines of a high-performance race car.

"Change of plans," the lieutenant told him. "The Fiftieth up in the North Bronx just found Vinnie Arata with half his head blown off."

"Jesus," Dante grunted. "Where? How?"

"Van Cortlandt Park. Some poor fucker stumbled across the body while walking his dog. The rats were at it, and I don't imagine it was pretty. Shotgun, they say. I'm on my way up there now. Swing by?"

"Sure," Dante told him. "I'll be out front."

It was the eighth of November, but the weather made it feel like at least a month later in winter. A solid cold front down from Canada hadn't met much resistance from the usual warm air mass up from the Gulf. It settled cold and gray over the entire northeast, bringing a chilling wind with it.

Dante and Manley parked on an access road in the middle of the park, unable to get any closer to the scene because of vehicles blocking their path. There were quite a few of them, medical examiner, IAD, Bronx Borough Command, the usual unmarked and prowl cars from the Fiftieth. Before long, Gus Lieberman, the chief of detectives, and the commissioner would also arrive. The murder of a cop, gangland style, made the hierarchy in the job very nervous.

Dante wore a tweed jacket over a bulky wool sweater, and even so, as he stepped out into the high, damp grass, he turned the collar of the jacket up against the chill. He could see his breath up here in the Bronx. The temperature was a good five degrees lower than in the heart of the city, where a thermal layer kept things a little warmer both summer and winter. Together, he and Vic Manley approached the patrolman securing the scene and flashed their shields. The cop pointed back into a thick stand of trees where a line of trampled grass led.

It was dark and gloomy back in the shade of the copse. The trees had begun to yellow but still hadn't dropped many leaves.

"How the hell did someone find him in here?" Dante asked the zone commander for the North Bronx area. They stood huddled together just a few feet from the corpse as flashes illuminated it in grisly detail. "Usually, a thing like this goes undiscovered until someone catches wind."

The inspector, a heavily built Irishman named Marr, shrugged against the chill, taking a sip of the coffee he held in a Styrofoam cup in his hand. "A guy was throwing a baseball to his dog. It rolled in here."

Dante didn't have to ask how the Fiftieth had made such rapid identification. The killer or killers had pinned the dead detective's gold shield directly to the flesh of his chest.

"Nasty stuff," Marr said. "Guy from IAD over there,—Willkie?—tells me you people were set to launch an investigation into this guy. This morning he turns up here."

Vic Manley had drifted over to join them, breaking away from the IAD man.

"A day late and a dollar short," he commented. "Not that anything we were gonna do could have prevented this mess. It looks like we weren't the only ones who suspected Vinnie might be out of control."

"Damn," Marr sighed, "Just yesterday the papers were all calling this guy a hero."

* * *

Gus Lieberman arrived ten minutes later with the chief of detectives, a big, silver-haired Irishman named Hennessey. He was just a year away from retirement, an event that prompted a lot of speculation as to who his successor might be. Gus himself had as good a shot as anybody with his Jewish–Irish Catholic background and distinguished record. Chief Hennessey would have liked him to get the nod, and that was a lot of it, as long as the PC saw eye to eye with him, which was about half the time.

"Looks like you were right on target," the inspector said to Dante as he surveyed the mess that had been Vincent Arata. "Somebody had Crowley done, and Vinnie knew who it was."

"The inspector filled me in on your little theory yesterday," the C of D added. "You sure got a nose for the shit in this world, friend."

"It was just one way of reading the facts," Dante replied. "One of many."

"That's what I mean," Hennessey replied. "Half a dozen guys read facts a half dozen different ways. Fact is, you tend to see 'em straight. Nice work."

"It didn't save Vinnie's life."

The C of D shook his head sadly. "You know what they say about playing with fire, friend. This ain't nobody's fault but his." He nodded toward the body, removing a cigar from his breast pocket and biting the tip off. "What's the prelim from the lab boys?"

"They say he was killed somewhere else and dumped here," Vic Manley told him. "No blood. Just some indistinct tire tracks in the weeds."

"I'd like to check out his house," Dante told him. "Whoever was responsible for this has probably already tossed it, but they may have missed something."

The chief nodded, turning to Manley. "You seen enough here, Lou? Let's have a couple of lab people meet you out there and give the place a good goin' over. I want this other case reopened on the quiet, and I want some quick action on this. The papers get ahold of this, the people responsible are gonna dig a hole so deep we might never find enough dirt to bury them.''

With traffic, it was nearly eleven o'clock before the two men reached Vinnie Arata's home in the Sheepshead Bay section of Brooklyn. They found two men from the central forensics lab waiting for them in a parked city station wagon. The house itself was not very large, just two bedrooms on one level, frame with a fake brick facade, enclosed porch, and a narrow driveway moving back past it on the left to a clapboard garage. The lot was cramped, with a weedy postage stamp of a lawn between the sidewalk and the front stoop. The lieutenant introduced them to the technicians, and all four of the men mounted the steps to the glass porch porch door and found it ajar. The actual front door, six feet farther in, was not only unlocked but hanging half open. The lab guys, in their rubber gloves, approached it carefully, easing it the rest of the way open and inspecting the lockset.

''It wasn't jimmied,'' one of them said.

Dante noticed that there was a Medeco dead-bolt in addition to the normal knob lock. Vinnie Arata knew enough about residential crime not to sit around with his front door unlocked.

''Good Christ!'' the second forensics man breathed, flipping on the lights.

Both Manley and Dante moved up to view the scene. The front room looked like a slaughterhouse after a tornado. There was blood splattered everywhere across overturned furniture, torn-up carpet, emptied book-shelves, broken lamps, and a smashed color television set. The blood was even on the ceiling, along with bits of blackened matter that would most certainly be pieces of Vinnie Arata's face.

"Somebody had to hear this," Dante said.

"You'd be surprised what people don't hear," the whip said.

"No, I wouldn't. But it must've sounded like a cannon going off in a confined space like this."

"How many times you hear explosions every day and not even look out the window?" Manley asked. "We can check with the neighbors, but my guess is that we'll strike out."

Together, the two detectives left the lab men to the living room and pushed on into the rest of the house. Every room they came to was completely wrecked. Cover plates had been removed from electrical outlets and switches.

"Somebody was looking for something," Manley grunted.

"Or making sure something *wasn't* here," Dante added.

"Good point. Looks like they did a pretty thorough job."

Joe shrugged. "If Vinnie was hiding something on them, do you figure he'd make it easy to find?"

"Not likely."

"Then I'm betting there's a decent chance they didn't find it. I think you ought to call in half dozen more of those guys in the living room and have them rip this joint apart."

George Scully felt nothing but numbness. His whole world, always precariously balanced, had fallen in around his ears. He doubted his own sanity now. All he knew was that it had happened. Just when it looked like he might be able to breathe deep and smell the flowers again, he was being blackmailed to the tune of sixty grand a year, not counting apartment maintenance of six hundred and fifty dollars a month. Almost seventy thousand altogether. That was between a fifth and a quarter of what he could expect to make in a usual year. After taxes, nearly half. But what the hell could he do?

All day Saturday, he sat in his Manhattan office and stared at the walls. His mood swung between murderous fury and suicidal despair. He needed a plan. Even with the hatred he felt for Fiona right now, he couldn't convince himself that he should kill her. There'd been too much killing. It solved nothing. He was in deeper now than ever. In fact, she probably had some backup should she fail to survive her avaricious enthusiasm. A letter left with someone to be opened in the event of death. That's how they always did it in the movies.

By late afternoon, George had managed to calm himself enough to focus some semblance of clear thought on the problem. He took stock of who he was and what he had. At this rate, he would never be able to pay the notes on his home and other real estate. If he tried to go on, the specter of Joan finding him out would forever lurk along with the rest of the demons in his closet. He hated Joan anyway, now more than ever. He hated the entire sparkling little Connecticut town with its well-scrubbed, aggressive-tennis-playing wives and spoiled children. He loved medicine but hated the circumstances that could turn him into a pauper for practicing it. He hated Fiona. In fact, he hated his whole sorry existence. He also knew he didn't have the guts to stick a gun in his mouth and end it all.

Escape. That was the only reasonable answer. Fugitive financial hustlers and train robbers had managed it. Living for years under assumed names. Comfortable in some out-of-the-way Third World country where the weather was always warm. Local governments were often willing to look the other way because these fugitives brought badly needed capital into their sagging economies.

George Scully was certainly not wealthy, but he did

have the lackluster offshore fund with four hundred thousand dollars in it. And there was the life insurance policy. He could get at least a hundred and a half out of that . . . and the Porsche. He began to calculate feverishly. By the time he finished digging into the corners, he figured that he could scrape together something in the neighborhood of six hundred and twenty-five thousand dollars. It represented more than a start. Money for getting lost and relocating. Seed money to begin investing in local opportunities. He could do it. He could disappear.

Sixteen

In a matter of half a day, the nature of the investigation into Benjamin Crowley's murder changed again. Instead of getting smaller with scrutiny, the thing continued to mushroom. It was no longer necessary for Joe Dante to be assigned out of squad to pursue a confidential line of inquiry. Now it was back in Lieutenant Vic Manley's lap, with the execution of a publicly praised cop added to it. The attitude from the big building was adamant. They were to climb all over this thing until something caved in. Blanket overtime, extra manpower, the works. There were conferences held in the squad all Saturday afternoon. Inspector Lieberman was involved. IAD was involved. The two teams from the other shift were swung in to take up some of the slack. Dante and Jumbo Richardson were assigned together again to investigate any angles suggested in the Crowley file. Everyone else would exhaustively research Arata's background. Family, friends, every connection or association he ever had on the street. The strategy was to push both ends of the case against the middle in hopes that something would pop from the strain.

* * *

Dante argued for his own involvement in the Crowley end of things. Others, including Lieberman and COD, thought his former narcotics background might help in covering the Arata side of the equation, but Joe believed that the break was going to come from the motive behind the Crowley killing. He'd spent quite a few hours now, poring over the file, including the Thompson and Koehl reports on the man's medical history and the whole malpractice thing. The lawsuit tickled his curiosity. Gus Lieberman respected Dante's hunches when they were that strong. He gave him the green light, encouraging Manley to let him work on it with Jumbo.

"Detail here is kinda sketchy as to why the old guy was suing in the first place," Richardson commented. He and Joe were in the squad room, huddled together across a pair of desks away from ringing phones and foot traffic. "We got these two doctors, Scully and Neisbaum, named along with the hospital. The amount being claimed is two and a half million. Does that sound high or low to you?"

Dante shrugged. "This sort of shit's gotten all out of hand in the past few years. It sounds like a lot of money, but we should find that out. Maybe it's pretty standard."

"Must be someone over at the hospital we can talk to," Jumbo suggested. "Place with liability like that's gotta have legal advice."

Probably a whole department," Dante said. "You want to take a run up there?"

Jumbo glanced at his watch. "If hospital administration's anything like city government, there won't be nobody up there at this hour on a Saturday.

"There isn't going to be anybody anywhere at this hour," Joe agreed. "I didn't realize it was so late." He yawned, threw his pen onto the blotter, and stretched. It was moving on six o'clock, and he'd been at it since early morning without a break. "What do you say we throw in the towel and hit this again first thing Monday. Both of these doctors have attorneys we want to talk to, but first I'd like to find out the particulars on the actual operation, like who's on the hook here. I doubt if anyone is going to want to talk to us on the phone about pending litigation. We're gonna have to get out there and pound the pavement."

Wendy Lee had made the bed before she left. There was a note on it thanking him for not waking her up when he'd had to leave. She couldn't have known that Joe often got called out of bed at all hours and long ago got used to leaving his guests to rise at their leisure. He only asked that they didn't let the cat out.

After stripping off his clothes, he took the shower he hadn't gotten to take that morning. He then dressed in a pullover sweater and Levi's. It felt good to be rid of the weight of his gun and the faint, lingering odor of last night's copulation. The gun reminded him that he'd seen far too much blood in the past couple of weeks. The smell of making love to a woman other than Rosa made him feel inexplicably guilty. And speaking of Rosa, he'd told her he would drive up and spend the night with her, upstate. Wendy's note had been scrawled on the back of Rosa's directions. She must have inadvertently picked up that scrap of paper off his dresser. He stared at the directions now. If he pushed it, it would take him no more than an hour and a half to make it up there. He could relax. Wake up in the country. Maybe split some wood and take a walk. He needed something like that right now. This city and all the crazies were getting him down. When the craziness started to seem normal, he was in trouble. He checked the time. Just a little after seven. It took him ten minutes to throw a few things in a sport duffle and leave extra food for the cat.

Joe almost collided with Wendy Lee as he hurried down the front walk.

"Hey, where are you off to? I was just going to knock on your door and see if you wanted to have dinner or something."

"Can't," he told her. "I'm heading upstate until tomorrow night late."

She looked disappointed. "What's upstate that you can't find right here at home?" she asked.

"Trees." He turned, hurried to the sidewalk, and down the block toward the parking garage.

Cindy Spinell was a compact, athletically lithe investment banker who had shared an apartment with Rosa in Bennington, Vermont, during their junior and senior years in college. She'd since gone on to earn an MBA at the University of Chicago and was currently fighting her way up the corporate ladder of a mid-sized Wall Street firm. Until a little more than a year back, she and Rosa had shared an apartment in the Park Slope section of Brooklyn. Cindy earned enough income as a single New Yorker to afford a modest house tucked away in the rolling farmland of Dutchess County. In the months since moving out of her situation with Dante, Rosa had become a frequent weekend visitor.

This was Dante's first drive up to Cindy's new place. He was surprised to see patches of snow just an hour and a quarter out of town. The growl of the Corvette's engine told him he'd been climbing for some time. There were actual *stars* in the night sky. It struck him as odd that he'd grown up in a place where there simply weren't any. Only on page six of the *Post*.

He spotted a liquor store and pulled in to purchase a couple of bottles of wine. It was late enough that he knew Rosa and Cindy would have finished dinner. In fact, when

Rosa extended the invitation that morning after showing up, after the Chief, to deal with the press at Arata's dump site, Joe told her it was looking like it might be a long day and not to wait on his account. He'd grabbed a burger and fries at a drive-in outside Brewster on Route 22. All he wanted now was a drink and a chance to let his brain freewheel for thirty-six hours. Even in her harried state at having also been called out of bed, Rosa seemed to be in good humor that morning. She hadn't put any pressure on. Just the suggestion that a day out of the city might act as a tonic.

Rosa and Cindy were sitting in front of a fire in a downstairs living room when Dante pulled up the long drive and parked. There was snow everywhere up here, the moon and stars reflecting off it to give the entire surroundings a soft, luminescent glow. Silhouettes of leafless trees stood stark in the gloom, one density of darkness against another.

"Hiya," Cindy greeted him, opening the door and standing just outside the threshold as Dante grabbed his single bag.

He hurried up the path and pecked her lightly on the cheek. "This is a great spot," he said.

"Thanks. Wait until you see it in the light of day."

They got him a glass of red wine and saw him settled. The room was big, with an old-fashioned farmhouse hearth and ten-foot ceilings. A big oriental carpet was stretched across wide plank floors, with a sofa and two chairs facing the fire. Rosa stretched out on the sofa with Dante at her feet.

"Rosa told me about your day," Cindy said. "God, it must have been awful."

"Worse for Vinnie Arata," Dante replied. "But yeah, it was less than considerate the way he brought the entire city down around our ears. It isn't like we weren't already plenty busy.''

"Our phone was ringing off the hook when I left at noon,'' Rosa said. "The chief issued a statement, I passed it out, and then got the hell out of there. Those people are like sharks in a feeding frenzy when something like this hits.''

Dante reached over and took one of her feet into his lap. He played idly with a toe as he sipped wine.

"What's the official line of shit?'' he asked. "Those pricks have gotta hate to backpedal away from a hero-cop story, what with all the negative press we're always getting.''

"Not an easy pill to swallow,'' Rosa allowed. "The chief filled the PC in on your angle, and the big boss doesn't like it one bit. The way I got it, the PC and the mayor went through the roof when they heard about it. Nobody likes having a feather snatched from his cap.''

"Bureaucrats,'' Dante muttered. "And you want to *be* one.''

"Vinnie Arata wasn't a bureaucrat,'' Rosa reminded him.

Joe smiled. "I guess you've got a point there.''

When Cindy finally stretched, yawned, and announced that she was going to bed, neither Rosa nor Dante was particularly tired yet. Joe suggested they take a walk.

It was a bright, knife-edged cold they strolled through, the snow with a frozen layer atop it that crunched beneath their feet. Bundled against the cold, Joe and Rosa made their way down across the back of Cindy's several acres, heading for the edge of a tiny frozen pond.

"I'm glad you came,'' she told him. "I wondered whether you would change your mind.''

"I need it,'' he replied. "Besides, I think I've come to a conclusion about us. Not an answer or anything. Just a sort of interim revelation. It's like a car with engine trouble. You work on it. You don't take it out and push it over a cliff.''

She smiled and looked up at him. ''Would you just hold me a minute?''

He stopped. ''Sure.''

She came into his arms, kissed his cheek, and then stood there, hard up against him and staring across the gleaming ice.

''Listen,'' she said. ''It's so quiet. No ambulances. No squealing tires.''

''It's beautiful,'' he admitted. He lifted her chin then and kissed her full on the mouth. When the image of Wendy standing at his bathroom door with her champagne surfaced, he pushed down hard on it. No one had ever said life wasn't going to be confusing.

The chief administrator of the hospital wanted to be cooperative. He also didn't want to jeopardize his institution's position in regard to the subject litigation. Now that Benjamin Crowley was dead of unrelated causes, he assumed that the suit would be dropped. On the other hand, he had received no verification of that fact. As Dante and Richardson waited patiently in his office, he placed a call to the legal department, requesting that they sit in. It was another twenty minutes before a trim, attractive, gray-haired woman appeared at his door.

''Hello, Fred,'' she said, stepping in. ''These are the two detectives?''

Murcheson, the administrator, stood and shook hands before introducing her. ''Gentlemen, this is Judith Cathcart, our chief counsel. Detectives Dante and Richardson.''

The counselor nodded, took a seat facing them, and straightened her skirt. She smiled in a noncommittal, businesslike way, giving them her full attention. ''Fine. Now what exactly is it that you need to know about the Crowley suit?''

Dante took the ball. "We're not entirely sure ourselves. According to our preliminary investigation, the suit names three co-defendants and a claim of two and a half million dollars. One of the things we'd like to know is how that money would break out if a judgment was rendered in the plaintiff's favor.''

"Break out?" she asked, purposely forcing him to be more specific.

Dante shrugged. "In other words, would the liability be distributed equally or is one particular party on the hook for the bulk of it?''

The cards were on the table. Judith Cathcart glanced at Murcheson for an instant. She then shook her head as she cleared her throat. "This isn't the answer you want, officer, but let me put it this way. This hospital does not make a policy of discussing the personal situations of its medical staff. You have several avenues of inquiry there. You could address the various insurance carriers. We would be happy to provide you with that information. Or you could question the principals themselves. I *can* tell you that this institution has concluded that its exposure is minimal in this particular instance. Our insurance carrier concurs in that assessment.''

Dante nodded. "Fine. Maybe you can tell me how much malpractice insurance you require doctors to carry in order to practice here.''

"One million dollars. That is the maximum any carrier will underwrite at the present time. We are lobbying for legislation which would force raising that ceiling, in conjunction with the AMA.''

"So a million is as much as any individual can be insured for?" Joe asked.

"That's correct.''

"What happens if an award is made against a doctor for more than that amount?"

Again, the lawyer shot a glance at Murcheson. "Again, without meaning to be difficult, I suggest you speak to a specific physician's attorney if there are particular circumstances."

Dante realized that he wasn't going to get much more out of this bird. She was covering the hospital's collective ass, and he couldn't blame her. They probably weren't at risk here, and she saw no reason to jeopardize that status by shooting her mouth off about matters that were beyond her immediate concern.

"I'd appreciate it if you could get us those names," he told her. "And thanks for your time."

"Might I ask what this is in reference to?" the woman asked. "I understand that the Crowley murder had been solved."

"We're in the same jam you are, ma'am," Joe told her. "We've all got things we're free to talk about and things we're not. We would appreciate it if both you people would keep this conversation confidential."

"Let's see," Jumbo mused, checking the list of names in his notebook. "I say we start off on the other side of the legal fence. Hit the team that was bringing the suit. See what they were pursuing."

The two men were in an unmarked Plymouth outside the hospital on First Avenue. A little warm moist air had managed to creep up from the Gulf, colliding with the cold air mass and bringing a steady drizzle that didn't quite want to be called rain. The temperature was up a couple of notches from the chilly low of Saturday morning, but it was by no means warm.

"Good idea," Dante agreed. "Where to?"

"Not far. Holcroft-Hornsby on 51st and Madison."

Dante started the car and swung it out into traffic, heading north to the high-rent lair of this prestigious firm.

"Cool customer, that Cathcart," Jumbo commented.

"Just doing her job," Joe said. "Gotta be *vultures* circling a place like that. By the hundreds."

Crowley's representation in the two-million-dollar suit was Barrington E. Hornsby himself. There may have been only two names on the letter-head, but there were another thirty partners in fine print, and the law firm occupied a full eight floors of a major midtown office tower. Getting to see Barry Hornsby without an engraved invitation was something the whole organization seemed bent on preventing. When Dante and Jumbo were first dismissed out of hand with the information that the big man was both busy and absolutely not to be disturbed, they had to get a little heavy. The receptionist called the security chief, who called Hornsby's executive secretary, who called the man himself. By the time they reached his massive corner office on the forty-sixth floor, he was grumbling irritably in his best captain-of-industry peeve.

"I'll have you two know that I'm having a call placed to the commissioner at this moment," he growled.

"We wish you would, sir," Jumbo rumbled. "He'd be very interested to know we're hard at it in our investigation into the slaying of a police officer. It's right at the top of his list this morning."

Hornsby shot him a disturbed glance. "Slain policeman? I beg your pardon?"

"Take it easy, sir." Dante moved to put him at ease. "Please. We just want a few minutes of your time. We'd like to ask you some questions about a malpractice suit you filed on behalf of Benjamin Crowley against his hospital and two attending physicians."

Hornsby looked confused. "What does that have to do

238

with a dead cop? Crowley's dead. Killed by that red-haired punk you people shot downtown.''

"We have reason to believe the two circumstances may be related, sir. You'll have to trust that we know how.''

Hornsby glanced at his watch. "I've got a lunch meeting in fifteen minutes. What would you like to know?''

"The attorney for the hospital tells us that they had only minimal liability in the case. Is that your assessment as well?''

Hornsby nodded. "I suppose it's all academic now, but yes. The hospital *and* Neisbaum. They were named in the suit just to cover any contingencies that might have arisen later, anything the preliminary findings might have overlooked. It was Dr. Scully, the neurosurgeon, whom we were directly accusing of negligence.''

"Why?'' Dante pressed. "What made his position different?''

"He was unavailable when Benjamin Crowley almost died in post-op. They couldn't raise him on his paging device. In fact, he left the hospital without briefing the neurosurgical resident on the status of his patient. It's all in the record.''

"Nothing else has come up in your subsequent investigation?''

Hornsby shook his head. "Negative. We're very thorough. The only real change in status was a couple of expert opinions we were able to obtain from two of Scully's colleagues here on the East Coast. Very eminent in the field.''

"How would that affect things?'' Joe asked, his interest piqued.

Hornsby smiled, albeit tightly, for the first time. "I have no conclusive evidence of the fact, but experience leads me to believe that the carrier was probably on the verge of offering some sort of settlement. If I were their counsel, that is what I would have recommended.''

''Would you have gone for it?''

''That's purely speculation, Detective. Just between you and me, though, it would have had to be a very substantial offer.''

The claims agent at Colonial Mutual Insurance on William Street in lower Manhattan referred Dante and Richardson directly to the attorney retained by the carrier to handle Dr. George Scully's case. He was a Paul Thatcher of Weingarten, Shoop, Thatcher, & Loeb on nearby John Street. Thatcher was in a meeting when they arrived, and they agreed to wait until he was finished. They wanted him to be as receptive as possible.

The offices of this law firm were elegantly appointed but not nearly as impressive as those presided over by Barrington Hornsby. Wealth had it's advantages;—probably the reason why people indicted on securities fraud and the like seldom went to jail. Paul Thatcher had a nice thing going; Barry Hornsby had an empire.

The object of this round of questioning proved short, rotund, and almost completely bald. He wore an elegantly tailored gray wool flannel suit, and smoked a big cigar that looked hand-rolled.

''What can I do for you gentlemen?'' Thatcher asked when they were seated. ''I'm on sort of a tight schedule, so I hope you don't mind if we have to make this brief.''

''Everyone seems to be on a tight schedule today, Mr. Thatcher,'' Jumbo said, forcing a smile edged in irritation. ''I'm afraid we'll have to make it as long as it takes.'' He nodded to Dante, initiating the old good guy, bad guy routine.

Dante was a little more pleasant. ''We're looking into the murder of a Benjamin Crowley, sir. It's our understanding that you represented the Colonial Mutual Insurance Company in defending a Dr. George Scully against a malpractice suit brought by Benjamin Crowley.''

Thatcher frowned for just a moment and then nodded. ''That's correct. Represent. Present tense. The suit has not been withdrawn.''

''Fine,'' Dante agreed. ''Our information also tells us that Dr. Scully was insured for the maximum of one million dollars and that the claim against him is for two and a half.''

''Him and two other parties,'' Thatcher said.

''But that the two other parties are understood to have limited liability, correct?''

Thatcher frowned once more. ''I'm not at liberty to disclose the amount of liability any party is exposed for.''

Dante shrugged. ''Whatever. We believe our information to be accurate. There is also some speculation in other circles that Colonial Mutual was prepared to offer the plaintiff a cash settlement, that there has been damaging expert testimony, and that fighting the suit in court would be more or less futile.''

Thatcher stood up abruptly. ''I'm sorry, gentlemen, I'm afraid that's all I am going to say, off the record. There is a certain confidentiality in this sort of situation that I am not prepared to violate. If you wish to have any further questions put to me, you'll have to do it through the district attorney, under oath.''

Dante and Richardson didn't have much choice but to back off at that juncture. On the other had, neither felt that further questioning was necessary. Through a wall of double-talk and obstinance, Paul Thatcher had answered the only important question. Scully was indeed the liable party, and, yes, they'd been about to offer settlement.

Milt Carpfinger was tied up with trading until lunch and

only got back to George Scully after his third phone call. Scully was in his office, becoming more agitated by the minute, when Amy poked her head in the door.

"It's Mr. Carpfinger on two, Doctor."

Scully nodded and reached for the receiver, thought better of it, and stood to close his office door first.

"Milt. I thought you'd forgotten me."

"I know, George, buddy. Been insane down here this morning. First of the week and oil's going up and down like a yo-yo again. What can I do for you?"

"It's that offshore fund," Scully said evasively. "I've decided I want you to cash me out of it. And rescue what you can out of Biotechnics."

"Jesus, George. I'd have to advise against either one of those moves. There's a lot of good talk about the fund right now. It's ready to do maybe thirty-five percent in the next year. Everything's falling into line. These things take time."

"Sell it, Milt. Something's come up. I need cash. Fast. I've got a small account in Nassau. Rainy-day money. I want you to transfer the proceeds into it."

Against Carpfinger's further protestations, Scully read him the account and telex numbers of the Caribbean bank. Earlier, he'd done the same thing with his insurance agent, liquidating the life policy.

"George, what's going on? Maybe I can help swing something for you," Milt said. "You need a bridge loan? Done. This is terrible timing. Biotechnics has other projects on the board. In another year or two, they'll be back on their feet. You're writing seven hundred and fifty thousand off as a total loss. Are you nuts?"

"No loans," Scully told him. "Just take my word for it, Milt. I've got no choice. And all of this is on the absolute quiet. Got it?"

* * *

The coffee shop on lower Broadway was jam-packed and raucous with the press of working stiffs on lunch break. The cheeseburgers Joe and Jumbo ordered were overdone. The buns were as soggy with grease as the fries.

"Are you starting to think what I'm starting to think?" Dante asked, setting his root beer down and wiping his mouth.

"Depends on what you're starting to think," Jumbo said. "Why don't you elaborate?"

"We got a murder we suspect is a copycat killing and too close on its heels for comfort, a cop who we think was dirty and got his shit blown away because of it. Somebody who knew an awful lot about the Wembley thing had something to do with the Crowley thing. Vinnie whacks Wiems and shuts *that* door. Somebody whacks Vinnie and shuts *another* door. Now we got this fat-cat neurosurgeon who was being hung out to dry for what's looking like more than a million bucks. If it were me, it might be a serious temptation to take care of my problem before I left my fate in the hands of that bald fucker with the cigar and the court system."

Jumbo nodded. "I'm with you so far—but who? Scully? I've got my doubts about whether a man like that would walk into a bungalow in Sheepshead Bay, blow a policeman's face off with a shotgun, pin his badge to his chest, and dump him at the other end of the city."

"Somebody Vinnie was working for, then," Joe ventured. "Somebody who might get nervous when our hero cop goes gunning prime suspects down in the street before we can question them. Somebody who's not quite as stupid as Vinnie Arata was."

"What do you think our next move ought to be?" Jumbo wondered. "We've got two directions I can see. Lean directly on this Scully or see if we can pick the brain of the other doctor. I still don't quite understand what went down that night. Why it was Scully's fault that Crowley ended up paralyzed.''

Dante didn't see the harm in talking to the ear, nose, and throat man, Neisbaum, first.

''He's a colleague,'' Jumbo added. ''Maybe he knows something that might shed a little light. I'd love to have some way to get a hook into Scully. If he's our fish, that would make it a lot easier to land him.''

Seventeen

Dr. Philip Neisbaum was taken aback when the two detectives walked into his Park Avenue office and showed him their shields. George had called that morning to cancel their weekly golf game, leaving him some time to catch up on his reading and recover his breath. It was a busy time of year for him, with hayfever running high through autumn until the first hard frost. All morning, his waiting room was full of sniffling, ill-tempered patients expecting miracles. He hadn't even gone out for lunch, preferring the sanctuary of a locked door and a request to his receptionist to hold all his calls.

"We're sorry to disturb you, Doctor," Dante said. "It's a matter of some importance."

Neisbaum's first reaction was to presume something had happened at home. His face lost a little color and he sat up a bit straighter.

"Take it easy, sir," Jumbo told him. "There's nothing wrong. We just want to ask you some questions about a malpractice case you were involved in."

Neisbaum was more confused than ever now. "The police? In a malpractice case?"

"One that won't likely ever come to trial," Dante said. "The Benjamin Crowley suit. We understand that you were one of the two attending physicians. We're wondering if you could tell us what happened."

The doctor shook his head, reluctant now. "I'm not sure I should be saying anything about that. My attorney advised me not to. It looks like I'm pretty much in the clear, one way or the other. I'd like to keep it that way."

"Let's try a different angle then. How well do you know Dr. George Scully?"

The question seemed to hit Neisbaum from the blind side. He blinked hard and shook his head. "The man's an excellent surgeon. One of the best."

"Have you known him long?"

"Sure. We were both residents at University Hospital together. I've known George for almost fifteen years."

"Still friendly?"

"I don't understand what you're getting at. What does this have to do with the Crowley case?"

"Look, Doc, I'm gonna level with you," Dante said. "We aren't sure if it has anything to do with it—or if *you* have anything to do with it for that matter. Both of you guys had a malpractice suit pending, him in deeper than you. What we get from his insurance carrier says they were ready to offer settlement. They think there's reasonable evidence to suggest negligence."

"That's bullshit," Neisbaum said defensively. "They're a pack of ambulance-chasing bastards. All of them. The old man popped a blood vessel. Sure, it was a direct result of surgery, but whether they'd found George in five minutes or five days, the result would have been the same."

"The insurance company was going to settle," Dante said evenly. "Yes or no?"

Neisbaum's shoulders sagged. "That's what I gather," he admitted. "They're mostly too scared to fight this sort of thing head-on. Technically, George was supposed to be within immediate reach.''

"And you?'' Jumbo jumped in. "Where were you supposed to be, doctor?''

"I was just assisting. Crowley was my patient. I made the initial diagnosis. The surgery was George's show.''

"What happened to him. Where was he?'' Jumbo pressed.

"He forgot to switch on his beeper. It happens. He was within a hundred yards of the post-op recovery area.''

"He was in the hospital?'' Jumbo asked, skepticism in his voice.

"Not exactly.''

"Where then?''

"I'm not at liberty to say. You ought to ask him that yourselves. What's with this, anyway? I thought the Crowley case was closed. You people got the guy who did it.''

Dante looked at Richardson.

The fat man shook his head. "You know what obstruction of justice is, Doctor?'' Jumbo asked seriously. "We're in the middle of a confidential investigation here. There are irregularities. For all we know, you might be involved yourself. How do we find out? We ask questions and you answer them. If you don't, we wonder why. It makes us suspicious as hell. If nobody here done nothing wrong, what is it all you fellas got to hide?''

Neisbaum looked a little uncomfortable for the first time. "I think maybe I should have counsel here.''

"Why?'' Jumbo asked. "You done something wrong?''

"No!''

"Then relax, man. We're askin' a couple questions about your colleague, Dr. Scully. You tell us you and him been buddies since way back. Fine. I bet you two talk about things, then, right? We're running some checks of our own. Financial and that sort of thing. Seein' if your buddy could really afford to handle the sort of loss he was facing. From you we're lookin' for what we call substantiation.''

The sincerity lacing the fat man's address as he focused those big, bloodhound eyes on the uncomfortably shifting doctor had Dante suppressing a grin of admiration. He took over.

"Anything that you can tell us, Doc. We don't want to drag you or your attorney into this. It'd just get uglier all around than it has to be. We're interested in what you can tell us about George Scully. For instance, is there reason to suspect that he might have been in over his head somewhere?''

Neisbaum shifted nervously in his chair. He wanted off the hot seat. "Listen," he said. "Crowley's blood pressure was elevated slightly in post-op. Nothing radical but certainly something to be concerned about. It was late. I had a long drive home, and George was spending the night in the city. He told me to go on ahead, that he'd hang around to make sure the patient was stable.''

"Is that standard?'' Dante asked.

"Absolutely,'' Neisbaum replied. "One neurosurgical resident was going off duty and another was coming on. Technically, he and George should have done a consult before George left the building. But George wasn't going far. He figured the staff could find him just as quickly as the resident if something came up.''

"Just exactly where was it he was going?'' Jumbo pressed.

Neisbaum shrugged. "His office is directly across First Avenue. No more than a hundred yards away.'' He swallowed nervously.

Dante caught it. "What is it that you're *not* telling us, Doctor? If you need time to think about it, maybe we can take you back to the station and you can wait for your lawyer there.''

Neisbaum glanced at his watch, anger flashing in his eyes. "You people are incredible," he groused. "Okay, he has a fucklet stashed upstairs. One of the recovery nurses. He was with her when Crowley had the bleed."

Jumbo nodded with satisfaction. "Now we're gettin' somewhere. Your buddy's gettin' his end off and the hospital can't reach him. He's clearly at fault then, and they're gonna crucify him. So tell us, Doctor, *was* he in over his head? *Could* he afford to drop a million bucks?"

"No," Neisbaum said weakly, shaking his head. "George is in financial trouble right now." He went on to describe Scully's situation, the floodgates opening. He told them about Biotechnics, the forged signature on the house note.

"So the man's in deep shit," Jumbo concluded.

"That's about the size of it. The bioengineering thing really hurt him. I was amazed when he told me. I'd been under the impression George was a wealthy man. Everything is on paper. He's leveraged to the eyeballs." The doctor took a deep breath and then let it out, cheeks bulging and face red with chagrin.

"Lately he hasn't been the same George. Not the one I've played golf with for the past ten years. Jesus, taking up with an airhead like Fiona Hassey. Acting like an eighteen-year-old with a permanent hard-on. Hell, he's even promised her he'll get a divorce."

Dante nodded, scribbling the nurse's name in his notebook. "Only he can't," he said. "Because in executing a separation agreement, his wife would find out about the forged signature on the second mortgage, right?"

Neisbaum shrugged. "That's about the size of it. He could afford to play both ends against the middle while he tried to get his finances back together. Until this malpractice thing, that is."

"Other than acting like a teenager, have you noticed anything else odd about his behavior?" Dante asked.

"Everything," Neisbaum replied. "He about bit my head off the other day. Over nothing. He has these mood swings—seems distracted all the time. Just this morning he canceled our weekly golf game for the first time in almost six years."

"Any particular reason?" Joe asked.

"Just that he had some things he had to take care of."

Dante glanced at his watch. It was just after three in the afternoon. "Do you have an address for the nurse?"

"Directly across the street from the hospital's front door," Neisbaum told him. "You'll see his name on a brass plate just to the left of the awning. She's in an apartment George bought when the building went co-op. I think it's on the fifth floor."

The neatly uniformed brunette at the rostrum next to the boarding gate announced that they would begin by boarding first-class passengers as well as women with small children and any people in need of special assistance. The boarding area of British Caledonia's Flight Seven from John F. Kennedy Airport to London's Heathrow was crowded with travelers. George Scully glanced impatiently at a clock on the wall. It was 3:20 P.M. He'd been at the airport since one thirty, on the run and scrambling madly all morning. Still, he'd done it. The Porsche dealer on Eleventh Avenue had promised the previous day to have him a check by noon. Even after waiting for Milt Carpfinger's call until half past and then rushing across town, it still hadn't been ready. With running to the bank to cash it and the subsequent chain of approvals, he'd almost missed the two-hour pre-boarding cutoff imposed on all international flights. This new security beef-up was a true nuisance.

The Porsche people saw him coming. With time on his hands and an ad in the Connecticut paper, he might have gotten as much as thirty-five thousand for the late-model

928. As it was, the thieves forced him to settle for twenty, take it or leave it. After paying for his reservation with cash in order to avoid easy tracing through credit records, he was left with nineteen thousand, five hundred dollars. More than enough to take him from London to Madrid to Paris and on to Nassau for an overnight. Buenos Aires was rumored to be nice this time of year. It was spring there. He would find someone to get him a different passport, maybe spend the summer there and then make a more permanent move. Already, the prospect of it all seemed less threatening and more like an adventure. A new life. Maybe even to practice medicine again someday. With the money he had, in the Third World, there could be other women like Fiona. Exotic beauties who would worship him. God, he would love to see the look on Joanie's face when she found out he'd skipped town without a trace. Fuck her. Fuck them all.

By five o'clock, when it was time for them to think about getting back downtown and signing out, Dante and Jumbo still couldn't find Doctor George Scully. They'd made calls to his home, office, and the hospital. They checked with the doorman of the apartment building across the street from the hospital on First Avenue to learn that the nurse had just left for work and that the doctor was not upstairs. The hospital confirmed that Fiona Hassey was on duty in the recovery room on the sixth floor. She would be off at midnight and return again for the same shift the next afternoon.

"Where the hell is he?" Jumbo asked. He was slouched against the passenger door of the Plymouth as Dante piloted them through sluggish rush-hour traffic, moving south toward the Village.

"Tough to guess," Dante said. "Our four-to-midnight boys could give his place up in Ridgefield a call again about ten and leave word that we'd like him to come in for questioning tomorrow morning. If that doesn't do it, I'd say this nurse is our next-best bet. Once the wife finds out about his financial hocus-pocus, she'll be hostile as hell.''

Lieutenant Vic Manley was very interested in the progress report Dante and Richardson delivered at the end of their tour. In one day they'd covered a lot of ground, making progress at each stop along the way. In counterpoint, the investigation into Vinnie Arata's possible connection to the underworld was hurrying nowhere fast.

"This guy looks pure as the driven snow." Manley grumbled. He looked tired, the muscles in his face sagging and bags heavy under his eyes. The big building had to be putting a lot of pressure on him with this one. Even if a man proved dirty, they didn't like people running free who thought it was okay to murder policemen. "The family, parish priest, pals in the job, everybody thought he was a wonderful guy.''

"Who's shittin' who?'' Jumbo grumbled.

"Vinnie was one of those guys who would stand at a bar, tell you how he fooled a hooker into sucking his dick for free, and buy you a drink. Other guys who ain't gettin' much either eat that shit up. He was a Brooklyn-style good-old-boy.'' Manley rubbed his face with his open hands, working the heels into his eye sockets. "Another problem with people he knew in the job is the whole idea of talkin' shit about a dead cop who can't defend himself. There's guys who know stuff. Seen shit go down over the years. But they ain't talkin'. Some of 'em ain't all that lily-white themselves. You gotta suspect people who *like* a guy like that.''

"How about his informants?'' Dante asked. "He must have had a string of them while he was working narcotics.''

"Lost in the cracks mostly, except a dude named Pinky

Cole. Been in the joint in Ossining for the past year and a half. He had to know some people that Vinnie musta met. I'm takin' a drive up there in the A.M. to pick his brain. Not a particularly charming character. No guarantee he'll do more than spit in my face.''

''You look like you could use a beer, Vic,'' Dante told him. He turned to Jumbo. ''How about it, big guy? You game?''

Both Manley and Richardson shook their heads.

''Not tonight,'' the whip begged off. ''I'm dead on my feet as it is. About all I'm good for is crawling into the sack.''

Jumbo had to get home and make sure no homicide had occurred since he left that morning. The change of the guard had happened after a week's respite. Now *his* mother was in from Detroit. She was making the old lady crazy with suggestions on how a household ought to be run.

''By this time of night it's bare knuckles, no holds barred,'' he told them. ''Thank God she's goin' to my sister's tomorrow. The minute I walk in the door, the both of them start insisting I choose sides.''

There was a Monday-night game on the tube, but Dante wasn't much interested in the match-up. Hell, a little more than a week ago, the Mets had won the god-damn World Series, and the excitement of *that* had passed him by in his preoccupied fog. He considered stopping by the video joint and renting a tape, but his feet took him wandering instead. Along the way, he noticed through the gloom that the trees were finally beginning to shed their leaves in earnest. They always took several weeks longer to fall in the city than they did just twenty miles upstate. Something about that extra five degrees of trapped warmth, he supposed.

Sometimes it felt good to just stroll. Getting out of the city for a day had only served to focus him on how wound up he'd let himself get. He knew he needed to pay more attention to it, to make the actual effort to relax. There were times he could set aside, like now. He had the luxury of not having to do a commute into the city every day. Sure, it was space and trees and the wife and kids, but you ended up spending half your life at the wheel of a car. Living in the city, he would drop by someplace for a beer, do his grocery shopping, hit the liquor store—all within a five-minute walk of his place. This evening he took his time, dawdling at D'Agostino to shoot the shit with a schoolteacher from Bank Street who'd been a mugging victim a few years back. They'd remained acquaintances, a couple of straight bachelors in the Village. Once in a while they'd have a burger at the Bistro. Compare notes. Maybe watch a game. They walked back up Bank to West 4th, where they parted company, Dante continuing on east.

Rosa was sitting in her parked car out front when he arrived home. They hadn't made any arrangement, and it was in surprise that he approached to tap on the glass, distracting her from the Sunday *Times Magazine*.

"There you are," she said, running down the window. "I called the squad and they said you left half an hour ago."

"One thing led to another," he confessed. "To what do I owe the honor?"

Rosa smiled. "I wanted to see if I could catch you and con you into having dinner with me."

Dante hefted his bag of groceries. "Penne with putanesca sauce. A tossed salad?" he asked. "I've got a nice bottle of Chardonnay."

"You're sure you didn't have any other plans?" she asked. "This was strictly spur of the moment."

While she drove off to circle the block and drop her Supra in front of the church on 11th Street, Joe waited,

leaning against the cast-iron fence in front of his building.
A cab pulled up and Wendy Lee climbed out.

"Fancy meeting you here," she said, beaming him a
broad smile. "I left a message on your answering machine,
inviting you for dinner. Accept?"

Dante glanced quickly toward the corner. No sign of
Rosa. "Can't," he apologized. "Made other plans."

She looked instantly disappointed. "Oh. What's a girl
got to do to wedge herself into your busy schedule? Take a
number?"

"It isn't all *that* busy. The pressure's been on the past
couple of weeks because of the big murder case I've been
working. Lots of odd hours. It isn't always like this."

"Maybe another night this week?" she asked. "Tomorrow?"

Joe nodded. He also spotted Rosa rounding the corner at
the periphery of his vision, coming their way. "Sure. I'd
love to."

"Drinks first? Around seven?"

"Sure. That would be great."

Rosa approached before Dante could break it off and get
Wendy on her way.

"Rosa Losada," he said. "Meet the new upstairs neighbor. Wendy Lee. She's just across the hall from Becky."

Rosa nodded and smiled. "The entertainment show at
five o'clock. I've seen you. It's much better since you've
been on."

"Becky's spoken of you," Wendy said, extending a
hand. "You don't look much like a detective—and I mean
that as a compliment."

"Thanks," Rosa replied. "How do you like it so far?
The building and the neighborhood?"

"It's sure a lot different than L.A. But everyone's been
very friendly. They're making me feel right at home." She
glanced at her watch. "Listen, I'd better be running. It's

255

nice to be able to put a face with a name. I suppose I'll see you around."

"She seems nice," Rosa said when Wendy was out of hearing. "*And,* she's gorgeous."

A heavy bead of sweat rolled down Dante's back, tickling his spine. He ushered Rosa in the front door, breathing again in relief.

"I'll bet she doesn't know all that many people in the city," Rosa continued. "Maybe we ought to invite her down for a drink or maybe coffee after dinner."

"We will," Joe told her, his deodorant starting to break down. He carried the groceries into the kitchen. "But not tonight, huh? It's been a long day. I'd rather just spend the evening with you."

She wandered into the kitchen behind him. "Are you sure you don't mind me just dropping in like this? I mean, if you're tired . . ."

Dante whirled to face her, too quickly. "No. I'm fine, really. It's just that I'd like to have a relaxing evening, just the two of us. We'll invite Wendy another time, all right?"

It was much later, with the two of them relaxing in bed after making love, that Rosa turned her head and confronted him. "How long have you two been sleeping together?" she asked.

"What?" Dante shot back.

"You and Wendy. She left her diaphragm cream in the bathroom cabinet."

"Jesus." He swallowed hard. "How did you know it was her?"

"An educated guess. There was something about her body attitude when I first spotted you together on the street, like she owned a piece of your space."

Dante stared at the ceiling. "It isn't a question of how long. Just once, actually."

She rolled over onto her side and propped her head up on one elbow. "New thing?"

"Friday."

"Want to talk about it?"

He snorted. "Do you?"

A short silence intervened as Rosa gathered her thoughts.

"I was the one who moved out, Dante. I can't very well expect to dictate the terms of your personal life. On the other hand, I don't enjoy having other women rubbed in my face."

"That shit in the medicine cabinet was none of my doing," he retorted. "I sure as hell wouldn't have left it there if I'd seen it first."

"Just don't play games with me, Joe," she said quietly. "It's one thing I'm proud of about us. The cards have always been on the table. I don't want that to change."

Dante drifted off to sleep feeling like absolute shit.

Joe Dante and Jumbo Richardson hit the trail just after signing in Tuesday morning. The nurse girlfriend of George Scully would have gotten off her previous night's shift at midnight. They wanted to catch her before she had a chance to leave for the day, and that put them in front of her building at nine A.M. To the entire City's surprise, the weather world that morning was experiencing a return to summer. A big, balmy low pressure system had drifted into the area overnight, carrying warm air from the Gulf. Without a high to fight it, there wasn't a cloud in the sky, and the day sparkled. Both detectives were overdressed. They found themselves shedding pullover sweaters in the car before locking up and approaching the doorman of the nurse's building. After being shown ID, the man confirmed that Fiona Hassey was indeed home. They asked him not to buzz her, preferring to make the approach unannounced. In their experience, mistresses had a way of getting very nervous very quickly. No sense giving her a chance to get all worked up before they had the opportunity to ask an opening question or two.

Fiona answered the door. Statuesque at five foot eight or nine, the woman had straight blond hair, ice-blue eyes, and a face that was all chiseled angles and cheekbones. She wore a fitted peignoir that left little to the imagination and a scowl.

"What the hell is this?" Fiona Hassey demanded. "You're not from the building."

"We're police, ma'am," Jumbo told her. "I'm Detective Richardson and this is Detective Dante."

She stiffened involuntarily at the first mention of the law.

"It's nine o'clock in the morning, and I don't get off work until after midnight, gentlemen. Are you sure you have the correct apartment, and if so, can you come back later?"

"If you're Fiona Hassey, we're sure, ma'am," Jumbo replied. "And no, we're sorry, but we need to talk to you now. May we come in?"

She demanded to see their identification and then stood back, allowing them to enter. "You have to excuse me while I get a robe," she said. "Sit down."

As the woman disappeared into the bedroom, Dante and Jumbo studied her amazing backside. They took seats on the sofa. Dante grinned at Jumbo and Jumbo rolled his eyes. She was gone longer than it should take to slip into a robe, and in the interim, Joe was sure he heard her clear her sinuses in a manner more characteristic of drug ingestion than *con*gestion.

"So," she asked, emerging in an expensive, floor-length royal blue terry robe. "What is it that I can do for you gentlemen?"

Dante observed that while the redness persisted in her eyes, that telltale eyelid puffiness of recent sleep was all but gone. Her fingers and bare toes moved nervously. Her jaw muscles were tighter than they'd been. Nine A.M. The woman had a little nose habit.

258

"We'd like to ask you a few questions," Jumbo told her.

She nodded, her attention more on Dante than on the big black man. Joe took the ball, laying the best understanding look he had on her.

"We know this sort of thing can be . . . ah . . . delicate, Miss Hassey. But we have information that you and a George Scully are good friends. Is that correct?"

Again, that momentary and involuntary tightness. "Friends?" she asked, a coolness in her voice. "We've gone out a few times, if that's what you mean. Is George in some sort of trouble?"

"We're trying to determine that," Dante replied. "Just 'gone out'? Isn't it true that George Scully owns this apartment and is planning to divorce his present wife in order to marry you?"

Fiona Hassey's eyes flashed. "Who told you that?"

"We try to protect confidentiality," he told her.

"It's crap," Fiona said flatly. "Yes, Scully does own this apartment. I *rent* it from him. The rest of it's a lie. Ask him yourself. He was kind enough to help me out when he heard I was looking for a place."

Dante looked around the room. It was big for a Manhattan apartment. The living room was half again as big as his own and expensively furnished. From the glimpse he'd gotten of the bedroom in passing, it also appeared quite large. There was a dining room. This was *nice*

"He must be a pretty generous guy," Dante observed. "What's a place like this run? Two grand? Maybe more? On a nurse's salary, no less."

Joe and Jumbo watched as the woman became very theatrical. Indignation punctuated by a fluttering of hands. A sigh of resignation. A shrug of surrender.

"All right," she admitted. "George and I had an affair. Once. A long time ago. He felt badly. Said he felt like he led me on. My rent here just covers the maintenance. It was sort of a gift from him. A consolation prize.''

''Very generous,'' Joe commented. ''Had you heard anything about Dr. Scully being in any sort of financial trouble?''

This time it was only a blink. ''I can't imagine. I have a quite contrary impression. George is pretty well off, I believe. This is only one of half a dozen apartments he owns in the city. It must be worth three hundred thousand at least in today's market.''

''Then you won't mind if we *do* confirm what you've told us with the doctor, do you?''

''Certainly, I mind. What was between George and me was in the past. His wife Joan never knew. I would be very upset if any of this got out now.''

''We'll be discreet.''

''Do you mind my asking what all this is in connection with?''

''Yeah,'' Dante said. ''We mind. If it's like you say and you broke it off with George ages ago, then we're mistaken. It couldn't have anything to do with you. Thanks for your time, and both Detective Richardson and I apologize for getting you out of bed.''

''It'll be a while before she gets back to sleep,'' Jumbo commented once they reached the street.

''You heard it too, huh?''

''Heard it. Saw it. Musta been pretty good blow. She was jacked to the tits in no time.''

''And what a pair of tits to be jacked to.''

''You *noticed*.'' Richardson grinned. ''What's she up to, Dante? You figure it?''

Joe shrugged. ''Real hard to say. But I know one thing— whatever it is, us showing up made her jumpy as hell. I want to talk to this Scully character, but right now it might pay to cool our heels in the car for twenty minutes and see if the ants in her pants make her dance.''

Jumbo shot him a conspiratorial grin. They climbed back into the Plymouth. As they were splitting the driving every other half shift, and it was the big man's turn at the wheel. He started the car and rolled half a block up the street to park next to a hydrant. After adjusting their side view mirrors, they settled back to wait.

And not long. Within five minutes, the nurse exploded from the starting gate, hailed a passing cab, and headed uptown. Jumbo followed about three cars back as the taxi rounded the block and then took Park Avenue all the way north to where it was Park Avenue in name only.

"Spanish Harlem?" Jumbo asked.

"Right about now, anything could happen in this case and it wouldn't surprise me," Dante said.

"Up in this neck of the jungle, anything *could*."

"That's what I like about this job."

"Oh yeah. Me too." Jumbo rolled his eyes.

At 110th Street, the cab veered left across the top of the park and then jogged north once more at Lenox Avenue. At 129th Street, it turned left, pulling to the curb about three buildings in. They watched as Fiona hopped out and hurried into a building on the south side of the street.

"Feel like checking to see if there's anything interesting on the mailboxes?" Dante asked.

Jumbo shrugged. "*You* might look a little conspicuous, white man."

After parking, Jumbo climbed out onto the sidewalk. "Make sure you keep the windows rolled up and lock all the doors."

"Fuck off."

Dante watched as his partner ambled nonchalantly toward the lobby of the building into which Fiona had disappeared. For a guy well over two hundred and fifty pounds, he was amazingly light on his feet, like a young Jackie Gleason. Joe had decided some time back that he liked working with Richardson because he was one of the rare naturals. He was smart, intuitive, and had amazing retention. In a tight spot, he showed a lot of grit. He insisted on living in the East New York section of Brooklyn, even though he could afford to move, because that's where he was from. He didn't have any cards in the vulva file because he never fucked around on his wife. Still, Jumbo Richardson didn't *act* like a straight arrow. He just felt comfortable with who he was, and fuck what the rest of the world thought.

"Bingo," the big man said. "You won't believe this." He slipped back behind the wheel. "Nothin' to give it away on the boxes themselves, but there's a mailman in there makin' the delivery. You know how the whole row of boxes pops down when the man puts his special key in? There's another label *inside* one of them boxes. Different from the one on the intercom and the outside of the box. Does the name Reginald DuQuesnay strike a familiar note?"

Dante's eyes widened. "You're shittin' me. Here?"

"Here. On the fifth floor."

"What'd I tell you?" Dante asked, cracking a broad smile.

Jumbo grumbled. "That's what you like about this job, right?"

Eighteen

Vic Manley digested the recent glut of information with great interest.

"Your other doctor tells you that Scully is gonna divorce his old lady and marry this bimbo nurse, and she denies it outright. How close a friend is this Neisbaum?"

"They play golf every week," Jumbo said. "My guess is that they compare a few notes out there. It's hard to talk about the stock market for an entire eighteen holes."

"How would you know?" Dante quipped.

Jumbo scowled at him as the lieutenant cleared his throat.

"I think Reggie DuQuesnay is a fascinating factor in this equation. He's a big-time uptown operator with an arrest record as long as your arm and just as many downtown dismissals. One famously slippery sonofabitch—and almost strictly dope. How's he fit here?"

"He's got the kind of muscle it takes to hire dirty cops," Dante mused. "Hell, it was almost a definite once upon a time that he had them riding shotgun for some of his big deliveries. What if he's figured out some other way to use them? Then it might follow that, if the Hassey woman is in contact, George Scully had the means of reaching him and contracting the Crowley hit.''

"How do you prove it?" the whip asked. "Every time we've thought we had the drop on Reggie, it turns out he's so clean the shit squeaks comin' out his ass.''

"George Scully," Jumbo said. "I think it's time we jump down this motherfucker's throat with both feet.''

"For what?" Manley asked. "Arrest him on suspicion of murder? We've got nothin'. A whole house of cards sittin' on circumstance. He wouldn't be in jail for three hours. A man like that turns around and sues the city for false arrest. I need some sorta *proof*. Concrete. Find me something that ties this shit together.''

"We can at least talk to him," Dante said. "Put the fear of God into him. Right now, he probably figures he's gotten away with it. He'll do something stupid if we let him know he hasn't.''

George Scully was dead on his feet. In the past, he could never sleep aboard a plane. Now, as he sat wearily in the departure area of the airport in Madrid, preparing to embark on the third leg of his escape, he could barely keep his head up and his eyes open. Paris lay only six hundred and fifty miles to the north. A flight of less than two hours, which would land him at Charles De Gaulle at 7:30 P.M. their time. By then, he would have been up almost thirty-two hours without a wink of sleep. He had to lay over, trusting that no one would have the wherewithal to trace Milt Carpfingers transactions to the Caribbean before he arrived there late Wednesday. It would mean waiting until Thursday morning for the bank to open. Meanwhile, he needed sleep. He couldn't think straight like this.

* * *

Fiona Hassey lay alongside Reggie DuQuesnay in that huge circular bed. The words of reproach had failed to materialize when she arrived. She'd been ordered never to come there without first clearing it by phone. She'd violated that command, but Reggie didn't seem to be mad. He was doing her right that very moment, wasn't he? God, she loved the way he touched her. Took command. Told her to do things to him. Did things deliciously pleasurable to her.

"You been so panicky about your visit from the cops that you never told me how Georgie took the news," Reggie cooed. "You think he'll be a problem?"

"He doesn't have much choice, does he?" Fiona asked confidently.

"You talked to him since?"

She shook her head. "He left pretty mad. Sort of stormed out. Can I have another line?"

"Sure, sugar," Reggie agreed. He reached over to lift the hand mirror off the nightstand and used the shiny new razor blade to cut out a couple of fat ones for them. "You snort yours and then I want you to rub the rest on me."

When she eventually came up for air, Reggie stroked her perfectly straight blond hair, his eyes encouraging her.

"No problem with old Georgie then, you don't think?" he asked.

"I can't see how. He's over a barrel. I know he's got money in a fund in the Bahamas, so when he asked me where I thought he was going to get that sort of money, I told him that was his problem."

"That's good," Reggie said.

Fiona bent her head to drag her tongue the length of him again, a frown of worry furrowing her brow. "What about the police? They know more than they were letting on. Something's up. I could feel it. It scares me."

"Don't you worry, sugar," he soothed. "C'mere." he

265

reached to take her in his arms as she moved to accept the embrace. Gently, he rolled her onto her back and pushed her thighs apart. She guided him as he pressed forward, the heat of her enveloping him. "Don't you worry sugar. You know, you shouldn't have come here like that today. We agreed that you wouldn't do that. It's dangerous. Somebody might follow you and then they'd know that *we* know each other. That wouldn't be good."

"I was afraid," she whispered, writhing beneath his deep thrusts.

In one smooth movement, he reared back on his knees, took her hips in his big hands, and flipped her onto her stomach like a rag doll. She was too surprised to resist. As she started to lift her head, mouth coming open and eyes wide, he dropped forward onto one elbow, pinning her face into the pillow. With his other hand, he spread the cheeks of her buttocks and forced himself up her anus. She screamed muffled hysteria and pain into the pillow, her body alive in panic beneath him. His breath came hard and labored now as he thrust, sweating, while his testicles began to constrict. With a forearm planted along the back of her neck, he took a deep breath and shoved down with all his might. Her neck snapped as he ejaculated.

It was another five minutes before her corpse ceased convulsing and Reggie had recovered from the resultant wild ride. Still panting with the exertion of staying with her, he rolled off and stumbled into the adjoining bath. Such consummate delights had an unfortunate, rather messy aspect.

The chief administrator at the hospital told Dante and Richardson that Scully had cancelled all surgery the previous day and then failed to show up for the postponed procedures that morning. Calls to his home and office failed to turn him up. The two detectives obtained his home address and drove the hour and a half northeast to Ridgefield, Connecticut, to interview the wife.

They arrived in the kind of storybook Connecticut town where everything is in its proper place. Impeccably maintained clapboard homes. Manicured lawns and gardens. Cutesy boutiques and shops. The children all well scrubbed and dressed. Everyone was white. Women strolled the sidewalks in their crisp tennis outfits or drove the pin-neat streets in their European performance cars. For Joe Dante and Beasley Richardson, already having made a stop in Harlem that day, it was like passing through a reality warp into fairyland.

George Scully owned a palatial spread. Perched atop a small rise, it was surrounded by just the right mix of controlled horticulture and shamelessly rampant nature. His wife, Joan, was the appropriately pert and perky Ridgefield housewife in her short tennis jumper. Well scrubbed, with little or no makeup; that "Ivory Girl" sort of good looks framed in straight but expensively cut chestnut hair. Well muscled legs. There was also something tighter than an overwound clock about her.

Joe and Jumbo sat in the museum-quality living room, hoping none of the city's grime, having crept onto their clothes, was being transferred to the chintz sofa they sat on.

Joan Scully insisted on serving them coffee. They sipped it now. It was good. Fresh ground.

"We're worried about your husband, ma'am. We believe he may be in some sort of trouble and would very much like to contact him before he gets in any deeper," Dante told her.

"What sort of trouble?" she asked.

"That would be speculation at this point, ma'am. Let it suffice to say we're concerned."

"I have a right to know, Detective. I'm the man's wife."

"He hasn't bothered to share any of this with you?" Dante asked skeptically.

"What?" she asked in frustration.

"That's just what I'm getting at, ma'am," Joe insisted. "Are you aware of any financial difficulty your husband might be in?"

She shook her head. "Not really. Our finances are in very good order, I believe. My father has helped George with a number of expert investments."

"Are you aware that he took a second mortgage on this house just eight months ago?"

Joan Scully was shocked to the soles of her perfect size sixes. "I beg your pardon. That isn't possible. The house is in both our names."

"We were advised that Dr. Scully may have forged your signature on the contracts, ma'am. A check of the title company and lending bank would seem to bear that out. A second *was* taken out last March."

The shocked woman was barely able to hang on to her coffee cup. She leaned forward and set it on the saucer, trying at the same time to compose herself. "You're saying that George forged my signature on a mortgage contract?"

"We believe so."

"In what amount?" it came out somewhere between a croak and a whisper.

"Seven hundred thousand dollars."

She went white. "Oh my God."

"You are aware your husband was being sued for malpractice?" Dante asked.

"Yes," she answered, nodding weakly. "He was insured to the maximum."

"Not maximum enough," Jumbo interjected. "The carrier was prepared to offer settlement. The suit was in excess of his coverage."

It was coming at her from all sides now. She held up a

hand, trying to catch her breath. "The forgery is a crime only so long as I choose to press charges," she said. "What else is it that my husband's done, gentlemen?"

"Nothing that we can prove at this point, ma'am," Dante said noncommittally. "I'm afraid we're not at liberty to simply speculate. The man who was suing your husband for malpractice was murdered."

He might as well have punched her in the face. The blow of absorbing this information physically turned her head aside and caused her to wince.

"You think George had something to do with this?" It was asked without emotion. Cool, dispassionate.

Dante shrugged. "There are a lot of unanswered questions. We hope he might be able to shed some light on a few things."

"His passport is gone," she said hollowly.

"What?"

"This morning. I was putting away a bond my father gave me. In the safe. We kept them there together. His and mine. His is gone."

Dante and Richardson glanced at each other in concern. They'd gone to great pains not to spook their quarry until they had a good, clean drop on him. Yet he'd cut and run. Just when they thought they were making progress on this thing, someone dropped a brick in it and the water got muddy all over again.

"Wait till it gets dark and then dump her," Reggie told Bobby as he turned away from the corpse in disgust.

"What about the doctor now, boss?" Bobby asked, unable to take his eyes off that body. It was beautiful, even in death. Reggie was crazy.

"He don't know shit about us, and we know everything about him," Reggie snorted. "We got the motherfucker by the balls. Bitch here was pure liability. The last thing that could link us to the hit. Now we got us a situation. Once that white-ass chickenshit discovers his bitch is no longer in the picture, we'll have properly scared the shit out of him. Nothing to split. No one hooverin' up the stash. You check the nose on her? Gone through a good couple thou inside three days. We don't need that bullshit. Plenty of pussy with nose habits already failin' to earn their keep around here.''

Lieutenant Vic Manley threw a single-page typed report on the desk toward the two detectives. They were just back from Ridgefield and only a half hour from signing out for the day. The frustration was written in the set of their shoulders as they slumped in their chairs.

"We've got an idea of where he's probably headed, anyway,'' the whip said.

Dante reached and picked up the sheet. One of the people from the Securities Fraud Squad downtown had been sent to interview the stockbroker Phil Neisbaum fed them the previous afternoon. Milton Carpfinger. The name had come up again that afternoon in their conversation with Joan Scully.

Dante whistled. "Look at this,'' he said. "I thought the son of a bitch was tapped out.''

"Apparently not,'' Manley replied. "But if what you tell me about the house mortgage is true, he might as well have been. Think about it. Seven hundred on the house. Another million for the lawsuit. Look at that investment disaster with the biological engineering lab. A couple million flushed down the can. Add it all up and that's a pretty deep hole. Deeper than the six hundred grand he has could ever cover.''

Richardson was craning his neck, leaning over Dante's shoulder to scan the report. "But plenty enough to set him up nice in some little backwater.''

270

"More than enough," Manley agreed.

"The Bahamas?" Dante asked thoughtfully. "Can we have him pulled in down there?"

"On what charge? Taking a vacation? We still don't have shit to pin him with. Foreign countries don't extradite on spec."

"Fuck!" Joe spat, slapping the report back down on the desk. "He picks this money up, he's gone. We might never find him again."

"We're trying to delay the transfer on this end," Manley told him. "It hasn't been made yet. Should be able to stall it for a couple days. The bulk of it's gonna have to be let go sooner or later. All offshore investments. The only way we could get this much cooperation was to threaten the money man with demand for a field audit by the state and IRS. He's already plenty steamed."

"We need something fast," Jumbo said. "You ask me, I think Reggie DuQuesnay and this nurse are the keys. Did you feed him to our guys chasing the Vinnie angle?"

The lieutenant nodded. "They're out workin' it right now. So far, goose eggs. I think it's time we staked him out."

"I'm game," Jumbo said. "Cowboy?"

Dante shrugged. "You're the one with the wife and kids."

"And the mother visitin' from Detroit."

"I thought she left this morning."

"Decided she was havin' such a good time, she'd stay another couple days. Give me stakeout."

"Gonna have to split you," Manley said. "Don't have the manpower to work teams."

Beasley shrugged. "No sweat, huh, Joe? Somethin' starts to shake, we call each other. I'll take the first one."

Dante agreed, making plans to relieve Jumbo in front of DuQuesnay's place at midnight. He'd keep his dinner date

271

with Wendy and maybe get a couple of hours of shut-eye. He gave the big man her number and then scribbled it on a card in the vulva file almost as an afterthought. The rule didn't have anything to do with how you felt about someone. If you spent nights babysitting your invalid granny, she went in the file.

"Wendy Lee," Jumbo read off the scrap of paper. "Hey, ain't that the name of the new broad on the entertainment show?"

"Mind your own business," Dante growled.

"Starfucker," Jumbo chuckled.

Reggie DuQuesnay slammed down the receiver of the telephone in disgust.

"I can't find the motherfuckin' prick anywhere!" he snarled. "Fuckin' bitch at his answerin' service says his office is closed and he ain't pickin' up his messages. Hospital says he ain't there. What the *fuck* is goin' on with this dude?"

"You think the bitch spooked him?" Bobby asked. "He lit out?"

"What? You fuckin' kidding? Man with a fancy pad in Connecticut somewheres? Respectable job as a motherfuckin' *neurosurgeon*? Man knows he got a murder rap hangin' over his motherfuckin' head? Where do you think a man like that goes? To dig a hole and hide his head in the sand? On vacation? Where?"

Bad Bobby shrugged. "Maybe he just freaked out."

"Freaked out?" Reggie ranted, still in a rage. "You bet your motherfuckin' ass the dude's freaked out. But that don't mean shit to me. He done danced, and now it's time to pay the fiddler. Sonofabitch better show his sorry ass soon or I'll get mad and decide to take it *all*!"

Something was gnawing at Dante. Something about Fiona

Hassey showing up at Reggie DuQuesnay's. Deep in his gut, his "hunch center," he knew that Reggie had to be Vinnie's contact man. It was the only way the puzzle fit. How else could Vinnie be connected to George Scully if it wasn't through a common link. The nurse knew what Scully'd done. He was sure of that. Her bolting from the apartment and heading uptown minutes after he and Jumbo left sealed it. Reggie was in on it too. So why hadn't Vinnie's "insurance" surfaced? That little something every dirty cop kept stashed to make sure that the evil he consorted with didn't turn on him. Only it had. Before or after it located the damning evidence? The way the man's place was torn apart like that suggested that Arata hadn't surrendered it. Vinnie may have been dirty, but he wasn't stupid enough to hide it in any of the usual places. Maybe he'd been too smart for his own good, burying it someplace no one would ever look.

Wendy Lee was dressed to kill—all body-hugging slink out of some fabric that shimmered with her every move. Her hair, usually held back by combs, was down around her face and cascading over her shoulders. Mesmerized, Dante had to rein in a rampaging case of the hots. Before he started trying to figure women out, he thought maybe he'd better decide what it was *he* wanted. Right that instant, it was to crawl up those shimmering hips to pay dirt.

He handed her the tube of contraceptive cream. "You, uh, forgot something the other night. Rosa thought you might want to carry your own with you instead of leaving spares."

"I hope I didn't get you in any trouble."

"Like hell you do."

Her brow knit. "I don't understand why you're doing this."

He smiled affably. "We play a clean game here. No shots below the belt. No cute tricks. That"—he pointed at the tube of cream in her hand—"was both."

All the seduction drained from the pose she struck. Anger flashed in her eyes. "I beg your pardon?"

"C'mon, Wendy, the door swings both ways. We fucked once and it was swell, but that doesn't give you the right to start messing up my life."

"Listen," she said stiffly, "maybe this wasn't such a good idea tonight. I think you'd better go."

Dante shrugged. "Suit yourself. I'm not much in the mood for games anyway." He looked her up and down. "Too bad. All dressed up and nowhere to go."

He walked downstairs feeling a number of conflicting emotions. Still, he'd known how he was going to play it before going up there. And the night wasn't a total loss. There was still the matter of Vinnie Arata's house. The night was young. He had plenty of time to drive out to Brooklyn, have a good look around, and still make it up to Harlem to relieve Jumbo at midnight. Before hitting the road, he let himself back into his apartment and re-recorded the message on his answering machine. It told Jumbo to leave any messages for him at the squad.

Beasley Richardson sat parked on 129th Street with the window rolled down. It was balmy for so late in the year. Even after dark, pedestrians were strolling the sidewalks in their shirtsleeves. Up the block, a couple of kids were shooting hoops, their backboard and rim bolted to a light standard. Passersby paid him little mind. An overweight black detective sitting in a parked, unmarked car. He wasn't fooling anybody, but then nobody was doing anything wrong. Nice and cozy, having a vigilant policeman parked on your block. Jumbo often wondered why the city chose to make their so-called unmarked cars so goddamn conspicuous, almost as though they wanted to provide the criminal element with a fighting chance. The boxy Dodges and Plymouths bore a conspicuous absence of frills. No chrome. All one standard color. The only cars in town with no white stripe on the tire sidewalls. Real people didn't buy cars like that. Rental companies didn't even *rent* them.

From where he sat, Richardson could plainly view the lit windows of Reggie Duquesnay's fifth-floor apartment. From time to time, shadows passed in front of the closed curtains. Down on the street, five cars up and diagonally across the way, the hustler's extravagant stretch Mercedes gleamed under a street lamp. Jumbo wondered how much a car like that might run. It had to be in the neighborhood of a hundred grand. Maybe more. Probably more than Reggie had declared in earnings for the past five years. Reggie was smart, though. If he wasn't, they'd have nailed him years ago for one of the dozen operations he was suspected of controlling. If checked, the car would prove to be leased by a corporation, controlled by a second corporation, and by the time you decided to stop digging, you'd have a massive headache and little else to hang your hat on.

Jumbo checked the time. Eight thirty. It was as dark as it was going to get now. Prime TV time too. Foot traffic was starting to thin on the sidewalks. People were starting to think about having to get up in the morning. Peeling the tab back on a tepid Diet Coke, Richardson eased it to his lips. A gate squeaked off to his left, across the street, and he swung his head around. Well, well. A big, hulking man he recognized almost instantly as ex-heavy Bobby ''Badness'' Burke scanned the sidewalk in both directions before stepping out of the service gate and walking briskly to open the trunk of Reggie's Mercedes-Benz. Jumbo thought he remembered hearing a rumor that after super-pimp Willie Davenport went down in mid-Manhattan, a couple of the other real dreadnoughts of the Harlem underworld had seriously beefed up security. Bobby Burke might not have been much of a boxer, but he was mean and quick enough to make a formidable bodyguard. Right now he was looking a little nervous, and that piqued Jumbo's interest.

With the trunk lid ajar, Burke hurried back to the service gate, stooped, scanned the sidewalk once more, and then hefted an awkward bundle onto his shoulder. He was a big man, and as such wasn't exactly struggling under the weight. It appeared to be about five and a half to six feet long and was wrapped in a blanket. After dumping it unceremoniously into the trunk, Bobby slammed the lid, hurried around to the driver's door, opened it, and climbed behind the wheel.

The detective wasn't sure he should believe what he was seeing. Could this be some sort of ruse? Had they spotted him down there and were now conspiring to lead him on some sort of wild goose chase? Twisting the key, he fired up the Plymouth, waited until the Mercedes was well down the block, and then pulled away from the curb without headlights. At the same time, he eased the handset of the radio to his lips and called central, requesting that they get hold of Dante at Wendy Lee's number.

Vinnie Arata's neighborhood in Sheepshead Bay appeared tranquil as Joe Dante piloted his Corvette up the block to the little two-bedroom, white frame and stone facade bungalow. He was still dressed in the same duds he'd slipped into for dinner;—sneakers, tan cotton chinos, and a striped rugby shirt. Before climbing out of the car, he removed his automatic from the glove box, slid the clip-on holster into the waistband at the small of his back, and pulled on a light jacket.

A neighbor parted the front drapery to peer out at him as he crossed the lawn to the front porch. A crime scene seal dangled from the lockset. He snapped it with the can opener of his Swiss Army knife and used the blade to trigger the spring lock. The electricity was still on in the place, and the phone worked. He used it to call the squad. There was no message from Jumbo yet, at just after eight thirty. He figured he would dig around for half an hour and then check again.

"Detective Dante is not at that number," the female dispatcher informed Jumbo.

"Try his home number then," the detective requested. He read it to her out of his notebook. Ahead, the Mercedes had turned right on 130th, done a jog south of Fifth Avenue to 125th, and was now heading toward the approach to the Willis Avenue Bridge. With headlights switched on now, Jumbo followed two cars behind as they climber over the Harlem River and into the South Bronx.

"There is a message on Detective Dante's machine," the dispatcher told him. "You're to leave a message with the squad."

"Great," Jumbo said. "Leave this then: Subject's body-guard on the move. Strange package in his trunk. Turning east on Bruckner Boulevard in the South Bronx."

Vinnie's living room appeared much the same as when Dante had first seen it. The gore of murder was now dried almost black on the floor, ceiling, and walls. Forensics techs had moved furniture and other debris around in an effort to determine whether the frenzied search might have turned up anything obvious. The image of Vinnie's body lying faceless in the weeds of Van Cortlandt Park sprang into his mind's eye as he forced himself to contemplate the carnage here. The odor of the place was sickening. Carefully, he began to work his way through, tapping on the floor for evidence of loose boards and a possible cavity beneath. Outside, the bright search beam of a prowl car suddenly illuminated the room through the curtained windows. A few minutes later, the barrel of a flashlight rapped on the front door. Dante stopped what he was doing to step over and open it.

One partner remained standing by the open door of the squad car as a second stood on the stoop. "What's going on here? the tall, curly-haired uniform demanded. "This is a crime scene."

Dante extracted his wallet from his back pocket and showed his shield and ID to the guy. "I should have called and let you guys know I was coming over," he apologized. "It slipped my mind."

"You one of the people who caught this?" the patrolman asked.

"Afraid so."

"Making any progress?"

"Slow but sure."

"Nail their asses," the young guy told him enthusiastically.

"We will," Joe told him. "Can't have the citizenry going around killing cops."

Back inside, Dante gave up on the front room and started in on the rooms to the rear. He took his time, going over every square inch. At nine o'clock, he took a break to call the squad. Composto, one of the guys on duty, delivered Richardson's message of twenty minutes earlier.

"Nothing since?" Dante asked.

"Not a peep, Joe."

Dante gave him Vinnie's number and told him to call if anything came across the wire. Meanwhile, he'd call back in half an hour just to check in.

As the Mercedes continued on Bruckner and then veered into East 133rd Street, Jumbo became increasingly convinced that this was no ruse. 133rd ran beneath the approach to the Triborough Bridge where it started south across Randall's Island. It paralleled the Penn Central rail yard on the Bronx Kill. Bleak, desolate territory. Dead ahead lay the north estuary of the East River where it eventually opened out into Long Island Sound and Flushing Bay to the south. Around Randall's Island ran the part of the river called Hell's Gate, its passage narrow and the current treacherous. For years, this had been a favorite dumping ground for victims of underworld retribution.

As traffic thinned, Jumbo cut his lights. The car ahead turned south a block at the terminus of 133rd Street at Locust. This was known as the Port Morris section of the Bronx. At that hour, the sprawl of decrepit warehouses lining adjacent streets was virtually abandoned. A cyclone and razor-wire fence enclosed the rail yard where it ended at the water. Bobby Burke parked the Mercedes alongside. Jumbo, a block behind, switched off his own engine. Before opening his door, he popped the cover of the dome light and removed the bulb. Up ahead he saw a faint glow from the Mercedes trunk as the lid yawned open. Jumbo hurried toward it, hanging with the shadows as best he could. After three hours of sitting on his butt, he was grateful for the opportunity to stretch his legs.

Bobby stood for a moment at the rear of the Mercedes. He scanned the surrounding landscape for prying eyes and listened to the engulfing darkness. Jumbo observed him from the cover of a three-yard commercial dumpster. He was perhaps twenty-five yards away now. The light was not very good. Carefully, he removed his service revolver from the holster inside his jacket and checked the cylinder. Up ahead, Bobby stooped to reach down inside the trunk and gather up his bundle. The blanket-wrapped bulk passed through the soft glow of the interior light as Jumbo pushed off from his concealment and sprinted diagonally across the street to the rail-yard fence. Hugging it, he covered the remaining few yards to the Benz.

"Freeze, motherfucker, or I blow your head off," he commanded. He was breathing hard from exertion, arms extended in a two-handed grip on the gun. He was careful not to get too close.

Bobby Burke dropped his burden into the street. The blanket came apart and an arm flopped out. Bobby's head came around until his eyes met those of his captor.

"Real slowly," Jumbo told him. "Close the lid of the trunk and spread your hands on it."

Burke complied, standing with his back to Jumbo now. Jumbo released the gun with his left hand and groped into his back pocket for his cuffs.

"Right hand behind you, asshole. Again, real slow."

When Burke's wrist lay against the small of his back, Richardson took one long stride forward and slapped the bracelet around it. The other end, still clutched in his left hand, was suddenly torn from his grasp as Burke vanished beneath the barrel of his gun. Excruciating pain shot up his arm from the torn flesh of his fingers. A split second later, he was temporarily blinded when the ex-pug, down on one knee, whipped the free cuff hard across the detective's left temple. Jumbo fought for control, flailing out hard in the direction the blow came from. He connected with something solid and Burke let out a grunt. It was dark, and everything was a blur. He swung hard again, missing as a fist slammed up into his solar plexus. The air went out of him in a *whoosh*. Another fist slammed into his jaw with the force of a wrecking ball. Jumbo tried to get his hands up to protect his face. The effort proved too little too late. A second fist clubbed him hard on the back of the neck. The lights went out.

Nineteen

From Vinnie Arata's kitchen, Dante phoned into the precinct again at nine thirty. In the intervening half hour, he'd meticulously gone over both bedrooms, the bath, and most of the kitchen itself. Next to where the phone hung on the wall was the door to the basement. When he learned there was no further word from his partner, he decided it was time to try downstairs. It was either that or dig up the entire yard, and he wasn't quite ready for that.

Whoever had torn apart the ground floor hadn't spared the basement area in his desire for thoroughness. There was a work-shop that looked like the aftermath of a train wreck. Pegboard was torn from the walls. Workbenches, cans of nails, and boxes of potentially useful junk were overturned and scattered across the concrete floor. Adjacent to them, the oil burner was torn apart. The washer and dryer were a shambles, pushed over and apparently pried apart. It was difficult to tell what of the destruction had been wrought by the perpetrator and what had been done since by the forensics team.

There were a series of overhead bulbs with pull-string

switches. Dante went around turning them all on until the basement was brightly illuminated. Starting at one end, he began to carefully inspect the joisting and underside of the floor above. Most of it was clearly visible, but here and there ducting and plumbing got in the way. He concentrated on these, even going so far as tapping out the entire length of the duct system in hopes of hearing the dull thud of an object concealed inside the sheet-metal channel. It was only after he'd completed this laborious process and made a fourth call to the squad that he attacked the foundation itself. Jumbo still hadn't called in. That seemed odd.

The foundation was quite solid, done entirely in stone. The neighborhood was probably a hundred years old, each house built individually over a span of perhaps thirty years. This one had to be one of the first. You just didn't see all that many stone foundations much later than the turn of the century. Not in the city, anyway. Joe started working his way along the head-high wall at the rear of the house. There was nothing that seemed even vaguely uncharacteristic about it. He turned the corner, stepping over debris as he went, until he reached the wrecked furnace. There, behind it, down low next to the floor, he thought he saw something out of the ordinary. Maybe it was wishful thinking, the product of having been at it a little too long. The mortar around one particular stone appeared to be slightly discolored. A darker gray, as though it were new.

It took another five minutes to locate a two-pound hammer and rusty cold chisel, clear away enough debris so that he could kneel in the cramped space, and get started. His excitement grew as the mortar chipped away easily, actually falling off in chunks at some points. It was a good-sized stone, maybe eighteen inches long by a foot in height. When he finished freeing the mortar around it, he found it loose to the nudge.

A pry bar of some kind. He scrambled through the pile of junk, digging for something that would suffice and coming up with the exact tool for the job;—a Stanley Wonderbar. The slightly upturned, flat end fit nicely between the loose stone and the rest of the foundation wall. When he tugged on the leveraged end of the fulcrum, the stone gave way, causing him to sit hard and suddenly. After getting back onto his knees, he leaned into the gap and reached back into the resultant hole. His fingers touched something cool and metallic, wrapping around a wire handle. He tugged on it and pulled a small steel lockbox out into the bare bulb-light of the basement.

The box contained almost one hundred thousand dollars in cash, as close as Joe could tell. All in hundreds and twenties. In addition to the money, there was a Colt Python .357 Magnum revolver and a small, imitation-leather bound notebook. Bingo. He took the lot upstairs to the kitchen where he could spread it out on the table. There were still ten more minutes before he made his ten-thirty call to the squad. He opened the notebook.

It didn't take long for Dante to ascertain both why Arata had kept it and why Reggie DuQuesnay wanted so very much to find it. There was little question, given the information contained therein, that the initials "R.D." were DuQuesnay's. There was also little question about another thing: records of large lump-sum payments with dates and names, culminating with "$25,000 — 10/24 — Crowley." It could mean only one thing. Vinnie wasn't just supplying the big man with information. Not for that kind of money. For that kind of money, you wielded the knife. Sweet Jesus Christ. George Scully must have paid a fucking fortune.

Dante repacked the lockbox, lifted the receiver from the wall phone, and called Vic Manley at home.

*   *   *

283

When Beasley Richardson regained consciousness he found himself on the carpeted rear floor of Reggie DuQuesnay's limousine with a rag stuffed into his mouth and his hands cuffed behind his back. Lying face-down, he could feel the vibration of the road against his cheek. At every slight bump, a searing pain shot through his head behind his left eye. With the rag in his mouth, he had difficulty drawing a decent breath.

How long had he been out? What the hell had happened? It was coming to him in bits and pieces. The arm coming loose from the blanket. A woman's arm. White. Bobby Burke getting the jump on him. He'd never looked that fast in the ring. Probably just a matter of split seconds could make you look slow and clumsy against an Ali. Plenty fast enough for the street. *Too* fast for old Jumbo. Damn, why hadn't he radioed in? That was just dumb.

The car slowed and came to a stop. Richardson tried to move his head. There was the searing pain again and a sticky wetness beneath his right ear and cheek. His own blood. Bobby'd clipped him good. The rear door just ahead of him came open, and Reggie Duquesnay climbed in, stepping on his outstretched hand.

"He came outta nowhere, boss" Bobby said from the front seat. "Musta been stakin' out the pad. Followed me. He's good. I checked half-dozen times and didn't see him."

"What do we have here?" Reggie asked with a snarl. He kicked out hard, his boot heel finding Jumbo's ribs and partially knocking the wind out of him. The detective tried to close up, but the movement caused such pain in his head that he nearly blacked out again. Reggie was leaning over him now, roughly tugging at his wallet in the breast pocket of his jacket.

"Well, well. We got us a nigger detective here, Bobby. Big old fat Tom with a shiny gold shield name of Richardson.

Ring any bells?'' He reached to snatch the rag from Jumbo's mouth. ''What you got to say for yourself, Uncle Tom Richardson? You bein' where you were tonight's gonna end up causin' me a lot of trouble. I think there's a story behind it that you're dyin' to tell me.''

Beasley was busy trying to work some saliva around the inside of his parched mouth. The direct access to a supply of oxygen was nice too. He stared sullenly up into DuQuesnay's eyes, hatred in his own. What good would it do to reply. He shook his head and got another foot in the ribs for not answering. Reggie bent over him now as he gasped. The interior of the car was spinning wildly, and the hood's breath was hot in his face.

''Don't *fuck* with me, cop. You ain't but shit in my world.''

His hands worked inside Jumbo's jacket, eventually finding his notebook. As he extracted it, the slip of paper with Wendy Lee's number on it fluttered to the carpet. Reggie retrieved and unfolded it. The number and woman's name didn't attract as much attention as the last names ''Dante.'' It was the name of the other pig who'd visited Fiona. Things were falling into place. Somehow these bastards had made some connection. When the bitch panicked and came running uptown to him, she'd left a trail right to his door.

''My, my,'' Reggie said. He quickly flipped through the notebook to see his suspicions confirmed. Visits to the hospital, Scully's old lady in Connecticut, lawyers. He stared down at Jumbo.

''We got us a real problem with you, Tom. Why don't you tell me where this honky partner of yours is now.''

Jumbo just continued to glower at him, steeling himself for the next crushing blow.

Bobby glanced up into the rearview mirror, addressing Reggie. ''If they were staking out the pad, we'd better get these wheels to ground and use the backup, boss.''

Reggie waved him on. "Let's do it. I'm havin' an interestin' one-way conversation with our pet whale back here. I think he wants to tell me how we can find his partner and nip this thing in the bud."

Joe Dante and Vic Manley arrived almost simultaneously at the squad. From his home, Manley had called Inspector Lieberman at Manhattan South Command and received authorization to issue an APB on Reggie DuQuesnay. Units in the South Bronx had been dispatched to search the last reported location of Jumbo Richardson and the immediate area. During their separate drives to the station, both men experienced increasing panic, not wanting to dwell on what might have gone wrong. Something had *definitely* gone wrong. Dante figured he must have broken all standing records for running the length of Flatbush Avenue from Avenue U to the BQE.

It was nearly midnight before bench warrants were issued and a small army of cops assembled from the Sixth and Twenty-fifth precincts descended on Reggie Duquesnay's domicile. Inside, they found two women in residence, one black and one white, in addition to a cache of cocaine, the derivative crack, heroin, and over two hundred thousand dollars in cash. They didn't find Reggie.

Gus Lieberman arrived in the middle of the raid, followed shortly by the commander of the Manhattan North Narcotics Task Force and the C of D. Dante wasn't surprised to see Rosa straggle in a few minutes after her boss. When something like this broke, the brass hats didn't take long to crank up the smoke machine and start it blowing at the newshounds outside the door.

Dante went into a huddle with the various bosses. It could only be assumed that Jumbo had run afoul of DuQuesnay. DuQuesnay, they concurred, was most likely responsible for the execution of a NYPD detective and three citizens of Fifth Avenue. The cop-killing by itself was enough to see him fry in the electric chair.

"I want that limousine located," Lieberman growled to the chief of detectives. "And Richardson's fucking car. I don't care if it takes every uniform in the five boroughs."

"What was the last location?" the chief asked.

"Somewhere on Bruckner running east," Vic Manley told him. "We've got units from both Harlem and the South Bronx blanketing the area."

A patrolman from the Twenty-fifth hurried into the room, out of breath from skipping the elevator and running upstairs from the street.

"They found the unmarked unit, Lou," he informed his immediate superior. "One thirty-two and Locust. Where the Penn Central yards end at the East River."

Dante, piloting the Corvette out of Harlem and across the South Bronx with Gus Lieberman in the cockpit beside him, arrived at the scene before Manley and C of D. The desolate street was now ablaze with the headlights of a half-dozen prowl cars from three precincts and another three unmarked cars from the Bronx Borough Detective Task Force. Dante pulled in among them, killed his own lights, and hurried forward to the abandoned Plymouth. He heard one of the detectives address Gus as he approached behind him.

"No sign of the officer, sir. But just a few minutes ago, we did a sweep of the river and found a floater about fifty yards up. Female Caucasian. Maybe twenty-five. Neck broken. Hadn't been in the water long by the look of her."

"Where?" Dante demanded.

"Huh?" the guy asked, taken aback by his intensity. "Oh, uh . . . just down there where those guys are standing. We called it in to the ME . . ."

Dante didn't wait to hear the rest of the man's sentence. He hurried down the street to where the knot of uniformed patrolmen huddled at the water's edge. There on the ground, with a regulation raincoat spread over it, lay the corpse.

Joe approached one of the cops. "Let me borrow that flashlight a sec, would you?"

The young guy handed him the four-battery torch, watching curiously now as the detective bent to one knee, lifted the raincoat, and played the light across the dead woman's face.

"You know her?" It was Gus, standing over his right shoulder.

Dante nodded, swallowing hard. "Since just this morning," he said quietly. "Her name is Fiona Hassey. The girlfriend of the doctor who was being sued by Crowley for malpractice."

"Do you understand this?" Lieberman asked.

Dante stood slowly, handed the cop his flashlight. "I think maybe I do," he replied, leading the inspector away. "One thing we couldn't understand was why the doctor, Scully, spooked and ran before we even had a chance to talk to him. There was no way he could have known there was pressure coming from us. That meant it had to be coming from somewhere else. I think I know where it was coming from now."

"The girlfriend?"

"Not by herself. Jumbo and I could have sworn we heard her do a quick toot this morning when we questioned her. She was antsy as hell. Ten minutes after we split, she goes running to Reggie. If she had a nose candy habit and he had the candy, I'm betting they were in it together. Reggie hires Vinnie to do the hit and then gets rid of him. Once he did Wiems, he was expendable. Then Reggie was in a perfect position to turn the screws on the doctor.

"Scully bolts. The nurse feels the pressure from us and

288

freaks out as well. That leaves DuQuesnay exposed. He kills Fiona Hassey, and Jumbo is sitting out front of his building when he leaves to dump the body in the drink.''

"Jesus Christ," Lieberman said.

"Right now, if Beasley's still alive, he's in real deep shit," Dante muttered. Fear and frustration edged his voice. "Reggie's the kind of guy who thinks of himself as always being in control. I doubt he imagined that the cops were anywhere near him. Now we've made a good bust of his stash and his money. We just knocked him out of the ballgame in the middle innings. He won't take it sitting down."

"We've gotta find that car," Gus insisted. "God knows it oughta stick out like a sore thumb."

"Chances are he's ditched it by now," Joe replied. "A man in his precarious position has contingencies all planned."

"You think he'll make a run for it, then?"

"Sooner or later."

"And Jumbo . . . ?"

Dante shook his head, sadness in his eyes. "We've just gotta pray, boss. We don't have much choice."

The two-tone Ford Fairmont sped south on the Henry Hudson Parkway past the West 79th Street exit. It was quarter to one in the morning and traffic in both directions was light. Bobby Burke and Reggie DuQuesnay, riding in the front seat together now, wore ball caps and were rid of any flashy gold neck chains and rings. The car had to be considered safe so long as no one inspected the trunk. The bound and gagged cop had looked half dead when they'd dumped him in. He was their holecard if they decided to make a run for it. Right now, Reggie was hoping maybe they wouldn't have to. Maybe they could plug the leak and buy an easy out. The way he saw it, the two cops Fiona met must have followed her from her pad near the hospital and staked out the building she entered. The cop's notes told him they'd been hot on the trail. Still, Fiona was the only link. One of the cops was the fatso in the trunk, and the other was this Dante. They obviously split the duty for the night so Dante could screw the pussy whose name was on the piece of paper. He'd left the number with the fat man just in case something came up. Unfortunately, the nigger detective decided to be a hero and make the collar all by himself. Lucky for them. Now all they had to do was hit this Dante while his dick was still damp and hope it'd fox their boxes. If not, at least they'd be buying some time. Reggie was prepared for any eventuality. There was at least ten million stashed in the bank in the Cayman Islands and close to that in Lucerne. He prided himself in being smart enough to know when his string of luck ran out. Once it did, there was no turning back. You moved on to new circumstances and made new luck. If you tried to breathe life into the old, you lived to regret it.

"Once you get off down there, I want you to find me a phone booth," he directed Bobby. "In a coffee shop or a bar."

The coffee shop Bobby drove them to on 14th Street was perfect. Like most of the major cross streets in Manhattan, 14th seemed to attract riffraff. A couple of black guys in a six-year-old Ford weren't going to garner any special attention. While Bobby idled at the curb, Reggie took time to first purchase a pack of Kools before asking the woman at the cash register if he could borrow her telephone directory. "There ain't one by the phone," he explained, pointing.

"What's wrong with information?"

"I'm lookin' for an address, Mama. With all that computerized shit, you barely talk to a real person no more."

With a heavy dose of bored reluctance, the woman produced the Manhattan directory and proceeded to watch Reggie like a hawk while he paged through it. To his dismay, there were only a couple of Wendy Lees and none at the number he held in his hand. If the woman lived out of Manhattan, he'd be all night trying to locate her. Thanking the woman, he handed the directory back and wandered over to the phone on the wall to drop a quarter. He dialed directory assistance and asked to be connected with a supervisor. When the woman came on the line, he peered at the number on the badge in Jumbo's wallet.

"Police business," he told her in his best authoritative voice, "Detective Beasley Richardson." He read her the shield number. "I have a number I'd like you to run in your reverse directory."

It was almost too easy. The operator told him it was a new listing on Perry Street, registered to a Wendy Lee. She read him the address and he made a note. It was same address fatso had for Dante in his book. Real cozy. That block of Perry was only a hop and skip away.

The tail lights of the medical examiner's meat wagon faded to red pin-dots in the distance, bearing the water-logged corpse of Fiona Hassey to the morgue on First Avenue in midtown. Dante watched it disappear. In that moment, he realized how bone-weary he was. He'd been on the go, one way or another, since before eight that morning, and had covered an immense amount of territory in the intervening seventeen hours. The anxiety of the current circumstances, not knowing if his partner was alive or dead, prevented the weariness from taking complete control of his faculties.

To one side, the chief of detectives was conferring with the other bosses on hand.

Rosa broke away from them and moved to his side. "I know how you feel about him," she said.

"Thanks."

"You look beat."

"I'm dead," he admitted. "Right now, it looks like it'll be a while before I see the insides of my eyelids."

"Give me a call when this is over?" she asked. "I'll probably still be at the office."

"I gave Wendy her cream back," he said with a grin. "She wasn't much interested in a frank exchange of views."

"Why should she be?" Rosa asked. "She can have anything she wants."

Dante reached out and touched his lady liaison on the cheek. "So could you. Stop selling yourself so short."

"Be in touch?" she asked as he started to turn away. Manley and Lieberman appeared to be finishing up with the chief.

The inspector stepped over. "Go on home, Joe," he said. "There's nothing more you can do right now."

Dante shook his head in frustration. "My partner's out there somewhere. I'm supposed to go home to bed and just leave his ass to fate?"

"What choice do you have?" Gus asked. "We've got fresh troops flown in from all over the five boroughs. the PC's ordered checks at every toll booth, airport, and bus station out of the city. There are people combing the streets. What the hell difference are you going to make in your condition? Go home. Get some sleep."

In his condition, Dante thought. "Maybe in a few hours," he conceded.

Lieberman looked at Rosa in exasperation. "Can you talk any sense to him?" he asked.

"Since when?" she replied.

"Try," he pleaded. "I'll see you at eight, Joe. We're setting up the operation command straight from the big building." He looked hard into Dante's eyes. Both of them were old soldiers. Both knew that this sort of thing could happen to any one of them, at any time. The knowledge didn't make it any easier. Jumbo was one of the good ones. Even though it would be tough to lose him, both men were now facing the fact that his chances for survival were slim. "I know how you're feeling, Joey. Like you've been kicked in the gut. I'm feeling it too."

Dante stared back into those perpetually tired eyes. He knew that coming from Gus, it wasn't some placating line of brass-button bullshit. The man was feeling it.

"I'd love to take you home with me and *sit* on you," Rosa told him once Lieberman had moved off. "Fortunately, there *is* something I can do. Go home, Joe. Do like he says. I'll be right on top of it downtown. If anything happens, I'll call you."

The hotel lounge was crowded as George Scully entered it from the casino. Even at one A.M., revelers ashore from the cruise ship in the harbor and other vacationers were still trying to cram as much recreation into a day as humanly possible. George himself was beginning to find his spirits lifting. The night in Paris had helped some, giving him a much needed respite from the rigors of nonstop jet travel. He had left Charles de Gaulle just a little after three that afternoon, landing in Nassau after having lost little more than an hour in transit. His room in the hotel was big and airy, with a view of the lagoon and the sea out beyond the reef. He ate, showered, and napped for several hours into the evening, waking refreshed and truly relaxed for the first time in what seemed like months. Tomorrow morning he would go to the bank, collect the funds transferred to his account, and catch the afternoon flight to Mexico City. From there he would make the hop to Panama. An unscrupulous ship captain would certainly take him south from there for a price. He could sneak off the ship once it made port in Brazil, Uruguay, or Argentina. He'd let six hundred thousand dollars speak for him then.

There was a stool vacant at the bar. Scully strolled over and climbed up. He'd just dropped a little over fifteen hundred dollars at the craps table;—part of his therapy. Now he wanted to have a couple of drinks before turning in. Fuck Fiona and Joanie. George Sculley was his own man now. He was free. When the bartender approached, the neurosurgeon ordered a Tanqueray and tonic. As it was being mixed, the stool next to him was momentarily vacated before the most stunning black woman George Scully had ever seen moved to occupy it. When he glanced over, she flashed him a friendly smile.

"Buy you a drink?" he asked boldly.

She shrugged a pair of expressive shoulders, the gesture tugging the tiny straps of a skin-tight sheath barely containing a pair of exquisite breasts. Scully eyed the heaving cleavage hungrily.

"Why not?" she asked, her accent that wonderful, lilting island British.

"No reason in the world," he replied gallantly. He flagged the bartender a second time, buying her a banana daiquiri.

The rich American told the prostitute that his name was George. She knew he was rich because she'd spent two hours in the casino watching him lose his money. Twice, when he'd run out of money on the table, he'd opened his wallet. It was stuffed full of hundred-dollar bills. Again, at the bar, as he paid for the drinks, she had an opportunity to peer into that open wallet. There were some American twenties in there and many more hundreds. Maybe as much as three thousand U.S. dollars. More money than the prostitute could make in two months.

The American grinned at her. "Don't you think my

room would be a lot more comfortable than this?'' he asked. ''It's overlooking the water. Maybe we could go for a swim.''

She returned his smile. ''I think that I would like that, George. You have rum in the room?''

''We'll have some sent,'' he promised, sliding down off the stool and taking her by the elbow. Damn, she had a spectacular set of tits on her. To say nothing of how friendly and willing she seemed. ''Gin, too. We'll have our own little party.''

''You're fun,'' she told him, laughing gaily. ''Not like so many other Americans who come down here. I can tell you know how to have a good time.''

Scully winked slyly. ''Do I ever, honey. Do I ever.''

Nestled in the heart of the city that never sleeps, Perry Street at two o'clock in the morning was doing a good job of faking it. Reggie and Bobby had traded places at the coffee shop, Reggie now driving while Bobby rode shotgun. There he would be free to hop out and do the dirty work while the boss kept it idling at the curb for a quick getaway. DuQuesnay now eased the Fairmont up the right-hand side, Bobby peering out his open window at the addresses.

''Right up there.'' He pointed. Dante and his bitch lived in a building distinguished from some of the others by being set back from the curb an additional five feet. There were two steps to descend before entering the tiny vestibule.

Reggie pulled it up, setting the transmission in PARK and leaving the engine idle. ''Don't leave no doubts,'' he said.

Bobby checked the load in the clip of his Llama 9mm parabellum automatic before screwing a three-inch noise suppressor into the muzzle. With a nod to Reggie, he slid from the front seat onto the curb, waited for a fast-moving cab to pass, and then strolled to the low cast-iron gate, unlatched it, and continued down the two steps to the door. The name W. LEE was on a recently typed label, stuck over the glass of the building register to obscure the name of a former tenant. He noticed that Dante was listed in apartment two. The woman was in three. Four floors and eight apartments in the building. Two per floor. That put her on the second. From inside his jacket he extracted an eighteen-inch spring-steel jimmying wand he always kept in the trunk of the Mercedes. You never knew when you might have to boost a car in a hurry, and besides, it came in handy for other things—like snaking down past the angle iron prevalent on most New York apartment building doors and depressing the latch tongue. Most of the lockset mechanisms themselves were primitive fare, beveled back and sprung for automatic closure. It took him all of thirty seconds to get the door open. Once inside, he took to the stairs, climbed to the second floor, and checked the numbers on the two doors.

Wendy Lee lived in the apartment facing Perry Street. Bobby counted three separate cylinders mounted in the steel-clad fire-proof panel. There was no sense wasting time and making noise trying to gain access there. He climbed two more flights to the roof access, slid back the simple gate latch, and stepped quietly out onto the flat tar surface. Fire escapes ran down both the front and back of the building. It was one of those fluke, warmish nights that caught an old building's boiler by surprise. He'd already noticed that half the windows in the neighborhood were open to allow for an excess of steam heat. Bobby climbed down the escape, slowing to creep by the windows of the fourth and third floors. He discovered open windows at each level, the premises beyond protected by metal security gates. Wendy Lee's apartment was no different. The window was open about twelve inches. The ex-fighter paused a moment outside, listening hard before easing the sash up an additional foot.

There was a low table with a framed photograph and a flower-filled vase on it just inside the window. Bobby set himself, eased the hammer back on the parabellum, and reached through the grate to knock the vase off onto the floor. His action was followed by a loud crash. He pulled back to hug the exterior bricks and waited.

The lights in the room came on. Perfect. Macho detective Dante hurrying to investigate in a display of bravery. A shadow approached the window, probably wondering why it was open so much wider now. Several beats while the shadow stood stock-still. Listening, no doubt. Bobby held his breath. The shadow moved, hands now reaching through the gate to grab the sash of the window to close it.

Bobby grabbed a wrist and yanked as hard as he could, coming around to face the window at the same instant. The automatic came up, muzzle of the silencer jammed beneath the jaw of a pained face just inches away now. His finger was already applying pressure on the trigger when he froze. The face was female. Oriental.

"Where is he?" Bobby hissed menacingly.

Wendy Lee turned pale and almost passed out. Terror froze her face in a grimace of horrible expectation. There was a gun at her throat, a giant black face, puffy with scar tissue, behind it. In the shadows of night, with only the ambient light of the lamp behind her to illuminate it, the face looked demonic. It was gripped with rage. She was unable to speak.

Bobby yanked the arm and jammed the barrel of the pistol harder into her neck. "Where is the motherfucker?" he repeated insistently.

Wendy found some remote cousin of her normal voice. Who?"

"Dante," Bobby snarled in reply, as though the answer were obvious.

She blinked and started to shake her head before thinking better of it. "He's not here," she said weakly.

"What you sayin', bitch?"

"He's not here. He left. Just after he got here." Wendy knew she was going to pass out. Already, the urine released with her initial terror ran down her legs and onto the bare oak floor underfoot.

"When?" Bobby pressed.

"Just after seven."

"Home?" he demanded. "Did he go home?"

Tears formed in her eyes, her lips began to tremble, and she shook her head now, all judgment and control gone to the wind. "I don't *know*." she blubbered, the dam bursting. I don't *know*."

In disgust, Bobby Burke leaned as far back as he could without letting go of the arm and pulled the trigger. He was unable to avoid splattering tissue fragments and blood as the woman's head exploded at point-blank range.

Twenty

Joe Dante still hadn't been able to shake his burden of helplessness as he guided the Corvette across West 4th Street and turned up into Perry. Gus was right, of course. There *wasn't* anything he could do that wasn't already being done. On the other hand, how could he expect to get any sleep under the circumstances? On any other night, he'd grab a six-pack and get just bombed enough to pass out. Now, that was out of the question. He had to be fresh when he got out of bed. Clearheaded. It didn't matter to him that looking for Jumbo now was like trying to find a needle in a haystack. He owed the man nothing less than an all-out shot at it.

Par for the course, there were no parking spaces on his block. He noticed a two-tone Ford parked at a hydrant a couple buildings up from his place. Fool probably dropped it in there out of frustration. He would be sorry in the morning when he found his wheels towed away—but then this city was full of people with shit for brains.

At two thirty in the morning, there was little risk of encountering one-way traffic on the short stretch of Waverly

Place between his block and West 11th. Whenever he came home late, he took advantage of this little illegal shortcut to the yellow zone in front of St. John's. Before reporting in at the squad, he would drive the car to his usual parking garage. He hated leaving his baby on the street, but the place closed at eleven thirty. Damn inconvenient.

The street was quiet as he walked down it toward his place in the middle of the block. It was cooler now than it had been just an hour earlier in the South Bronx. Up ahead, a couple climbed unsteadily out of a cab, both in black leather with his-and-hers yellow mohawks. Seeing them reminded Dante of his night combing the clubs with Diana for Stuart Wiems. God, it seemed like years ago that he'd entered this labrynth. He felt no closer to finding his way out now than he had before Nancy Epstein told them of the redheaded punk's existence.

At his front gate, Dante stooped to lift the latch. Something on the walk beneath him caught the light from the street lamp at just the right angle and caused him to pause. Perhaps an inch in diameter, it looked for all the world like drying blood. The fob of his keyring was a tiny flashlight. He stooped now and played the beam across the pavement. There were several more splotches of crimson present, spaced fairly randomly several feet apart.

The fire escape was directly above where the blood would have come from if it hadn't come from someone on the walk itself. He stepped back and craned his neck. Wendy's window appeared to be closed, while the two windows above it were several inches ajar. The beam of his light was weak at any distance, but he aimed it overhead in hopes of maybe making something out. The knot that had been sitting in his stomach all evening suddenly tightened. The casement, glass, and fire escape surrounding Wendy's closed window were spattered with blood.

Jumbo had been carrying Wendy's phone number in his pocket.

Joe eased back into the shadow of the building now and pulled his Walther P-5 from the holster clipped to his waistband. He was thinking fast now. Was it possible? DuQuesnay figuring Jumbo had stumbled on the dumping of the Hassey woman's body by accident? If Jumbo hadn't talked, all the pimp had was the big detectives' identification, notebook, and a scrap of paper with Dante's name on it along with Wendy's name and phone number. Fiona would certainly have told Reggie about their little visit. Hell, they'd both given her their *cards*.

Only he hadn't *been* at Wendy Lee's.

Dante swallowed hard, breaking into a cold sweat. The knot in his stomach turned into a sudden urge to vomit.

Bobby Burke and Reggie DuQuesnay crouched together in the shadows of their quarry's bedroom. Somewhere there was a goddamn cat in there because Reggie's eyes and nose itched something fierce. Neither man was willing to risk lights at that point to try to find it. The hair was everywhere anyway. Reggie sneezed.

"Maybe we makin' a mistake here," Bobby ventured. "Maybe this asshole was supposed to meet fatso someplace and he didn't show. We'd be wastin' precious time here then."

Reggie was weighing this possibility when the night came apart around them.

Joe Dante had hung heavy curtains on the garden doors and window to block out the morning light. The wrought-iron gates on the doors, being on the outside of the building, were unlocked by a keyed cylinder facing in. To get them open from outside was a matter of removing that particular key from his ring, working it around to the inside, and fitting it into the lock. This was easier said than done; he was also trying to do it noiselessly.

About halfway through the procedure, he heard a muffled sneeze come from inside, followed by hushed voices in conversation. With his wrist bent back around almost double and his other hand cupped beneath the cylinder lest he drop the key, he worked it slowly and painstakingly into the lock. Once it was all the way home, it turned easily enough, ending with what seemed like a deafening click as the dead bolt was thrown over by the internal mechanism.

They were undoubtedly waiting just inside the bedroom door, lying in ambush for his anticipated entrance through the living room. He got down low to the ground now, gripped the Walther in his right hand, and lifted the front of his jacket to protect his face. The gate was almost certainly going to squeal because he'd put off oiling the hinges. He had to do it all at once. Fast. He also had to hope to God that Jumbo wasn't in there.

His cold sweat turned hot now, the rivulets running freely from his armpits, forehead, and down his back. The beat of his heart thundered in his ears. This wasn't the night or the way he'd planned to die. The iron of the gate was cold against his hand as he gripped it, breathing in concentration, steadying his respiration. He lowered his head in his crouch, yanked the gate hard, and sprang. Glass exploded around him as he aimed for a spot on the floor about five feet inside, shards raining down like lethal hail.

Reggie DuQuesnay froze in confusion as the door behind them erupted and a dense object hurtled through in a shower of glass. Bobby was a little quicker to react, trying to bring the silenced Llama around as the man on the floor rolled right, staying low and using the cover of the bed.

"Down!" Bobby roared, his voice seeming to come from somewhere remote from the unfolding events. Beside him, he felt Reggie unfreeze and react. The hurtling shadow was now fully extended on the floor, something glinting out in front of it. Bobby wasn't set. It was like seeing the KO blow coming out of nowhere at the last split second before the lights went out. A muzzle flash blinded him as a massive jolt slammed his chest and threw him back into the closet doors. Almost in reflex, his own weapon jerked crazily in his hand as he pulled the trigger. Bobby could see and hear nothing. The floor came up hard. He was dead before he came to rest on it.

"Freeze!" A voice screamed as Reggie DuQuesnay scrambled frantically up the short hall, trying to gain cover of the living room. He was already deafened from the first gunshot. The one that got Bobby. Two more cracked in surreal succession, far off like limbs snapping in the forest. Terror pumped adrenaline through his veins by the quart. Goddamn, he had to get to the street.

Dante watched the first target slam into the wall and then covered up. The sizzling snarl of a silenced discharge was followed by falling plaster. There appeared to be two of them, the second now making his break up the hall. Joe rolled through broken glass, firing again from a prone position. The shadow ahead melted into the gloom of the front room. The two additional shots he sent after it were probably fruitless. He could hear gasping and frantic movement.

"I know who you are, Reggie!" he roared, moving cautiously forward. The dead bolts on his door were being thrown. "You're dead fucking meat! Now!"

Diving forward, he shoulder-rolled into the living room from the hall, bringing the gun up just as the front door slammed shut. Shit. He'd probably parked somewhere close by, and the Corvette was halfway around the block. He jerked open the door, checked the hall, and took off in pursuit.

Reggie made it out onto the street with about thirty yards on the cop. He was fast, maybe even widening the distance a little by the time he got to the Ford.

"Start, you motherfucker," he begged, jamming the key into the ignition and turning it over. The engine caught almost instantly as a bullet slammed through the back window and burrowed into the passenger seat headrest.

With his head down so low that he could barely see over the dash, Reggie whipped the wheel hard to the right, jammed his foot on the accelerator, and shuddered away from the curb. Another bullet thudded into the back quarter panel. He had no idea of where to go, but he was behind the wheel of a car now, and the man with the gun was on foot. Seventh Avenue lay just ahead. He aimed for it, his pulse thundering in his head and his heart in his mouth.

On the street, Dante quickly dismissed the notion of trying to stop a moving car with a handgun. As Reggie wheeled the Fairmont away from the hydrant at the curb, Joe scanned quickly up and down the block, the idea of going for the Corvette now abandoned. Just down the way, a car was idling, waiting for a space being vacated by a late-model silver Honda Prelude. As it eased away from the curb, he leapt into it's path, waving his arms. The driver got no explanation. Joe flipped his tin at the startled woman and yanked open the door.

"Get out! Police emergency!" When the woman hesitated, stunned, he screamed at her. "Now!"

The Fairmont careened around the corner ahead and

fishtailed across three lanes of Seventh Avenue before getting straightened out. Dante moved on after it, surprised by the spunk of the import. Out of the corner of his eye as he skidded onto the avenue he spotted a cruiser with its lights flashing, coming on. They must have spotted Reggie skidding out of control onto the avenue and given chase.

A second squad car appeared, swerving onto the avenue with smoking tires and nearly broadsiding the Honda as Dante shot past. He barely had a visual on the Fairmont now as it streaked down Seventh Avenue South toward the Holland Tunnel. The highly responsive little Honda was closing on the Fairmont as it swung into the entrance to the tunnel. Dante gripped the wheel hard, road vibration shooting all the way to his shoulders. The speedometer was riding just past a hundred and five miles per hour. The Ford up ahead wasn't capable of that. In the near abandoned tunnel, Dante was forced to back off a hair, and he was still gaining ground. His heart roared, and the blood pounded in his ears as he rocketed through the fluorescent-lit tube. Thousands of information bits were being processed in his adrenaline-hyped brain. Mileage on the clock told him this car was 25,000 miles old. The way the car handled under the circumstances told him that the tires were relatively new. He had half a tank of gas. How much did Reggie DuQuesnay have? They crossed over into New Jersey. Fuck jurisdictional boundaries. This was hot pursuit.

Just as suddenly as the tunnel had closed in on them, it opened again. Dante was fifty yards off his quarry's bumper. Together, they flew through the toll area as a state trooper, most likely radioed by NYPD, sprinted toward his parked cruiser. Joe jammed the pedal all the way to the floor, the glow of the digital speedometer passing one fifteen. Reggie was just twenty-five yards ahead and losing ground steadily.

The black man couldn't have known what he was doing. This was a panicked, blind run. Instead of getting off the road and down into Jersey City where there was some remote chance he might lose his pursuit, he was taking the Turnpike Extension all the way out. The stinking marshlands between Jersey City and Bayonne spread out beneath them as Dante crawled right up on his tail.

Reggie guessed within seconds of spotting the silver Prelude in the rearview mirror that it wasn't some guy giving his fuel injectors a cleaning out.

"Cocksucking bastard!" he seethed, slamming his hand on the wheel. Beneath him, the Ford was doing everything it could and threatening to shake itself apart in the process. The needle of the speedometer was topped out at the far end of its range. The fucking little Japanese car on his tail was closing fast.

Continuing ahead was suicide. Sooner or later, the cops back at the toll plaza would be joining the pursuit. His only hope was to get off this thruway and onto some city streets. Below him, some godforsaken place like Bayonne or Jersey City was spreading out in both directions. He'd only passed one exit ramp.

The sign came up fast. Route 169 into Bayonne. He had to do this right. Stick to the left lane. Look like he was intending to stay on the fly. The Honda couldn't have been but twenty or thirty feet off his rear bumper now. At the last possible instant, Reggie gripped the wheel and swung hard. The tires of the Ford screamed as it rocked up on two wheels, whipping wildly and all but out of control toward the ramp. Reggie watched it coming up, unable to dictate the sequence of events. It was happening too fast.

"Oh my fuckin' God!" he screamed. A tire had clipped the curb and launched the car free of the pavement. He was airborne, flying head-on into a concrete barrier. He screamed again, wordlessly now, and tried to shield his face with his arms.

*   *   *

Dante saw only part of the scene unfold as he slammed on his brakes and slewed wildly across the Turnpike Extension. From the shoulder where he came to rest he saw the Ford go airborne, slam into a barrier, and Reggie thrown clear like a rag doll. He put the car in reverse and rolled back along the all but abandoned roadway. He was no longer in a hurry. Even in darkness, the high-intensity street lamps along the ramp adequately illuminated the scene. Reggie DuQuesnay lay nestled unnaturally against the concrete abuttment, his gray matter oozing from a gaping hole in the back of his head. The collision had sprung the trunk lid and hood. Gasoline ran in a pool on the pavement from a ruptured gas tank. Joe rolled down the incline and parked. He got a couple of flares from his trunk and set them out. The Port Authority and State Police were taking their sweet time about getting there. He didn't want them to drive right by.

He was standing wearily and surveying the carnage, the far-off wail of sirens growing louder, when he thought he heard something in the trunk of the wrecked car. He shook his head, sure that his ears were playing tricks on him. Right about now, he was all but out on his feet. His knees were shaking.

A soft *whump* drifted over on the still air. Something was moving in the trunk area. Holy shit! There was someone in that car. Someone alive.

The gasoline fumes seared his nostrils as he started forward. The ignition of the car was still switched on. A spark could touch off the fumes and turn the whole mess into a ball of fire at any instant. Up on the Turnpike Extension the sound of sirens swelled to fill the night like the wailing of banshees. The cops must have spotted the flares. They were coming down. Dante hurried forward to the rear of the demolished Ford.

It was Jumbo, bleeding profusely from a head wound,

bound and gagged but definitely alive. The gasoline fumes were so heavy that it would only have been a matter of minutes before he succumbed to them. He was in pretty bad shape.

"Beasley!"

His eyes were unfocused and he didn't respond to his name being screamed in his ear. Dante swallowed hard. The gasoline was now splashing on his shoes. He'd never lifted two hundred and fifty pounds of dead weight in his life.

Rubber squealed behind him and the hubbub of voices drifted in and out as he focused every fiber of his being. With his arms wrapped beneath the giant man's girth, he bent his knees and braced them against the bumper of the car. Then he heaved with single-minded intensity. The huge mass came slowly up over the lip of the trunk and free of it. Momentum carried Jumbo over on top of Dante, and the two partners tumbled across the pavement. With the adrenaline still coursing through his veins, Dante rose, to his feet and began frantically dragging the all-but-unconscious man free. More hands came to his aid. The world swam in front of his eyes. His legs refused to support him any longer. He staggered, fell to his knees, and threw up.

Gus Lieberman turned to Dante as an ambulance bearing Jumbo Richardson streaked off into the night. All around them, camera strobes flashed and newsmen spoke with animation into their microphones, the smoldering wreck of Reggie DuQuesnay's Ford as backdrop. Rosa Losada was decked out in a dress uniform, a set of sergeant's stripes on her sleeve. She fielded queries as the chief of detectives stepped away from the bright lights. By the look of it, every brass asshole in the job, both sides of the river, had shown up to get his picture taken. Such opportunities were rare. Dante could give a damn. Vic Manley was already in the back of the ambulance, riding with Jumbo. Joe was eager to follow as soon as he could.

Lieberman contemplated Rosa as she worked the clamoring press with charm and poise. He nodded in her direction. "She's on her way up, Joey. That's always a tough thing for a street cop to handle."

Dante smiled, perhaps a little sadly. "I'm learning something about that. But . . . one day at at time, right, buddy?"

Lieberman had begun to reply when he caught movement in the younger man's eyes. He turned to follow what had caught Dante's attention. A pair of coroner's men wheeled Reggie DuQuesnay's corpse past in a blue rubber body bag.

"Right," he grunted. "Come on. I'll give you a lift to the hospital."

Together with his conquest in his room, George Scully again mentioned the idea of going for a swim. "You ever been skinny-dipping, honey?" he asked her. God, he was hungry for a look at that pair of hers. They looked to be every bit as spectacular as Fiona's. A great build all over, in fact, and she was hot to trot; eager to have a smooth American guy treat her nice and spend a few bucks on her. What a score. His luck was really on the upswing now.

Instead of hemming and hawing around the idea, the woman got a conspiratorial little grin going and peeled back the shoulder straps on the dress. The tits he was so hungry to see were revealed in all their glory, and he hadn't even had to get wet.

"How about we skinny-dip in your nice big bathtub instead?" she asked. "Wouldn't you like that better?"

Scully wasn't going to argue. Hell, all he asked was that

someone didn't pinch him and wake him up to the nightmare that had been his life just forty-eight hours ago.

"That'd be just fine," he said agreeably.

There was a knock at the door, and the woman slid discreetly out of sight while George accepted the rum, gin, mixers, and ice.

"Why don't you just slip in there and make yourself comfortable while I make you a drink?" she asked, reappearing.

He could hear the water running in the tub. This broad was really on the ball. He gave her a big friendly leer. "I think I might just do that," he told her. "Make mine about half and half, huh?" He slipped a hand under her arm to fondle a breast as he passed.

The water in the tub was a little warm. He ran in a bit of cold while he stripped down and then stepped in. She was right. It *was* a nice big tub. Plenty big enough for the two of them if you didn't mind it a little cozy. Hell, *he* didn't mind it a little cozy. He already had one hell of a hard-on just contemplating how she'd feel next to him in there.

She padded into the bathroom, naked from head to toe now and carry his drink in one hand. Reclining, he took it from her, met her seductive smile, and raised it to his lips.

"Ah," he enthused appreciatively. "Perfect. Hop on in here."

She smiled as she stepped to the edge of the tub, grabbed hold of his hair, and shoved him under with all her strength. He started kicking hard, struggling against her. A straight razor flashed in her other hand. She plunged it beneath the surface and slit his throat.

The prostitute removed the money from the dead man's wallet and slipped back into the seductive cocktail dress. Within the hour, she would be changed into something less conspicuous and asking one of the fishermen on the quay to take her back home to Freeport. Eleven thousand U.S.

dollars. She'd had no idea how providential this night would be.

Before leaving the room, she pulled the plug on the crimson water in the tub, turned on the shower and drew the curtain closed.

About the Author

CHRISTOPHER NEWMAN lives in New York City. His first novel, MIDTOWN SOUTH, was published by Fawcett in 1986.